Sherryl Woods

Harbour Lights

A Chesapeake Shores novel

MIRA

First published in Great Britain 2012
MIRA Books, an imprint of Harlequin (UK) Limited,
Eton House, 18-24 Paradise Road,
Richmond, Surrey, TW9 1SR

ISBN 978 1 848 45135 3

54-0712

MIRA's policy is to use papers that are natural, renewable and
recyclable products and made from wood grown in sustainable forests.
The logging and manufacturing processes conform to the legal
environmental regulations of the country of origin.

Printed and bound by
CPI Group (UK) Ltd, Croydon, CR0 4YY

Dear Friends,

From the time I was four, I spent my summers along the Potomac River not far from the Chesapeake Bay. My love for this locale has grown out of those carefree days spent swimming—not very well—in the river, walking along the beaches and, more recently, sitting on my front porch watching a bald eagle sit high in an old oak tree peering out at the water. There's no place on earth quite like this in terms of beauty and tranquillity.

Though my love of the area grew over time, another member of my family was far more pro-active in seeking to save this vast estuary. My mother's cousin, Tayloe Murphy, while in the Virginia House of Delegates and later as Director of Natural Resources for the state, has been heavily involved in both creating legislation and in oversight. He and others were my inspiration for some of the characters in *Harbour Lights*, including Mick O'Brien's brother Thomas.

Of course, Mick's son, Kevin, has his own love of this region and it helps him to begin the healing process as he returns to the fictional town of Chesapeake Shores with his son after his wife's death in Iraq. I hope you'll enjoy Kevin's very emotional story and enjoy being back with all the O'Briens.

And if you ever have the opportunity, I hope you'll visit the Chesapeake Bay and come to understand why the fight to preserve its natural beauty is so important.

All good wishes,

Sherryl Woods

Prologue

Former army medic Kevin O'Brien had seen his share of combat, violence and death. He'd served two tours in Iraq before being discharged a few months ago. In his current job as a paramedic in Arlington, Virginia, he'd been on plenty of accident scenes, treated gunshot victims, and gone on domestic violence calls where arguments had turned nasty. None of it, though, had prepared him emotionally for spending a day with a sick kid—his sick kid.

He'd spent the night pacing the floor of his Northern Virginia town house, his miserable eleven-month-old son cradled against his shoulder. Davy intermittently squalled and whimpered, leaving Kevin frustrated and anxious and about ten seconds away from calling his grandmother back home in Chesapeake Shores for advice…or maybe hopping into his truck and driving straight over there. Gram would be thrilled to take over for him.

It was times like this when Kevin missed his wife the most. He could handle the basics of day care and meals, even the everyday medical stuff—baby aspirin, eardrops, whatever—but Georgia had the soothing voice down pat. He was almost certain that Davy never cried this loudly—as if his little heart were breaking—when he was being held by his mom.

Unfortunately, Georgia had another six months to serve on her latest stint as a medic in Iraq. With a new baby in the house, she could have gotten out of the overseas assignment, but she had refused. She'd insisted on going where she thought she was most needed by the military and her country. If she kept her promise—and it was a big *if* in Kevin's mind—this would be her last tour before she, too, was discharged. Then they planned to move to Maryland to be close to Kevin's family in Chesapeake Shores, the quaint seaside town his father had built.

As terrified as Kevin had been of staying behind and being a single dad to an infant, he'd understood Georgia's devotion to duty. She wasn't the only mother who'd made the difficult decision to leave her family behind to serve in the army. Besides, her very dedication to the mission was one of the things he'd admired the most about Georgia when they'd met on the job at a hospital in Baghdad's Green Zone, supposedly the safest spot to be in that war-torn country.

Kevin paused in his pacing to look at their wedding photo, sitting on the mantel. It was practically the only time he'd seen Georgia in public wearing anything other than her medic's uniform. He hadn't been able to get over how beautiful she'd looked in the simple white gown, her golden hair in unaccustomed curls, her smile so bright it made his heart ache with missing her.

That they'd married in a rushed ceremony at the Baltimore airport had hardly mattered, because her father, a minister in Texas, had flown in at the last minute to officiate. Her mother had accompanied him. Georgia had sworn it didn't matter that they wouldn't have the lavish ceremony most girls dreamed of. It had been enough to have her family beside her when she and Kevin had wed.

Kevin's only family member present for the brief service had been his dad, because he'd wanted the rest of the family to meet Georgia for the first time at home on the banks of the Chesapeake Bay, not in a whirlwind in some sterile room at the airport. He'd taken plenty of grief over that decision, especially from his sisters.

Now he picked up the wedding picture and held it in front of Davy, as he did almost daily. "Do you see this pretty woman, kiddo? This is your mom. I know you're sad without her, but I'm doing the best I can. And your Uncle Connor is coming over here tomorrow to hook us up with a camera so we'll be able to talk to her and see her on the computer. It'll be almost as if she's right here with us."

Davy hiccuped, his eyes wide and shiny with unshed tears. "Mama," he said, reaching toward the picture.

Kevin beamed at him. "That's exactly right. That's your mama. She's a real beauty, pal. The sweetest woman in the whole world. Feisty, too, and brave. Boy, does she have a mind of her own. She's going to keep both of us on our toes once she gets home."

Davy whimpered, then laid his head on Kevin's shoulder. He could feel his son's breath, warm and soft, against his neck. Maybe Davy was finally falling asleep. Maybe they'd both finally get some much-needed rest.

The wistful thought had barely come to him when the doorbell rang, snapping Davy awake with a start. The crying started up all over again, even as Kevin cursed under his breath and headed for the door.

When he opened it, the sight of two somber men in uniform on the doorstep sent him staggering back. He knew why they were here. God help him, he knew.

"No." It was the only word he could manage with Davy still sobbing and his own heart about to break.

"Sir, we regret to inform you—"

Kevin cut them off. "No," he repeated more forcefully. "I have to…" He looked around, uncertain what he had to do. Something, *anything,* to prevent them from saying what the family of any soldier dreaded hearing.

"My son," he said finally. "Let me put him down, please."

The two soldiers regarded him with compassion. "Of course, sir."

He carried his son into the nursery, but in the end he couldn't let go. He needed that tiny bit of warmth, the human contact, to steady himself for what was coming. He needed to be reminded that, no matter what, he had to keep a grip on things. His boy needed him. From here on out, he and Davy had to be a team, just the two of them.

Because even though he hadn't heard the words yet, he knew: Georgia was dead. How and when hardly mattered, only that one truth with its ultimate finality: Davy's mom—Kevin's wife—wouldn't be back. Their all-too-brief life as a family was over, practically before it had begun.

1

Thirteen months later

Kevin glanced out the window of his childhood bedroom. The yard that sloped down toward the Chesapeake Bay was decorated with balloons. Piles of presents sat on a picnic table next to a cake decorated with toy trucks, Davy's favorite things. All of the O'Briens had gathered to celebrate his son's second birthday, but Kevin could barely summon the energy to get out of bed. Despite his resolve to be strong for Davy, he'd pretty much been a wreck since Georgia's death, not able to get a fix on anything, unable to make even the most basic decisions about his life.

He had made three decisions, though. He'd quit his job as a paramedic, he'd sold the town house, which was filled with memories of his too-brief marriage, and he'd moved home. At least here, he knew there were plenty of people who would love and look out for his son while he figured out what came next. That was something he really needed to get to…one of these days.

Someone pounded on the door of his room—his younger brother from the sound of it.

"Get your butt downstairs!" Connor bellowed. "The party's about to start."

Given his choice, Kevin would have crawled back into bed and pulled the pillow over his head to block out the sound of laughter coming from outside. He wouldn't, though. For one thing, even if nothing else in his life made sense, his son was the most important person in it. Kevin wouldn't let him down. For another, either Gram or his dad would be up here next, and either one of them had the power to shame him into doing what was right for the occasion.

"On my way," he assured Connor.

He showered in record time, pulled on jeans and a T-shirt and slid his feet into an old pair of sneakers, then went downstairs. Only his youngest sister, Jess, was in the kitchen. She surveyed him, then shook her head.

"You're a mess," she declared.

"I showered. These clothes are clean," he protested.

"Did you lose your razor? And maybe your comb?"

"Who are you?" he grumbled. "The fashion patrol?"

"Just calling it like I see it, big brother. Everyone else spruced up for the party. Turning two is a big deal."

"Do you honestly think Davy's going to care if I shaved?" he asked as he rubbed his hand over his unshaven jaw. He had shaved yesterday—or was it the day before? He couldn't recall. Mostly the days slipped by in a blur.

"No, Davy won't care today, but you'll look like some derelict in the pictures. Is that the memory you want him to carry with him throughout his life? Last year on his first birthday it made sense that you looked ragged. It was only a few weeks after Georgia—"

"Don't mention her name," he snapped.

"Someone has to," she said, looking him directly in the

eye without backing down. "You loved her, Kev. I get that. You're hurting and angry because she's gone, but you can't pretend she didn't exist. She was that little boy's mom. What are you planning to do, let him go through his entire life with the subject of his mother off-limits? What about his grandparents? Do you expect them never to mention their daughter's name?"

"*I* can't talk about her. Not yet." He knew it was irrational, but somehow he thought if he didn't talk about Georgia or her death, it wouldn't be real. She'd still be out there, on the other side of the world, saving lives. She'd still walk through the door one day, back into his life.

"When, then?" Jess asked, her gaze unrelenting.

If he hadn't been so annoyed, he might have admired her persistence. For a woman who rarely stuck with anything for long, Jess had certainly dug in her heels on this. Just his freaking luck.

"What do you expect me to say?" he snapped again. "A day? A month? Hell if I know when I'll be ready." Even as he spoke, he felt the sting of tears in his eyes. He hated the sign of weakness almost as much as he hated this whole conversation. "Just drop it, okay?"

Of course she didn't. "Sit down," she ordered, not cutting him any slack.

He didn't like that Jess was turning the tables on him. His little sister had always come to him for advice. Now she was obviously planning to dole it out. Just like Georgia, once Jess got stirred up, she was going to speak her mind, whether anyone wanted to listen or not. Apparently this was one of those times. Kevin sat, mostly because he was too shaky not to and because she'd plunked a cup of much-needed coffee on the table to go with whatever words she was intent on dishing out.

She pulled a chair close and sat so that her knees were brushing his. She covered one of his hands with hers. The show of sympathy was almost his undoing.

"Listen to me, Kev. You need to get out of this house."

Alarm shot through him. "Why? Has Gram said something? Is having Davy underfoot too much for her? Do she and Dad want me out of here?"

She rolled her eyes. "You know better," she said impatiently. "This is your home. I wasn't saying you should move. I was saying you need to get a life." Her gaze, locked with his, was filled with compassion. "I know this is going to sound harsh, but somebody needs to say it. Georgia died. You didn't. And Davy needs his dad, the real one, not the one who walks around here all day in a daze."

He frowned at her. "I'm not drinking, if that's what you're suggesting."

"Nobody said you were. Look, I'm saying all this now, before everyone else has a chance to gang up on you. You know it's coming. You must. This family can't keep their opinions to themselves worth a damn. It's amazing we've all been so quiet for this long."

He smiled, despite his sour mood. "You're right about that."

"Will you at least think about what I've said? If you promise to do that much, I'll run interference and keep the others at bay a while longer. Abby, the mother hen, is champing at the bit to offer her own special brand of tough love. She's worried sick that you haven't snapped out of this dark mood."

Since he would do just about anything to keep from being surrounded by all that well-meaning concern, especially from his oldest sister, he nodded. "There's just one thing."

"Oh?"

"I don't have any idea at all what to do with myself."

"You're a paramedic," she reminded him at once. "There are openings right here in town. I've checked."

He shook his head. "No. I'll never do that again." His career was all twisted up in his mind with Georgia and how she'd died on a call to a market in Baghdad after an explosive device had been triggered, killing and wounding a bunch of innocent civilians. She and her team had arrived just in time for the second bomb to be detonated. Kevin knew his reaction, his refusal to put his EMT training to good use, wasn't rational, but then he wasn't operating much on reason these days.

"You sure about that?" Jess asked.

"A hundred percent."

Her expression brightened. "Then I have an even better idea."

He didn't like the glint in her eyes one bit. Jess had always had a knack for getting into mischief. Ideas came fast and furiously with her. It was the follow-through that was lacking. Or had been, anyway, until she'd opened The Inn at Eagle Point. That seemed to have captured her complete attention. After a shaky start, she had the place running smoothly and successfully.

"What's your idea?" he asked warily.

"A fishing charter," she said at once, then rushed in before he could utter an immediate objection. "You could lease dock space at the Harbor Lights Marina. Come on, Kev, at least think about it. You spent half your life on the water as a kid. You always claimed it calmed you, even if you didn't come home with a single rockfish or croaker. And naturally, because you didn't really give two hoots about catching them, the fish practically jumped into your boat."

"You want me to become a waterman?" he asked incredulously. It was a hard, demanding life, especially with the impact that farming and other human misdeeds were having on fish, crabs and oysters in the bay's waters, to say nothing of what skyrocketing fuel costs had done to profit margins.

"Not exactly. I want you to take people out on your boat to fish."

He gave her a wry look. "The only boat I currently own is barely big enough for me and one passenger, and I wind up rowing home more often than not because the motor's unreliable."

"Which is exactly why you'll spend some of that trust fund money that's sitting in the bank on a bigger, more reliable boat. Dad set up those funds for us to buy a home or start a business. I know you haven't touched yours, so the start-up money's there, Kev."

"And you think this can become an actual career?" he asked skeptically.

"It's not up there with saving lives," she said pointedly. "But I get requests practically every day from guests at the inn who want to go fishing. There's no one in town who does charters. Once in a while I can convince George Jenkins to take someone out, but he has the conversational skills of a clam."

Kevin thought about the long, lazy days he and Connor had spent on the bay as boys. They were some of the best in his life. He hadn't cared a fig about catching fish, just as Jess said, but he'd loved the peace and quiet of being on the water. Of course, if he had a boat full of strangers along, the tranquillity would pretty much be shattered. Yet somehow the idea took hold.

Jess regarded him hopefully. "You'll think about it?"

There were a thousand practical things to be considered, but the idea held promise. He'd have to take classes to become licensed to be a captain, for example, and that would get him out of the house. Maybe that alone would be enough to keep everyone off his case.

He nodded slowly. "I'll think about it."

"Good! Now let's go outside and spoil that son of yours rotten," Jess said, dragging him to his feet. "You should see his haul of presents. They're piled high. Davy doesn't entirely understand yet that they're his, so this should be fun."

Fun wasn't something Kevin had had in his life for a while now, but when he saw Davy running around on his chubby little legs, his mouth already streaked with chocolate frosting, he couldn't help but feel a little lighter. And when Davy spotted his father and a smile spread across his face, Kevin felt a split second of pure joy. It was Georgia's smile, as bright and carefree as she had been.

For the first time since his wife had died, the sorrow lifted briefly and he felt hopeful again.

Despite his promise to Jess, Kevin spent two more weeks holed up at home, passing his days with Davy and his evenings hiding out in his room away from Gram's pitying looks and his father's increasing impatience. Mick clearly had plenty to say to him, Kevin could tell, but apparently an edict from Gram had kept his father silent. He doubted that would last much longer.

To his surprise, it was Gram herself who broke the silence first. She joined him on the porch at dusk one evening, handed him a glass of iced tea and a plate of his favorite oatmeal raisin cookies and said, "We need to talk."

"About?" Kevin asked, even more wary than he had

been when Jess had made the same announcement. If Jess was good at uncomfortable, straight talk, it was because she'd learned from a master—their grandmother. Nell O'Brien had stepped in to raise them after their mother and father had divorced. She had a huge heart and a tart tongue.

"The way you're moping around this house day in and day out," she replied. "It's not good for you, and it's certainly not good for your boy. A child needs to expand his world, to see other children."

Kevin frowned at that. "His cousins are here all the time."

"Caitlyn and Carrie are almost eight now, and while they love playing with Davy, he needs to be with some youngsters his own age." She gave him a penetrating look. "He needs to laugh, Kevin. When was the last time you got down on the ground and rough-housed with him, made him giggle?"

"Seems to me that Dad's filling that role." In fact, Mick seemed to delight in it.

"It's his father who ought to be doing it, not his grandfather. When was the last time you took Davy into town for an ice-cream cone?"

"You took him just yesterday," Kevin reminded her.

Gram gave him an impatient look. "Is that what I asked? I want to know when *you* took him."

"I haven't," he admitted. "But I don't see why that's such a big deal. Davy's got plenty of attention around here. That's why I moved back to Chesapeake Shores."

"So we could raise him for you?" she asked. The question was pointed, though her tone was gentle.

"No, of course not," he retorted, then regretted his tone and sighed. "Maybe."

"Kevin, we all know you're grieving over Georgia, and

there's not a thing we wouldn't do to help out, but you have to start living again. You have to give Davy a more normal life. I know Jess has talked to you about this, so I waited, but you're showing no signs of changing. I can't go on watching you shortchange Davy or yourself like this. It's just plain wrong. You're a vital young man with a lot of years ahead of you. Don't waste them and live to regret it."

As much as he hated to admit it, Kevin knew she was right. He just had no idea precisely what he could do about it, not when he was filled with so many conflicting emotions. He was angry about a war that had taken a child's mother and left him a single dad. He was guilt-ridden about not having tried harder to make Georgia reconsider taking another tour in Iraq, even after just about everyone in his family had begged him to. And he was grieving for a vibrant young woman who would never know her son, who wouldn't be there for his first day of school, his college graduation, his wedding.

He finally lifted his head and faced his grandmother. "Gram, I have no idea what to do. Some days just getting out of bed seems like a triumph."

She nodded knowingly. "That's the way I felt when your grandfather died. I'm sure it's the way Mick felt when your mother left him alone with all of you children to raise. You know how he handled that."

"By taking off for work every chance he got," Kevin said bitterly.

"Do you think staying here and hiding out is any kinder?" she asked him.

The soft-spoken words hit him like a slap. "But I—"

She reached over and covered his hand with hers before he could argue that this was different.

"He didn't intend any hurt, either, Kevin," Gram said. "Mick was managing the only way he knew how. So are you. But both of you are better than that. Mick's a little late in trying to make up for those absences. I don't want you to wait till Davy's grown before fixing this."

"Where do I start?" he asked, genuinely at a loss. Plunging into a career taking out fishing charters, while it held some appeal, was more than he could cope with. It might require him to be civil to strangers, and he didn't trust himself to do that. Not yet. Just look at how quickly he lost patience with the people he actually cared about.

Gram gave his hand a squeeze. "You take one step at a time. Tomorrow, I expect you to get away from this house. This first time, go into town while Davy's down for his nap. Have lunch at Sally's. Stop by Bree's flower shop. Visit Jess at the inn and help her out for a couple of hours. It doesn't matter. Just do one thing tomorrow that's a step forward. The next day, take another."

When she said it like that, when she didn't ask for an overnight transformation or a leap into a whole new career as Jess had suggested, it seemed possible. Reasonable, even.

"I can do that," he said eventually.

"Well, of course you can," she said reassuringly.

He thought back to all the years when Gram had been left virtually on her own with him, his brother and sisters, while his mother was making a new life for herself in New York and Mick was roaming the world for work.

"Gram, did you ever have doubts after you moved in here to help Dad raise us?"

She laughed. "I didn't have time for doubts, not with the five of you to run me ragged. Besides, I had the advantage of having raised your father and uncles. I already knew a thing or two."

"I've been in a war. I've worked as a paramedic. None of that's easy or predictable." He shook his head. "But despite all that, there are days when the thought of raising Davy on my own scares me to death."

"But you're not on your own now, are you?" she reminded him lightly. "None of us are going to abandon you to the task. We just don't want you to miss out on being the kind of father I know deep down that you want to be."

"How'd you get to be so smart?" he teased, feeling lighter than he had in a long, long time.

"Live long enough and it's amazing what you pick up," she said as she stood. She leaned down and pressed a kiss to his cheek. "I love you, Kevin. Never forget that."

"As if you'd let me," he grumbled.

She chuckled. "Yes, as if. Don't stay up too late."

"Thanks, Gram, for the cookies and the talk."

She winked at him. "Can't have one without the other."

It was true, Kevin thought, as she left him alone. Gram's serious talks had always been accompanied by freshly baked cookies—oatmeal raisin for him, chocolate chip for his sisters and peanut butter for Connor. The advice had always gone down more easily because of it. Just as it had tonight.

One step forward, he reminded himself. That's all she was expecting.

Chances were, he thought wryly, one step was just about all he could manage.

The cappuccino machine was a complete mystery. If she'd had money to burn, Shanna would have tossed it across the room and let it shatter. But the success of her new business depended on making coffee and tea sales as brisk as selling books and games. And she needed this business to succeed in the worst way.

She'd poured every last dime she had into Word Games. She was hoping to combine her love of reading and board games like Scrabble, Clue, Sequence and Monopoly with her obsessive need for frequent caffeine fixes and turn it into something that would help her bring her life back into focus.

She'd picked Chesapeake Shores because it was a small seaside town, rather than an overwhelming city. On a prior visit, she'd been drawn in by its serenity, its friendly people. She'd noted the absence of any business similar to the one she wanted to open. Who could be at the beach without wanting a good book? Or a few games and puzzles to keep the kids occupied? She'd probably need to look into handheld electronic games, as well, but not only was the technology pricier than she could afford, it was a complete mystery to her. How could she sell something she couldn't explain to her customers? Of course, half the teenagers in town could probably explain those games to her.

Though the idea of starting her own business was scary, it was exciting, as well. She'd loved every second of placing her initial orders. Now, she had plenty of stock, most of it still in boxes, and lots of ideas, jotted on Post-it notes stuck on a refrigerator in the shop's back room or on the beat-up old desk she'd salvaged from a thrift shop.

What she needed next, more than anything, was a caffeine fix. Unfortunately, the stupid machine wasn't cooperating. She couldn't even read the instructions, which seemed to be in every language except plain English. There were, in fact, recognizable English words on the page, but added together they were indecipherable.

Since the cappuccino machine was too costly to replace, she heaved the world's ugliest mug—a joke goodbye gift from her best friend—across the room instead. Naturally, it didn't shatter, which Shanna would have counted as a blessing. Instead, it was caught by a startled man who'd just opened the front door.

She was about to apologize, but he was studying the awful orange mug with fascination. When he lifted his gaze to hers, there was a faint, but unmistakable twinkle in his dark blue eyes. It died quickly, but that glimpse of it had made her heart catch.

"The mug is pretty hideous, but do you really think that's cause to put it out of its misery?" he inquired lightly.

"Actually the coffeemaker was on my hit list. The cup was just a less costly substitute."

"Lousy instructions and a need for caffeine," he guessed. "It's a dangerous combination. Sally's is a couple of doors down. Why don't I buy you a cup of coffee before you try to break something else?"

Embarrassed, Shanna shook her head. "I think I can control myself until I figure this out."

He hesitated, looking oddly torn, then stepped all the way inside. "At least let me take a look at those instructions," he offered. "Maybe I'll have better luck. I'm Kevin O'Brien, by the way. My sister owns the flower shop next door. Any idea where she is? There's a closed sign on the door."

Shanna shrugged. "Not a clue. I haven't met a soul on the block yet. I've been totally focused on trying to get this place ready to open. I'm Shanna Carlyle."

"I'm surprised Bree hasn't been in here pestering you for information about your plans. She prides herself on knowing everything going on in town."

"This all happened pretty fast," Shanna said. "There was a waiting list of people looking for retail space on Main Street. I got a call that the prior occupant wanted to move to a bigger space and I could take over her lease. That was two weeks ago, and here I am." She was babbling, but something about this man made her as nervous as a teenager meeting the sexy new kid in school for the first time.

"You've accomplished all this in two weeks?" he said, his amazement plain as he took in the fresh coat of paint and the stacks and stacks of boxes.

She gave him a wry look. The place was a disorganized mess. Still, it did look as if something might happen in here soon.

"I'd done a lot of my homework, knew the kind of inventory I wanted to carry and where to get it. All I had to do was establish my credit, which thankfully is good, and make some calls to vendors." She shrugged. "Besides, I couldn't afford a lot of downtime once I signed the lease. I need to get money coming in if I'm going to keep up with the rent on the shop space and the apartment upstairs."

He surveyed the room and the piles of boxes. "What's your target date for opening?"

"A week from Saturday."

He looked skeptical. "Then you need help."

"I can't afford help."

Once again, she noticed a faint hesitation, as if he thought he was going to hate himself for uttering what came next.

"Then it's a good thing I don't need to be paid," he said eventually, his hands shoved in his pockets, his expression bland. "I have a little time to burn while I wait for Bree. I'd be glad to pitch in."

Shanna stilled. Big-city jitters kicked in. Kevin O'Brien was definitely intriguing. And probably safe enough, if his sister owned the florist shop next door. She'd heard the name O'Brien around town, knew that a man named Mick O'Brien, in fact, had been the architect who'd designed and built Chesapeake Shores. The woman she'd dealt with at the management company had been an O'Brien, too.

"So, are you one of *the* O'Briens?" she asked. "I've read a little about Mick and I met Susie."

"My father and my cousin," he told her.

That was reassuring, but still, old habits kept her cautious. "I appreciate the offer to help, but I probably should do it myself. I have to figure out the placement for all this stuff as I go. And, as you can see, the shelves aren't in yet. They're not coming till tomorrow."

He didn't seem especially disappointed by her refusal. In fact, he almost looked relieved.

"Okay, then, no coffee from Sally's, no help in here," he said easily. "How about the cappuccino machine? Want me to take a crack at that?"

Not wanting to seem ungracious, Shanna finally nodded. "Sure. If you can get it working, your first purchase is on me."

"You shouldn't be offering to give books away," he scolded as he studied the instructions, then sorted through the tools she'd spread out until he found the one he wanted. "Though my son will be delighted. Picture books are among his favorite things. I'm sure we'll be frequent customers."

Her heart did an odd little stutter step. She couldn't have said for sure if it was disappointment or delight. Kevin was an attractive man, after all, but she loved kids. She was hoping the store would draw a lot of them.

"You have a son?"

He nodded. "Davy. He's two."

"Well, you or your wife will have to bring him in as soon as I open. I have a huge selection of picture books on order."

For an instant, it looked as if Kevin had been frozen in time, almost as if he weren't even breathing. Then he exhaled slowly and frowned as he concentrated on the cappuccino machine. Shanna could tell instantly that she'd said something wrong, but she had no idea what it might have been. Perhaps it was mentioning his wife. Maybe they were divorced, but wouldn't she have their child? It sounded as if the boy lived with his dad.

Then she remembered. When she'd first come to Chesapeake Shores for a visit a year ago, recovering from her own very complicated and shattered marriage, she'd stayed at the inn. It, too, was run by an O'Brien. And the whole place had been buzzing because the owner's brother had lost his wife in Iraq and had just moved home with his son. Her heart had ached at the news, not just for the man who'd lost his wife, but for the little boy who would grow up without a mother.

That man was Kevin—it had to be. She felt awful, but had no idea how to apologize, especially since her inadvertent mention of his wife had caused such a strong reaction. Maybe it was better to let it pass.

Even as she was debating with herself over the best tactic, he stood up. "Where's the nearest plug?"

She gestured toward a table she'd set up temporarily to hold the machine. The foam cups, gourmet coffee beans, and supplies were already sitting on it.

Within minutes, he had the coffee brewing, the rich aroma filling the space.

"Milk?" he asked.

"In the refrigerator in back. I'll get it."

When she brought it back, he deftly frothed it to perfection, poured it on top of a cup of fragrant coffee and handed it to her. "There you go," he said with a grin. "You're all set."

"I'm eternally grateful," she said, meaning it. "The coffee's fantastic." She met his gaze and asked impulsively, "What are you doing a week from Saturday? If you'll man this machine, I'll not only give your son his pick of any book in the place, but I'll pay you, too. I can't afford to hire anyone even part-time just yet, but I can certainly pay you for one day just to keep the customers in coffee."

His expression closed down as if the offer offended him. "If I'm around, I'll help out, but I don't want your money."

"You work, I pay you," she said, not sure why she was so insistent that it be a business arrangement. From what she'd gathered, the O'Briens were probably not in need of the kind of paltry money she could afford to pay. Still, paying her way was a matter of pride to her. Accusations from her former in-laws that she'd been a gold digger were still a little too raw. She didn't want to start her life in Chesapeake Shores feeling indebted to anyone.

"Let's table that discussion until we see if I'm around."

She studied him curiously. "Commitment issues?"

"Something like that," he said evasively. "I'll be in touch. It was nice to meet you, Shanna."

"You, too, Kevin."

But as he walked away, she had the strangest sensation that she still knew next to nothing about him beyond his name and her speculation that he was the man who'd lost his wife in a war halfway across the world. The fact that she found him fascinating was probably a sure sign that she ought to be grateful he was gone. Wounded souls were a bad bet. She'd found that out the hard way. Trying to save another one would be a monumentally stupid idea.

2

It was after six and Shanna was still unpacking boxes and stacking books according to the sections she'd sketched out on a floor plan for the store. She planned to be ready the instant the shelves were put into place. The supplier had promised delivery by nine tomorrow morning.

When her cell phone rang, she grabbed it and answered without checking caller ID, something she hadn't done since her divorce. Avoiding calls from her ex-husband had become a way of life. This time, thankfully, the impulsive action didn't cost her.

"How's the book business?" Laurie asked.

Shanna smiled at the sound of her best friend's voice. "I'll let you know when I've sold my first book."

"Well, if it's too soon to answer that question, then tell me how you are. Still happy about making this move to the middle of nowhere? How can you possibly get through the day when you're miles and miles from the nearest gourmet coffee shop?"

"Because I'm opening my own," Shanna replied, sinking down on the floor and leaning against the wall. She felt relaxed for the first time all day. Talking to Laurie, who'd been there through the ordeal of her marriage and her divorce, always grounded her and invariably cheered her up.

"And for the record, I really am happy," she added emphatically. "This is the best thing I've done for myself in a very long time."

"Met anyone interesting yet?"

She stiffened at the oft-repeated refrain. "What is this obsession you have with my social life?" she asked, instantly annoyed. "I've only been divorced for a year and it's been a rocky one. You should know that better than anyone. I'm hardly ready to rush into anything new."

"My, my," Laurie said. "Aren't you defensive? That must mean you have crossed paths with someone attractive. Tell me."

Shanna sighed, an unwanted image of the very attractive Kevin O'Brien now locked in her head. "Nothing to tell," she insisted. A ten, maybe fifteen-minute encounter was not worth mentioning, though she seriously doubted Laurie would agree. Recently engaged, Laurie thought the entire world should be traveling in pairs.

"Well, that's just a plain shame," Laurie declared. "I suppose I'll have to listen to you go on and on about inventory, instead."

"I'll restrain myself just this once," Shanna promised. "You tell me about Drew. How are the wedding plans coming?"

The last she'd heard, the occasion was to be opulent and excessive, every little girl's dream wedding. Of course, a few weeks ago, it was going to be on a Hawaiian beach at sunset. It all seemed to be evolving at a breakneck pace that suited Laurie, but would have given Shanna hives.

"Actually, that's one of the reasons I called," Laurie

said. "Didn't you tell me that the inn where you stayed last year was really wonderful and that they do weddings?"

"The Inn at Eagle Point?" Shanna asked, surprised. "Here in Chesapeake Shores?"

"That's it," Laurie said. "I couldn't recall the name to save my soul. What would you think about us having the wedding there, something small and intimate?"

"I'd love it, of course. The inn is charming, the food's outstanding and the setting is spectacular, but I thought you wanted something huge, splashy and extravagant."

"I found out just how much huge, splashy and extravagant cost," Laurie admitted ruefully. "Drew had a cow. He said if we spent that much on the wedding, we'd be ninety before we'd have enough money to buy a house."

"A good point," Shanna agreed. "And fancy and expensive doesn't guarantee happiness. I'm a living testament to that."

"So, would it be okay if I came for a quick visit, maybe weekend after next, to look over this inn, maybe talk to the owner about costs and available dates?"

"That's my store opening," Shanna reminded her. "I won't have a spare second."

"Two birds with one stone," Laurie said happily. "And great planning on my part, if I do say so myself. I can help out at the opening. I'll be your go-to girl for any last-minute details. You can send me out for ice or make me dust the shelves. You know how you love bossing me around. You'll be in heaven."

"Are you sure this is about checking out the inn?" Shanna asked. "Or are you just anxious to get a look at this new life of mine, so you can give it your seal of approval? I know you weren't overjoyed that I made this leap without consulting you."

"Well, you have to admit, you made the decision practically overnight. That's not like you. You're a lot of things, Shanna, but impulsive isn't one of them. I'm worried about you."

"I'd been thinking about this for an entire year," Shanna reminded her. "It was hardly impulsive. You have nothing to worry about."

"I suppose," Laurie conceded. "But I will feel better if I see for myself if this suits you. So, how about it? Can I come to help you celebrate your grand opening?"

Though she'd barely have time to breathe that weekend, Shanna found it impossible to resist the offer of help or a chance to show off Chesapeake Shores to her friend. She realized she did want Laurie's blessing. Despite an occasional flighty moment or two when it came to her wedding, Laurie was as levelheaded as anyone she'd ever known.

"Absolutely. I want you here. It wouldn't be the same without you," Shanna told her, even as an image of Kevin O'Brien and his promise to help out if he was around came and went. She could hardly count on him, now, could she? Of course, if he did turn up, Laurie would spot Shanna's interest in two seconds flat and do everything in her power to encourage it. Worse, subtlety wasn't her strong suit. Oh well, she'd just have to risk it. "Please come, Laurie."

"I can't wait," Laurie enthused.

Just then the bell, left behind by the previous tenant, rang as the shop door opened. A pretty woman with what she'd come to realize were the brilliant azure eyes of the O'Briens stuck her head in. Shanna waved at her to enter.

"Laurie, I've got to run. Someone just dropped in. Make your plans and let me know when you're coming, okay?"

"Will do. Love you, girl. See you soon."

Shanna clicked off the phone, then turned to the woman who was wandering through the shop unabashedly checking things out. "Hi. Can I help you?"

"I'm Bree O'Brien from next door," she announced, turning back to Shanna. "Bree Collins, actually." She gave a rueful shake of her head. "I can't get used to the fact that I'm married. I'm afraid I'm giving Jake—he's my husband—some kind of a complex about never remembering to use his name. Anyway, I just wanted to welcome you to Main Street." Her grin spread. "And to get a look around, so I'll have something to report to all the people who're asking questions. A new business is big news around here. I'm getting at least a half-dozen extra customers every day just from the curiosity factor."

Shanna instinctively liked Bree's candor. "Well, you can report that it will be a books and games store with a tiny café, no threat to Sally's. Be sure she knows that. Just coffee and tea and maybe a few pastries if I can find a bakery to supply them."

"Sounds fabulous. Just what we've needed in town, a place to browse for books and kick back over a cup of coffee." Her expression turned thoughtful. "You know, you might check with my sister Jess at the inn. She has a fabulous baker on staff. Maybe you can work something out. Just remember that Sally has the croissant concession locked in. We try not to trample on each other's business toes."

"Absolutely. Got it," Shanna said. "You're welcome to keep looking around, if you can maneuver around the stacks of books. Shelves are coming in the morning, so hopefully the floor will be clear by this time tomorrow and this place will be starting to look the way I've envisioned it."

Bree somehow found her way straight to the gardening and flower-arranging books. She picked them up, all but cooing her enthusiasm over each one. "Mind if I put a stack aside for myself?" she asked. "There are three here I absolutely have to have."

"By all means. I'll put them in back with your name on them." She decided now might be a good time to get some of her questions about Kevin answered. "By the way, your brother Kevin was here earlier. Did he find you?"

Bree looked startled. "Kevin was here?"

Shanna nodded.

"Was he civil?" she asked worriedly.

"Of course. Why?"

"Sorry. I shouldn't have said it like that. It makes him sound, I don't know, unpredictable or something. It's just that he's been going through a tough time. He pretty much keeps to himself these days."

"Why?" Shanna asked, then could have kicked herself. "Sorry. I'm being nosy."

"It's okay. Most people around here know, and they're pretty understanding about his need for privacy and his moods. His wife died a while back, and I guess you could say that he's lost his way."

"That explains it," Shanna said. "I inadvertently mentioned his wife, and he shut down. I had a feeling something awful had happened."

"She died in Iraq. One of those improvised explosive incidents. It just about killed him. If it weren't for his little boy…" Bree shrugged. "I'm not sure what would have happened, if he didn't have Davy in his life. He's only two, so he still needs a lot of attention. At least Kevin knows he can't go completely underground and brood."

With her guesswork confirmed, Shanna felt another

burst of sympathy. Here were two people who needed mothering, one of them practically a baby, the other a grown man who'd been through his own personal hell. The situation was right up her alley. Once again, she warned herself to steer clear.

But when she thought of Kevin's sad eyes and what a difference it had made the few times he'd smiled, she knew in her gut she wasn't going to be able to resist, not if he gave her half a chance. He might be lost and needy, but she had a void inside that she'd been trying to fill for years. It had made her love well, but not wisely. Not wisely at all.

Kevin sat in an Adirondack chair in the yard, his bare feet propped on a stool, a beer in his hand as he watched Davy play with his trucks. Thank heaven he was the kind of kid who, even at two, could entertain himself, at least for short stretches of time. They were waiting for dusk and the arrival of the fireflies, which Davy found endlessly fascinating. Then they'd go inside, Davy would get a quick bath and a story before bed, and finally, Kevin would have the rest of the night to himself.

As Charles Dickens had once said about something else entirely in the opening to *A Tale of Two Cities,* "It was the best of times, it was the worst of times." Those few hours before sleep claimed him were too often filled with memories, good ones, yes, but painful because of it.

"Hey, Davy, look what I caught," Bree called out from somewhere behind him.

Davy looked up from his trucks, squealed with glee and took off toward his aunt, who had two fireflies trapped in a jar with holes punched in the lid. If Kevin wasn't mistaken, that was probably the very same Mason jar they'd used as kids to gather lightning bugs on evenings just like this one—humid and thick with the promise of a storm in the air. Whitecaps were already stirring on the bay and the leaves on some of the huge old trees were turned inside out in the stiffening breeze.

With Davy's hand tucked in hers, Bree came over to join him, plopping down on the grass and setting the jar where Davy could watch it, his brow furrowed now in concentration.

"I can see lightning in the distance," she commented, her gaze directed toward the bay. "Heat lightning, most likely."

"Maybe," Kevin said.

"Then, again, it could storm in an hour or two," she said, clearly making small talk. "I hope so. We could use a good rain."

Kevin didn't respond, just waited, wary. Bree rarely dropped by for no good reason now that she was married. She had better things to do with her evenings than to sit with him and chat about the weather. Usually if he kept quiet, she'd eventually get to the point.

Tonight, however, the tactic didn't seem to be working. Bree just sat there, gazing out at the water, seemingly content. He knew better. Like him, she was biding her time.

"Why aren't you home with Jake?" he asked eventually, hoping to forestall whatever had brought her over here by guiding her toward what was usually her favorite topic, her new husband.

"Mrs. Finch had a lilac emergency," she said with a smile.

Mrs. Finch's obsession with her lilacs was legendary. She nearly drove Jake crazy with her insistence on overseeing the annual mulching and trimming he did for her, but she was one of his landscaping business's best customers, so when she called, he went. Kevin grinned. "Better him than me."

Bree laughed. "That's right. I'd forgotten you used to do lawn work for her when you were a kid."

"I only helped Jake, so he'd finish sooner and we could go out chasing girls," he corrected.

"You and my husband chased girls together?" she asked with a narrowed gaze. "I don't remember that."

"Oops!" Kevin replied, trying to inject a note of contrition into his voice. He couldn't quite manage it. If he'd just thrown Jake to the wolves, so be it. Maybe it would get Bree's focus off him.

Apparently, though, she was more than capable of multitasking, because she turned her attention right back to him.

"I met Shanna today," she said, all innocence. "She said you'd been looking for me."

"I was."

"Any particular reason?"

"I mentioned I might go into town and Gram immediately claimed she wanted a few flowers to fill in an arrangement." Gram's request had been a blatant lie, and they'd both known it.

"But you never picked up any flowers," Bree said, looking confused.

"Because her garden's in full bloom," he said. "I know a manipulation when it slaps me in the face. She just wanted to be sure I kept my word and got out of the house. It's her latest mission in life."

Bree grinned. "She's not half as sneaky as she likes to think she is."

"Never was," he said, waiting for another shoe to drop.

"I hear you hung out for a while at the bookstore," she finally said, her tone oh-so-casual.

He shrugged. "I was waiting for you. Shanna was having trouble with her cappuccino machine, so I offered to set it up for her. It was like the one I used to have at home. No big deal, certainly nothing to bring you running over here with all these questions."

Her brow lifted. "She didn't mention that you'd helped her out."

"Like I said, it wasn't a big deal. Is there some point you're trying to get to?"

"Not really," she said, sitting back in companionable silence just long enough to lull him into a false sense of complacency before asking, "What did you think of her?"

"Who? Shanna?"

She rolled her eyes. "Isn't that who we've been talking about?"

He regarded her evenly. "A second ago we were talking about Gram."

"Oh, please. I know what you think about our grandmother. Yes, Shanna, dolt. She's attractive."

"I didn't notice." It was a lie. He'd noticed that her cheeks flushed easily, that her hair had a tendency to curl haphazardly, that she barely came up to his chin. But he'd also seen something else: trouble. She was vulnerable and needy, and not because she couldn't get her cappuccino machine working, either. It was something else, something he'd read in the depths of her eyes. He couldn't cope with needy. He could barely cope with his own life these days.

"Well, she is attractive," Bree said. "Single, too. At least she wasn't wearing any kind of a ring, and she never mentioned anything about a husband."

"Do most people you know spill their entire life story the second you meet them?"

"Of course not. I'm just passing along what I observed."

Kevin scowled at his sister. "I hope you're not planning to indulge in some unsolicited matchmaking," he said in a tone he hoped would quell any ideas she had along that line.

"No one in this family approves of meddling," she said piously.

"That doesn't seem to stop 'em from engaging in it," he retorted sourly. "Before you go getting any ideas, keep in mind that I'm so far from wanting a woman in my life, I might as well be living in a monastery."

"Which is a waste, if you ask me."

"I didn't ask, did I?"

"Come on, Kevin," she coaxed. "Live a little. You don't have to marry the woman. You don't even have to date her. Just have coffee with her, help her out getting the store organized, something that will bring a little human contact back into your life."

"With you, Jess, Abby, Gram and Dad on my case, I have about as much human contact these days as I can handle," he grumbled.

"We don't count. You need to interact with the outside world."

"Leave it alone, Bree. Leave *me* alone."

He stood up, then reached down to scoop Davy off his feet. "Bath time, kiddo."

"No! More flies," Davy protested, clinging tightly to his jar with both hands.

"Two's enough," Kevin told him. "That's quite a catch. Thank your Aunt Bree and tell her good night."

Davy dutifully smiled at his aunt. "Bye, Bwee."

"Good night, lovebug." She grinned at Kevin. "Night, pain."

He laughed. "Ditto."

She fell into step beside him as he crossed the lawn. "Shanna says her shelves are being delivered first thing in the morning," she said casually.

"So?"

She stood tall and gave him a peck on his cheek. "Just thought you might want to know."

He let that pass. And tomorrow, if he had a grain of sense in his head, he'd find some excuse to be anywhere other than Main Street. Not only did he not want to get sucked into Shanna's life, but he also didn't want to give his sister even an iota of encouragement for this undisguised matchmaking scheme of hers.

Mick was sick of seeing his son hanging around the house. For months now he'd cut Kevin some slack. He'd figured it took time to recover from losing his wife. Maybe just as much to recover from being in a war zone, despite Kevin's claim that he'd put all that behind him when he'd been discharged. Kevin had had enough nightmares under this very roof to make a liar out of himself, though Mick was sure Kevin thought no one knew about those.

Mick had listened to everyone else's opinion that Kevin needed time, but to his way of thinking, time was up. A thirty-year-old man needed a focus in his life, a reason to get up in the morning, something beyond a demanding two-year-old. Mick intended to see that Kevin got busy finding that new direction for himself.

He found Kevin on the beach, staring out to sea while Davy built a lopsided sand castle beside him. The structure of it offended Mick's architectural eye, but he shook off the desire to sit down and teach his grandson how to build something that would withstand the first lap of a wave. This walk down to the beach wasn't about giving his grandson an engineering lesson he wasn't ready for.

"Grampa," Davy said, looking up at him with glee. "Play with me, okay?"

"Maybe later, sport," Mick told him. He turned to Kevin. "You have plans for the day?"

Kevin shook his head.

"Good. Then you can come with me."

"Where?" Kevin asked suspiciously.

"I'm managing one of the Habitat for Humanity sites. I could use some help."

Kevin pulled his sunglasses down on his nose and eyed Mick skeptically. "Really? You're volunteering?"

"Yes, I'm volunteering," Mick said irritably. "It was your grandmother's idea, and it was a good one."

"And your company?"

"Can pretty much run itself these days," Mick said. At first that discovery hadn't pleased him. He'd always thought of himself as indispensable, but now he'd recognized the advantages of having more free time. He was spending quite a lot of it in New York with his ex-wife. The rest he was devoting to building these houses for Habitat for Humanity. They'd been thrilled to have someone with his level of expertise on a site. With his contractor skills, he could juggle several locations at once and keep construction flowing on all of them. And he had contacts in the trades all over Maryland and wasn't above twisting anyone's arm to get a few free hours of help with the skilled carpentry, electrical and plumbing work.

"Okay, let's say I can swallow this new, compassionate, giving role of yours," Kevin said, his tone wry. "Where exactly do you see me fitting in? You pretty much banished me from every job site you were ever on. As you were so fond of pointing out, I have absolutely no construction skills. I believe you mentioned a time or two that I was a disgrace." He grinned. "You weren't wrong."

To Mick's dismay, Kevin was right about that. It had been a sad day when he'd realized that neither of his sons knew one end of a hammer from the other and, worse, didn't care. They couldn't even paint a room without making a mess of it.

Still, he said optimistically, "You're not too old to learn. A lot of volunteers aren't experienced."

"But won't it be embarrassing when the son of the great architect Mick O'Brien puts up a wall that falls right back down?"

Mick chuckled despite himself. "You have a point." He studied his son with a worried frown. "So, what are you going to do with yourself?"

"Today? I thought I'd hang out here for a while with Davy, then maybe run some errands."

Mick barely managed to keep his irritation out of his voice. "You know I'm not just asking about today. What's your long-term plan, Kevin?"

"No idea," he said succinctly and without remorse.

"There are paramedic openings here in town," Mick said.

"So I'm told," Kevin admitted. "I'm not interested."

"Then what does interest you?" Mick asked impatiently, then could have bitten his tongue. He'd vowed to build a bridge with his son, not destroy the rare bit of peace between them.

At his raised voice, Davy looked up, his chin wobbling precariously, his eyes filling with tears. The look tore at Mick's heart. He bent down and scooped up his grandson.

"Hey, big fella, what about you? You want to come with Grampa today?"

Kevin frowned at that. "You can't have a two-year-old running around a construction site," he objected.

"I'm only going by for an hour or two to check a few things. I have a hard hat somewhere around here that's just his size. I won't let him out of my sight. You could ride along with us, if you're worried about him."

"Nice try, Dad, but contrary to whatever impression I gave you earlier, I actually do have things to do."

"Such as?" Mick pushed.

The simple question seemed to throw Kevin. Clearly he needed time to invent an excuse.

"I'm going into town," he said eventually.

"For?"

"What difference does it make why I'm going? Isn't the goal to get poor, depressed Kevin out of the house?" He stood up and stalked off.

Mick stood, staring after him, and sighed.

"Daddy go bye-bye," Davy said sadly.

Mick gave his grandson a hug. "That's okay, pal. We're going bye-bye, too, and something tells me we're going to have a lot more fun."

And, truth be told, knowing that ripped him apart inside.

3

Despite his resolve the day before, Kevin found himself on Main Street in front of the bookstore. He was only here because he was so annoyed with his father, and he might have walked right on past, but his sister chose that moment to step outside of Flowers on Main, the shop she'd opened over a year ago.

"Well, well, look who's here," she said cheerfully. "You came to help Shanna, after all. Good for you."

"Maybe I came to help you," he muttered, embarrassed at having been caught anywhere in the vicinity after making such a big show about his determination to steer clear of the town's new bookseller. He watched anxiously to see if his sister would buy that he'd come to see her.

Bree regarded him with a speculative expression. "Okay," she said eventually, as if taking his claim at face value. "What did you have in mind?"

"I could deliver flowers," he offered impulsively, seizing at straws.

"You could," she said agreeably, "but I already pay someone to do that." She seemed to be fighting a smile.

"Maybe your place needs to be swept out. I could do that."

She laughed then. "You are so pitiful, big brother. Go inside and give Shanna a hand. She's the one who could really use some help today. Being a Good Samaritan to a newcomer in town will make you feel better. Who knows? You might even enjoy yourself."

She was probably right about that. Gram had always taught them that reaching out to someone else was the best way to forget about their own problems. He regarded his sister with a narrowed gaze. "Only if you don't mention it to anyone else," he bargained. "I'll do it, if you promise you won't go blabbing to Jess, Abby and Gram, making some kind of big deal out of it or hinting around that I'm interested in Shanna."

"You didn't mention Dad," she noted. "Can I tell him about it?"

"Actually, he sort of knows," he admitted sheepishly. "Not about Shanna exactly, but that I was coming into town today for a reason. I used it as an excuse to get out of going with him to a work site."

She stared at him in astonishment. "Dad wanted you to go to a construction site with him? Seriously?"

Kevin laughed at her reaction. "Yeah, it shocked me, too. Obviously he's desperate to get me out of the house." He sobered. "So, is it a deal? If I help Shanna, you'll keep quiet about it? I just don't need the aggravation."

"What aggravation?" she asked, her expression all innocence.

He rolled his eyes. "We both know Abby and the rest of them would be down here before the day's out to check out Shanna. Whatever antimatchmaking resolutions they supposedly live by would be tossed out the window. If Shanna passes inspection, they'll be throwing her at me every time I turn around."

"Would that be so awful?"

"Exactly how much of their meddling did you find tolerable?"

Her smile spread. "You have a point. It's a deal. I won't say a word."

"And you won't poke your head in every two seconds to see what's happening in there," he added.

"Why? You scared I'll catch you sneaking kisses behind the bookshelves?"

Kevin turned on his heel. "That's it. I'm out of here."

Bree caught him before he'd taken half a dozen steps back toward his truck. "I'm sorry," she said. Her tone was serious, but there was still a wicked twinkle in her eyes. "I just can't resist teasing you. You're so cute when you get all flustered."

"How old are we? Thirteen?"

She held up a hand. "I'll behave. I promise. Now, go. It's a good deed, Kevin, not a lifetime commitment."

Kevin hesitated, then walked back to the bookstore. He cast one last warning look at his sister, then turned the knob and went inside.

He found Shanna sitting in the middle of the floor with a screwdriver in one hand and tears tracking down her cheeks. She was surrounded by piles of unassembled shelves.

"Uh-oh," Kevin said, immediately recognizing the problem.

Shanna swiped impatiently at the tears, then regarded him with a chagrined expression. "I thought they came assembled. When the delivery guy piled up this huge stack of boxes, then headed for the door, I almost went after him with a hammer. I begged him to stay. I offered him money. It was pitiful. I even offered him a lifetime of free books if he'd put these together for me, but he just waved and walked out the door. What kind of customer service is that? I'd call and complain, but there's no time. I have to get these put together."

She stopped babbling and gave him a watery smile. "Have I mentioned yet that I am really, really glad to see you, especially if you have any idea how to assemble these things?"

Kevin wanted to be the hero she needed, but the sight of all these pieces of wood, little plastic bags of screws and nails and other unidentifiable pieces of metal made him want to curse a blue streak himself. If his father heard about how Kevin's day had turned out, he'd laugh himself silly.

Still, she looked so frantic, he had to do something. He took another survey of the materials. How hard could it be?

"Instructions?" he asked at last, resigned to taking a stab at putting the shelves together.

She held up a sheet of paper with a diagram on it.

He looked at it. "Okay, this looks easy enough," he said, faking confidence.

She frowned at that. "Really? It makes sense to you?"

He considered lying to reassure her, then shrugged instead. "Not really, but we're two intelligent adults. Surely we can figure this out. If not, I have an ace in the hole."

"Oh?"

"My dad," he said succinctly. It might be humiliating to call in Mick, but in the interest of making sure these shelves didn't tumble down on top of Shanna the instant the first books were stacked on them, it might be necessary.

"Isn't putting bookshelves together a poor use of his

skills?" she asked. "He's an architect, right? A really famous one?"

"He is, but he'll see this as an act of kindness," Kevin said. "He seems to be open to all sorts of unusual opportunities these days."

She studied his expression. "You sound bitter."

"Maybe, just a little," he said. "But that's a story for another day. You read and point. I'll assemble."

"Works for me," she said.

An hour later they had the frame for the first set of shelves assembled and the backing nailed on. It even seemed relatively sturdy. Kevin stood it upright and gave it a gentle shove, just to be sure. It sat squarely in place. "Not bad," he murmured.

"It's excellent," Shanna said.

He laughed at her enthusiasm. "Let's not get carried away. Where do you want it?"

When he'd positioned it to her satisfaction, they installed the movable shelves.

"Perfect," she announced, then met his gaze. "There are only fifteen more units to go."

Kevin swallowed hard. "Fifteen?"

She nodded, her expression apologetic. "You don't have to help with all of them. I think I've figured it out from watching you. And the units for the children's books are smaller. I can handle those, I think."

It was the *I think* that kept him squarely in place. He resigned himself to a very long day. "I'm here. We might as well finish, or at least get as many done as we can today."

And as long as they were focused on the shelves, there was little time for personal chitchat, no time for his gaze to linger on her soft curves and the shapely legs revealed by a pair of shorts. There were only a few spare seconds for that quick hint of betrayal that flashed through him when he did feel a stirring of interest in this woman who wasn't Georgia.

That thought was so troubling, he stood up abruptly. "First, though, I think we need some lunch. I'll run over to Sally's and pick something up. Anything in particular you want?"

Shanna looked startled, but she recovered quickly. "Sure, a tuna on whole wheat would be great. Maybe some chips." She met his gaze. "But I'm buying. I'll get my purse."

"I'll pay for it," Kevin said, but she'd already turned and headed to the back room.

He stood staring after her. In that instant, he realized for the first time that she was as skittish as he was, maybe even more so. If looking at her aroused his masculine appreciation, then this sign of vulnerability intrigued him in a way that was far more frightening. It was one thing to be here, helping out a newcomer to town. It was something else entirely to allow himself to be fascinated by her. Bree would gloat from now till doomsday if she ever found out her scheme just might be working.

Shanna had recognized the panic in Kevin's eyes earlier in the day. She was pretty sure it was reflected in her own. After that one moment of disconcerting awareness, she'd been careful the rest of the day to avoid his gaze, to keep the conversation impersonal.

Of course, there was only so much to be said about the assembly of the bookshelves, especially since after a while it had become almost routine. An awkward silence had fallen between them. She'd had no idea how to break it without venturing through the minefield that was apparently his life these days.

It occurred to her that if she couldn't converse with a man who was spending hours out of his day helping her put together bookshelves, it might not bode well for her ability to come up with small talk with which to engage her customers. That gave her a whole different reason to panic.

She had to stop sitting here pretending to help him when he obviously no longer needed her to read the instructions. She needed to focus on some other task.

Standing up, she announced to some point behind his left ear, "I'm going to start shelving books while you finish up, if that's okay."

He didn't even glance up. "Good idea. I can finish up these last few units by myself."

Shanna opted to start in the children's section, which was as far from Kevin as it was possible to get without leaving the store. The shipment of picture books had come in at midmorning, so she started by unpacking those, her eyes lighting up as she studied the colorful artwork in each book before placing it on the shelf.

She was exclaiming over each one until a shadow fell over the pages of the book in her hands. She looked up and saw Kevin grinning at her.

"It's going to be slow going if you stop to read every book," he said.

"I'm not," she protested, then chuckled. "Okay, I am glancing through every one of them. The artists who illustrate these books are amazing."

"Thus all the excited exclamations," he guessed. "I was hoping maybe you were back here looking at erotica."

Shanna blushed furiously. "I'd hardly have it anywhere near the children's section."

"Good to know." He studied her with obvious interest. "What sorts of books are you planning to stock, besides the picture books for kids?"

"I figure people at the beach will want escapism, so mostly bestsellers, mysteries, thrillers, romances, as well as some nonfiction such as cooking, gardening and regional books. If people start asking for things I don't stock, I'll special order it for them. I think customer service is going to be critical if the store's to be successful."

He hunkered down beside her and glanced at a few of the books spread around her. "Davy's going to love coming in here," he said.

"Pick a book and take it home to him," she encouraged. "I owe you at least that for all your help today."

"Nope," he said flatly. "Any books I get from here, I'll pay for. This is your business and it's a new one. A few months, a year from now, if you offer me something for free, I'll accept it graciously."

"I'll make a note of that, then. On my first anniversary, you get your pick of any book in the store."

Kevin nodded. "That'll work. Now, how about a break? I'm starving again, and we've been at this for hours. I'll come back in the morning and finish up. In the meantime, why don't we walk to Sally's or one of the places along Shore Road and grab a bite to eat?"

She glanced at her watch and saw with dismay that it was after seven. "I had no idea how late it was," she protested. "Shouldn't you get home to your son?"

"I called and he's already out like a light. He had a big day with my dad, apparently."

"He's really lucky to be surrounded by so much family," she said, unable to keep a wistful note out of her voice.

She couldn't help thinking about another little boy whose life was nowhere near as idyllic. Because despair lay down that path, she deliberately stood up and went into the back room for her purse. "I'll have dinner with you on one condition," she told Kevin. "I'm buying. It's nonnegotiable."

"In that case, I should insist on going to Brady's. It's the most expensive place in town, next to the inn."

Shanna's expression brightened. "I hadn't even thought of the inn. Let's go there. I stayed there last year, and the food is fabulous."

"I don't think so," Kevin said flatly.

"If it's the cost, don't worry about it. And I think we're dressed okay. It's fairly informal."

"Not the cost or our clothes," he said. "My youngest sister owns the place."

"Oh, that's right," she said. "Jess, right? I really liked her." She frowned at his expression. "Why is that a problem?"

"Apparently you don't have siblings," he said direly.

"No, but..." Her voice trailed off as understanding dawned. "They meddle!"

"They meddle," he confirmed. "I've already made Bree take a vow of silence about me helping you out today. If we show up at the inn, Jess will try to make something out of it, and the next thing you know Abby will be chiming in with her two cents. She's the worst of the lot. She's the oldest, and she stepped in as a surrogate mother hen when our mom and dad divorced. She thinks that gives her the right to an opinion on almost everything related to our lives."

Kevin sighed dramatically. "The only one not likely to chime in is my brother, Connor, but that's only because he's in Baltimore and won't hear about this for a day or two. He's in his first year with a big law firm, so he barely has a minute to himself, much less time to listen to the family grapevine."

Though she understood the problem, Shanna thought it all sounded rather wonderful. As an only child who'd lost both of her parents a few years ago, she'd always longed for a great big family of exactly the kind he was describing. That was one reason, she now believed, that she'd been so eager to marry Greg Hamilton. It had nothing to do with his wealth or his family's prominence in Philadelphia society. Greg was a single dad with sole custody of his son, and she'd had an instant family. That had overshadowed all of the warning signs that she was making a terrible mistake.

"I hear the French bistro around the corner is really good," Kevin prompted. "How about that, instead? Please. Take pity on me and keep my family out of both our lives."

"Sure," she said, though not without some disappointment. "That makes sense. It's close and I'll be able to get back in here and do a few more things before I quit for the night."

Kevin looked so genuinely relieved, she was glad she'd acquiesced.

To her surprise, Shanna found herself adding, "On one condition."

"What?" he asked, instantly suspicious.

"You'll tell me more about your family."

"Why?" he asked, clearly bewildered by the request.

"I was an only child and have what I used to refer to as *Little House on the Prairie* syndrome. I idealize big families. I always imagine these amazing holiday gatherings, brothers and sisters pestering each other but being there for each other, no matter what. Is it like that with your family?"

"It is," he said, then gave her a wry look, "though it's not always the blessing you seem to be envisioning."

"I want to hear about that, too," she said eagerly, leading the way out of the shop and locking the door behind them.

"You're going to be bored silly," he warned her as they strolled down the block and turned onto the road that ran along the beach. There were several sidewalk cafés along the block, all of them busy. Across the street, couples and families strolled along the beach.

"You won't bore me," she said with certainty.

Even if his stories turned out to be dull, she had a feeling she'd find them fascinating, because of the insights they'd give her into who Kevin O'Brien really was. Or maybe who he had been before his life had been turned upside down by tragedy.

"I don't like this," Megan O'Brien declared to Mick. "I don't like it one bit."

During one of their now-nightly phone conversations, Mick had been filling her in on Kevin's ongoing lack of motivation. She'd seen for herself how lost he was on her visits to Chesapeake Shores, but like everyone else she'd been making excuses for him. Clearly, though, it had gone on long enough. Everyone might grieve at their own pace, but sooner or later it was time to get on with life, especially with a child to consider.

"Have you tried to get through to him?" she asked Mick.

"Of course I have," Mick said. "I tried to get him to go with me this morning, just to give him something to do. He turned me down flat, then stormed off. I haven't seen him since."

"Oh, Mick, you don't think he's drinking, do you?"

"Absolutely not," Mick said at once. "I haven't seen him have more than a beer or two in the evening since he moved home, and he hardly leaves the house, so I think I would know."

"Well, something has to be done. He can't go on like this," she said.

"That seems to be the general consensus around here, but not one of us has been able to come up with a plan."

"I'm coming down there," Megan announced. "I'll be there on Friday."

"Not that I won't be happy for any excuse to have you here," Mick said, "but what is it you think you can accomplish that the rest of us haven't?"

"I'm his mother. Surely I can think of some way to get through to him, even if having me around does nothing more than make him angry. At least that would demonstrate *some* kind of emotion."

"Meggie, are you sure?" Mick asked worriedly. "He's not been very receptive on your last visits."

"Because I've been tiptoeing around like everyone else, trying to give him space. He's mad at me. We all know that. I left and he took your side and he can hold a grudge with the best of the O'Briens. It's time to put that in the past. Like it or not, I *am* his mother, and I *will* make him listen to me."

Mick chuckled. "I'm impressed by your determination and I agree he should let go of the past, but this may not be the best time to get through to him," he warned. "He already has a lot on his plate."

"Since when did you give two figs about timing?"

Mick chuckled. "Never," he conceded. "I just don't want him trampling all over your feelings."

"I can take it," she assured him. "I deserve whatever he

wants to dish out. And maybe if he's venting all of his anger at me, he'll release some of the pent-up emotions he has about Georgia. Where is he now?"

"I have no idea," Mick admitted. "Like I said, he took off this morning in a huff, and Ma says she hasn't seen him since."

"What about Davy?" she asked incredulously. "He didn't just go off and leave Nell to take care of him, did he?" Even as she asked, she saw the irony, since that was exactly what she'd done years ago, left Mick's mother to raise her children. It had been unintentional, but that's how it had turned out when her plans to bring them to be with her in New York had been ditched for a whole variety of reasons that she now knew were nothing more than flimsy excuses.

"No, he's very reliable when it comes to his son. He knew Davy was with me. He called earlier to check on him, but when Ma told him Davy was already asleep, Kevin said he'd be home in a couple of hours."

"Maybe he's spending time with one of the girls," she suggested. "Or Jake. They used to be good friends."

"Maybe," Mick said, though he sounded doubtful. "He's not been in any mood to socialize, though. Jake's stopped by more than once, suggested a guys' night out, but Kevin's refused. I suspect he's off somewhere by himself, brooding."

"For hours on end?" she asked, her concern growing. "He was always a social kid, not a loner. This really isn't good, Mick. I'm worried."

"You think I should go look for him? I could take a ride around town."

"He'll be furious if he thinks you're checking up on him," Megan said. "Then, again, it would put my mind at ease if I at least knew he wasn't in real trouble."

"Then I'll go right now," Mick said at once.

The immediate response surprised her. There'd been a time when Mick wouldn't have wanted to involve himself in messy, emotional situations. He'd been focused almost entirely on his career. His family had taken a distant second place. It was the reason she'd finally left him.

All that was water long since under the bridge, she reminded herself. Lately Mick had been proving time and again that he'd changed his priorities, that he was putting his family first. More and more, Megan was reminded of the caring man she'd married. That he was as attentive to her as he'd been when they'd first been courting helped, as well.

"You'll call me when you find him?" she asked him now. "No matter how late it is."

"I'll call," he promised.

"In the meantime, I'll make my flight arrangements for this weekend," she said. "Even if he rejects me again, at least Kevin is going to know that I care enough to be there for him."

"As long as you're prepared for things not to go smoothly," Mick said.

"No one ever said the path to reconciliation was destined to go smoothly," she reminded him. "I still have a long way to go with each of our children."

"As do I," Mick conceded.

"The point is to keep trying. Now, go find our boy, Mick. Make sure he's safe."

"He's not a boy," Mick said.

"I don't care how old he gets to be, when he's hurting, he's still my boy," she said fiercely. "And I'm always going to want to make it better."

She had to wonder, though, if this time that was going to be beyond her capabilities.

4

Shanna frowned as a classic Mustang convertible passed by on Shore Road for the fourth time. Though he made a halfhearted attempt to disguise his interest, it was evident the older driver was studying her and Kevin on each pass. There was no question that he was looking at them, because they were the only two people left at the café. They'd been lingering over coffee for a while now. Kevin hadn't noticed the man's odd behavior because his back was to the street. When she spotted the car yet again, she reached for Kevin's hand.

"Turn around," she said in an urgent undertone. "There's someone watching us. I thought I might be imagining it, but he's back again. This has to be the fifth time he's gone around the block and slowed down right in front of us."

Kevin regarded her blankly. "What? Who?" He shifted around, took one look at the approaching car, and groaned. He turned back to her with an apologetic expression. "That would be my father."

"Your father?" She took another look and saw the resemblance: the same square jaw, the same thick black hair, though his had some gray and Kevin's was cropped short in a way that kept its natural wave under control. If she'd been able to see them at this distance, she suspected the man's eyes would be the same vivid blue. She turned back to Kevin with a puzzled expression. "Why on earth do you think he keeps circling the block?"

"I don't know for sure, but if I had to hazard a guess, he's spying on me."

Shanna stared at him, then glanced back to note that the car had, indeed, slowed to a crawl. The driver lifted his hand in a casual wave, then made a sharp left into a metered, pull-in parking space across the road.

"Maybe he's looking for you because something's wrong at home," she suggested.

Kevin shook his head and gestured toward the cell phone on the table. "He and my grandmother both know how to reach me."

"Well, he's definitely coming this way, so obviously he was looking for you."

"More's the pity," Kevin said grimly. He stood up and met his father before he reached the table. "Dad."

She watched as Mick O'Brien gave him a jovial slap on the back as if this meeting had been totally accidental. "Son, I didn't expect to find you here." He glanced in Shanna's direction. "And with this lovely young lady."

Kevin gave a dramatic roll of his eyes. "Dad, this is Shanna Carlyle. She's opening a bookstore next to Bree's shop. I was helping her at the shop earlier."

"Good for you," Mick said, retrieving a chair from a nearby table and pulling it up to theirs. "Think I'll join you for a cup of coffee, if you don't mind." Then as an obvious afterthought, he added almost hopefully, "Unless I'm interrupting."

Kevin, his expression resigned, sat back down. "You're not interrupting."

"Well, that's good then." He beamed benevolently at them as if bestowing a blessing.

It took every bit of restraint Shanna possessed not to chuckle at Mick O'Brien's undisguised eagerness to figure out what was going on between the two of them. If Kevin weren't so obviously miserable at having been discovered with her, she probably would have laughed. She hadn't had anyone so blatantly checking out any of her dates since she'd left home for college, and back then it had been *her* dad.

"Mr. O'Brien, it's a real pleasure to meet you," she said when Kevin remained silent. "I fell in love with this town when I visited last year. I'm so excited that I was finally able to get some retail space to open my shop."

"You're exactly the kind of young, energetic person the town needs," Mick said. "You'll keep Main Street interesting, just the way it was intended to be." He paused long enough to order a decaf coffee from the perky young waitress, who'd been hovering nearby, her rapt gaze on Kevin all evening. When she'd left, he asked Shanna, "How did you and my son meet?"

"Dad!"

He blinked at Kevin's reaction. "What? It's a logical question." He winked at the waitress when she brought his coffee. "Thanks, Mary." He turned his attention back to Shanna. "So, how did you meet?"

"He was looking for Bree yesterday and stopped in my shop. He came back today and saw that I was practically buried under a pile of unassembled bookshelves. He offered to pitch in."

She was surprised by the look of dismay that passed over the older man's face.

"Kevin put your shelves together?" he asked, sounding worried.

"He did."

"And they're still standing?"

She frowned at his reaction. "Well, of course they are. Why wouldn't they be?" she asked, indignant on Kevin's behalf.

"Dad's not a fan of my construction skills," Kevin told her.

"You said yourself this morning that you don't have any," Mick reminded him. "This isn't news."

"Well, he did a fine job on my shelves," Shanna insisted. "You can inspect them yourself."

Mick backed down, obviously chagrined at having maligned his son in front of her. "No need for that. I guess I'm just surprised."

"For any number of reasons, I'm sure," Kevin added wryly. "Dad, is everything okay at home? Davy's not sick, is he?"

"No, no. I just decided to go for a ride. You know I like to take the Mustang out on a nice night from time to time."

"Which necessitated circling this block several times?" Kevin inquired.

Mick actually blushed at that. "Thought I saw you here, but I wasn't sure at first. Then I had a bit of trouble finding a parking space."

Kevin took an exaggerated look up and down the street, where parking spaces abounded. "Really? There are plenty now."

"Well, there weren't ten minutes ago," Mick told him, taking a final sip of his coffee and then standing. "Nice to meet you, Shanna. You let me know if you need any more help getting your store ready to open. I'd be glad to help out."

"Thanks, but I think it's all under control now," she said.

"See you at home, Kevin," he said, then turned on his heel and walked away.

Beside her, Kevin released the breath he'd obviously been holding.

"For a minute there, I thought he was going to tell me not to stay out too late," he grumbled. "Do I look like I'm sixteen?"

"I think he was sweet. He was obviously curious about what was going on with the two of us."

"Which he will now report far and wide," Kevin said, his expression grim. "You should have locked your shop door when you saw me coming today. You could have saved yourself a lot of grief."

"But then my shelves wouldn't be up," she reminded him. "That's worth a little meddling."

"We'll talk again in a day or two," he said direly. "See if you still feel that way."

She studied him for a moment, then risked a question that had been on her mind most of the day. "How is it that you have time to help me out? Is your job really flexible?"

The frown, which she'd come to recognize as an immediate response when she was cutting a little too closely to a nerve, returned.

"I've been taking some time off."

The response told her a lot, yet nothing at all. "Vacation?" she asked. "Or are you between jobs?"

His frown deepened. "Is there some reason you're so curious about my employment history?" he asked testily.

Shanna backed down at once. She'd *definitely* hit a nerve. "I'm sorry if I was prying. Sometimes my curiosity gets the best of me."

He sighed then. "No, I'm the one who should be sorry. I'm just sensitive, because my family's been bugging me to get back to work. Not because I'm sponging off of them. I have money and I'm paying my share of expenses around the house. They think I'm drifting."

"Are you?" she asked before she could stop herself. "Sorry, there I go again."

This time he didn't take offense. Instead, he shrugged. "It's true. I am drifting. I was a paramedic before I went overseas. I was a medic in Iraq. That's how I met…" He drew in a deep breath.

Shanna stayed silent and waited, sensing that he was struggling to find the words to finish the story.

"It's how Georgia and I met," he said at last, a catch in his voice. "When I came back, I got a job with a rescue unit in Virginia, while she was stationed at Fort Belvoir. Then she went overseas again. Six months into her tour, that's when she was killed. I quit my job and moved home."

"With all that training, I'm sure—"

Kevin cut her off. "Never again. I don't want to go back to that kind of work. I can't explain it, but I don't."

"Then what will you do?"

He gave her a wry look. "That's the million-dollar question." He stood up abruptly. "Look, it's late. I need to be getting home. I'll walk you back to the shop."

"It's just around the corner," she protested. "I'll be fine."

He gave her an impatient look. "My truck's just around the corner, too. I'll walk you back."

She gave in. "Thank you," she said. "Let me get a cup of coffee to go and pay the bill."

His eyes widened. "You planning on an all-nighter?"

She laughed. "I'll get decaf, but I can't seem to get anything done without a cup of coffee."

"Maybe you should consider getting some sleep instead. I'll be over here first thing to help you again. We'll have everything in place by the end of the day tomorrow."

"I can't ask you to spend another day dealing with shelves and boxes."

"You didn't ask. I volunteered. Besides, consider it a favor to me. If I'm with you, I'm not being subjected to questions and worried looks at home."

"Then this is a good deed on my part?"

"Something like that."

"In that case, I'll see you tomorrow."

"You get the coffee going, prove you've mastered that machine of yours, and I'll bring some of Gram's scones. She always bakes on Friday morning."

"Now, that's an offer I can't resist," she said as she accepted her change and the take-out cup of coffee from their waitress, who thanked her politely, though her gaze never left Kevin's face.

"Good night, Kevin," Mary said, her tone breathless. "Come back soon."

"Good night," he replied distractedly, clearly oblivious to the young woman's undisguised interest.

"I think you have a fan," Shanna said as they walked away.

He regarded her blankly. "Who?" At her gesture, he glanced back. "Mary? She's a kid."

"She's old enough," Shanna said, though she was vaguely relieved that he didn't share the girl's interest.

A few minutes later, in front of her shop, Kevin said, "I'll wait till you're inside with the door locked. I still think it would be better if I walked you up to your apartment. I don't like the idea of you in here all alone late at night."

"First of all, it's not that late, barely ten o'clock. Second, Chesapeake Shores is a very safe town. It says so in all the brochures."

"Do you think the local Chamber of Commerce would announce it if we'd been having a crime wave?"

Shanna laughed at that. "Probably not, but everyone I've asked, including the local police chief, has told me it's true."

"You spoke to the chief?"

"Of course. I wanted to know if I'd need an alarm system."

"Very smart."

"Just because I get flustered over putting together a few shelves doesn't mean I didn't do my homework," she said, bristling at what she took as a hint of condescension in his voice.

"Hey, I wasn't suggesting you didn't go into this business with your eyes wide open. I was just praising your foresight."

Shanna winced. "Sorry. My best friend's skepticism about all this has made me a little touchy."

"She thought the store was a mistake?"

"She thinks it's insane, actually. But she's coming to check it out for herself next week. I intend to prove her wrong."

"Good for you." He held open the door so she could go inside, then advised, "Lock up."

She gave him a quelling look that had him backing away, hands in the air in a gesture of surrender.

"Just a suggestion," he said.

"Top of my to-do list," she assured him, closing the door, then making a dramatic show of turning the lock.

Kevin gave her one last wave, then headed down the

block toward his truck. She stared after him, wondering at the feeling of disappointment that swept over her when he was out of sight. She felt a moment's empathy for poor Mary back at the restaurant. What was wrong with her? Had she expected him to come inside, sweep her off her feet and smother her with passionate kisses? Of course not. But a friendly peck on the cheek might have been nice, she thought wistfully.

As soon as the thought came to her, though, she reminded herself that Kevin O'Brien was off-limits. He had more baggage than a passenger jet. So did she. It was a lethal combination. She needed to remember that.

But the scary truth was, it was getting harder and harder.

To Kevin's very deep regret, his father was at the kitchen table when he walked in there in the morning. The lingering scent of his grandmother's fresh scones was in the air. An airtight container, filled with the traditional scones, sat on the counter.

"You're up early," Kevin commented as he poured himself a cup of coffee. "You going back to the Habitat site this morning?"

"Nope. Getting up early's a habit that's hard to break. Thought I'd go over to the inn later. Jess has a few little projects that need doing."

Kevin lifted a brow. "And she's letting you do them?"

"As a matter of fact, she asked if I would," Mick responded, clearly delighted about that. "Depending on how long that takes, I thought I might drive into town afterward and check on Bree."

"Really?" Kevin said with undisguised skepticism. "Has she mentioned a few chores, as well?"

His father scowled. "Can't a man visit his own daughter?"

"Of course, if that's all you're doing. Are you sure you're not more interested in checking out the new bookstore, maybe seeing if I'm hanging around there again today?"

Mick gave him a bland look. "Might as well, as long as I'll be in the neighborhood."

"You are so transparent," Kevin accused. "There's nothing going on between Shanna and me."

"Never said there was, but I wouldn't mind taking a look at those shelves you put together. I consider that a civic duty."

Kevin couldn't help chuckling at that. "I think they're safe enough, but it actually wouldn't hurt to have a second opinion."

Mick gave him a considering look. "Did I mention your mother's coming into town tonight?"

Kevin stilled at the news. "Why?"

"She and I have plans, if you must know," Mick said, though it wasn't very convincing.

"You called her about me, didn't you?" Kevin said flatly. "Dad, why would you do that? Don't you think I have enough family on my case, as it is? I don't need Mom chiming in with her two cents. She has no right."

"Get over yourself," Mick retorted. "Your mother and I are trying to patch things up. We talk every night. I try to lure her down here every chance I get."

"Then she's not developing some sudden need to be the mother that she stopped being over fifteen years ago?" he asked skeptically.

Mick flushed angrily. "She never stopped being your mother," he told Kevin. "She stopped being my wife. Both of us made some lousy decisions back then, and you kids suffered because of it. That's my fault as much as hers."

"You weren't the one who chose to date while you were still married," Kevin said just as heatedly.

Mick's fist came down on the table. "Dammit, she did not have an affair, Kevin. You know that."

"Maybe not, but she was seen all over town in the company of some other man while you were away on business. How am I supposed to respect her after that?"

"You give her another chance, same as me," Mick retorted. "Every one of us has made mistakes, Kevin. Your mother, me, even you, I suspect. All we can hope for after is that we'll be able to make amends and be forgiven."

Kevin thought of the mistakes he'd made with Georgia, not by betraying her, but by letting her go back to Iraq without a fight. How could he make amends for that? How could he ever be forgiven, when she was gone? To his regret, he could see his father's point, but he wasn't ready to let go of the past, not his own mistakes or his mother's.

"I think maybe I'll see if I can stay with Bree and Jake this weekend," Kevin said.

"They're practically newlyweds," Mick objected. "They don't need you and Davy underfoot. And Abby and Trace have little enough time alone as it is, in case that was your next excuse for getting out of here."

"Then I'll book a room at the inn," Kevin said.

"Jess is all booked up. Told me so herself last night."

Kevin resigned himself to staying put. Running was cowardly anyway. Why should he be the one to leave? This house was as much his home as it was his mother's. More so, in fact.

"Dad, do you seriously think you and Mom will get back together?"

"I'm counting on it," Mick replied without hesitation. "There's never been another woman for me, Kevin.

Never." He gave him a pointed look. "And there's never been another man for her, either, in case you were about to offer your opinion about that."

"You really believe that, don't you?" Kevin said, wondering at the fact that a man as smart as his father could be so gullible.

"I *know* that," Mick told him. "And if you took a few steps back from your own pain at having your mother move away, looked at the whole situation back then, you'd know it, too. Her seeing that other man meant nothing. It was a cry of desperation, but I had too much pride to see it for what it was. I reacted the same way you did, judging her without asking for one second if I was responsible for her needing a little attention from someone else."

"So cheating is okay, if she was feeling neglected?" Even as the words left his mouth, he knew the bitterness behind them had little to do with his mother. For weeks before she'd died, he'd worried and wondered if Georgia was being faithful to him. He knew what it was like over there, knew how hard it was to face the danger alone. He'd had not one shred of evidence to support his suspicions, but each time she'd mentioned another soldier's name in passing, his jealousy had deepened. If his worst fears had been confirmed, he wasn't sure how he would have handled it. It wouldn't have been like this, that's for sure. His mother's behavior years ago had hardened his heart toward cheating, no matter the excuses behind it.

"I can't believe you'd just turn the other cheek, Dad," he said.

"Your mother never cheated," Mick repeated emphatically. "She might have thought about it, might even have wanted me to think she would, but she never did. I believe that with every fiber of my being." He looked Kevin in the eye. "And even if she had, it's in the past now. We're moving on, finding our way back to each other. It's what we both want, and if you can't embrace that, then just stay out of our way."

"So you don't care what I—what any of us, for that matter—think about this reconciliation?"

"We care," Mick said. "But it's not going to be the deciding factor. You're adults now, not children. Your opinions count, certainly, but you're old enough to understand that love is what matters in this life, and we shouldn't let anything stand in the way of that."

"You let work get in the way," Kevin reminded him.

"And I was a damn fool," Mick replied without hesitation. "That's a lesson I'm passing on to you here and now. If you're lucky enough to love someone, make that your top priority."

His father's belated transformation was hard to buy, but there was at least some evidence to support it. "Is that why you've cut back on work, taken to volunteering?"

"Yes."

Kevin tried to grapple with this turnaround. "And you don't feel like you're sacrificing your identity?"

"I have plenty of testaments to my identity as an architect all over this country," Mick said. "The identity that matters is how well I've done as a husband and father. That one's still evolving."

Kevin looked into his father's eyes and saw a serenity there that he couldn't recall ever seeing before. He was at peace with the choices he was making lately. Kevin would give anything to find some measure of peace these days. He didn't think he was going to find it in work, despite what everyone else seemed to be pushing him toward. As for love, what had that ever gotten him but a broken heart?

* * *

By midafternoon Shanna couldn't stand it another minute. Beyond asking where she wanted things, Kevin hadn't said two words to her all morning and only a half a dozen since lunchtime. The silence was making her a little crazy.

She poured two cups of coffee, frothed milk and added it to hers, then walked over to where Kevin was sorting the books for the nonfiction section according to category.

"Time for a break," she announced, holding out the coffee.

He accepted it with obvious reluctance and eyed her warily. "What's up?"

"That's what I want to know," she said. "You've hardly said a thing all day. Is something wrong? Is everything okay with your son?"

"Davy's over at my sister's playing with his cousins. Abby has a nanny who watches them during the summer."

"Okay," she said. "Then, if you're not worried about him, what's on your mind?"

He sat back, leaning against an overstuffed armchair she'd placed in the middle of the room. There were similar chairs scattered throughout. Most had been thrift shop finds, but all had been fitted with bright new slipcovers. Kevin's gaze finally met hers.

"Why does something have to be wrong?" he inquired testily. "Don't you ever have a day when you simply don't have much to say?"

"Sure," she said readily. "Usually when something's wrong."

His lips quirked up at that. "Okay, you got me there. Look, it's nothing for you to worry about. My mood has nothing to do with you."

"You're here, so it does affect me," she told him.

"I could leave."

"Now you're being ridiculous," she said irritably. "I don't want you to leave. I want you to talk to me."

"Shanna, I appreciate the concern. I really do, but you don't get to try to fix what's wrong with me. Believe me, others have tried and failed."

"So, you're a real hard case, is that it?"

Again, his lips twitched. "Something like that."

"You know, I'm actually a good listener," she said, not sure why she was so determined to get to the bottom of his mood. "I don't even have to offer any advice, though that might be a test of my willpower."

He laughed then, which was a breakthrough of sorts. She grinned back at him. "That's better."

"Can we consider your work here done?" he asked hopefully.

"For the moment. Laughter really is the best medicine, don't you think so?"

He gave her a somber look, then. "If only it were that easy," he murmured, putting aside his coffee cup and standing up. "I'm going to finish with these books now."

She watched as he went back to the task, deliberately shutting her out.

"You might take a look at a couple of those books on positive thinking," she called out as she went back to her own section of the store.

To her delight, he laughed again.

Maybe, she thought, if she worked at coaxing that laugh out of him, in time it would get easier. It might not chase away all his demons, but it could be a start.

She sighed at the thought. Here she was again, trying to save a wounded soul. She thought of her ex-husband.

She'd worked so hard to try to save him from himself, convinced that she could make things better for him and his son, but in the end alcohol had won.

It had taken a very long time, but she knew now it had never even been a fair fight.

5

With all of the physically demanding work finished at Shanna's store, Kevin needed to find an excuse to be away from the house over the weekend, so he could avoid an encounter with his mother. Despite his father's willingness to let bygones be bygones, Kevin wasn't interested in a reconciliation with the woman who'd left them. It still shocked him that his sisters seemed to be mellowing toward their mother, especially Jess, who'd suffered the most when she'd gone.

Friday evening, assured that Davy was welcome to spend the night at Abby's, he'd called Jake and scheduled a guys' night out with him, Will and Mack. The quick agreement to the last-minute suggestion was one of the few benefits of having everyone worried about him. Bree had immediately given Jake her blessing to join the outing. Apparently she considered the invitation to Jake a sign that Kevin was finally on the mend.

Kevin wondered what she would have thought if she'd known how little he'd had to say all evening. Jake and Mack had filled the conversational gaps, while Will had studied him with way too many speculative looks. That was the risk of having a shrink for a friend, though Will was halfway decent about waiting to be asked for any kind of advice. If Kevin had been in a better frame of mind, he might have chuckled at the number of times he caught Will practically biting his tongue to keep silent.

Since Kevin had nursed a single beer most of the evening and gotten home early, he was up barely after dawn on Saturday and heading for Abby's a half hour later. He was fairly confident that he'd be long gone before anyone else in the house awoke. He hadn't formulated a plan for the rest of the day, but he definitely wouldn't be spending it here waiting for his mother to pounce with advice or comfort.

Unfortunately, he'd just stepped off the porch, when he spotted his mother crossing the lawn, obviously returning from an early-morning walk on the beach. She offered him a tentative smile.

"You're up early," she said, her voice determinedly upbeat. "Going somewhere?"

"Over to Abby's. I need to pick up Davy."

He was about to walk on by, but she faced him with a penetrating look that halted him.

"Then you weren't hoping to avoid me again this morning?" she inquired lightly.

He flushed guiltily. "So what if I was?" he asked defensively.

"I never took you for a coward," she responded, her tone deceptively mild. "Certainly no one in this household raised you to be one, not your father or Nell or—"

He cut her off before she could add her name to the list. "At least you acknowledge it was Dad and Gram who raised me."

The barb didn't seem to humiliate her as he'd intended it to. Instead, she kept her gaze steady.

"Of course I do, Kevin, though if we're both being honest and direct, I did have a hand in raising you until you were in your teens. It wasn't until then that Nell stepped in."

He was about to speak, but she apparently wasn't through, because she silenced him with a hard look, then added, "And though I'm quite sure you think otherwise, I never intended any of it to turn out the way it did."

"Oh, really? Then you just went to New York for the weekend and got lost? Maybe developed amnesia?"

She sighed and gestured toward the beach. "Let's go for a walk, Kevin. We might as well have this out here and now. This fight has been brewing for years."

She was right. It had been. He'd stored up plenty of things he wanted to say to her, but now that the opportunity had presented itself, he felt tongue-tied.

"You're just back from a walk and I need to get to Abby's," he argued, but he could tell from her unrelenting gaze, she wasn't going to give in. Maybe it was best to get this over with, let her know there was nothing she could do or say to make amends for the past. In fact, a part of him admired her for not backing down. In her shoes, he wasn't so sure he'd have been as strong. Recent history certainly suggested quite the opposite. He was lousy at facing hard truths.

"I'm not so old that I can't take a second walk on the beach, and those children over at Abby's are probably still in bed," she said, regarding him with amusement. "Any other excuses?"

"None," he conceded and turned toward the beach. He strode off across the lawn, then went down the steps without slowing his pace. Let her chase him, if she wanted to talk to him.

To his surprise, she actually kept up with him, despite being several inches shorter and a good many years older. When he glanced over at her, she gave him a faint smile. "Everyone walks fast in New York," she said with a shrug. "Do your worst. I can keep up."

The knot in his chest seemed to ease just a little at her show of determination and defiance. He suddenly recalled that it had been a matter of pride to her that she could keep up with him and Connor. With Mick so often away, she was the one who'd even organized the occasional camping trip for the two of them, or gone with them on hikes. She might have looked out of place with her perfect hair and stylish outfits, but she'd never complained and she'd matched them step for step.

Because he didn't want to dwell on the good memories and because the question had been nagging at him for more than fifteen years now, he finally blurted it out. "Why'd you do it, Mom? I know why you left Dad, but why us?" He couldn't seem to help the pain that was revealed in that single question.

"Oh, Kevin, I never meant to leave any of you behind," she said, reaching out to touch his jaw, but drawing back before she made contact. Her expression turned sad. "Not even your father."

What the devil was she talking about, Kevin wondered. She'd left. What had she expected to happen? Suddenly it dawned on him. "Did you expect Dad to come running after you?" he asked incredulously.

She shook her head at once, then sighed deeply. "Okay, maybe at first I hoped for exactly that, but I knew your father well enough not to expect it."

In an odd way he was relieved that she hadn't been that delusional. "Then what did you expect?"

"To have my children with me in New York."

She said it so wistfully that it stunned him, especially when he knew it was a lie. "Come on," he scoffed. "You never wanted that. I overheard you tell Dad more than once that you hadn't signed on to be a single mom. Am I supposed to believe that changed just because you'd divorced him? Did you suddenly get all warm and fuzzy over the idea of raising us on your own?"

She looked stung, then shook her head. "Sometimes I'm still astonished by how much you all heard, when your father and I tried so hard to keep our arguments private. You heard just enough to be hurt, but not enough to understand."

"Come on, Mom, what's to misunderstand? If you ask me, you made yourself pretty clear."

"Actually the point I was trying to make to your father was that we'd agreed to be partners in our marriage, that if he wasn't going to be around to share in the responsibilities of parenting, I might as well be a single mother. At least then I'd know that everything was up to me."

Kevin knew she was trying to make a distinction, but he wasn't sure he bought it. "What's the difference?"

"I'll give you an example," she said at once. "Do you remember the first thing that would happen every time your dad came home from a business trip?"

Kevin thought back, but couldn't think of anything specific. He shook his head.

"Then I'll remind you. You or Connor or one of your sisters would greet him at the door with a laundry list of things you wanted to do that I'd already refused to let you do. Mick would automatically say yes, undermining my decision without knowing any of the relevant facts. He loved being the good guy, which left me to be the hard-nosed disciplinarian. Then he and I would end up fighting about it."

Though he hated admitting it, Kevin did recall exactly how they'd used Mick's absences to their advantage. On some level, they'd known that their dad's guilt at being away so much would keep him from saying no to anything. They'd also known that Megan wouldn't overrule him.

"You're saying it would have been easier to be the final authority," he concluded.

"Pretty much."

"Couldn't you just have told Dad to butt out until the two of you had a chance to talk? Wouldn't that have made more sense than divorcing him?"

She smiled at that. "We're talking about your father. Have you ever known him to butt out? Besides, you know the divorce was about much more than that."

"I still think you're revising history," he said bitterly. "It's easy to say now that you wanted us with you. How are we supposed to prove otherwise?"

There was a quick flash of hurt in her eyes at his remark, but then she said, "Don't you really mean how am I going to prove that I'm telling the truth? Okay, fair enough. Do you remember my first visit back here after I left?"

Kevin shook his head. He'd made it a point to be away from the house as much as possible whenever he knew she was coming. He'd been so angry then. And Gram and Mick had let him get away with it, buying whatever excuse he'd offered. They'd gently tried to coax him into sticking around, but the minute he'd balked, they'd given in.

"You spent the weekend with Jake," she reminded him.

"On a camping trip." She let that sink in, then asked, "How about my next visit?"

He tried to think back, but nothing specific came to mind. "How do you expect me to remember something from that long ago?"

"You seem to remember pretty clearly that I supposedly abandoned you."

"Well, of course, because that's exactly what you did."

Her gaze steady, she said, "No, Kevin, I didn't, not the way you're implying, anyway. I was here, time after time. You were all so angry, and who could blame you, but I kept coming back. I encouraged all of you to come to New York. I was supposed to share custody with your father. Mick and I had agreed to that. He provided enough alimony and child support for a place big enough for all of us. My apartment was filled with empty bedrooms intended for you. I had schools picked out. Ask Abby if you don't believe me. When she moved to New York, she visited the apartment, saw the room I'd decorated for you and Connor with all sorts of sports posters, the one for Bree and Abby with a computer, the perfect little girl's room for Jess."

Shaken, Kevin regarded her with disbelief. "Why did you do all that, then never take us with you?"

"Because I was convinced you'd be miserable if I took you away from here. It was the wrong decision, no question about it, but I did what I thought was best for you at the time. Your friends were here. You had family here. In New York, with me working, you all would have had too much time on your own in a strange place, even if I'd arranged for a housekeeper. And, on top of all that, most of you were barely speaking to me. Eventually I had to face the fact that you all wanted to be here, rather than with me. I finally gave up that ridiculously expensive apartment and got one I could afford without any help from your father."

He hated the image that came to mind of his mother sitting all alone in that large, empty apartment. For an instant, his heart filled with compassion, but it took only a moment before it hardened again. He'd had years to perfect the anger and no time at all to absorb this other side to the story.

Apparently his mother wasn't expecting a response or even a reaction, because she continued, each word another blow to the wall of defenses he'd erected.

"Instead, I settled for being the outsider," she said. "I settled for coming again and again for uncomfortable visits, trying to chip away at all that anger." She gave him a rueful look. "Every one of you kids inherited the O'Brien gene for stubbornness in spades. Not one of you ever cut me any slack."

"Did you expect us to?"

"I hoped, with time, you would. That's why I never stopped trying."

The conversation made him look back from a different perspective, see that period of his life in a new light. Maybe she hadn't been quite the monster he'd turned her into in his own head.

She looked at him thoughtfully. "Now that I've answered your questions, will you answer one of mine?"

He shrugged. "I guess."

This time when she reached out to touch his cheek, she didn't pull back. "Tell me why you're in so much pain?"

He stared at her incredulously. "I lost my wife! How do you expect me to feel?"

"Oh, Kevin, I know grief when I see it, and that's not what I'm seeing with you, not entirely, anyway."

"You think you know what it's like to grieve for someone?"

She didn't even hesitate. "I grieved for you children every day of the past fifteen years."

"Not the same. You could have had us back. All you needed to do was move home, or at least back to Chesapeake Shores. There's nothing, *nothing,* I can do to get Georgia back."

To his dismay he saw something in her eyes that scared him, an apparent understanding of every emotion that was in his heart.

"If you could wave a magic wand and bring her back, would you?"

"Of course," he said at once, stunned that she'd even ask such a ridiculous question.

She waved off the quick response. "I don't just mean having her safe and alive," she amended. "Of course, all of us want that. I meant here, with you."

He was slower to respond this time, though he once again insisted, "Of course."

"Sweetheart, that tiny hesitation speaks volumes," she said.

"What?" he demanded. "What did it say?" He honestly wanted to know, because for the life of him he couldn't figure out all of the conflicting emotions rampaging through him on a daily basis.

"Think about it," she said. "When you've figured out the answer, I think you'll finally be ready to move on with your life."

"If you know so much, you tell me," he said. He barely kept himself from begging. He had a feeling she was right, that if he knew the answer, he could get beyond these endless days of living in a fog.

"It's not up to me to put words in your mouth," she said, then shrugged. "Could be I've got it wrong, anyway. But if you ever want to talk it through, I'm here to listen."

Impatient, he snapped, "No, you'll be back in New York. As usual."

This time when he strode away, she didn't even try to keep up with him. She let him go. Astonishingly, that hurt almost as badly as when she'd walked out on them.

Laurie arrived in town on Thursday to see Shanna's shop and pronounced it amazing.

"I love the pale green color of the walls and all the white trim," she said, as she stood in the doorway. "And the bright seaside pattern in the upholstery on the chairs looks fabulous. The whole store is warm and cozy and inviting. Not only is the mix of books and games perfect, but it smells like coffee and the tables and chairs in that area are charming. Who could resist coming here for a chat with a friend or a book club meeting? You are planning to start a book club, aren't you?"

"Absolutely," Shanna said. "I'm going to have a sign-up sheet at the opening. I love the idea of women getting together right here to talk about books."

Laurie continued to walk slowly around the shop, surveying the room more closely. "There's not another single thing you could do to make it better," she said, then added with a grin, "So, let's go book the inn for my wedding."

Shanna regarded her friend with amusement. "What happened to coming to town to help me get ready for my grand opening?"

"You don't need my help," Laurie said blithely. "Frankly, I'm a little miffed about that, but since you don't, we can focus on me. That's always my favorite thing."

"If I didn't know you so well, I'd think you were a totally self-absorbed human being," Shanna told her, even as she grabbed her purse and prepared to take Laurie to the inn for an inspection to see if it would meet her needs.

Fortunately, she'd anticipated exactly this scenario and had worked doubly hard to get ahead for the opening, so she could spend a few hours focused on the wedding.

"I've made an appointment with the owner," Shanna told her. "We'll walk around, look things over and have lunch, then meet with Jess."

"You're an angel," Laurie said, giving her a hug. "I knew I could count on you. And once we've done this, you can count on me a hundred percent to do whatever you need me to do. I'll even bake cookies, if that's what you want."

"Given your cooking skills, I think it's probably a good thing that I'm having the food for the opening catered, by the inn, as a matter of fact. I'll go over those details while we're with Jess, too."

"Then it won't be all about me," Laurie said with an exaggerated pout.

Shanna laughed. "Sorry, sweetie, you are not the center of the universe, at least not this week. When the time comes for your wedding, I promise you'll get all of my attention."

Laurie put on her seat belt, then managed to turn sideways and tuck a leg under her. "So, tell me about the men in this town."

"Haven't we had this conversation? Besides, you're engaged. Other men should be the last thing on your mind."

"Not for *me.* For *you.* And we haven't discussed this since you've met someone," Laurie said confidently.

Shanna regarded her with shock. "What makes you say that?"

"There's a glow in your cheeks and a sparkle in your eyes. It wasn't there when you left Philadelphia."

"Maybe it's there because I've been walking on the beach every morning. Or because I'm excited about opening the store day after tomorrow."

"I like my reason better," Laurie said, undaunted. "Who is he? What's his name? How'd you meet?"

"Not talking about this," Shanna said. "And here we are at the inn. Isn't that fortunate timing?"

Laurie tried to stare her down, then relented. "These questions aren't going away," she warned. "I'm just hitting the pause button."

"That'll do for now," Shanna said, relieved.

Of course, an hour later when Jess joined them in the dining room, it didn't help that the first words out of her mouth were, "So, what's going on with you and my brother?"

Laurie's eyes lit up at once, even as Shanna groaned. Laurie turned to Jess.

"Shanna's been seeing your brother?"

"No!" Shanna said emphatically. "Kevin has helped me out at the shop a couple of times. No big deal."

Jess shook her head. "It's a big deal to all of us. Kevin's wife died in Iraq a little over a year ago," she explained to Laurie. "Other than taking care of his son and dealing with family when he has to, he's been pretty much isolating himself since then. Not that half the women in town haven't tried to get his attention, but he's been oblivious, at least until Shanna arrived on the scene."

Shanna saw the precise moment when the full import of Jess's words registered with Laurie. The excitement in her eyes dimmed. It was immediately replaced by concern.

"I see," she murmured, turning to Shanna with a worried frown. It was evident that Jess's words had doused her enthusiasm for this new relationship.

"Let's talk about available dates for the wedding," Shanna said pointedly. "I have a million last details to take care of at the store, so we don't have much time."

"Of course," Jess said at once, opening her event planner.

As she and Laurie discussed the details of the wedding, Shanna sat back and tried to figure out how on earth to explain to her best friend that she really wasn't about to leap from the frying pan of one lousy relationship into the fire of another.

The ride back to the shop was made in uncomfortable silence. Shanna made it clear at the outset that any discussion of Kevin O'Brien was off-limits. Since he was the only subject on Laurie's mind, she apparently could think of nothing to say. That suited Shanna just fine.

After parking in the alley behind the shop, Shanna said, "Why don't you go on upstairs and settle in? Take a nap while I finish sorting through the last boxes of inventory."

"I can help with that," Laurie said.

"Not really. I'm the only one who can figure out which things should go on display and which should be held back. I want to keep some things till after the opening, just in case it goes really well and the customers buy everything that isn't nailed down." She grinned as she said, "I should be so lucky, right?"

"You're going to be a huge success," Laurie said with unfeigned enthusiasm. "I can already tell. You have a knack for this. All those years of working as an accountant apparently stifled this creative side of you."

Shanna could hardly deny that. Being a CPA had been a safe, but boring career. It was ironic that she'd met Greg while working for his family's corporation. He'd encouraged her to quit right after the wedding, and she'd been only too eager to get away from the tedium. She hadn't gone back to accounting until after the divorce, and she hadn't been any happier the second time around, though her work environment had been a new one with coworkers she'd really liked.

"At least I know exactly how to set up a bookkeeping system and work with spreadsheets," she said finally. "My education and experience weren't a total waste of time."

She unlocked the back door to the shop, and Laurie followed her inside. Shanna removed her spare apartment key from the small safe she'd had installed and handed it to her, but Laurie didn't budge. Instead, she poured herself a cup of leftover coffee and nuked it in the microwave.

"We need to talk," she announced, peering at Shanna over the rim of the mug.

"Not if it's about Kevin O'Brien," Shanna said firmly. "There's nothing to discuss."

"Lost soul. Little boy. I'd say there are at least two things we need to address."

Even though she'd drawn the comparisons herself, Shanna remained insistent. "It's not Greg all over again. You've heard the expression once burned, twice shy. Well, I'm at least three or four times shy. No way am I walking into the middle of this situation. Not that Kevin is actually like Greg. For one thing, he's not drinking."

"You have proof of that?"

"Proof, no, but he's been around the store enough that I would surely have seen some evidence of it."

"You missed it when you were dating Greg, even though the signs were there all along."

Shanna sighed. She couldn't deny that. "True, but now, believe me, I'd notice."

"I wish I could believe that," Laurie said. "But I know you, Shanna. You have the biggest, most generous heart in the world."

"You make it sound as if I'm a sucker for a sob story."

"Hardly, but I know one thing about you that very few people know."

"Oh?"

"You want to be part of a family in the worst way. I know part of Greg's attraction was, well, Greg. Add in his son and that whole impressive, if seriously dysfunctional, family of his, and you never stood a chance. I sense the same thing happening now."

"You're wrong."

"How many people are there in this O'Brien clan? I'm guessing there are quite a few of them. I've met Jess. You've mentioned the woman with the flower shop next door. She's an O'Brien, too, as I recall. Any more?"

"There's another sister, but I haven't met her," she admitted. "And another brother."

"Parents?"

"His father was the architect who designed the town. I'm not really clear on where his mother is. And there's his grandmother."

"Any more?" Laurie pressed.

"Isn't that enough for you to make this point you're so anxious to make?"

"There are more," Laurie concluded.

"Okay, yes, his cousin is the rental agent who leased me the property, and his uncle manages all the properties." She shrugged. "There are others, I think. Someone at Sally's mentioned they refer to Chesapeake Shores as "O'Brien's town"—because there's such a slew of them or because Mick designed it. I'm not sure which."

Laurie nodded triumphantly. "Either way, I rest my case. Big family, wounded man, little boy in need of a mom and you. It has destiny written all over it." She gave her a knowing look. "Or disaster."

"Don't you think I know that?" Shanna snapped impatiently. "Which is exactly why I keep telling you there is nothing going on between Kevin and me. And there's not going to be."

Laurie started to speak, then sighed. "I suppose I'll see for myself soon enough."

"Meaning?"

"The second he walks into the shop on Saturday, I'll know."

Shanna turned away to hide the look of dismay she knew must be on her face. It was true. When it came to men, women and chemistry, Laurie would be able to read the situation in a heartbeat. And the only way to avoid it would be to call Kevin and warn him to stay far, far away.

The instant Laurie left and went upstairs to settle in, that's exactly what she did. Unfortunately, she got his voice mail. Though she tried to explain in a message that it would be a bad idea for him to show up on Saturday, she suspected she wasn't making much sense.

"Call me," she said at the end. "It's important." Not sure if she'd even identified herself at the beginning of the call, she added, "This is Shanna, by the way. Call, okay?"

She hung up then, almost regretting the fact that she'd called in the first place. She was probably making too much of the entire situation. Then again, after the way his father had been checking out their relationship the other night, Kevin would surely understand about one well-meaning, meddling friend. He'd also likely want to avoid her like the plague.

6

"Why aren't you dressed?" Gram demanded on Saturday morning, regarding Kevin with disapproval.

He glanced down at his perfectly respectable shorts and T-shirt. The shirt wasn't even wrinkled. "I am dressed."

"Not to go into town for the opening of the new bookstore," she said. "This is a special occasion. I'd think you'd want to look nice."

He'd worked really hard trying to block this particular special occasion from his mind. Unfortunately Bree hadn't been able to resist dropping frequent hints and a few blatant reminders. Shanna had even called his cell phone while he'd been out fishing—or more specifically drifting around in his old boat. She'd left some cryptic message about the opening that hadn't made a whole lot of sense. It had almost sounded as if she were warning him to stay away, which, frankly, he was more than happy to do. It was everyone else in his family who seemed to have other ideas.

"You're going, right?" he asked his grandmother. "You can take Davy."

She scowled at him. "Yes, I could do that," she agreed. "But I'm not going to."

He stared at her in surprise. Nell had never once backed down from an opportunity to have any of her grandchildren all to herself. "Why not?"

"Because he needs to pick out books with his father," she said. "Reading is something the two of you do together. And you mentioned yourself that the shop owner promised you a free picture book for Davy for helping her with the coffee machine and her shelves."

"I'm not taking a free book from Shanna," Kevin said. "Starting a new business is tough. She doesn't need to be giving away freebies to anyone who helps her out."

Gram's jaw set stubbornly. "Well, whether you take the book or not is up to you, but you are going. Davy's already dressed and he's looking forward to it. Abby's taking Carrie and Caitlyn. They'll meet us there."

He was about to seize that opening and suggest sending Davy with Abby, but a hard look from his grandmother kept him silent. It was plain she would disapprove of that plan, too.

As if on cue, his son toddled in, dragging his tattered Winnie the Pooh bear. "Story, Daddy? Want new one."

Kevin sighed. "Okay, buddy. We'll find you some new stories. Give me a minute."

Gram gave him a triumphant look. "I knew you'd listen to reason."

Reason had nothing to do with it, he thought sourly. It was looking into his son's eyes and knowing the disappointment he'd see there if he refused to go. For a kid barely past his second birthday, Davy had an amazing capacity to induce guilt. Apparently that was something he'd inherited from his great-grandmother.

"I'll meet you at the car," he told Gram tersely.

He waited until she and Davy were gone before rummaging in his closet for something to wear. He had more than enough choices since he rarely wore his so-called good clothes. His shirts were ironed and his slacks were all hanging in bags straight from the dry cleaners. He grabbed two hangers at random.

It seemed ridiculous to him to be changing clothes just to go to a store opening in a beach town like Chesapeake Shores, but he dutifully pulled on a pair of pressed chinos and a long-sleeved shirt. Though he dispensed with socks, he even shoved his feet into almost-new boat shoes, instead of run-down sneakers.

Grumbling under his breath, he was almost out the bedroom door, when he stopped and splashed on a couple of drops of aftershave. It was probably a mistake. One whiff of that and Bree, Abby and Gram were going to start making wedding plans. It wouldn't take much to send those three into a hopeful frenzy.

Gram would be delighted because she was worried sick about him. Bree would leap to conclusions because she was still in a romantic haze from her own marriage. Abby was simply a mother hen. Besides that, her own wedding to Trace was coming up in a few months, if she ever got around to planning it. Neither she nor Trace seemed to be in a rush, much to Gram's dismay and Mick's annoyance.

The last time Kevin had been by Abby's house, she'd had a huge stack of bridal magazines on the kitchen table, dropped off by various family members as less-than-subtle reminders that she needed to get started. He could envision those suddenly appearing in his room. He shuddered at the thought.

Then there was Jess. How had he forgotten about her? She was catering today's event. She would be underfoot, too, watching him like a hawk to see if any sparks were flying between him and Shanna. If she spotted any, she'd be doing her part to fan them into flames. She'd felt totally left out when he'd basically eloped with Georgia with only Mick present. She'd do everything in her power to make up for that by meddling in his relationship with Shanna.

Well, they could observe, exult, plot and scheme all they wanted. There'd be nothing to see. He'd make sure of that.

This day was about buying his son a couple of new picture books, nothing more. The fact that the owner of the store's image had popped into his head more than once when he'd been drifting along in his old boat had nothing to do with anything. Really.

Kevin had to park all the way around the corner on Shore Road. Every single space on Main Street had been taken and, to his shock, there was a line outside the bookstore waiting for it to open. Were people in Chesapeake Shores this starved for excitement? It wasn't as if Shanna had James Patterson or that wildly popular Maryland writer—what was her name? Oh, yes, Nora Roberts—there for a signing.

"Just look at that," Gram said, beaming with pleasure. "She's going to be mobbed today. What a wonderful welcome for a newcomer to town!"

All Kevin could think about was how inept Shanna was with that coffee machine of hers. "Gram, could you please take Davy to the store?" he implored.

"You are not turning right around and going back home," she said heatedly. "I won't allow it."

"Yeah, I get that," he acknowledged ruefully. "It's just that Shanna has this new cappuccino machine she doesn't totally know how to work. Remember, I told you about that? She's obviously going to be way too busy to be worrying about that with this crowd. I told her I'd help out if I was around."

Gram's expression brightened at once. "Oh, well, by all means. We'll see you inside. I see Abby and the girls just up ahead. We'll join them in line."

The gleam in her eyes gave Kevin pause, but he consoled himself with the reminder that a promise was a promise and letting Shanna down when she was in for this kind of impending chaos was out of the question.

Avoiding curious gazes from those already in line, he went around to the back and rapped on the door. A woman he didn't recognize opened it, then surveyed him thoroughly with undisguised interest.

"You're Kevin O'Brien," she concluded.

He blinked at her certainty. "How would you know that?"

"Lucky guess," she said, beaming at him in a disconcerting way. "Your sister Jess and Shanna are in the front. They told me I was in the way. You probably will be, too, so why don't you sit down right here and you and I can get to know each other." She patted a stool, then took a seat on the one right next to it. "I'm Laurie, Shanna's best friend. I came down from Pennsylvania to help her with the opening."

Kevin cast a longing look toward the front of the store, but he sat as requested. He scrambled to come up with the small talk the situation required. "Shanna mentioned you were coming." he said at last.

"Really? Do the two of you share a lot of things with each other?"

Something in her tone made him instantly wary. "Such as?"

"Intimate little secrets?"

He grinned at the deliberate innuendo behind her

words. "I don't know. Does something like, 'Hand me the Phillips screwdriver' count?"

She looked disappointed. "Absolutely not."

"Then sorry, no intimate little secrets." Okay, that was a blatant lie, but he had the distinct impression that discretion was called for. Laurie sounded as if her meddling genes rivaled those of the O'Briens.

"Too bad," she said with unmistakable regret, "because I'll bet you have some fascinating ones."

"Well, you'd be wrong. My life's an open book and a pretty boring one at that."

"I'll be the judge of that after I get to know you a little better," she said.

Kevin frowned at her determined tone. "Just how long are you planning to stick around town?"

"Just through tomorrow," she conceded. "But I'll be back, Kevin O'Brien. You can count on that."

"That sounds like a warning."

"You're very intuitive," she said. "I like that."

He frowned at her. "Maybe you ought to spell out this warning of yours, just the same, because I'm not all that clear on why you feel the need to issue one."

She was apparently only too eager to fill him in, but Shanna rushed into the back room, took one look at the two of them and blanched.

"Kevin, I…I didn't think you were coming today."

Laurie's brow rose. "You called him and told him to stay away, didn't you?"

Shanna winced at the accusation, then her chin jutted up. "As a matter of fact, I did," she said, then turned to him. "Why didn't you listen to me?"

He finally realized the missing piece of that cryptic message. "That phone call was about her?" he said.

Shanna nodded. "If I were you, I'd run for your life."

"And hide where?" he asked. "My grandmother's outside with Davy and she's expecting to find me manning the cappuccino machine. My sister Abby and her daughters are with them. And I gather Jess is already here. Sticking around and dealing with your friend here might be awkward, but bolting is no longer an option."

Laurie looked from one of them to the other. "Now isn't that interesting," she said. "A knight in shining armor, willing to sacrifice himself for the greater good."

Kevin was about to reply that his armor was seriously tarnished, when Shanna stepped in.

"The only knights around here are in the children's storybooks," she snapped. "Leave the man alone."

Despite himself, Kevin chuckled. "I'll go check on that coffee now, okay?"

"Please do," Shanna said.

As he left the room, he could hear her whispering something to Laurie in an urgent undertone. He had a hunch she wasn't asking her to help him with the coffee. If anything, she might be sending her all the way to Baltimore to get some hard-to-find-but-vital something or other for today's event. That was probably the only way she'd keep her friend from asking him all the questions that were so clearly on her mind. From Kevin's perspective, Siberia would be the better destination.

He turned to find Jess standing in his path, beaming at him. "Well, don't you look handsome! Did you get all dressed up to impress Shanna?"

"I got all dressed up because Gram made me," he said, then chuckled at how ridiculous that sounded. He really was pitiful if he was letting a bunch of women run his life.

This, more than anything else that had happened lately,

suggested it was past time for him to get his act together. Otherwise he'd lose all respect for himself as the testosterone-driven man he'd once been. He'd served in the army, for heaven's sake. He'd been in a war. He was tough, dammit! It might be smart to keep reminding himself of that.

He glanced past Jess and saw that several tables had been set up along the wall in the café area. They were laden with tempting hors d'oeuvres and cookies.

"Nice spread," he commented.

"And you're not to touch it till after the customers have seen how beautiful it looks," she warned him. "This kind of event is great advertising for the inn's catering services. I bet I'll pick up half a dozen parties because of this."

"Good for you." He hesitated, then asked, "Jess, how did you know the inn was the perfect career for you?"

"You mean after all the other jobs I held for a nanosecond and quit?"

He nodded.

"When I saw the For Sale sign on that property, I remembered how much I'd loved it and thought about owning it, even when I was a kid. I just knew it was what I'd been waiting for." She studied him thoughtfully. "Is this about the charter fishing boat idea I mentioned to you?"

"Yeah, at least I think that's why I'm asking."

"You're still not sure it's the right fit?"

"I'm not sure *anything's* the right fit," he admitted. "But I have to do something, and I want to be as excited about it as you are about the inn. Bree has the flower shop and her writing. Abby's passionate about all that Wall Street financial stuff. Connor loves practicing law. I don't have anything I feel that way about, not since..."

"Not since you ruled out being a paramedic again," she said. "Have you even been down to Harbor Lights? Maybe if you spent some time looking at the boats the marina has for sale, the pieces would start to fall into place."

"Good idea," he said. It was another of those steps that Gram had been encouraging him to take. Just one step forward. He didn't have to buy a boat. He just had to look at them. Maybe take a couple out to sea to get the feel of them, then sign up for the training to become certified as a charter boat captain. Even after taking the course and becoming licensed, he never had to actually start a fishing charter.

"Thanks, Jess," he said, pressing a quick kiss to her cheek. "Now let me man my station at the cappuccino machine, because I think the doors are about to open."

His sister gave him a hard hug. "I think it's great that you came to help out."

"It doesn't mean anything," he said defensively.

She grinned at him. "Did I suggest otherwise?"

"No, but—" He cut himself off in midsentence. Protesting would only convince her, convince the entire family, of the exact opposite. Better to drop this and stay as far away from both his family and Shanna as possible for the rest of the day.

Shanna had never expected a turnout like this. The store was so packed and sales so brisk, she'd barely been able to leave the cash register since she'd unlocked the front door at 10 a.m. At least that hadn't given her a single second to worry about what Laurie might be up to with Kevin. She'd warned her to leave the man alone, but a stern warning had never stopped her friend from doing exactly as she pleased, especially when she was worried.

And Laurie was worried, even more so now that she'd met Kevin. She'd had plenty to say once he'd walked out of the back room. The only thing that had saved Shanna from hearing every single one of her concerns was Jess's timely arrival announcing that the food was set up and it was 10 a.m. After that, everything had been a blur.

Everyone in Chesapeake Shores, it seemed, had been starving for reading material. Stacks of paperbacks and children's books had flown out the door. She'd even sold every single one of her deluxe Scrabble sets, the ones on a turntable. Jigsaw puzzles were selling well, too. Apparently the summer people loved keeping a supply of things like that on hand for rainy days and visiting grandkids.

Bree had been the first customer in line. She'd brought over a huge arrangement of flowers for the opening, then insisted on buying the books she'd put on hold.

"I want to give you your very first sale," she'd said, "Sorry to be in such a rush, but I can't leave Jenny there alone for too long on a Saturday, not with this crowd you've drawn into town today. I was afraid I wouldn't have a chance to get by later. Your opening is the big news on Main Street today, but I'll get the spillover clientele who'll want to talk about you."

Laughing, Shanna had rung up her sale, already feeling as if the day was off to a promising start. She'd never expected the outpouring of support and sales that had followed.

It was midafternoon before she finally drew in a deep breath and took a minute to look around. There were still several customers browsing through the shelves, but the surprise was the sight of Kevin refilling the cappuccino maker. She'd expected him to vanish long before now, either out of boredom or because Laurie'd been badgering him. She walked over to him.

"I'd say your first day has been a success," he said when he saw her. "Congratulations!"

"And I'd say you deserve accolades for sticking around," she replied. "You must be worn-out."

"Hey, this is easy. All I have to do is keep this thing filled and make sure there are cups."

"And fend off women," she teased. "I saw quite a few lingering over here and, trust me, it wasn't the coffee that fascinated them."

Kevin actually blushed at the observation. "It's a small town. Most of them were women I'd gone to school with."

"And dated?" she asked.

"A few of them," he admitted.

She couldn't seem to stop herself from pursuing this now that she'd started. "And how many wanted to pick up where you'd left off?"

He chuckled. "I wasn't keeping count." His gaze narrowed. "You almost sound jealous. What would your friend Laurie have to say about that?"

Shanna shuddered. "I don't even want to think about it. I owe you after the inquisition she put you through. I'm really sorry about that, but she worries about me."

"Is there some reason she needs to?"

"Long story," she said. "And there's no time for it today. I met your sister Abby and her girls earlier. They're a handful, aren't they?"

"You have no idea," Kevin said.

"Is your son still here?"

"There are books. I doubt he's ever going to want to leave," Kevin said. "I do think Gram took him next door long enough for lunch, but they came back a few minutes ago." He gestured behind her.

Shanna turned, immediately recognizing the dark-haired toddler snuggled next to a white-haired woman and studying an Eric Carle book with total fascination. They'd bought several books earlier—cozy mysteries and a new photographic tour of Ireland for her, picture books for him. She grinned with delight as she realized which book they were looking at now.

"He's looking at the one about fireflies," she told Kevin. "It's one of my favorites. It even has tiny lights in it. Did you see that?"

"About thirty times so far," he said. "Gram finally took over." He hesitated, then said with obvious reluctance, "You should probably meet her—my grandmother, that is."

"We spoke earlier when she bought the books, but we didn't really have a chance to chat."

"It might be better to keep it that way," he said direly.

She studied him curiously. "Is there some reason you don't want me to talk with her?"

"You'll see soon enough," he said in that same grim tone, then led the way. "Gram, this is Shanna Carlyle. My grandmother, Nell O'Brien, and my son, Davy."

Shanna gave his grandmother's hand a warm squeeze. "I know we met earlier, Mrs. O'Brien, but it's nice to have a chance to speak to you when things aren't so rushed."

"Please call me Nell," she said. "Davy and I love your shop. I'm sure you'll be seeing a lot of us."

Shanna knelt down beside Davy, who was still gazing with rapt attention at the book. "I'm so glad you could come today, Davy." She pointed to the book. "Something tells me you like fireflies."

Davy regarded her shyly. "Uh-huh."

"You know what I think? I think this book about them is magic."

Davy nodded solemnly, then turned to the back of the book to make the lights twinkle. "'flies," he pronounced happily.

Shanna's heart melted. "Well, I guess you've picked out your favorite book today," she concluded. "You'll be able to read it every night."

"That'll be three or four times a night," Kevin muttered behind her. "Thanks."

She grinned up at him. "Well, it is a magical book."

She noted that his grandmother was watching the exchange with a speculative gleam in her eyes. That's when Shanna realized why Kevin had been so hesitant about the two of them meeting. The woman apparently wasn't above matchmaking, even after he'd made it plain that he wasn't interested. She'd caught similar looks from all three of his sisters today, as well. Add in his father's behavior a few nights ago and she could see why Kevin dreaded more meddling.

She stood up, backing away so quickly she almost tripped over the low table in front of the chair. Kevin caught her arm and steadied her, his eyes glinting with amusement. She had a hunch there would have been an I-told-you-so if they'd been alone.

"I'd better get back to the front," she said. "Thanks again for coming, I hope I'll see you again soon."

"Oh, I think you can count on that," Mrs. O'Brien said, a wicked twinkle in her eyes that suggested the next visit would be less about books and much more about Shanna herself.

If her own grandson found that twinkle worrisome, it was nothing to what Shanna was suddenly feeling. She found it terrifying. And she still had to face Laurie and several hours of her interrogation before the day was done.

* * *

It was after seven by the time Jess had cleaned up the empty dishes and trays and loaded them into her van. Laurie had tidied the bookshelves while Shanna tallied the day's receipts. It had been a very good day. She knew better than to think every day would be this good, but it was an excellent start.

"I think we should go out to celebrate," she announced to Laurie and Jess. "And not at the inn, because then you'll be fretting about work, Jess. How about Brady's? On me."

Laurie gave her a look that said she knew exactly what Shanna was doing by inviting Jess along. And she was right. The last thing Shanna wanted was to be alone with her inquisitive best friend.

"I don't know…" Jess began. "I'm pretty beat."

"So am I," Shanna said, "but I want to do something special to mark the occasion, and you absolutely have to be a part of it. Your food was a huge hit today. I think that's what kept people browsing and buying."

Jess beamed with pride. "I think you're exaggerating, but thank you anyway. Just about everyone asked for my card, so I'm sure we'll get more catering jobs from this. I can't wait to let Gail know. I may be the face of the business, but she's the wizard in the kitchen. If we get even one job from today's event, I'm knocking ten percent off your bill."

"Come on now," Shanna protested. "You can't do that. You're in business to make money, too."

"Well, all this talk of food and money is making me hungry," Laurie said. "Come on, ladies, let's get out of here. I want a big juicy steak."

"Crab cakes for me," Jess said at once.

"Me, too," Shanna added, then gave Laurie a chiding

look. "How can you be in one of the world's great seafood regions and eat a steak?"

"What can I say? I love my meat."

"You'll have to come more often, so we can convert you," Jess told her.

Jess was about to climb into her van when Shanna stopped her. "Leave that here. I'll drive. Since I live right upstairs, I'll be coming back here anyway."

"Works for me," Jess said at once.

Ten minutes later they were in the packed parking lot at Brady's. The waterfront restaurant had a line at the door.

"Oh, no," Shanna groaned. "I didn't even consider what it would be like here on a Saturday night. I don't think I'm up for a wait for a table."

"Leave that to me," Jess said. "Stick close behind me and don't stop."

"You're going to break in line?" Laurie said, awe in her voice.

"Not exactly," Jess said.

Instead, she led the way around to the back of the restaurant and opened the kitchen door to complete chaos. A tall, redheaded man the size of a truck took one look at her and bellowed, "What are you doing in my kitchen?"

Shanna and Laurie immediately fell back a step, but Jess marched right on in and straight into his arms. To Shanna's shock, the man scooped Jess up and spun her around.

"I thought I told you never to sneak in this way again," he scolded.

"Have you seen that line outside?" Jess demanded. "Ladies, this is the best chef in Chesapeake Shores, next to mine at the inn, of course. Dillon Brady, meet Shanna

Carlyle, owner of the town's hottest new store, and her friend Laurie, who's visiting from Philadelphia. How could I not bring them here to celebrate Shanna's grand opening today? Surely you can find one small table for us."

"For you, anything," Dillon said. He turned to Shanna and Laurie. "Even though she abandoned me, I have chosen to forgive her." He sighed dramatically. "Jess was one of the best waitresses I ever had."

Jess rolled her eyes. "I was a disaster," she said. "He just kept me around because I flattered him endlessly about his food."

"Yes, that was part of it," he concurred unrepentantly.

"And what was the other part?" Jess said, feigning forgetfulness. She snapped her fingers. "Oh, yes, I introduced him to the woman who is now his wife."

He beamed. "Yes, there is that, for which I will be eternally grateful. Now, give me a minute. I'll find you a table, even if I have to hurry the mayor and his party."

Shanna watched in fascination at the obviously orderly chaos that was the kitchen. She'd never been in a restaurant kitchen during the height of the evening rush…or ever, for that matter. "I couldn't do this," she declared after several minutes.

Jess laughed. "Neither could I. I was jumpy all the time. I barely lasted three months and that long only because Dillon took pity on me. He was convinced I'd get the hang of it eventually."

"How does he feel about you now being his primary competition for fine dining in town?" Shanna asked.

"He just tells everyone that anything I'm doing right I learned here," Jess said, then shrugged. "He's probably right about that. It helps that he and my chef get along really well. They have dinner every couple of weeks and compare menus to be sure we're offering different choices. Obviously there are certain dishes both places are expected to carry around here, but there are enough distinctions that people can also get some variety."

Dillon returned with his arm around the woman who was apparently the restaurant's hostess. "My wife, Kate," he announced to Shanna and Laurie as the woman hugged Jess. "She'll take you to your table." He shook his finger at Jess. "Next time you come in the front like everyone else."

Jess grinned at him impudently. "What's the fun in that? Besides, Kate's far too diplomatic to let us butt in line."

"Exactly," Dillon told her. "Now, go."

As soon as they were seated and Kate had gone back to her station at the door, Shanna ordered a bottle of wine. Before the waitress could get away, they also placed their orders for food.

Shanna sat back with a sigh. "Just sitting down like this is heaven. I had no idea how hard it would be to stay on my feet most of the day. Don't tell, but I've kicked off my shoes. Don't let me walk out of here without them."

The waitress brought their wine and some crab dip. "Dillon sent this out to tide you over. The kitchen's slow because we're so packed, but he'll get your meals out as quickly as he can."

"Please tell him thanks," Jess said, then turned to Shanna. "Okay, let's get to the important news of the day. How'd you get along with Davy and Gram?"

Shanna winced. Why hadn't she considered that Jess was at least as nosy as Laurie? Now there were going to be two of them ganging up on her. She held up a hand.

"The subject of Kevin, his son and the rest of your family is off-limits," she declared.

Jess turned to Laurie, her eyes wide with innocence. "Did I mention Kevin?"

"I never heard his name," Laurie confirmed.

"He's obviously on her mind," Jess said, then added thoughtfully, "You know her best, Laurie. What do you suppose that means?"

"I'm guessing she's a little sensitive on the subject because she's interested in him but doesn't want us to know it."

Shanna scowled at them. "I hope you two are enjoying yourselves."

"Immensely," Jess said.

"Haven't had more fun in ages," Laurie chimed in, though her expression sobered quickly. "Seriously, Shanna, do you have any idea what you're doing?"

"Absolutely," she said at once. "Nothing. I am doing absolutely nothing. This thing about Kevin and me is all in your heads."

"You seem to be forgetting I saw you together earlier today," Laurie said. "There were unmistakable sparks."

"I saw them, too," Jess added. "Even Abby commented on it."

"I barely met her," Shanna protested. "And she has never seen your brother and me together."

"He was there. That was enough for her."

"Oh, for heaven's sake, you're all making way too much of this. Kevin has baggage. I have baggage. It's not a good mix."

"In any relationship these days, both people have their share of baggage," Laurie said. "Amazingly, it doesn't always scare either of them off, even when it should."

"Then I'm an exception," Shanna said. "So is Kevin. Now stop this before you spoil our dinner, or mine, anyway."

"I just have one more thing to say, sweetie, and then I'll drop it for tonight," Laurie said. "Despite my teasing, Kevin is all wrong for you. He's a nice guy, and all those sparks are lovely, but the two of you would be a disaster. Surely you can see that."

Jess regarded her with indignation. "Hey, that's my brother you're talking about."

"It's not personal. I like him. I really do. I'm just saying he and Shanna are a bad fit. If you knew her history, you'd agree."

"So tell me," Jess said, leaning forward with obvious fascination.

Shanna glared at Laurie. "Not if you expect to have a place to stay tonight."

That only stirred Jess's curiosity. "Why? What are you hiding?" She turned to Laurie. "Do I need to warn my brother off?"

Laurie shook her head. "It's complicated, though."

"Complications aren't always a bad thing," Jess said thoughtfully. "Tell me and I can decide for myself."

Shanna gave her a pleading look. "I swear I will tell you anything you want to know, just not tonight. Dwelling in the past will ruin the evening, at least for me."

Jess nodded slowly. "Fair enough. This is your night to celebrate," she said, then added, "But I will be on your doorstep one of these mornings with questions."

Shanna sighed. Of course she would. She was as protective of Kevin as Laurie was of her.

"I'll have the coffee ready," she said, resigned to the inevitable.

Both of her companions dutifully changed the subject as their meals arrived. Jess and Laurie dug in happily, chatting about inconsequential topics now, but Shanna couldn't eat a bite of her food. Just thinking about her unfortunate and short-lived marriage had ruined her appetite and her mood. Talking about it, whether tonight or any other time, could fill her with despair.

7

On Sunday, Kevin walked into the dining room as Gram was setting the table and noted more place settings than usual. Even if Bree, Jake, Abby, Trace and the girls were joining them, the extra leaf in the table seemed excessive. Still, it wasn't all that rare for someone in the family to invite a few more people to the family's traditional Sunday gatherings.

"You need help?" he asked his grandmother.

"If you could finish setting the table, I'd appreciate it. I need to check my pot roast."

"Exactly how many people will be here today?" he asked, picking up where she'd left off and arranging another place setting.

"You and Davy, all three of your sisters, Trace and Jake, Abby's girls, of course, your father and me. Jess has invited a couple of friends, too." She ticked the numbers off on her fingers. "That's thirteen of us, plus your mother, assuming she and Mick are around. They have a habit of not filling me in on their plans."

Kevin frowned at the prospect of dealing with his mother again, even though they'd had something of a breakthrough on her last visit. "Wouldn't she have flown in on Friday if she were coming?"

"More than likely, but her days off can change, so she sometimes turns up on Sunday. Since I haven't seen your father this morning, something tells me he's run off to the airport to get her."

"And you're okay with them not giving you any notice?" Kevin asked, annoyed on her behalf.

She shrugged. "I wouldn't mind a little consideration, but when did I ever require any of you to give me more than a few minutes' notice before inviting a friend to a meal? There's always enough food for a few extra people."

"I suppose," Kevin said, but it still struck him as yet another example of his mother's thoughtlessness. Or maybe the fault was Mick's, he conceded, deciding to cut his mother some slack for once. After all, it was his father who was bringing home the parental version of a playmate.

The possibility that Megan was going to be around for a few days soured his mood, but it was too late now for him to come up with an excuse to take off. Besides, he'd resolved to stop running from things—people, issues, whatever.

A few minutes later he had a hard time remembering that resolution when he walked outside and spotted Jess crossing the yard with Shanna and her friend Laurie in tow.

Why the devil hadn't he considered for even a second that his sister might be inviting these particular friends? It was just like Jess to try to stir the pot. What he didn't understand entirely was why Shanna had gone along with it, especially with her overly inquisitive friend still on the scene.

Shanna glanced his way, caught his eye and silently mouthed, "I'm sorry."

Kevin grinned, despite his initial exasperated reaction. Apparently she was not much happier about this than he was, though it begged the question of how she'd let it happen. Then he caught Jess's cat-swallowed-the-canary look of triumph and knew she'd deliberately masterminded this meeting. As he knew all too well, she wasn't the kind to take no for an answer.

"Kevin, be a sweetheart, and take Shanna inside for something to drink," Jess called out to him.

So, he thought, she'd set the game into motion. Unless he or Shanna did something to prevent it, they'd be thrown together from here on out as frequently as his sisters could manage it.

He caught a quick frown on Laurie's face, but then Jess was linking arms with her and walking briskly toward the beach, either to show her the view or simply as a blatant attempt at distraction, so he'd have no choice but to deal with Shanna.

He turned to Shanna, whose cheeks were flushed with embarrassment. "I warned you about getting caught in the O'Brien web," he told her.

"What you didn't warn me about was how sneaky and persuasive your sister can be," she said. "I said no to coming today. I said it at least a half-dozen times. Even Laurie protested, and she's a lot tougher than I am."

"And, yet, here you are," he said. "Maybe I can get Davy to teach you how to say *no* and mean it. It's currently one of his favorite words."

Her eyes lighting up at the mention of his son's name, she immediately looked around. "Where is he?"

"In the kitchen with Gram and his cousins, last time I checked. They love hanging out there with her because she lets them sneak cookies, even though she knows perfectly well that's not allowed before a meal. When we were kids, she stuck very firmly to that rule. With Davy, Caitlyn and Carrie, the rules have flown out the window. Whenever I've dared to mention that, though, she says a great-grandmother has a right to spoil anyone she wants to. I haven't come up with an argument that'll work when she pulls rank."

Shanna chuckled. "What do you suppose the odds are of us sneaking a cookie if we join them? I'm starved. I slept late and skipped breakfast. Laurie, Jess and I had kind of a late night."

Kevin regarded her with dismay. "You were out partying with my sister? Are you nuts?"

"Apparently so, since that's when she talked me into coming here today. And we weren't partying, exactly. We just had dinner after the store closed, then sat around talking for a while afterward. Dillon Brady and his wife joined us."

"Really? Then it must have been a late night. Dillon's rarely out of the kitchen before eleven."

She nodded. "Which meant it was after midnight by the time we got home. We were having so much fun, I didn't even notice the time until I crawled into bed."

"Then you're making friends," he said, oddly miffed by that. It was ridiculous, since he didn't especially want to get any more involved with her himself. Of course she should have friends here. And it wasn't as if she'd been out with, say, Will and Mack. This was his sister, Dillon Brady and his wife. It couldn't have been more innocent. There was absolutely no reason for this strange little twinge of annoyance or jealousy or whatever it was.

She was studying him curiously. "Does that bother you for some reason?"

"No," he lied. "Why would it?"

"I'm not sure, but there was something in your tone of voice."

"You're imagining things. I'm sure now that you have the store, you'll be making a ton of new friends."

"I hope so," she said at once.

"Speaking of the store, aren't you planning to be open on Sundays? That's a big day for tourists around here."

"I will be, starting next week," she told him. "I knew yesterday was going to be really demanding, so I planned it that I don't officially start my regular hours until Tuesday of this week. Thank heavens I did that, because in my wildest dreams I never imagined an opening like yesterday."

"I'm pretty sure everyone in town stopped in," he said.

"It certainly felt like that. Anyway, from now on I'll be open six days a week, taking Monday off. That'll give me a chance to get some new stock on the shelves after the weekend, place orders and so on."

"Six days? Won't that wear you out, especially if you're using Monday as a catch-up day for paperwork and that sort of thing?"

"Probably," she admitted with an air of resignation, "but at first there won't be any money in the budget for even part-time help. Hopefully I'll be able to hire one or two teenagers part-time over the holidays and then full-time help by next summer. Everyone I spoke to told me it was the only way I'd be able to take a salary myself and pay the overhead. Small businesses in a town this size take a while to get established and on an even keel financially. I'm prepared for having virtually no life of my own for the time being."

Kevin wasn't sure whether to be relieved by that or disappointed. He was saved from too much introspection by Caitlyn, Carrie and Davy exiting the house at full throttle. Davy couldn't keep up with his older cousins. The farther they got away from him, the stormier his expression, until he recognized Shanna. He immediately detoured in their direction.

"Book?" he asked her hopefully, holding out his arms to be picked up.

Instead, Shanna hunkered down to be on his level. "I didn't bring any books with me, but if you have one you'd like me to read to you, I would love to do that."

Davy looked up at Kevin. "Book, Daddy?"

Kevin glanced at Shanna. "You sure about this? He's relentless once you give in."

"It's fine," she assured him.

With Davy clinging to her hand, they went inside and upstairs to Davy's room. He led her to his bright blue bookshelf and grabbed the firefly book, then another one about trucks. He was reaching for a third, when Kevin stopped him.

"That's enough, pal. You can't take up all of Shanna's time. She's here to see the grown-ups."

"I don't mind, really," she insisted, picking up the book Davy had been reaching for. "Can we read outside? Do you have a favorite place?"

Again, Davy held out his arms to be picked up. "I show," he said.

Before Kevin could protest, Shanna scooped Davy up as if he weighed next to nothing. "Tell me where," she instructed.

Then, walking away as if she'd forgotten Kevin's existence, she took off with his son. Davy was babbling a mile a minute in her ear. Kevin could hear her laughter drifting back up the steps. The sound sent another one of those unexpected little zings of jealousy straight through him.

"Ridiculous," he muttered to himself. First he was jealous of his sister, Dillon and Kate. Now he was envious of his two-year-old. Clearly he needed to get his own life, and he needed to do it in a big, fat hurry.

After dinner, Shanna was sitting in the shade, her back resting against an old oak tree, Davy asleep in her lap, when Laurie found her. Her friend's arrival shattered the few minutes of complete tranquillity and contentment she'd been feeling.

"Are you out of your mind?" Laurie demanded, taking in the scene at a glance.

"Hush! You're going to wake him up."

"Don't you see how wrong this is?" Laurie asked, her tone lower, but no less urgent. "You can't substitute one child for another, or one father for another, for that matter."

Shanna sucked in a horrified gasp. "That is not what I'm doing."

"Aren't you?" Laurie asked, her gaze unrelenting. "Oh, sweetie, I know how much you must miss Henry. I know how devastating it was when you had to walk away and leave him with Greg, but you had no claim to custody. He'd only been your stepson for a few months when you divorced Greg."

"And a part of my life for a lot longer than that," Shanna retorted heatedly. She and Greg had dated for nearly a year before marrying, and she'd fallen in love with his son the instant she'd met him. Henry had been so desperate for a mom, he'd taken instantly to Shanna, as well, pleading to call her Mommy almost from the beginning.

"My point is that you're repeating the same pattern that wound up breaking your heart," Laurie said.

"Not now!" Shanna ordered angrily. "And certainly not here."

She was not going to discuss her ex-husband or his son where anyone might overhear. She could barely utter Henry's name without wanting to cry. Walking away and leaving him in that toxic environment might have been her only legal option, but that hadn't made it easy. She'd regretted it every day since, although she knew she'd done everything in her power to protect him.

Even now, over a year later, she made regular calls to Henry, convinced she'd be able to tell if he was okay by the way the seven-year-old sounded on the phone. At least Greg hadn't denied her those calls, though he had fought her request for visitation. She'd vowed that if she ever once heard anything that suggested Henry was anything other than happy and well-adjusted, she wouldn't hesitate to stir up a ruckus that would set the staid and powerful Hamilton family on its collective derriere.

Now, Laurie gave her an apologetic look and lowered herself to the ground next to Shanna. "I'm sorry, but I had to say something."

"Look, I understand why you're concerned. I really do. I'm not blind to the similarities in the situations. But there are significant differences, too. Still, I swear to you that I'm not going to let myself get too involved. I'm not interested in getting my heart broken again, either, you know."

"You're saying all the right words, Shanna," Laurie said, sounding resigned. She gestured toward Davy. "Your actions, though, they're shouting something else entirely. You're already in over your head. You've spent most of the day out here with Davy."

"I'm not in over my head," she said firmly. "And you're not taking into account Kevin. He's no more interested in getting involved than I am. He can barely be around me without getting skittish."

"Hasn't it occurred to you that neither of you would be skittish if there was no attraction?" Laurie suggested. "Acquaintances, even friends, don't get skittish around each other. It's only men and women who are fighting or denying all those rampaging hormones."

"Have you considered writing an advice column, instead of recipes?" Shanna inquired testily. "Even though you edit cookbooks, you seem to think you have all the answers when it comes to relationships."

"No," Laurie said. "But maybe what I should be doing is telling fortunes, because I can see disaster written all over this."

Shanna could hardly pretend that she hadn't seen the same signs and portents, but wasn't that enough to keep her from doing something stupid? She'd fallen for Greg because she'd missed all of the most ominous signs.

"My eyes are wide open," she assured Laurie. "I promise."

Her friend apparently heard the finality in her voice, because she sighed even more deeply. "You know I'm only a phone call away if that ever changes."

"I know," Shanna said. "And you'll never know just how much I appreciate that. I couldn't have gotten through the past couple of years without you."

And she hoped with everything in her that she'd never need to lean on Laurie in that way again.

Kevin went down to Harbor Lights Marina first thing on Monday morning to buy a fishing boat. It was an impulse, but it was also a necessity.

After spotting the warm and inviting picture Shanna

made with Davy sound asleep in her lap after Sunday's midday dinner, half of his resolutions about her had flown right out the window. In that instant he'd seen how much Davy needed a mother, someone warm and gentle to hold and comfort him. Gram and his sisters were excellent substitutes, but it wasn't the same.

An instant later with his willpower wavering, he knew he needed to do something to assure that he and Shanna wouldn't cross paths. He would not allow himself to get involved with anyone just to give his son a mother. If he was out on the water for hours on end, then he'd be far away from temptation in the form of the pretty bookseller who seemed to have a way with his son. Buying a fishing boat became an immediate priority.

At Harbor Lights, he wandered the docks until he spotted Hawk Cooper with his bald head, leathery skin and sharp eyes. The son of a waterman, Hawk hadn't been able to give up living by the sea; he had built his marina at the same time Mick had been developing Chesapeake Shores. Old friends, they'd coordinated their plans to ensure that the docks would complement the town. Residents of Chesapeake Shores had docking privileges at special rates, though there were plenty of nonresidents whose yachts and speedboats could be found there during the summer months.

Hawk's customers ranged from the superwealthy owners of sixty-foot cabin cruisers to those who owned only a small sailboat for weekend excursions. In the past year or two, he'd even added a section for the growing number of kayakers in town who wanted to store their crafts by the water, rather than in their garages.

In touch with boaters and marinas from Maryland, Delaware and Virginia, he also brokered deals on boats of every size and description.

"Well, look at you," he said to Kevin. "It's been a long time since you've come poking around down here on my docks. Heard you were back home. I'm real sorry about what happened—"

Kevin cut him off before he could say more. "You still selling boats, Hawk?"

"Of course. You in the market for one? Maybe a pretty little sailboat? I've got a real nice one in stock right now."

"Actually I'm looking for something bigger, something I could use for fishing charters."

Hawk stared at him, clearly taken aback by Kevin's request. "Son, do you have any idea what that business is like these days?" Hawk demanded, his tone gruff, his concern apparent. "The life was hard enough when my father was working these waters, but with fish and crab supplies dwindling and the regulations about catches getting stiffer all the time, a man can't hardly make a living that way. Add in the cost of fuel, and it can ruin you before you get started, especially if you're thinking of going clear out to the ocean."

"I think I'll stick to the bay," Kevin told him, though to be truthful he hadn't given the matter much thought until just that minute.

"Well, that's something, I guess." Hawk studied Kevin, his expression thoughtful. Then he gave another shake of his head. "I've known you since you were a boy. I know you're going through a rough time. No offense, but maybe you should think this through some more."

"No offense taken, but I've made up my mind," Kevin insisted. "Can you find me a boat or not?"

"Well, of course, I can," Hawk said indignantly. "There's not a boat for sale within a hundred miles of here that I can't get for you. I'll negotiate a fair deal, too. Give me a couple of days."

"I want it today," Kevin said, afraid if he waited, second thoughts would start to creep in. At Hawk's startled look, he said, "I don't mean I have to take possession today, just that I want to find the boat and make the deal."

"What's your hurry?"

Kevin tried to explain, but words failed him. "It's a step forward, that's all. I need to take it now."

"Give me a few hours at least," Hawk said, compromising. "Come back after lunch. I'll have some material faxed in here."

Since there wasn't a fishing boat actually docked in the marina, Kevin knew that was the best Hawk could do. "I'll be back at one."

"Make it two. They might have something down at Mitchell's place. Might be able to get it up here for you to see by then."

Kevin nodded in agreement.

That afternoon at two-fifteen, after walking through the boat stem to stern and getting Hawk's assurances that it was mechanically sound, he signed the papers and wrote his check, then made arrangements with Hawk for dock space.

He'd expected to feel relieved that he had not only a plan, but an actual boat. Instead, all he felt was overwhelmed.

"Why on earth did you buy a boat?" Bree demanded when she caught up with him one evening a week later. He was sitting on the still-warm sand, while Davy splashed around at the edge of the water.

"Jess's idea," he said succinctly.

"Well, what was she thinking?" Bree grumbled.

"That I could take out fishing charters," he said.

"And are you planning to do that?"

"Not yet. I need to check into getting certified for a captain's license."

"Have you checked into it?"

"Not yet."

She nodded triumphantly. "Just as I thought. This wasn't about fishing at all. You could care less whether you ever catch a croaker or a rockfish, much less whether anyone else does. This is all about running scared."

Saints protect him from all the women who thought they knew him so damn well. "You don't know what you're talking about."

"Five-two, green eyes," she said. "Ring any bells?"

"If you're so sure that Shanna wants a man in her life, why don't you fix her up with one of Jake's friends. Mack and Will are both available." But even as he said the words, the thought of Shanna going out with either one of them made him a little crazy.

Bree frowned. "You really wouldn't mind? I mean I thought of you first, but she and Mack might get along, too. Of course, he's spending a lot of time with Susie, doing something they both describe as definitely *not* dating. I'll have to see if that leaves room for something that actually *is* dating."

"Whatever," he said, his voice low and suddenly hostile.

A grin spread across her face. "Thought so. You hate the idea."

"It's none of my business," he insisted.

"It is if you want her for yourself."

"Which I don't," he said adamantly.

"Liar."

"Pest."

In what was becoming an all-too-familiar pattern, she

kissed him on the cheek before leaving him with one last gibe. "Coffee, Kev. Just meet her for coffee one day. It's not a big deal. Men and women do it all the time. It doesn't have to lead to something huge, but you'd be keeping your options open."

No matter what his sister said, though, he knew it was a big deal. When a man was still pining for the wife he'd lost, the prospect of having coffee with another woman was almost paralyzing. He felt disloyal even thinking about it. As for actually uttering the invitation, he knew the words would get stuck in his throat.

As it turned out, the whole thing was taken out of his hands. By his son. Even if it was a little scary and a whole lot exasperating, he had to love that his kid had somehow inherited the matchmaking gene of his sisters and grandmother.

Shanna glanced out the window of the store and saw Kevin walking down the street, his stride paced to accommodate the boy beside him. The picture the two of them made filled her with that now-familiar sense of longing. This had to stop. One of these days, Kevin was going to catch her staring at him like some kid peering in at a display of forbidden candy. The probability of such a totally humiliating moment had her drawing away from the window.

After several minutes, when it became clear that they hadn't been coming here after all, she sighed and the feeling of anticipation died. She had six new boxes of books to unpack. She needed to focus her attention on that and not stand around like some lovesick fool.

A moment later, she heard a commotion outside and a high-pitched squeal, followed by a demand for books. She glanced up as a resigned-looking Kevin came into the store, his eager boy tugging on his hand.

"Hi, guys," she said, her heart thumping. "You here for more books, Davy?"

He tore free from his father's grip and toddled toward her. "You read," he commanded.

She immediately fell under his spell. "I can do that. Let's pick out a book." She glanced at Kevin. "Do you mind?"

"Please, be my guest. I'll just sit quietly over here with a cup of coffee."

"It's fresh. I just made it a few minutes ago. I think I finally have the knack for it. It's almost as good as yours."

He nodded and turned his back on them.

Shanna led the way to the picture books, then knelt down beside Davy to help him choose. He found three right away. The first, one with few words, had lots of pictures of trucks, which she'd noticed was a favorite theme of his. Another was about a fire engine and the third about a train. When Shanna took them over to the sofa and sat down, he snuggled in right beside her. She breathed in the scent of baby shampoo and little boy and nearly sighed with contentment.

Since the store was usually deserted at this hour, she read to Davy for nearly an hour without interruption. Then Kevin took pity on her.

"That's enough, pal. Pick out the one book you want and then we need to give Shanna a break."

"It's fine," she protested. "As you can tell, it's dead this time of day. I usually close for a half hour and run down to Sally's to grab some lunch."

"You haven't eaten yet?" Kevin asked.

"No."

He looked at Davy, toward the front of the store, everywhere but directly at her, seemingly mulling over what he was going to say or do next. "We could, that is, I'd like to take you to lunch, you know, as thanks for spending all this time with Davy."

No man had ever sounded more nervous—or endearing—as he stammered out the invitation.

"I mean, Davy and I were heading to Sally's for grilled cheese sandwiches when he spotted the books. You should join us." He hesitated. "If you want to."

"Okay," she said, unable to resist.

And that was how it began, what turned into almost-daily outings to Sally's. With each occasion, Shanna fell a little bit more in love. What she couldn't be sure about was whether it was the man or the package she was coming to love. And after all Kevin had been through, she knew she didn't dare get the answer to that wrong.

8

Bree had been right about coffee—or lunch, as it had turned out—not being such a big deal. Kevin was growing increasingly comfortable during the hour or two he spent with Shanna almost every day. He no longer felt the need to hide out down at the docks on a boat he still wasn't convinced held the key to his future.

Their conversations were light and breezy, mostly about books they were reading, places they'd traveled, his certification classes for his captain's license or his uncle Thomas's well-reported environmental fight to improve the quality of the Chesapeake Bay. They were both appalled that the nation's largest estuary continued to deteriorate despite the legislative act passed by several states to protect it. Kevin loved that Shanna was as passionate about this as he was.

Neither of them ventured into personal territory, either by unspoken mutual consent or because Davy's frequent presence precluded it.

By the time Shanna was able to take her break, Sally's was mostly deserted, so they weren't even subjected to the scrutiny of the locals. That limited the gossip around town, though Kevin knew that his sisters and grandmother were all aware of these outings. He didn't doubt for a second that Bree had taken note and filled them all in, but to his relief, they'd kept astonishingly silent on the subject, probably intent on not jinxing whatever might be developing.

Today, he and Shanna had just finished their cups of crab soup when his cell phone rang. Since Davy was at Abby's with the girls, he had to answer in case there was an emergency with his son.

"Kevin, this is Martha," his late wife's mother said, sounding emotional. "I was just sitting here thinking about Georgia today, and I figured you would be, too, so I had to call. She would have turned twenty-nine today." Her voice broke, and it was a minute before she was able to continue. "I'm sorry. I thought I was okay when I dialed your number, but sometimes it just hits me like this. I can't believe my baby girl is gone."

Her sobs cut right through him, partly because he understood her grief and partly because until she'd mentioned it, he'd forgotten all about today being Georgia's birthday. How had the date gotten past him? And what was he doing spending the occasion with another woman, however innocently? Today of all days, he should be mourning his wife.

"I'm sorry," he said, his own voice choked. He mouthed an apology to Shanna, then walked outside to finish the call in private. "I should have called you," he told his former mother-in-law.

"It's okay," Martha said. "I understand. Believe it or not, I really am fine most of the time. I thought maybe I'd feel better hearing Davy's voice. Is he there? It's not his nap time, is it?"

"Actually Davy's over at my sister's with her girls.

Abby and Trace organized a picnic for the kids on the beach."

"Oh, I'm sure he's loving that," she said. "Would you mind if John and I come up for a visit soon? I don't want my grandson to grow up without knowing the Davis side of the family."

"You have an open invitation," Kevin assured her. "Just let me know whenever you want to come." He thought of the awkward visit he'd paid to his former in-laws in Texas after Georgia's death, but still made himself say, "Or I can bring Davy down to visit you in Beaumont again, if you like. I want you to spend as much time as you can with him. Extended families are important. And he should hear all the stories that only you can tell him about his mom."

"Oh, I'm so relieved to hear you say that. In situations like this, it's so hard to know what to do. I know someday you'll move on, perhaps even marry again, but Davy's all…" Again, her voice grew thick. "Well, you understand."

"Yes, I do," he said. "Make those arrangements to come for a visit, okay? And if you can't find the right time, I'll bring Davy there. I promise."

"I'm sure we'll be able to work something out," she said. "Please give Davy a huge hug for me."

"I will," he promised. "And you tell John I said hello."

"I most surely will. We love you, Kevin. I know things didn't turn out the way any of us hoped or expected, but you are family to us."

Kevin felt an unexpected sting of tears in his eyes at these words from a woman he'd never found particularly demonstrative. She'd remained dry-eyed and detached during their wedding and during her daughter's funeral. Apparently, though, her stoicism had finally shattered. His own was taking a hit right now, too.

"Thanks," he managed to say at last. "We'll talk again soon."

"Yes, we will," she said.

He clicked off the phone, drew in a deep breath, then glanced inside the café and saw Shanna watching him with a worried frown. Something about the genuine concern he read in her expression eased the pain Martha's call had stirred. It also filled him with guilt. How could he be out enjoying himself with another woman on Georgia's birthday, of all days?

He walked slowly back inside, not sure what he could or should say about the call that had darkened his mood, provoking an unexpected surge of guilt.

"Is everything okay?" Shanna asked as he slid back into the booth. "That wasn't about Davy, was it?"

"No, it was Georgia's mother," he replied, the words tumbling out before he could stop them. "Today would have been Georgia's twenty-ninth birthday. Martha was upset."

"Oh, Kevin, I'm so sorry," she said, covering his hand, her expression instantly sympathetic.

He withdrew his hand. He didn't deserve her sympathy. "I'd forgotten," he said bleakly. "Georgia's only been gone a little over a year, and I'd forgotten about her birthday."

"How many birthdays did you celebrate together?" she asked.

He blinked at the odd question. "Just two," he said. "Why?"

"Then is it really so surprising that you forgot? From what little I know, the two of you were together a very short time and living in an intense environment for much of that time. I imagine there are a lot of dates that you never had a chance to commit to memory."

"Don't make excuses for me," he said. "I should have remembered." He met her gaze. "And I shouldn't have been here with you."

She looked dismayed at that. "Kevin, we're friends. At least I hope we are. Who else should you be with on a day that brings up such sad memories?"

"Family," he said without hesitation. "Davy."

"You'll be going home to both," she said easily.

"That's not the point."

"I doubt you'd be feeling this way if someone other than Georgia's mother had been the one to remind you about the significance of today's date."

He considered that, then nodded. "You're probably right. Martha doesn't call often, and I know she doesn't mean to stir up my guilt, but somehow I always wind up feeling as if I'm in the wrong. She makes me feel as if I'm not grieving the way she and John are."

Shanna regarded him incredulously. "I didn't know there were rules about such a thing. Is one way better than another? Are you supposed to shed so many tears for a set number of days? Explain that to me."

He chuckled at the questions. "Okay, maybe I'm making too much of what she said. It isn't as if she accused me of not mourning her daughter. Not even close." He turned serious as he met Shanna's gaze. "Have you ever felt so guilty about something that it almost paralyzes you?"

For an instant, she looked taken aback by the question, but then she nodded. "More often than you can possibly imagine," she said quietly.

There was something in her voice, something in the stricken expression in her eyes, that stunned him. In that second, he realized that she did know exactly what he meant, and yet somehow she had managed to go on. Though he was trying to get on with his life, she had actually done it.

One of these days, when the ground stopped shifting under him from one minute to the next, he'd have to ask her how. And then he'd have to ask what tragedy had forced her to learn that painful lesson.

Megan was about to call it quits and walk out of the Upper East Side art gallery where she'd worked for over fifteen years. Though Phillip had always been a moody and difficult boss, today he was taking his temperamental mood swings to new heights. A shipment of expensive paintings hadn't shown up earlier and he was acting as if she personally was responsible.

At the conclusion of his tirade, she stood up.

"Where are you going?" he demanded.

"For a walk."

"You can't just leave here now. We have a crisis on our hands."

She leveled a look directly into his eyes. "I am well aware of that, and yelling at me isn't going to change it. I'll be back when you've had a chance to calm down."

"I insist that you stay!"

"If I do, and you say one more word blaming any of this on me, when I walk out it will be for good," she warned. "Is that a risk you're willing to take?"

For an instant he looked stunned. "You'd quit?"

"In a heartbeat," she responded, realizing with a sense of shock that it was true. For the first time since she'd come to work here, she no longer felt as if this job was her only option. There was Mick.

Not that she intended to run back to her ex-husband

simply for the sake of security, but Mick would be here for her if she decided she'd had enough of Phillip Margolin and his tantrums. It was a comforting thought.

Phillip gave her a considering look. His heightened color began to fade. "Sorry," he mumbled, which was a major concession from him. "Go, take that walk. I do know none of this is your fault, but having paintings worth a million dollars or more wandering around somewhere in Manhattan when they're supposed to be here has made me a little crazy."

"Totally understandable," she agreed. "But not my fault."

He gave her a rueful look. "Again, very, very sorry if I implied that it was."

"I'll be back in fifteen minutes," she assured him. "And we will find the paintings, Phillip. I'm going to pick up an iced mocha. Can I bring you anything? Something without caffeine, preferably."

He lifted a brow at that. "A decaf iced cappuccino," he responded dutifully. "The biggest one they make."

Megan nodded, grabbed her purse and headed outside. She'd barely walked half a block when she bumped into someone and nearly stumbled. She looked up into Mick's startled gaze.

"Where's the fire?" he inquired, steadying her. "And why weren't you looking where you were going? That's a good way to get mugged."

She scowled at his chiding tone. "I've lived here for more than fifteen years, Mick O'Brien. I certainly don't need you to remind me of the dangers of not paying attention to my surroundings," she said testily.

He held up his hands at once. "Sorry. You're obviously in a mood of some kind."

"How condescending of you to phrase it that way," she snapped.

Worry knit his brow. He clamped a hand on her elbow and guided her straight into the coffee shop on the corner. Since that had been her destination in the first place, she didn't waste time arguing.

"Sit," he commanded. "What do you want?"

"A little less bossiness would be nice," she replied.

"To drink," he said, clearly fighting to cling to his last shred of patience.

She told him her order and Phillip's, then sat there and drew in several deep breaths while he went to get the drinks. She needed to calm down. It was crazy to be taking her frustration with her boss out on Mick. And what was he doing here anyway? He hadn't mentioned coming to New York when they'd talked last night.

He returned with their drinks and sat across from her. Waiting until she'd taken several sips of her coffee, he then regarded her with his most unrelenting gaze.

"Mind telling me what the devil put you in this mood?"

"Phillip's on a tear. Over a million dollars' worth of paintings weren't delivered on schedule, and we can't seem to track them. I'm sure it's just some ridiculous snafu with the delivery service, but he's convinced that we're the victims of a major art heist and that I know more than I'm telling him."

Mick regarded her with an expression that ranged from incredulity to outrage. "He's suggesting you're involved in some art theft?"

She waved off his indignation. "Not seriously. You've met Phillip. You know how dramatic he can be. He's just upset and I'm there." She shrugged. "Which is why I'm here, if you can follow my point. I had to take a break or quit."

"I vote for quitting," he said at once.

She lifted a brow at the quick response. "And you don't think you might be trying to take advantage of the situation for your own nefarious purposes?"

"Well, of course I am," he said without hesitation. He grinned at her. "If it'll get you back in Chesapeake Shores, I'll use any weapons at my disposal. You shouldn't be working for anyone who doesn't fully appreciate you."

"I was married to a man exactly like that," she reminded him.

Mick winced. "Okay, I deserved that, but I'm trying to make amends, aren't I? Give me a little credit here."

She reached for his hand. "I do," she told him. "I give you a lot of credit, in fact. What are you doing here, by the way?"

"I woke up this morning with a need to see your face. Since you were working and couldn't come to Maryland, I decided to come to you."

"Well, your timing was impeccable. I needed to see a friendly face."

He looked pleased by the comment, then gave her an earnest look. "Megan, seriously, think about moving home. You can open your own art gallery. You know the business. You have the contacts. And I have the money to back you."

"Which wouldn't make it my business now, would it?" she countered. "No, Mick. It's a generous offer, but I can't accept it."

"Then marry me again, dammit, and just come home."

She looked into his eyes and laughed. "Now, if that isn't the loveliest proposal a woman has ever heard," she said, shaking her head. "It absolutely makes me want to swoon right into your arms."

"If you want the whole hearts and flowers thing, I'll do it," he vowed. "Come to dinner with me tonight, and I'll arrange for candlelight and music and I'll bring along the biggest rock you can wear and still lift your finger."

"Oh, Mick," she said, squeezing his hand. "I don't need a diamond ring. Truth be told, I don't even like diamonds all that well. And I can't marry you again, so please don't drag out all the romantic gestures."

He pulled his hand away, the hurt in his eyes unmistakable. "Are you saying I'm wasting my time courting you? Have you already made up your mind that you'll never come back to me?"

"No," she said, immediately regretting the way she'd phrased her response. "I haven't decided anything."

"Well, you sounded pretty darn sure of yourself not a minute ago," he groused.

"I just meant I couldn't marry you *now,* or even say yes now. We still need time, Mick. Neither of us are who we were when we met, or even when we divorced. We can't drift back together and expect to fit together the same way."

"I suppose I should be relieved by what you're saying, but all I feel is aggravated," he admitted.

She smiled at that. "Because patience has never been one of your virtues."

"True enough." He stood up. "Well, since you won't let me set up some fancy dinner, I suppose we should get back to that gallery of yours and find those missing paintings."

She regarded him with surprise. "You don't have to help."

"I do if I expect to spend any time with you this evening," he said. "And I didn't come all this way just to wander around the city on my own."

She gave him a coy look. "With all the attractions New York has to offer, you care only about me?"

He laughed. "Meggie, don't you know by now that for me, you'll always be the main attraction?"

"There's more of that Irish blarney I always loved," she said as she followed him from the coffee shop.

"It's not blarney," he said indignantly. "It's the gospel truth."

Heaven help her, she thought. She was beginning to believe he meant it.

Shanna didn't see Kevin for more than a week after he'd gotten that call from his former mother-in-law. She knew what he was going through and why, but she hated that he seemed to have lost some of the forward momentum in his life. Bree had stopped by yesterday morning and mentioned that he was moping around the house again. The only positive thing he seemed to be doing was going to the required classes to get his captain's certification.

She'd picked up the phone half a dozen times to call him, then put it back. Friends certainly called friends, but she knew that wasn't exactly what they were. There was too much attraction sizzling between them for the label to fit.

Even more worrisome than her indecision about calling Kevin was the fact that she was spending so much time thinking about him in the first place. Every casual remark Bree had made about her brother when they'd chatted in front of their shops had been as welcome as rain drenching the parched flowers in a garden. Shanna recognized that it wasn't a good sign.

Of course, thinking about Kevin did keep her from dwelling on her former stepson. Whenever she saw children running eagerly toward the beach in the morning or families waiting in line to get ice cream at the shop around the corner, she thought of Henry and her heart sank. Today it was a toss-up which of the two worries ran deeper—Kevin or Henry.

Since Kevin was an adult and his problems weren't hers to solve, the next time she reached for the phone, she called the number that had once been her own. It was the nanny who answered.

"Greta, it's Shanna."

"Oh, Mrs. Hamilton, how are you?" She clucked at her mistake. "Sorry. I know it's Ms. Carlyle now. I just can't get used to that."

"Shanna is fine," she told the woman who'd been caring for Henry since his mother had died in an accident when he was three. "How's Henry? Is he there?"

"Standing right here beside me," Greta said. "As soon as he heard me say your name, he came running. I'll put him on."

"First tell me if he's okay."

Greta hesitated, then said unconvincingly, "Everything's fine."

Hearing an off note in her voice, Shanna persisted. "No, it's not. What's going on?"

"I really can't get into that now. Here's Henry."

"Mommy, is it really you?" Henry asked.

Relieved by the familiar excitement in his voice, she put aside her fears. She saw no need to correct him for calling her Mommy, either, though Greg and his family had objected to the continued use of it after the divorce.

"We gave him permission to call me that even before the wedding," she'd reminded Greg. "If someone else comes into the picture, then we'll worry about which of us he calls Mommy." Her ex-husband had finally relented.

For a moment now, she simply basked in knowing that her boy sounded happy. Then she asked, "Hey, buddy, how are you? Have you grown another six inches since last time we talked?"

He giggled. "Nobody grows that fast."

"I think you do. I had to buy you new school clothes three times when you were in kindergarten. How about that sweater I sent you for your birthday. Have you outgrown that already?"

"No way," he said. "It's awesome. I'm going to wear it forever and ever." He paused, then said, "Guess what, Mommy?"

"What?"

"Daddy promised to take me to a Phillies baseball game next week, and maybe to a Baltimore Orioles game later this summer. He said someday we'd go to every ballpark in the whole country. Isn't that the best?"

Knowing how much Henry loved baseball, she agreed. "It's definitely the best." She just hoped it didn't turn out to be one of the hundreds of promises that Greg broke. Each time it was harder and harder for Henry to bounce back from the disappointment. Each time the light in his eyes dimmed a bit more.

"Tell me what else you've been doing," she encouraged him. "Are you having a good summer vacation?"

"Greta took me fishing at the lake," he said, mentioning another of his favorite things. They'd gone almost daily when she'd been there. He sighed heavily. "But she didn't like baiting the hook. I don't think she'll take me again." He paused then asked, "Could you maybe come and take me?"

"I wish I could, buddy. I'll talk to your dad, and maybe one of these days we'll be able to work something out. No promises, though—understood?"

"I know. It's because the court said so," he said glumly. "I hate the dumb court."

Shanna wasn't especially fond of it, either. The judge had been a close friend of Greg's father; she'd never stood a chance. A more compassionate and less well-connected judge might have taken into account the bond she'd had with Henry rather than focusing solely on the legalities. These infrequent calls weren't satisfying to either one of them. Still, they were better than being cut out of Henry's life completely, which would have been the Hamiltons' preference.

"Did you open your bookstore?" Henry asked.

"I did and it's wonderful."

"I wish I could see it," he said wistfully. "Maybe Grandma will bring me."

Shanna had her doubts about that. Loretta Hamilton had never been one of Shanna's biggest fans. All evidence to the contrary, she'd blamed Shanna for the breakup of the marriage after only a few months. Though she was well aware of the tight bond Shanna and Henry had formed, she'd backed her husband and son a hundred percent in their efforts to keep Shanna out of Henry's life after the divorce.

"I need to go, but I love you, Henry," Shanna said. "Can you put Greta back on?"

"She went downstairs," he told her. "I think she's fixing lunch."

"Okay then," Shanna said, hiding her disappointment at not getting to ask the nanny a few more questions. "I'll speak to you again soon."

"Really soon?" he asked plaintively.

"Really soon. Love you," she said and waited.

After a moment came the hard-won response, "Love you."

Shanna hung up, tears in her eyes. It had taken her months of repeating the phrase every time she said good-night, both before and after the wedding, to get Henry to utter those words. In a family that thought effusive emotions were a weakness, he'd rarely heard them and learned to distrust them when they were spoken.

Sadly, when she and his dad had split up, he'd felt betrayed by the simple phrase yet again. At the age of six, when she'd left, he'd learned that love didn't mean people stayed in his life. He'd remained stubbornly silent when she'd uttered them during their conversations. It was only in recent weeks, when he'd begun to believe that she still cared despite being separated from him, that he'd started to say the words again.

"Oh, Henry," she murmured, brushing at the tears dampening her cheeks. "What have we done to you?"

It wasn't the first time she'd asked herself the question, and she knew it wouldn't be the last. Greg, in his own highly dysfunctional way, had gone on after the divorce. So had she, building a new life that promised to be fulfilling in ways her marriage had never been.

But Henry, living in the midst of the chaos that was his father's life, had no choices open to him, no defenses against the turmoil that was a daily occurrence with a man like Greg, who lost himself in an alcoholic haze more frequently than not.

Shanna had tried so hard to make all of that clear to the judge, but her word had been up against the testimony of Loretta and Harrison Hamilton, even against the word of Greg himself, who'd sobered up sufficiently to make his case to the court. Charming and intelligent when sober, Greg had given testimony about their marriage that had been impossible to refute with his powerful parents there to back him up and no one at all to support her claims. Even with a stack of exorbitant liquor store receipts as evidence, she couldn't place those bottles in Greg's hands. For all anyone knew, they'd been gifts to business associates or supplies for extravagant parties, as Greg's counsel had suggested.

She'd walked away from the brief marriage with her heart in tatters but her dignity intact. Yet the real damage had been to a then-six-year-old boy who'd been left with no one to protect and love him beyond a nanny too frightened of her boss to speak up in court when it might have counted.

Shanna sighed. The call had been unsatisfying in so many ways, but hearing the wistful note in Henry's voice had accomplished one thing. It had stiffened her resolve to watch over him as best she could from a distance.

And if the time ever came when she suspected that he was being hurt—emotionally or physically—by his father, she would act in a heartbeat and damn the legal consequences.

9

Tired of the pitying looks he was getting from just about everyone in his family, Kevin invited Jake, Trace, Will and Mack to go fishing with him on Sunday. It would give him a chance to test his skill at handling his new boat. More important, it might reassure everyone that his life was on track.

The other four men met him at the Harbor Lights Marina at dawn. Of all of them, only Mack was looking a little the worse for wear.

"Late night?" Kevin inquired.

"He was out on another one of those nondates with Susie O'Brien," Will said. "For two people who insist they're not even remotely into each other, they spend an awful lot of time together."

"We're friends," Mack said, giving him a sour look, then jumping on board the fishing boat to get away from them. No sooner had Kevin brought his cooler aboard than Mack popped open a beer.

Jake frowned at him. "What's going on with you? It's not even seven in the morning."

"I'm telling you, he's totally messed up," Will said.

"Is that your professional opinion?" Mack retorted. "What kind of shrink tells someone they're messed up?"

"One who cares, dammit!" Will retorted. "This nonsense has to stop. Either date the woman or don't, but this ridiculous denial you're both in isn't working. The last time I ran into Susie, she was as much of a basket case as you are."

"Did you share that insight with her?" Mack asked.

Will looked appalled by the suggestion. "Of course not."

"Well, FYI, I'm not the one you need to be lecturing," Mack said. "Now, can we please drop this? If not, I'm going back home."

Trace took out a beer and dropped down into the chair next to his. "I think I'll join you," he announced. "Misery loves company, right?"

Kevin's head snapped around at that. "Misery? What do you have to be miserable about? You and my sister are about to get married."

Trace shrugged and took a long, deep drink from his bottle of beer. "Couldn't prove it by me. Have you heard a date? I haven't. Every time I ask, I get the look."

Mack nodded sorrowfully. "I know that look."

"Me, too," Jake said.

Kevin stared at all three of them. "What look is that?"

"The one that says we're idiots for pushing something, am I right?" Trace said glumly. "Wouldn't you think Abby would want to get on with this? I'm surprised that ex-husband of hers hasn't raised a ruckus about us living together with the twins under the same roof. Of course, Wes has his own relationship issues, which is probably the only reason he hasn't been on Abby's case about this."

Feeling the need to defend his sister, Kevin said, "Abby's been pretty busy whipping that brokerage office into shape. She's in Baltimore as much as she's here."

"And that's another thing," Trace said, seizing on the remark. "You're exactly right, Kevin. She's hiding out up in Baltimore half the time, and I'm down here with the twins."

Before Kevin could question why he thought Abby was hiding out, Trace gave him a quelling look.

"Not that I don't adore those little girls as much as if they were my own," Trace added. "And taking care of them is not a problem, since I'm working at home. Believe me, that is not the point."

Kevin regarded him with skepticism. "Not a problem? Are you sure you're talking about Carrie and Caitlyn? I love my nieces, but those two are a handful."

"We have a system," Trace insisted.

All three men stared at him.

"A system?" Will echoed. "Really?"

Trace scowled at their doubting expressions. "I'm telling you, I have everything under control at the house."

"Are you locking them in their rooms?" Kevin asked, not entirely in jest.

"Absolutely not," Trace insisted. "Could you all please focus? The girls are not the problem. Abby is. I think she's getting cold feet. Why else would she get that look on her face every time I mention setting a wedding date?"

Kevin didn't believe for a second that his sister didn't want to marry Trace. He was the man she should have married years ago. "I'm telling you, you're wrong. She's just been too focused on work."

"You know what I think?" Will said to Trace. "I think you need to leave the girls with someone here and go to Baltimore to be alone with your fiancée for a few days. Abby jumped into a new job. You jumped into living together and being a parent. All of that requires some significant adjustments. You need some time to be a couple, to get your emotional feet back under you and remember why you fell in love in the first place."

Trace regarded him with a thoughtful expression. "You could have something there," he agreed.

Will grinned. "I don't get to charge those big bucks without having some credible insights every once in a while."

"I'll take the girls," Kevin offered. "Gram will love having them at the house for a few days. And it's the least I can do after all the times you and Abby have bailed me out by looking after Davy."

"There you go," Will said. "Problem solved. Am I good or what?"

Mack grinned and draped an arm over his shoulder. "Oh, you're good, all right. Maybe one of these days you'll use all that expertise to hang on to your own relationship for more than a few weeks."

Jake nudged Will in the ribs with an elbow. "He's got you there, pal."

Will sighed. "Give me one of those beers."

Kevin stared at the other men and shook his head. "Do any of you actually want to go fishing? Or did you just want to sit here at the dock and drink?"

"Staying right here works for me," Trace said.

"Me, too," Jake confirmed.

"Never did care that much about catching fish," Will added, settling into one of the lounge chairs on the deck. "Sitting here like this, though—" he sighed deeply "—now, this is the life."

"Amen," the others chorused.

Kevin grinned and reached for his own beer. "At the price of fuel, this suits me just fine, too."

"And there are some mighty fine-looking women who wander around these docks wearing next to nothing," Mack said.

"Look all you want," Jake taunted. "But it's not going to change the fact that you're hooked on Susie."

Mack sighed heavily. "Yeah, you're probably right," he said glumly.

And though he wasn't about to say it aloud, Kevin knew that no amount of babe-watching was going to change the fact that recently he hadn't been able to get Shanna out of his head, either. Maybe, though, it would distract him from the overwhelming guilt that attraction was causing him.

It had not been a good morning. Shanna had walked into the shop to find water all over the floor in the back room. The pipe under the sink in the bathroom had apparently sprung a leak overnight. She'd turned off the water, but so far she hadn't been able to locate a plumber who could get here until tomorrow.

She'd had so many customers this morning that she hadn't been able to get into the back room to thoroughly mop and to check out the damage to the boxes of inventory that had been sitting on the floor. At least she'd managed to move most of them off the ground so they wouldn't be further damaged.

She sighed with relief when the last of the customers left right on schedule around one o'clock and the usual lull set in. She was halfway to the back room when the bell over the door rang. She heard a familiar squeal and turned to have Davy launch himself at her. He was followed at a slightly more sedate pace by Carrie and Caitlyn and Kevin.

She forced a smile for the sake of the children, but suspected it didn't quite reach her eyes. Kevin noticed at once.

"What's wrong?" he asked.

"A plumbing malfunction in the back," she told him. "And I haven't had two minutes to do more than shut off the water and get some boxes out of the puddles. I couldn't locate a plumber who could get here today, either. This is the first chance I've had all morning to get back there and try to deal with it."

"Show me," he said at once. He turned to Carrie and Caitlyn. "Girls, I want you to stay in the children's section and look at books with Davy, okay? If you'll do that for me for a few minutes, you can each pick out a book to take home."

"Yay," Carrie said, her expression eager. She grabbed Davy's hand. "Come on. What book do you want us to read to you?"

"I'll keep an eye on them," Shanna offered.

"After you show me the problem and sit for a minute," Kevin said. "You looked completely frazzled."

She tried not to take offense at the description, especially since he was right. She was frazzled. "It's been a hectic morning. If you can deal with this leak, you'll be a lifesaver. I think I could fix it, if I had the right tools, but I don't."

She showed him the pipe and where the water had been coming out.

"Sounds like a bad washer," he concluded.

Suddenly she recalled something his father had said to her a few weeks back. "Kevin, not to look a gift horse in the mouth or anything, but do you have any idea what you're doing under there?"

He poked his head out from under the sink and winked. "There are a few household repairs that not even I can mess up. I drove over here in Dad's SUV because I had the girls. His toolbox is in the back. I'll have this fixed in a jiffy."

Taking him at his word, she debated dealing with the damp boxes, then decided that she really needed to be with the kids. Though they were being fairly quiet, there was no telling what mischief they might be up to. Besides, nothing would more quickly take her mind off her problems than listening to those three chatter about anything and everything.

"Ms. Shanna," Caitlyn said as soon as Shanna had sat down with them, "do you have a book about girls?"

Puzzled, Shanna said, "I have lots and lots of books about little girls."

"No, it's about a family with little girls. Mommy told us about it. She said Grandma Megan read it to her when she was our age. It's a movie, too."

"Are you talking about *Little Women?*"

Caitlyn's expression brightened at once. "That's it. Do you have it?"

"Of course I do," Shanna told her, going to the section of classic children's books. She reached for the Louisa May Alcott book that had once been her own favorite. "This copy has wonderful illustrations, too."

When she'd pulled it from the shelf and sat down, all three children settled down with her, Davy in her lap and the girls on either side. The immediate feeling of contentment that stole over her was amazing.

As she began to read, the girls leaned in closer to study the illustrations. Davy fell asleep. When she finished reading the first chapter, she closed the book and looked from Carrie to Caitlyn. "Do you like it?"

Carrie nodded.

"Me, too," Caitlyn said. "That's the book I want Uncle Kevin to get us."

"Uncle Kevin would be happy to get that book," he said, startling Shanna.

She met his gaze. "How long have you been standing there?"

"Long enough to see what a pretty picture you make sitting there with all three of those kids," he said. "You have a way with them."

Shanna blushed. Because she didn't know how to respond to a comment like that, she asked, "How's it going with the pipe?"

"All fixed and the water's back on. I mopped the floor, but you're going to need to go through those boxes. I think a few things got pretty soaked."

"I was afraid of that. I'll go back there and deal with that now."

Kevin shook his head. "Not until you've had lunch. We're going for pizza. You're coming with us."

Carrie and Caitlyn immediately jumped up and reached for her hands.

"Yes, Ms. Shanna, you have to come," Caitlyn said.

"Please," Carrie coaxed.

"And we're going to have ice cream after," Caitlyn added.

Shanna regarded Kevin with amusement. "This is your idea of babysitting? Feeding them till they're so stuffed, they'll fall into a stupor?"

"What's a stupor?" Carrie asked.

"Nothing you need to worry about," Kevin told her. "They have big appetites."

"And small tummies," Shanna countered.

"Not these two," Kevin insisted.

"We can eat lots and lots," Caitlyn confirmed.

Carrie held her arms wide. "At least this much pizza and then ice cream."

Shanna handed Davy to Kevin, then stood up. "I need to see this," she said, then grinned at Kevin. "And I definitely want to see how you handle it when they start turning green."

"Former EMT and army medic," he reminded her. "It's all good."

She laughed at his confidence. "We'll see."

An hour later, Kevin was tucking two very sick little girls into his car and trying to avoid Shanna's told-you-so expression.

"I had no idea anyone could get so sick, so fast," he mumbled as the girls groaned in misery.

"Two and a half slices of pizza topped off by hot fudge sundaes could explain it," Shanna said. Though she'd jumped right in to take care of the girls when they'd thrown up, her sympathy boundless and her tone gentle and soothing, with him she hadn't even tried to hide her amusement.

"I'm never going to hear the end of this, am I?" he asked.

"Probably not," she admitted.

"Are you going to feel the need to spill the beans to my sister?"

"You mean Bree?"

"Bree, Abby, Jess. It doesn't matter. Once one of them finds out, they'll all know."

"They won't find out from me," she assured him, then glanced pointedly at the girls sitting in their car seats. "But they will find out."

Kevin frowned. “Maybe I could bribe them not to blab to their mother or father.”

Shanna immediately shook her head. “Not a great idea. Children shouldn’t be encouraged to keep secrets from their parents.”

“Yeah, I suppose you’re right. Oh well, maybe Abby and Trace will be in such a good mood after their romantic little getaway without the kids, they won’t yell at me about this.”

As they stood on the sidewalk, Bree walked out of her shop and joined them. She peered into the car, then frowned.

“What have you done to those girls?” she asked at once. “They look green.”

“Don’t start on me,” Kevin told her.

“Too much pizza and ice cream,” Shanna said.

He whirled on her. “I thought you weren’t going to say anything.”

“She’s here. She saw them for herself.”

“You could have stopped me, you know,” he accused.

Shanna chuckled. “Not me. You said you had it all under control.”

Bree looked from one of them to the other, a grin spreading across her face. “This is too good. I’m going inside to call Abby.”

“You most certainly are not,” Kevin said, latching onto her arm. “She and Trace are…well, let’s just say that interrupting them to rat me out is not a good idea.”

Instantly distracted from her pale nieces, Bree regarded him with fascination. “What do you know about Trace and Abby that I don’t?”

“They’re in Baltimore—alone, if you catch my drift,” he responded.

Bree's eyes lit up. "Really? A little prewedding honeymoon?"

"Something like that," Kevin confirmed. "Trace wanted to get Abby's mind focused on the wedding, so I volunteered to help out by looking after the girls for a couple of days."

"Really? And you did that by making them sick?"

He scowled at his sister. "Bite me."

Beside him, Shanna chuckled. "I love this family. You two are a riot."

"You think this is fun?" Kevin asked.

"I do," she confirmed.

"My own sister is bugging me, even though I've been doing a good deed, and you find that amusing?" he persisted.

"You know what they say about no good deed going unpunished," Bree chimed in.

"Yeah, well, see if I ever do a favor for you," he told her, then turned to Shanna. "As for you, is this the thanks I get for fixing your leaking pipe?"

Shanna flushed guiltily. The pink in her cheeks made her more beautiful than ever. "Oops!"

Bree studied her. "You let Kevin fix a plumbing problem?" she asked, looking worried.

"I can replace a washer," he said, scowling at the pair of them. Women really were more trouble than they were worth at times. Obviously these two didn't appreciate a good deed.

"Maybe I ought to get Dad over here to take a look," Bree said. "He's back from New York, isn't he?"

"Dad does not need to be involved. The pipe is no longer leaking," Kevin said. "Ask Shanna. Was it leaking when we went to lunch?"

"No," she said at once.

Bree glanced toward the bookstore, then gasped. "Then maybe you can explain why there's water coming out from under the front door now."

Kevin turned and felt the color drain out of his face. Shanna wore a horrified expression that he was pretty sure matched his own.

"Bree, take the girls and Davy home," he ordered. "Call Dad on the way and ask him to get over here, okay?"

"Done," Bree said, racing inside her shop to let Jenny know she was leaving.

"Give me your key," Kevin said to Shanna, who seemed to be immobilized by the sight of all that water flooding into the street. When she didn't budge, he took the key she was clutching in her hand.

Inside, he sloshed through the water into the back room and turned the cutoff valve until the water slowed to a trickle, then a few final drips.

Shanna waded in after him, looking around in dismay at the mess. "What happened?"

"Apparently the problem was more than the washer," he said succinctly. "Don't worry about it. I'll clean this place up for you. In a couple of hours, you'll never know anything happened in here."

"There's inventory that can't be salvaged," she whispered, obviously near tears. "I can't afford a loss like that."

Kevin stared at her in dismay. "Don't you have insurance?"

"Of course I do, but I can't make a claim on my insurance a few weeks after opening. My rates will go sky-high."

Kevin went to her and pulled her into his arms. "Please don't cry," he whispered into her hair. "I can't take it. This is all my fault and I'll make it right."

"You were only trying to help," she said, clinging to him. Her tears were soaking his shirt.

Kevin tilted her chin up and met her gaze. "No more crying, okay? The last thing we need in here is more water."

A smile tugged at her lips, just as he'd hoped.

"That's better," he said. "Don't worry. This looks worse than it is. Most of your inventory is up off the floor and we'll have this place dried out in no time. I'll rent a couple of big fans and get a cleaning crew over here." He met her gaze. "Will you be okay while I make a few calls and get things moving?"

She nodded, though her expression was bleak.

Reluctantly, Kevin left her alone and went outside to make the calls. When he came back in, she was pushing the water toward the front door with a broom.

"A mop will work better."

"I don't have one."

"Sally will," he said at once. "You go borrow that and I'll start soaking this up with some towels. Can I use the ones in the bathroom?"

She nodded. "There are more up in my apartment. The key's on the same ring. I'll be right back."

Kevin went through the back door, ran up the stairs to her apartment, grabbed an armload of towels, then went back downstairs. By then, Shanna was back, not only with a mop, but Jake, Mack and Will.

"I found backup," she announced, looking a bit dazed. "When they heard me telling Sally what happened, they insisted on coming to help. Thank heavens they picked today to have a late lunch."

Kevin doubted they were as interested in helping as they were in making his life miserable by reminding him from now through eternity that this was his fault. These guys did love to gloat about how inept the son of Mick O'Brien was when it came to anything handy. In fact, though they pitched in without comment, there was no mistaking the amusement lurking in their eyes.

To Kevin's surprise, Mick had nothing to say when he arrived. He just put an arm around Shanna's shoulders and gave her a reassuring hug.

"Not to worry," he told her. "We'll have this fixed and the mess cleaned up in no time."

A few minutes after Mick's arrival, Bree returned and took in Shanna's glazed expression at once. "You need coffee," she announced. "Let's make a fresh pot, okay? Then you and I are going to pour a couple of cups and take them across the street to the park."

"I can't leave here," Shanna protested, even as she went through the automatic motions to start a fresh batch of coffee.

"You most certainly can take a break," Bree insisted.

"Go with my sister," Kevin said. "Let us fix this."

Bree nodded in wholehearted agreement. "You have an entire crew of strong, capable men cleaning things up. Let them get that done, then you and I will take stock of the inventory and see where things stand."

Once again, Shanna looked as if she were about to burst into tears. Kevin's heart sank, knowing he was responsible.

"I'm so sorry," he said, just as Mick came out of the back room.

"This wasn't your doing, son," he said. "That whole pipe was a disaster waiting to happen. I'm calling your uncle Jeff. I can't imagine what they were thinking, leasing this space without making a repair like that. There's no excuse for it. Shanna, the management company will have insurance to cover any losses you might have. You won't need to file a claim with yours."

Her expression brightened visibly. "Are you sure?"

"I'll see to it," Mick said at once, a hard glint in his eyes.

Kevin had a feeling his father was going to relish the confrontation with his brother. Those two rarely spoke these days, except when Gram insisted on civility during the holidays. There'd been bad blood between them ever since they'd differed in their ideas for developing Chesapeake Shores. This would be just one more thing for Mick to throw in his younger brother's face.

"Maybe I should talk to Uncle Jeff," Kevin offered.

Mick's forbidding expression warned him off.

"It was just an idea," Kevin said at once. "Thought maybe it would be nice to keep peace in the family for Gram's sake."

"I'm not going to beat my brother up over this," Mick retorted. "But I'll see to it that he makes it right. Might be just what he needs to remind him that his obligations extend further than simply collecting the rent checks."

Kevin kept his doubts about his father's restraint to himself. Besides, from what he'd observed, his uncle had a strong sense of duty and had run the property management company just fine without any advice from Mick. Their differing points of view on just about everything were the primary cause of the rift between them.

Ironically, any outsider could see that Mick, Jeff and Thomas had balanced each other, each bringing something unique to the table when they'd developed the town. Chesapeake Shores was better because of it. Not that Mick would ever admit that. He'd taken every disagreement as a personal criticism, not only of his vision for the town, but also of his skill as a developer.

Rather than wasting his breath saying any of that to his

father, though, Kevin turned to Shanna. "Still love this family?" he asked.

Her smile wobbled a bit, then spread. "Yeah, I do."

For some reason, that made him happier than he had any right to feel on a day that had been as chaotic and accident-prone as this one.

10

Shanna sat on a bench in the park across the street from her store, clutching her second cup of coffee and trying not to cry as boxes of sopping wet books were carted outside and put into the back of Jake's pickup to be taken to the dump. Dusk was falling, and they'd been working nonstop all afternoon to dry the place out and remove anything that had been damaged beyond repair.

She was physically and emotionally drained from going through sodden books, making a note of the ruined titles so she could remove them from her inventory list and then reorder. Most of the damage had been to the children's books, because they'd been on the lowest shelves or, in many cases, on the floor where young readers had left them.

She looked up as Kevin crossed the street, and her heart did a weak little stutter-step that was about as halfhearted as everything else she was feeling.

"Hey," he said, dropping down beside her. "You okay?"

"I've been better," she said. "I honestly don't know what I would have done if all of you hadn't pitched in this afternoon. Everyone's been amazing. Even people I barely know stopped by to help."

"We take care of our own in this town, and people love the addition of a bookstore to Main Street," he told her. Studying her intently, he added, "You look beat. Why don't you grab a shower, change your clothes and I'll take you for a quick bite to eat? You could probably use a low-key, relaxing evening."

She was shaking her head before the invitation was out of his mouth. "There's too much left to do."

"It will still be there tomorrow. We've dried the place out, and that's the most important thing. Susie got here a few minutes ago, and she's helping Bree sort through inventory." He grinned. "At least when she's not scowling at Mack."

"I didn't even see her," Shanna said.

"Because you're so exhausted you can barely keep your eyes open," he said. "Add in the stress, and you need an early night."

She started to rise. "I need to speak to Susie about the insurance."

Kevin tugged her right back down. "She'll bring the claim forms by first thing in the morning. She says she'll even cut you a check as an advance against that, if you need it." He grinned. "My dad's doing, I'm sure. He was over at the management office ranting at Uncle Jeff, according to Susie."

Shanna winced. "I didn't want that to happen."

"Don't worry about it. Those two have spent their entire lives arguing about one thing or another. They thrive on it. You've given them something new to chew on for a couple of days."

She gave him a bewildered look. "Is that normal? For siblings to fight like that?"

"You're an only child?"

She nodded.

"Well, I can only tell you how it is in my family. Abby, Bree, Jess, Connor and I have gone at it from time to time, though it's mostly been passing squabbles that don't mean much. My dad and uncles are another story. Their personalities are as different as night and day. They can clash over whether the sky's blue. Poor Gram's been trying to bring about peace among them for years, but if you ask me, they enjoy fueling this feud they have going. My dad's an uptight control freak. Uncle Jeff is almost as bullheaded. Uncle Thomas is the calmest, most rational of the three of them, but even he can get his Irish up for the sake of a good argument."

"But you all seem to get along with Susie," she noted.

"We're bonded just because of the rift between our dads. None of us entirely get it, so we pretty much just stick together and ignore it unless we're forced to take sides."

Shanna was fascinated. "They insist you take sides?"

"From time to time," Kevin acknowledged. "Mostly, though, we've declared ourselves to be neutral and we stick to it. Sort of like Switzerland."

"I wish…" Shanna began, then cut herself off.

"Wish what?"

She shrugged. "What's the point in wishing for something that can never be? My family was what it was. My parents were great. They were supportive and loving. I just always wanted the kind of big, crazy, semidysfunctional family you see on TV." She met his gaze. "The kind you have."

Kevin chuckled. "Most of the time I find my family to be an annoyance. This is the first time I've viewed them as an advantage."

Shanna gave him a startled look. It almost sounded as if he was expressing a previously undisclosed interest in her. Though they'd spent some time together, for the most part it had been completely casual…at least if she discounted the sparks she'd been feeling from the very first time they'd met.

Almost as if he realized what he'd implied, Kevin stood up and held out his hand. "Come on. You can take another look around, issue whatever instructions will make you comfortable with walking away, and then we'll grab a bite to eat."

"It's not right leaving everyone else to finish up," she said as she followed him across the street. "I really should—"

"You really should go with my brother," Bree said, joining them on the sidewalk and apparently guessing the topic. "We've done just about everything that can be done tonight."

"I need to make lists of the rest of the inventory we're tossing," Shanna protested.

"Done," Bree said. "I wrote down the titles, authors and that number on the back you showed me. Any of the books that seemed merely damp, I set aside. You can make a final decision on those tomorrow. The shelves are wiped dry. The fans are blowing. The air-conditioning is running. I put a couple of boxes on the counter of other inventory you should probably look at. I think you could sell it at half price, but it's up to you."

Shanna regarded her with amazement. "I don't know how to thank you."

"No thanks necessary. You'd do the same for me. Now, take a break and relax. The rest of us are going to Sally's for burgers. You can come along, but I recommend you let Kevin take you someplace quiet so you can forget about all of this for an hour or two."

Tears welled up in Shanna's eyes as she gave Bree a hug. Even in such a short time, Bree had come to be almost as dear a friend as Laurie. On a day like today, when Shanna had really needed a friend to turn to, Bree had been here. After taking Davy, Carrie and Caitlyn back to Nell's, Bree had come back and pitched right in. Of course Laurie had offered to drive right down when Shanna had called her, for which she'd been grateful, but Bree and the others were already on the scene.

Inside, Shanna opened the cash register and took out a handful of twenties. "Take this," she said. "Dinner for everyone is on me."

Bree started to protest, but Shanna's jaw set stubbornly. "Take it," she insisted. "It's the very least I can do." She'd replace the store money with her own in the morning.

"It's not necessary, but thanks." Bree gave her brother a hug, then went off to join her husband and the others at Sally's.

Shanna released a sigh as Bree left. Kevin rested a hand on her shoulder.

"It's going to be okay," he assured her.

"I know that," she said as she stood in the middle of the room and glanced around at the chaos. Books and games had been pulled off lower shelves and piled on tables and chairs to get them away from the floor. They'd need to be sorted through and put back before tomorrow's opening. She met Kevin's worried gaze. "It's just really hard to see how right now."

"Which is why you're not tackling it till morning. I'll be here to help. In the meantime, how about that shower and then some food?"

She had a fleeting image of taking that shower with him. Now *that* would definitely get her mind off the mess.

She held back a smile at the thought. Kevin gave her a curious look, almost as if he'd read her mind. She blinked and looked away, her cheeks burning.

"Sure," she said at last. "Give me fifteen minutes."

That would be plenty long enough for a quick shower and a change of clothes. She had a hunch, though, that it wouldn't be nearly long enough to regain her equilibrium…either from today's events or from Kevin's attention. It had been a very long time since she'd been around a man she felt she could count on.

Kevin had planned to take Shanna to Brady's, where they could have a leisurely meal in a serene setting. Instead, to his dismay, she insisted on joining the others at Sally's.

"Any particular reason?" he asked, not even trying to contain his consternation.

Her gaze narrowed. "Any particular reason you *don't* want to join them?" she countered, calling him on it.

"I never said—"

"You might as well have."

"I just thought it would be more relaxing to go someplace like Brady's," he claimed, though the truth was, he didn't want everyone at the table studying the two of them and openly speculating about their relationship. That's exactly what would happen if they went to Sally's. There was enough speculation as it was. He'd already endured quite a few pointed comments from his so-called friends this afternoon.

"I'm not dressed for Brady's," Shanna said, gesturing to her shorts and T-shirt.

"No place in Chesapeake Shores is really formal, except maybe the inn," he told her, still pressing his point.

"If you're going to convince me to change my mind,

you're going to have to be clear about your objections to Sally's," she told him.

"Bree is there," he said succinctly. "And Jake, Mack, Will and Susie."

"All family and friends," she said, still looking blank. Then understanding apparently dawned. "And that's exactly why," she concluded.

He nodded. "They'll make too much of us being there together."

"Won't they make even more of it if we go off alone?" she asked reasonably. "I know Bree suggested that, but if we really want to avoid stirring up talk, we should be with everyone else."

Kevin hadn't considered it that way.

"There's safety in numbers," she added. "We'll just be part of the crowd if we're with them. There will be nothing left to speculate about."

He saw her point, and it was a good one. Somehow, though, he still wanted to press for Brady's. And *that* told him he wasn't being entirely honest with himself about his reasons for wanting to go there. He wanted to be alone with Shanna, wanted to be the one who put a smile back on her face after this dreadful day. He wanted things he had no business wanting.

"You're right," he said. "Sally's it is."

If she was puzzled by his abrupt about-face, she didn't say anything. It was just as well, because he sure as hell wouldn't have told her the real reason behind it.

When they walked into Sally's, he was surprised to see two empty chairs set up at the table. Bree gave him an amused look.

"Something told me the two of you would be along any minute," she said. "The only thing I wasn't sure about was which of you would make the argument for joining us. Your burgers are on the way. I told Sally to put them on the minute you walked in the door."

"Thanks for ordering and, for your information, we both agreed to come here," Kevin told her stiffly, pulling out the chair next to his sister's so Shanna could be the one to sit there. He took the remaining chair, which unfortunately sat him next to his brother-in-law. Jake was regarding him with amusement.

"Want me to tell your sister to go easy on you?" Jake inquired in an exaggerated undertone that could be heard by everyone at the table.

Kevin gave him a hard look but refrained from using the words on the tip of his tongue, because there were ladies present. Instead, he glanced down the table to see Mack staring at Susie with the kind of lovesick expression that Kevin feared might be his own destiny if he wasn't careful. Susie was pointedly ignoring Mack and talking to Will. Kevin shook his head and turned to his sister.

"Maybe you should focus your attention on those two," he suggested with a nod of his head in their direction.

Bree grinned at his obvious attempt to divert her attention from him and Shanna. "Oh, believe me, when it comes to matchmaking, I can multitask."

"Did I give you this much grief when you were dating Jake?" Kevin asked.

"You weren't even here," she reminded him.

"I was the first time around," Kevin said. "And I stayed out of your business."

"Ha!" Jake said beside him. "You and Connor ganged up on me every chance you got."

"I don't recall that," Kevin claimed, though he could barely contain a grin.

The bantering continued for several more minutes, until Sally set a cheeseburger and fries in front of him and another plate in front of Shanna along with tall glasses of iced tea. She paused long enough to give Shanna's shoulder a squeeze.

"You need any help tomorrow, let me know, okay? Once I open in the morning, I'm not due back in here till the lunch rush, so I have some time to spare."

Shanna, who'd been on the verge of tears all afternoon, suddenly began to cry. Kevin stared at her helplessly, then cast a desperate look at Bree. She merely scowled back at him until he slid his chair closer to Shanna's and put an arm around her. He tucked a finger under her chin and forced her to meet his gaze.

"The worst's behind you," he reminded her. "And it's all going to look a thousand times better in the morning."

"I know," she said, sniffing and reaching for a napkin to blot the tears.

"Then don't drown a perfectly good burger."

"It's just that you're all being so nice," she said again. "Even Sally, and I barely know her. I barely know any of you."

"You stop that right now," Bree chimed in. "We're friends, okay? And friends pitch in. What would your friend Laurie do if she were here?"

Shanna's lips quirked in a surprising smile. "She'd help," she said at once. "As long as I paid for her manicure if she chipped a nail."

Bree held out her own hands, nicked from working with roses with thorns, wire and scissors. "Hmm. I could use a manicure."

"Done," Shanna said at once. "You, too, Susie. I propose a girls' day out later in the week. My treat."

"You've already bought us dinner," Bree protested. "That's more than enough, but we will go with you for a manicure, right, Susie?"

"Count me in," Susie responded, though she regarded her hands with despair. "I haven't had decent nails in a very long time."

In fact, it was apparent they'd been bitten to the quick. Mack had driven her to that, Kevin suspected. Those two really did need counseling to get off the dime and own up to their feelings.

From across the table, Mack covered one of Susie's hands with his own. "There's nothing wrong with your hands," he said gruffly, then jerked away, looking embarrassed. "I have to go."

Susie backed away from the table, almost knocking over her chair in the process. "Can you give me a lift?"

Mack looked even more flustered, but he nodded, and then they were gone.

Beside Kevin, Jake shook his head. "Those two are pitiful."

"Amen to that," Will added. "Do you suppose Mack will remember that he drove me over here earlier today?"

Bree laughed. "Not a chance. Jake and I will drive you home or back to your car, wherever you need to go. And we should be heading out now, too." She caught her husband's gaze, heat climbing into her eyes.

Kevin looked away. He did not want to know what his sister and Jake had planned for the rest of the evening.

Within minutes, he and Shanna were alone at the table. She finished the last bite of her burger and dipped one last fry in ketchup. When she'd finished it, she turned to him and grinned, her usually sunny disposition obviously restored.

"Thank you," she said.

"For what?"

"Agreeing to come here. It was just what I needed."

"It made you cry," he reminded her.

"I needed that, too, I think, but now I'm about to crash."

Kevin stood and held out his hand. "Then, come on. I'll walk you back to your place."

She tucked her hand in his, and for the first time in more months than he cared to count, Kevin felt not just a spark of attraction, but a deep and powerful connection to another human being. Shanna had needed him today—needed all of them, for that matter—and it felt good knowing that he'd come through for her. Though he'd been strong for Davy's sake since Georgia's death, this was different. It made him feel like a man again, rather than the shell of a man who'd only been going through the motions of living.

It also gave him hope that one of these days he might actually start to feel something again…something besides guilt and despair.

True to her word, Susie O'Brien arrived at Word Games first thing the next morning with the claim forms and a check in hand. Her cheeks were glowing and her red hair was mussed, as if she hadn't had time to deal with it after getting out of the shower this morning. Or as if someone had tousled it right before she'd left home, Shanna thought, hiding a grin and wondering if Mack had been that someone.

"You and Mack have a good evening?" she inquired lightly as she poured cups of coffee for herself and for Susie.

Under her freckles, Susie's skin turned pink. "Mack's just a friend," she claimed.

Shanna gestured toward a chair. "You may not appreciate me saying this, but you and Mack may be the only people in town who actually believe that."

Susie's color heightened. "It's that obvious?"

Shanna nodded. "Afraid so." She hesitated, then said, "May I ask a personal question?"

"I guess," Susie said with unmistakable reluctance.

"Why are you both fighting it so hard? It's evident that he's crazy about you and vice versa."

Susie set her cup down on the table and leaned forward, her expression earnest. She almost looked relieved that someone had finally asked. "You're new in town, so you don't know that much about Mack, right?"

"I barely know him," Shanna agreed. "But he certainly seems like a nice guy."

"He is, but he's a player, if you know what I mean."

"He's dated a lot of women," Shanna concluded.

Susie rolled her eyes. "You have no idea. He was a big football star in high school, so the girls around here were competing for his attention."

"Except for you," Shanna guessed.

"Why bother? I couldn't compete. Mack dated the cheerleaders, the most gorgeous girls in the class. Nothing's changed since then. He was a big man on campus at the University of Maryland. Now that he's back here, he's been out with just about every female with a summer home here, plus most of the tourists, at least if they're attractive."

"And yet, you're the one he seems most interested in spending time with," Shanna pointed out. "Has it occurred to you that he's tired of the whole shallow dating ritual and is looking for someone with substance, someone like you?"

Though her eyes were filled with yearning, Susie waved off the suggestion. "He's never once asked me out on a real date."

"Then what was last night about?" Shanna asked.

"He walked me home," Susie told her. "He didn't stay, if that's what you're thinking."

So much for her earlier theory, Shanna thought. "Well, the way I've heard it, you've said hell would have to freeze over before you'd go out with him."

Susie grinned. "Yeah, I've mentioned that a time or two."

"Then maybe he's too intimidated to ask you out directly."

"Mack?" Susie scoffed. "Come on. Nothing intimidates him."

"I just know what I see. The guy has it bad."

"Really?"

"Really," Shanna confirmed. "And if you don't believe me, think back over the past few weeks or even the past few months, and count how many evenings Mack has found a way to spend time with you without actually asking you out on a date. Seems to me he can't possibly have much time left to be dating all those other women anymore."

Susie looked startled by the observation, but as the truth of Shanna's words sank in, she began to smile. "Oh, my gosh," she said, her delight unmistakable. "Mack and I have been almost dating for months."

"Looks that way to me," Shanna agreed.

Suddenly her face fell. "Oh, jeez, I really wish you hadn't said anything."

"Why?" Shanna asked, bewildered.

"Because now I'm going to be a nervous wreck every time I'm with him." In her haste to stand, she came close to knocking over her cup of coffee. "I have to go."

"Where?"

She reached up and touched her out-of-control curls. "I need a haircut, and that manicure we talked about, and maybe a whole new wardrobe."

"Slow down," Shanna said. "What you need to do is remember that Mack seems to like you just the way you are."

Susie closed her eyes and drew in a deep breath. "You're right," she said with more composure. "I don't think I'll throw in the towel on playing hard to get just yet, either."

She grinned at Shanna. "But I am going to get some sexy lingerie. You know, just in case."

Shanna stared at her, startled, then chuckled. In her zeal to give Susie a gentle push in Mack's direction, it appeared she might have created a femme fatale.

As Susie headed toward the door, Kevin came in. Susie threw her arms around her cousin and gave him a smacking kiss, then gestured toward Shanna.

"Don't blow this, Kevin. She's a keeper."

She breezed out the door while Shanna's cheeks were still flaming. Kevin stared after his cousin, then turned slowly around.

"What was that about?" he asked.

"I might have done a little meddling," Shanna admitted.

"Susie and Mack?" he asked.

"Uh-huh."

"Then what was that bit about you and me?"

"I believe she was returning the favor," Shanna said. "Pay no attention to her."

"Don't you think there are enough matchmakers and meddlers in my family without you joining their ranks?" he asked.

"I thought she might need an outside perspective," Shanna told him.

"Do I need to warn Mack that his life is about to get even more complicated?"

Shanna grinned at him. "Now what would be the fun in that? It'll be much more fun to see how he handles Susie's newfound self-confidence."

He blinked at that. "You're devious. Why didn't I realize that before?"

"Oh, I have lots of hidden depths you know nothing about," Shanna told him.

But even as she made the lighthearted claim, she realized that she was keeping one secret that might truly change the way Kevin looked at her. And increasingly that scared her to death.

11

Kevin didn't miss the shadow that passed over Shanna's face. One second her mood had been light, her tone bantering, the next it was as if she'd seen some sort of emotional ghost. Since those kind of moods hit him without warning from time to time, he recognized the signs and couldn't help wondering at the cause.

"What are you thinking about?" he asked, his gaze on hers.

She looked away and busied herself at the counter. "Everything I have to get done in here before I open," she said, carefully avoiding his eyes. "I only have a little over an hour. I should get busy."

He stepped in front of her. "And you will, with my help, but first tell me why your mood changed so abruptly just now."

"I wasn't aware that it did," she claimed.

"Really?"

"Kevin, I have a ton of things to do," she said impatiently. "Are you going to be a help or a hindrance? If you're not going to help, go home and take care of those kids you're supposed to be looking out for while Trace and Abby are away. Did you leave them with your grandmother again?"

"Gram volunteered to watch them so I could help you," he said, immediately defensive. "And since you seem to think I'm slacking off, you should know I'm taking over from her at ten. I figured once you're open, you won't want me underfoot, so I'll head back to the house. I think I can keep them all out of trouble until Trace and Abby get back later today. In the meantime, though, I'm here to help. I brought Dad's SUV in case there are more things to go to the dump."

She hesitated, looking faintly chagrined, then let the subject go. "Fine. Thanks," she said tersely. "There's a box of damaged merchandise by the back door, and I'm almost through tossing stuff into another one. I just need to take down a few inventory codes."

"You do that, and I'll take the first box to the car," he said, eager to get away from the tension he'd inadvertently stirred up between them. He had no idea why she'd been so touchy, but something told him he needed to figure it out. Today, though, wasn't the time, and this was definitely not the place. Obviously they were both too edgy to confront whatever was going on.

He deposited the first box in the back of Mick's SUV, then retrieved the second one. "Okay, now what?" he asked her.

She gestured around the store. "Everything sitting on tables, counters or chairs, needs to go back on the shelves." She frowned. "I probably should do that myself, since I know where everything belongs."

Kevin was beginning to get exasperated with her stubborn independent streak. "I think I can figure it out. I learned the alphabet at an early age, and the sections are pretty clearly marked."

Shanna blinked at his tone, then sighed. "I'm sorry if

it sounded like I was dismissing you or something. I really am in a foul mood. But I shouldn't be taking it out on you."

Now it was Kevin's turn to sigh. "No, I'm the one who's sorry. You have enough going on without me getting in your face about doing it your own way. Look, I can see how the children's section is organized, so how about I get in there and deal with those books? If I have questions, I'll ask."

She nodded. "Thanks. That would be a big help."

By ten o'clock, they had the store put back together. Though many of the shelves, especially in the children's section, were nearly empty, only someone who'd heard about the disaster would know anything had happened in here. Bree even brought over a small vase of brightly colored daisies to sit on the counter by the register. Shanna had spritzed the room with a lightly scented spray to cover any hint of dampness in the air, though in Kevin's opinion the air hadn't needed it. The store was dry as a bone, the broken pipe now replaced and every other pipe checked for potential problems. The plumber sent over by his uncle had seen to that. He gathered, in fact, that every store on Main Street was being checked thoroughly to avoid other potential problems.

"Looks as if you're all set," he told her.

"I think so," she said, taking a last look around. Her gaze settled on the flowers. "It was sweet of Bree to bring these by. And, Kevin, you really were a godsend this morning. Thanks for not walking out when I was being a pain in the butt."

He grinned at her. "You'd have to be a lot worse to reach the level of pain in the butt," he assured her. He dropped a kiss on her cheek, considered moving on to her mouth, then pulled back instead. "Call me if you need anything today."

"It's all good. You need to spend the day with the twins and Davy. Do something fun."

At the door, he lingered, though he couldn't explain why he was so reluctant to go. Shanna grinned.

"Are you trying to avoid going home to those kids?" she taunted.

He laughed. "Absolutely not. They're a piece of cake."

"We'll see about that," she said doubtfully. "You caught a break by getting to send them home yesterday when they were pea-green from eating too much. Call me later and tell me if your luck holds today."

"Maybe I'll bring them by instead. The girls never did get the book I promised them yesterday."

"Little Women," she said, her face falling. "The copy they loved was ruined. It'll be a few days before I can get it in again."

Sensing she was on the verge of tears again over the losses, he impulsively leaned in and kissed her. He'd meant it to be nothing more than a comfort, maybe a brief distraction. Instead, it unleashed something inside him.

She tasted so sweet. Her lips were so soft. She smelled faintly of lilies of the valley, a scent he'd always associated with home because of his mother's garden path. And the whisper of breath she'd exhaled as their mouths met did something to his restraint. The next thing he knew, he'd deepened the kiss, pulling her close, then tangling his fingers in her hair.

It was only the sharp tap on the door and a muffled laugh that dragged him away from her. He turned to find her friend Laurie on the doorstep, her eyes alight with amusement, though there seemed to be a shadow of worry behind the glint of humor.

Shanna took a shaky step backward, her expression

vaguely dazed. She didn't seem to realize they had company, so it was Kevin who unlocked the door to admit her friend.

"Well, well, well," Laurie said. "Looks to me as if everything here is under control. Almost, anyway," she added with a pointed glance in Shanna's direction.

Shanna blinked and stared at her, her cheeks now a vivid pink, her expression guilty. "What are you doing here?"

"You called. I came," Laurie said succinctly. "Though one crisis at least seems to be in the past." She glanced around the neatly organized store, then turned back to frown at Kevin. "Somehow, though, I don't think I wasted a trip."

"I was just leaving," he told her.

"Excellent timing," Laurie said.

Kevin disagreed. Something told him he should have been out the door five minutes earlier…before Laurie's arrival and most definitely before the kiss.

"Where's the coffee?" Laurie asked, standing in front of the cappuccino maker. "Shouldn't it be made when you open the door for business."

"I had a few other things on my mind this morning," Shanna replied, a defensive note creeping into her voice.

"Are you talking about yesterday's flood and cleanup, or are you referring to the man with whom you were sharing a lip-lock when I arrived?" Laurie asked, filling the coffee machine with beans and turning on the grinder.

With Laurie occupied for the moment, Shanna ignored the question and went into the back room. A quick glance in the mirror over the sink told her she looked as mussed and flustered as she'd feared. That unexpected kiss would have been disconcerting enough under normal circumstances. With Laurie here as a witness, it was a calamity. Shanna knew she wasn't going to be able to explain it away. Even if she tried, her friend would never believe that the kiss had been totally innocent. Heck, even *she* knew there'd been nothing innocent about it. There'd been enough heat in that kiss to sizzle a steak.

"You can come back out now," Laurie called a few minutes later. "The coffee's made."

Shanna dared returning to the front of the store. She found Laurie perched behind the register.

"It could be fun sitting here all day watching people walk by," she told Shanna.

"Sometimes I do have to move around, even help an actual customer," Shanna told her dryly.

"I know that," Laurie said with exasperation. "I'm just saying I kind of get why you enjoy being here." Her eyes lit with mischief. "And then there's long, tall and dreamy."

"Kevin?"

"Who else? Are there more like him roaming around town?"

"Quite a few, as a matter of fact, though as you're a soon-to-be-married woman, I'm not sure why you care."

"You're the one who should be taking note of those other available men," Laurie told her. "I won't go into all the reasons why. We've discussed them before."

"Yes, we have," Shanna said.

"And you're obviously ignoring common sense."

"No, I'm not," she said with exasperation. "I get why Kevin and I would be..." She tried to think of a word to describe just how risky their relationship could prove to be.

"A disaster," Laurie supplied.

"No, complicated," Shanna insisted.

"Have you spoken to Henry lately?" Laurie asked abruptly.

"Cut to the chase, why don't you?" Shanna muttered at the mention of her former stepson.

"I'm trying to. What I don't get is why the parallels don't scare you to death. Wounded man, lonely kid. It's a pattern for you, sweetie, and it's not a good one."

"Kevin is nothing like Greg," she said with absolute certainty for what seemed like the hundredth time. Her ex-husband had serious problems with alcohol. Kevin was merely lost in his grief, not in a bottle. "And Davy isn't in the same situation. He's not in danger. He's surrounded by a huge family, not a couple of stiff-necked grandparents like the Hamiltons."

"But every instinct you possess is telling you that Kevin and his boy need you, isn't it?"

"Maybe," she admitted. "But I'm not rushing into anything with Kevin, not the way I did with Greg. He and I were emotionally involved almost immediately, even though we did wait quite a while before marrying. Kevin and I aren't even dating. We're just hanging out from time to time. He isn't remotely ready for a new relationship, either."

"Then I must have imagined that kiss I walked in on," Laurie said.

"That was a…surprise, an anomaly," Shanna retorted. "We're not in the habit of kissing."

"And you don't think that now that the ice has been broken, so to speak, it will happen again?"

"No, I don't," she lied. If she had her way, it most definitely would happen again. Kevin, she suspected, would see that it didn't.

"Because it was so awful?" Laurie inquired, leveling a look into her eyes.

"No, of course not."

"Then it will happen again," her friend said decisively. "And you'd better figure out how to handle that before you're in so deep with this man, you wind up drowning."

"We're just friends," Shanna insisted, realizing even as she uttered the words that she sounded as delusional as Susie about Mack. "How's Drew, by the way? How are the wedding plans coming?"

"Drew's fine. The wedding plans are right on track. Jess has been amazing." She frowned at Shanna. "Stop trying to change the subject."

"I was trying to show an interest in you. You're usually only too eager to leap right into your favorite topic."

"Well, today I'm being selfless. I'm more concerned about you."

"You don't need to be," Shanna said emphatically. "As you can see, the store is in good shape again, and my personal life is just fine. Your job here is done."

Laurie looked startled by the dismissal. "You want me to go home?"

Shanna nodded. "I love seeing you and I really appreciate the fact that you dropped everything to come down here, but everything here is good and I have a ton of work to do dealing with insurance forms and reordering stock."

"You can't even go to the inn for lunch, can you?" Laurie said. "As long as I'm here, I thought we could go over a few wedding details with Jess."

Shanna heard the disappointment in her friend's voice and realized how unfair she was being. Laurie had dropped everything to check on her, and now she was sending her right back home as if the visit had been an annoyance rather than a sweet gesture.

"How about this? We'll call Jess and see if she can come here, maybe even bring lunch."

Laurie's expression brightened. "Really? You'll have time?"

"As long as we stay right here, yes. I'll make the time."

"And I won't be in the way until then?"

Shanna tried to find a diplomatic reply. "Maybe you could check out the rest of the shops on Main Street and the restaurants on Shore Road. You'll want to be able to tell your wedding guests the best places to go when they're here. This is the perfect chance for you to familiarize yourself with the town. The kitchen shop might even be someplace to find some of those accessories you're addicted to." Laurie's kitchen was a gourmet cook's dream already, but that didn't mean there weren't new gadgets to be found.

Though Laurie gave her a knowing look, she nodded. "Great idea. I'll be back here at noon, okay?"

"That's perfect. I'll give Jess a call and make the arrangements." She crossed the room and gave Laurie a fierce hug. "Thank you for coming down here. It wasn't necessary, but I'm so glad you did."

"Even if I did butt into your personal life?"

"That's what best friends are supposed to do," Shanna told her, then grinned. "Doesn't mean I have to take your advice, though."

Laurie gave an exaggerated sigh. "In that case, I'm claiming the right here and now to say I told you so."

"Duly noted."

It wasn't until Laurie was out the door that Shanna finally released a sigh and reached for her phone. She called Kevin's cell.

"Whatever you do, do not come back here with the kids later," she told him.

"Laurie," he guessed at once. "She's still here."

"Right now she's out exploring, but she'll be back here at noon to go over wedding details with Jess."

"Thanks for the warning," he said. "She's a little too intense with her cross-examinations."

"Tell me about it."

"I'll call you tonight, okay? Will she be gone then?"

"Yes."

"Shanna?" He sounded suddenly hesitant.

"What?"

"The kiss…" His voice trailed off as if he'd grown uncomfortable with the subject as soon as he'd introduced it.

"It was an excellent kiss," she said, a hitch in her voice.

"It was," he agreed. "But—"

"But we probably shouldn't repeat it," she supplied before he could. Hadn't she just told herself this would be his reaction? His deep sigh of relief at her words told her she'd been right.

"It's just that my life right now is a mess," he explained. "I have a lot of things to figure out."

"Believe me, I get that," she said. "Mine's not exactly on an even keel, either."

"Then this was a onetime aberration," he said.

"Agreed."

Even as she said the word, disappointment spread through her. She'd have to worry about that another time, though. Right now, she had way too much on her plate, including trying to find a way to get Laurie out of town before she crossed paths with Kevin again.

As soon as he'd hung up after his conversation with Shanna, Kevin went inside the house and rounded up Davy and the twins.

"Put on your bathing suits," he told them.

"We're having a picnic on the beach," Caitlyn guessed, already stripping off clothes as she went in search of her bright blue ruffled one-piece bathing suit.

"Yes," Kevin told them. He scooped Davy into his arms and took him into his room to change him into his bathing suit, then donned his own.

Then he gathered up all of the paraphernalia they'd need—sunblock, a blanket, beach towels, sand pails, swim rings. Gram walked into the foyer as he was eyeing the mounting pile of necessities with a frown.

"How on earth did you ever manage to take us all to the beach?" he asked.

"Each of you carried your own toys and towel," she reminded him. "I took the blanket and picnic basket. Let the girls help."

When Carrie and Caitlyn raced down the stairs, Kevin gestured to the assembled beach supplies. "Pick what you want to play with," he instructed. "And grab a towel."

That still left him with the picnic basket Gram had packed, the blanket and Davy, who was too little to tackle the steps down to the beach on his own. Gram grinned, clearly seeing the dilemma.

"Why don't I come down in an hour with the picnic?" she suggested.

"Would you mind?"

"Of course not. I'll drop it off before I drive over to the church." She gave him a considering look. "Are you sure you can manage all three of them? You won't have a minute's peace trying to keep your eye on them every second."

"You handled five of us," he reminded her.

"And you were all older than these three," she said.

"Except for Jess, and even she was Carrie and Caitlyn's age by then. You all helped by looking out for her."

"We'll be fine," he said with confidence. It was a couple of hours on the beach. No big deal. Then there'd be naps, and after that his sister and Trace would return and this nightmare of babysitting would be over. Not that he didn't love Caitlyn and Carrie, he adored them. But despite what he'd said to Shanna, he'd been in over his head from the beginning of their visit.

An hour later, he had more proof that he was out of his depth. He was more than half-buried under sand and nearly immobilized, thanks to an idiotic scheme he'd devised to keep the three kids occupied until Gram brought lunch. Carrie and Caitlyn had loved the idea of pouring bucket after bucket of sand over him. Davy's buckets were barely half-filled, but he followed suit.

"Now it's time to dig me out," he told them.

Carrie and Caitlyn merely giggled and dumped more sand on top of him.

"This is too much fun, Uncle Kevin," Carrie said. "When we get enough sand, we can build a castle on top of you. It'll be the biggest one ever."

"Not a good idea," he said, trying to kick the sand off his legs. It was too heavy. He tried lifting his arms, to no avail. Next time, if he was ever stupid enough to suggest this again, he'd know to keep his hands free.

Just then he heard laughter behind him and turned his head to find Abby regarding him with barely suppressed amusement. Trace, holding the picnic basket, was behind her, not even trying to hide his grin at Kevin's situation.

"Quite a predicament you're in," Abby commented, her eyes sparkling.

"Mommy," Caitlyn screamed and ran for Abby, immediately followed by Carrie. Davy tottered along behind the two of them and held out his arms to Trace, who set down the picnic basket in order to pick him up.

"Do you think one of you could get me out of here?" Kevin inquired testily. "Or are you enjoying this too much?"

"The enjoyment factor is pretty overwhelming," Abby said.

Kevin scowled at Trace. "I do you a favor and this is the thanks I get?"

"Hey, I'm not the one who buried you," Trace said. "And don't tell me these kids came up with the idea all on their own."

"It was my idea, okay?" he admitted.

"What would you have done if we hadn't come along?" Abby inquired curiously. "Say, if one of them decided to take off and go for an unauthorized swim?"

"I was just working on that," he insisted. "They were going to dig me out. And they know the rules about going in the water, right, girls? Not unless you're with an adult."

Caitlyn, the little traitor, said, "But you *are* here, Uncle Kevin."

"I rest my case," Abby said. "Besides, it sounded to me as if they had big plans to construct a castle on top of you. Dad would be proud."

The weight of all that sand was beginning to make him feel a little claustrophobic. He fixed a hard look on his soon-to-be brother-in-law, since his sister clearly wasn't interested in coming to his rescue.

"I'd appreciate a little help now," he said.

Trace grinned and set Davy down on the sand. "Okay, kids, let's dig Uncle Kevin out of the sand. Then we can have a picnic."

"Picnic now!" Carrie said, jumping up and down in excitement.

"Nope, not till Uncle Kevin can join us," Trace said firmly.

"We could feed him," Caitlyn suggested, her expression thoughtful.

"Dig, now!" Trace said more firmly.

All three kids started removing the sand, tossing it aside by the bucketful. It seemed to take a lot longer to remove than it had to cover him. Kevin finally kicked off the last of it and stood.

"Since reinforcements are here, I'm going for a swim to get the rest of this stuff off," he told his sister.

"Maybe leaving him in charge of our children wasn't such a great idea," Abby said, a hint of worry in her eyes.

He caught the glint in Trace's eyes as he met Abby's gaze. "Really? Are you regretting the past couple of days we've had to ourselves?"

"No, but…"

"The kids are in one piece," Trace reminded her. "Kevin's still sane, which makes him an excellent babysitter to my way of thinking. In fact, right this second, he qualifies for sainthood in my book." He gave Abby a lingering look. "Know what I mean?"

She blushed.

"I'm thinking we should enlist him again in another couple of weeks," Trace said, his gaze locked with Abby's. "What do you say?"

Abby moved toward him. "Maybe so," she murmured, lifting her face for a kiss.

Kevin groaned, not just because the idea of babysitting again made him a little queasy, but because watching the heat between those two reminded him a little too sharply of what he'd felt when he'd kissed Shanna earlier. And then he'd foolishly told her they shouldn't do it again. What had he been thinking?

Probably that it had been a mistake, he reminded himself.

Even worse, she'd agreed with him.

Right this second, though, he couldn't imagine why either one of them thought that anything that had felt that good could possibly be a mistake.

12

Mick was in the air somewhere over Kansas when he realized that he'd never even tried to reach Megan to tell her he'd been called to Seattle on another emergency. Any other week, it would have been no big deal to let her know when he landed, but at this very moment, she was probably arriving at the airport in Baltimore for a few days in Chesapeake Shores. And there would be no one there to greet her. The situation had disaster written all over it. She'd take the incident and blow it all out of proportion.

He grabbed the in-flight phone, used his credit card and dialed her cell phone. To his frustration, the call went straight to voice mail.

"Meggie, it's me. I got called to Seattle late last night, and I grabbed the first flight I could get out this morning. I know I should have called you right away, but it was late, and then with all the rushing around this morning, I didn't think of it until just now. I'm so sorry. If you get this message while you're at the airport, why don't you see if there's another available flight to Seattle and join me? You'd love it out there. Let me know if you decide to do that. Otherwise, I'll give you a call when I get to my hotel. I should be on the ground in another couple of hours."

He winced as he hung up. She was going to be fit to be tied, and he couldn't say he blamed her. He made his next call to Kevin.

"Dad, I thought you were on your way to Seattle," Kevin said.

"I am, but I just remembered something and I need your help, okay?"

"Sure, what can I do?"

"Your mother's on a flight down from New York. You need to get to the airport to pick her up or to help her switch to a flight out to the West Coast, whichever she wants to do."

"You forgot Mom was coming?" He sounded incredulous and maybe even a little amused by Mick's obvious predicament.

"I didn't forget it exactly," Mick said defensively. "I had a lot of things happening at once."

"Oh man, she's going to be furious," Kevin murmured.

"Don't you think I know that?" he said impatiently. "Which is why you need to step on it and get to the airport."

"Why me? Abby's a lot closer. She could be there from her office in a half hour."

"She could be," Mick acknowledged. "But seeing you just might distract your mother from how mad she is at me."

"Dad, you know how I feel about her," Kevin began.

Mick cut him off. "I also know you need to get over it. Take Davy with you. Pretend it's all about him. He'll love seeing the planes going in and out and being there to greet his grandmother. Come on, son, help me out here."

Kevin sighed heavily. "What time is Mom's flight due in?"

"The information's on a pad by the phone in my office, but you don't have much time. Grab the details I've written down and Davy, then hit the road."

"You realize there are now two of us annoyed with you, me *and* Mom?"

"You're wasting time. You can yell at me later, okay?"

"Believe me, I will take you up on that," Kevin said, hanging up on him.

Mick sat back and closed his eyes, trying to envision Megan's reaction to arriving at the airport and not seeing him waiting for her in the terminal. If Kevin wasn't there in his place, she might turn right around and go back to New York. She might never return to Chesapeake Shores again. Any reaction was possible. Megan's unpredictability was one of the things he loved about her, but it didn't always work in his favor.

Of course, he could try selling her on the idea that the mix-up was all her fault. If she'd been living back at home where she belonged, she would have known about this trip as soon as he'd found out about it, and she could have been right here next to him, sipping a Bloody Mary and watching an action movie. Yep, that was the way he should play it.

And then duck, when she took a swing at him.

Kevin held tight to Davy's hand in the crowded terminal and kept his eyes peeled for his mother. Based on the information he'd found in Mick's office, she should be walking in from the gate area any time now. The arrivals board indicated her plane had landed five minutes earlier, which meant it probably hadn't even reached the gate yet.

"G'ma," Davy said.

He'd been practicing the word ever since Kevin had explained who they were meeting at the airport. Apparently tired of looking at a sea of legs, he held up his arms. Kevin hefted him up so he could see.

"G'ma!" he shouted excitedly, pointing.

Sure enough, there she was, striding toward them with a hesitant smile on her face.

"This is a surprise," she said, setting aside her carry-on bag to take Davy, who was practically crawling out of Kevin's arms to get to her. "Where's your father?"

Kevin didn't want to be the one to break the bad news. Instead, he told her, "He said he left you a voice mail. Maybe you should check that."

Megan frowned, but reached in her pocket, turned on her cell phone, then listened to her messages. Then, she clicked it off and snapped it shut. "Well, that sounded familiar."

"Mom, it really was last-minute," Kevin said, surprised by the need to defend his father. "I heard the phone ring really late last night, way too late for him to call you, and he left the house at the crack of dawn. He was already gone when I got up at six to go for a run."

"My flight didn't take off till after ten this morning. The recording says he didn't call till nearly eleven, after I was in the air."

Kevin could see how angry she was and could almost understand it. For once, he realized how many times she must have been an afterthought when some crisis changed Mick's schedule at the last minute.

"He mentioned something about you joining him in Seattle," Kevin said. "I've checked and there's a flight leaving in two hours that has seats available."

Megan shook her head at once, her jaw set in a too-familiar stubborn line. "I'll come with you, if that's okay.

Now that I'm here, I'd like to spend some time with Davy and the twins. I'll fly back to New York tomorrow."

Kevin winced. His instructions had been to get her to Seattle or to keep her here. It seemed she wasn't inclined to cooperate with either plan. Big surprise.

"You won't wait for Dad to get back?" he asked.

Her quelling look was answer enough. Kevin grabbed her bag. "Any other luggage?"

She shook her head, then focused her attention on Davy, who was exclaiming over everything he saw en route to the parking garage.

"I'm predicting this one is going to be a journalist someday," Megan said with a laugh as she settled him in his car seat with surprisingly practiced skill. "He has a keen eye for details."

Kevin chuckled. "That's one way of putting it. Me, I think of him as a little motormouth."

"Broadcast journalism, then," she said, climbing into Mick's SUV. She turned to Kevin, her gaze warm. "I'm glad Mick sent you in his place."

"That was Dad being devious," he admitted. "He hoped my presence would distract you, so you wouldn't be quite as mad at him."

"Well, *that* didn't work," she said. "I can still be plenty mad at him and happy to see you at the same time. At least we'll have some time to talk."

"Mom, don't," he said, his mood promptly turning dark. "Let's not go over the same old ground again."

"I wasn't going to bring up the past. I was merely going to ask how you're doing. I hear you bought a fishing boat."

Kevin nodded.

"Have you gotten your captain's license yet?"

"No, I have a few more classes before I can be certified."

She leaned back, her eyes closed. "I remember how much you loved fishing," she said, her expression nostalgic. "It didn't matter how tiny the fish or how big, you'd get so excited when you'd reel it in." She glanced over at him with a smile. "And then you'd want to throw it back. Being so softhearted isn't an especially good trait for a man running a fishing charter."

Kevin sighed at the observation. "Tell me about it." This wasn't the first time it had occurred to him that he wasn't as well suited for this new career as Jess had assumed. He'd seized on it only because he hadn't been able to come up with an acceptable alternative.

"You know what I always thought you'd do?" Megan said.

Curious, he shook his head. He couldn't imagine that his mother had even the slightest insight into what kind of man he'd become. He'd been sixteen when she'd left, a year younger than Abby and light-years from having any direction in his life.

"I thought you'd follow in your uncle Thomas's footsteps," Megan said. "I was so sure you'd become an environmentalist, work to protect the Chesapeake or some other fragile, endangered ecosystem."

Even as the words left her mouth, Kevin felt an odd stirring of excitement. "We used to talk about that, didn't we?"

She nodded. "Whenever Thomas was around for holidays, you'd pester him with a million questions." She gave him a sideways glance. "Maybe you should talk to him now, get a feel for what he's doing these days. Have you even seen him recently?"

Kevin shook his head. "You know how it is with him and Dad."

"I also know how persuasive Nell can be. She wants them reconciled, so sooner or later it's bound to happen, and I don't just mean the polite lip service they pay to each other on holidays." She shrugged. "You don't need Mick's permission to see your uncle."

At Kevin's frown, she immediately said, "I'm not trying to tell you what to do."

"No, I know that. I'm just thinking about how Dad would react if I turned into one of those tree huggers he's so disdainful of." Even as he said it, he grinned. Mick would be appalled, especially if he thought his brother had influenced Kevin into joining forces with the enemy.

"I think you're selling your father short. Mick might not be the activist that Thomas is, but he cares about the bay. He made a lot of compromises with Chesapeake Shores—perhaps not enough to suit his brother, but enough to make a difference. He respects what Thomas does."

"Really? Then why aren't they speaking?"

"Because they can rile each other faster than a rattlesnake can strike. They do it without thinking, and then stubbornness kicks in."

Kevin laughed, thinking of how many ridiculously small rifts in their family had quickly escalated out of control. "You could be right about that. It's definitely a family trait."

"Unfortunately, one I apparently possess, as well," Megan admitted with obvious regret. "Without even having the O'Brien genes."

"That's what happened with you and Dad, isn't it?" he asked with sudden insight. "You had a fight, then both of you dug in your heels."

She nodded. "Not that we didn't both make mistakes, but they were definitely compounded by the heat of anger and pure stubbornness."

"Don't do that again, Mom," Kevin said, surprising himself by trying to play peacemaker. "I know what Dad did today is wrong, but he wants you back more than anything. I've had a hard time accepting that, but I do know it's true."

"And yet he's in Seattle and I'm here," she said quietly.

"You could join him," he suggested mildly. "Or at least stay here till he gets back. Don't compound his mistake by making one of your own."

She met his gaze, her chin set, then sighed. "We'll see."

Kevin turned aside so she wouldn't see his satisfied grin. Mission accomplished. More than that, his mother had given him a whole lot to think about in terms of his future.

Saturday was Shanna's busiest day at the store. Thankfully, she'd been able to get a new shipment of books in on Friday and the shelves were once again fully stocked. Today, there'd been no lull, no chance to run over to Sally's to grab a quick sandwich, not even long enough to call in a take-out order and pick it up.

When Kevin walked in the door around three o'clock, she was so relieved to see him, she almost threw her arms around him.

"If you can pick up a sandwich for me at Sally's, I will love you forever," she told him, barely aware of the startled expression her comment elicited. "I neglected to bring lunch with me today. I keep forgetting that Saturdays are too busy for me to get out of here. I'm starving."

Kevin pulled a familiar white sack out from behind his back. "Tuna on rye, chips and a diet soda," he told her.

She did throw her arms around him then. "You're an angel."

He lifted a brow at that. "Hardly. I passed by earlier and could see you were swamped, so I took a guess that you wouldn't have time for lunch unless it magically appeared."

"I do love magic," she said, ripping into the bag. She took a bite of the thick sandwich and sighed as if it were gourmet fare. "Did you get something for yourself?"

"I ate earlier at the house." He hesitated, then added, "My mother's here."

Her hands stilled and she met his gaze. "You don't sound entirely happy about that."

"We have our issues," he admitted. "But, actually, today it went okay. She mentioned an idea that I haven't been able to shake."

"What kind of idea?" Because he looked more excited than she'd ever seen him, she set the sandwich aside to listen.

"About what I should be doing with myself."

She gave him a puzzled look. "I thought you were getting your captain's license so you could do fishing charters."

"That was the plan," he agreed. "But she reminded me I always threw the fish I caught right back out to sea."

"Okay," she said slowly. "Which means?"

"I might not make the best fishing charter captain," he said, a twinkle in his eyes. "Fishermen usually prefer to take their catch home. They might not appreciate a captain who snatches it right back out of their hands."

"Aha," she said as understanding dawned. "But she planted another idea in its place."

"She did. You know my uncle Thomas is an environmentalist?"

"Of course I do. He's mentioned in just about every article I've read on what's happening to the bay."

"My mother thinks I should talk to him."

Again, Shanna saw the excitement lighting his eyes. It definitely hadn't been there when he'd talked about fishing. "What do you think?" she asked carefully.

"That she's right. I have to say it grates a little that she knows me so well, but I'm not going to ignore the idea just because it came from her. Do you have any books in here about the bay? Not tourist books, but the more serious stuff?"

"Of course," she said, her sandwich forgotten as she went to the right shelf. Kevin followed.

"Here are a couple," she said, handing him two heavily illustrated volumes. "I've glanced through these and I think they're the most comprehensive." She tapped her finger on the top book. "And your uncle is quoted extensively in this one. He's also acknowledged in front by the author."

"Perfect. I'll take them," Kevin said, setting them beside the register, then drawing a second stool up beside the counter.

Shanna sat back down, took another bite of her sandwich and chewed slowly. "You know," she said eventually, "it might be interesting to have your uncle give a talk in here sometime. I've been wanting to do that kind of thing. I could ask him which books he recommends, then have plenty of stock of those titles, and he could get people excited about the fight to save the bay."

"That's a great idea," Kevin said with enthusiasm. "Want me to ask him for you?"

"If you're planning to speak to him anyway, please do," she said, warming to the idea. "Saturdays are insane in here, but maybe on a Friday evening, late enough that the weekenders could attend. I could serve wine and cheese or have Jess cater something light."

"I'd come to that," a customer chimed in as he appeared from the back of the store, where he'd apparently found an armload of science fiction paperbacks.

"Me, too," another one said as she waited at the register.

Shanna went to handle the sales, then turned to Kevin. "This could be a really good thing. I think more people than we know care about saving the bay, but maybe they don't know what they can do. I hope your uncle will agree to come. This wouldn't just be good for business. It would be a great public service."

"He'll come," Kevin said confidently, then grinned. "If only to annoy my dad by giving the lecture right here in Mick's town."

"I thought they developed Chesapeake Shores together. Doesn't he live here?"

Kevin shook his head. "No, he lives in Annapolis. He vowed not to set foot in this town after he and Dad fought over every single tree that Dad took down when he was building here. The irony is that because of my uncle, Chesapeake Shores is probably the most ecofriendly development anywhere around here. Thomas just thinks Dad could have done more."

"No one's ever going to be a hundred percent happy in this fight," Shanna guessed.

"Not if they're an O'Brien, anyway," Kevin said.

"Where do you come down on the issue?"

"I can see both sides," he admitted. "But I lean toward my uncle's point of view."

"Which means working with him might suit you perfectly," she concluded.

He nodded. "I'm beginning to think it might."

She met his gaze. "Which is going to make that boat you bought a very expensive toy."

He shook his head. "Where better to study the bay than on a boat in the middle of it?"

For the first time since Shanna had met him, she saw a sense of renewed energy and purpose in Kevin's eyes. It appealed to her on a whole new level. If she'd thought him devastating to her system before, this man was beyond seductive. He was all but impossible to resist.

First thing Monday morning, Kevin turned Davy over to Abby, who was working from home for the day, and drove to Annapolis to his uncle's office, glad that he had his little hybrid car rather than his dad's gas-guzzling SUV. Otherwise, Thomas would have started their meeting with a stern lecture on his carbon footprint.

After reading the books he'd bought from Shanna, Kevin was more intrigued than ever about joining the fight to preserve the Chesapeake and its delicate ecosystem. It felt right to him in ways the fishing charter never had.

The offices of the Chesapeake Preservation League were housed in what had once been a ramshackle warehouse along the Severn River. The exterior had been spruced up with gray vinyl shingles and the interior had been carved into offices, but there was no mistaking the building's origins. Kevin thought Mick must cringe at the lackluster, piecemeal renovations every time he walked inside, assuming he ever did.

Kevin asked for his uncle and was directed outside to a dock. He found Thomas on board a boat that looked as if it was only days away from sinking straight to the bottom of the river. It mostly seemed to be held together by rust. To add to the impression of disrepair, his uncle had the motor apart on a grimy drop cloth and was studying it intently.

"I assume you know how to put that back together again," Kevin said, leaping on board.

"Of course I do," Thomas said, grinning up at him. The youngest of the three O'Brien brothers, he wasn't yet fifty. His skin was tanned and weathered, his curly hair sandy, as Nell's had been rather than black like Mick's, and without a single thread of gray. His eyes were the same vivid blue as the rest of the family's. He looked younger than his age.

He gestured toward the motor. "Of course, putting it back together's a whole lot different from fixing it."

Kevin hunkered down beside him. "What's the problem?"

"Old age."

"Looks to me as if that's affecting more than the motor," Kevin said, glancing pointedly around the boat.

"Yeah, we've budgeted for a replacement next year. In the meantime, I'm trying to baby this old girl along."

"I might have a solution for you," Kevin said.

Thomas lifted his perplexed gaze from the motor and studied Kevin. "Oh?"

"I just bought a fishing boat a few weeks ago. You'd have to take a look at it, but I'm pretty sure it could be outfitted to do the kind of work you need."

He definitely had his uncle's full attention now.

"You want to give us a boat?"

Kevin nodded. "I'd come with it. At least if you think I could make any kind of contribution."

Thomas wiped the oil off his hands with an old rag and stood. "Let's go inside and talk. It's too hot out here for me to be sure I'm not hallucinating."

Kevin grinned at his reaction. "Took you by surprise, did I?"

"Not exactly," his uncle said. "I've been wondering what took you so damn long to figure this out. And now that you apparently have, what Mick has to say about it."

"Dad's out of town. He doesn't know about this yet."

Thomas shook his head. "This gets more interesting by the minute," he said, leading the way inside and filling two glasses with iced tea. He handed one to Kevin, then shoved some papers off the only spare chair in his office. "Sit down and talk to me."

Kevin filled him in on the epiphany he'd had over the weekend, thanks to his mother.

"You sure you're not interested just because it will rile Mick?"

"You know better. Mom reminded me of the way I used to pester you with questions when I was a kid. Somehow I got sidetracked by being an EMT, then in the army, but I think the time is finally right for this. I need to do something new, something challenging and, most of all, something that really matters."

"In my view there's not much that matters more than this," Thomas said. "Our future depends on what we do right here and around the rest of the country to protect our natural resources."

"I get that," Kevin said. "My only question is whether I can be useful."

"If you can pilot that boat you said you're willing to bring with you, I can teach you everything else you need to know." He gave Kevin a hard look. "Did you pass biology?"

"Yes."

"Chemistry? Zoology?"

"And a lot more science besides," Kevin told him.

"Then you'll fit right in," Thomas said. "The pay's

lousy, but we'll pay you something for the boat and we'll cover the fuel."

"That's good enough for me," Kevin said. All he cared about at the moment was that this felt a hundred percent right. In recent months, very little else had. This…and kissing Shanna.

13

Before leaving his uncle's offices, Kevin met most of the other scientists and employees. There were a surprisingly small number of them, given the magnitude of the task they were trying to accomplish. He was also able to convince Thomas to agree to give a talk at Shanna's bookstore.

"Have her call me and we'll work out the details," he told Kevin, then gave him a penetrating look. "Does this woman mean something to you? It sounds as if—"

"I hardly know her," Kevin said out of habit.

Thomas chuckled. "When it comes to attraction, time doesn't always factor into it." When Kevin started to respond, his uncle waved him off. "Never mind the denials. I'll see what's going on for myself when I come down there to give this talk."

For the first time since Shanna had suggested inviting his uncle to speak at the store, Kevin was starting to view it as a bad idea. Thomas had been twice married and twice divorced. Ironically, he'd lost both wives because, like Mick, he'd really been married to his work.

But even though he had trouble sustaining a relationship, Thomas genuinely appreciated women. His intuition was finely tuned. He could read them in a way that Kevin sure as hell hadn't been able to.

Water under the bridge, Kevin told himself, even as he caught Thomas studying him with a knowing expression. He draped an arm around Kevin's shoulders as he walked him outside.

"I think I'll take a drive down to Chesapeake Shores tomorrow," he said, taking Kevin by surprise. "I should drop in and see Ma, maybe take a look at that boat and see what modifications it's going to need, if you're serious about selling it to us."

"I told you I'd donate it," Kevin reminded him.

"It's a new boat, Kevin. We have some money put aside. Let's make it a business deal, even if it won't be for the kind of money you could get elsewhere."

"Whatever you want," Kevin said warily.

"Then I'll see you tomorrow."

Kevin sensed that his uncle had something else on his agenda for this sudden visit. He was pretty sure the boat was the least of it. Thomas proved the point by adding, "After we take a look at the boat, I can drop in at the bookstore and finalize things there, too," he said, his expression all innocence. "I'll bring along a list of recommended books for your friend. Shanna, is it?"

Bingo, Kevin thought, his stomach sinking. There was the real mission in a nutshell. "Shanna Carlyle," he said.

"Okay, then," Thomas said cheerfully. "I'll be looking forward to it. You going to be at the house?"

Kevin nodded. Unless he could get a ticket to Antarctica before then.

"I'll meet you there. We can drive over to the marina, then into town. You can make the introductions."

"Sounds great," Kevin said, though he knew his voice lacked enthusiasm.

His uncle gave him a questioning look. "You're not having second thoughts about your decision, are you?"

"Of course not," he said at once, then shrugged. "Maybe a few."

"About the boat?"

Kevin shook his head.

"Working with me?"

"Absolutely not."

A grin spread across Thomas's face. "Then it's Shanna. Not to worry, I won't embarrass you with my questions. I'll just be observing, trying to get the lay of the land, so to speak. I'm sure she must be used to being under a microscope with O'Briens everywhere she turns in Chesapeake Shores."

Kevin regarded him with dismay. "What is it with this family?" he asked. "I know all the women are inveterate matchmakers, but you, too? Is it in our damn genes?"

"Since there's a long, long list of O'Briens here and back in Ireland, I'd have to say yes," Thomas said unrepentantly. "We want our own to be happy. And we'll do whatever it takes to make sure of it."

"By marrying them off?" Kevin asked incredulously. "You can say that after two bad marriages?"

"They weren't bad, any more than Mick's was to Megan. They were flawed, maybe, not bad. Both Gillian and Diana were wonderful women. I just couldn't give them the attention they deserved. Truth be told, I'd marry either of them again in a heartbeat, if they'd have me."

"Dad seems determined to win Mom back, as well," Kevin admitted.

Thomas seemed surprised by that. "Is that so? Well,

God bless him for that. It was a shame he ever let her get away. How does Megan feel about it?"

"She's a tough sell," he admitted. "But my money's on Dad." He was even starting to get used to the idea. Having her around recently hadn't been awful. And he did owe her for planting this idea in his head about working with Thomas.

"My money's on my brother, as well," his uncle said. "I'll have to give him a bit of encouragement if I see him tomorrow." He shrugged. "Not that he'll appreciate it coming from me. Will he be around?"

"He should be. He's coming back from Seattle tonight."

"And Megan?"

"She's gone back to New York in a huff," Kevin said. "Which probably means Dad will go chasing after her in a day or two. He'll want her to have time to cool down."

Thomas chuckled. "Now you've given me yet another reason to be grateful to you for turning up here today—the perfect excuse to watch the fireworks between those two. It was lively enough the first time around. Now that Megan obviously has her sass and vinegar back, it's bound to be spectacular."

"You certainly have an unusual outlook on our mixed-up family dynamics," Kevin said, wishing he could reach a similar combination of fascination and objective distance.

"It's hard to see things clearly when you're in the thick of it," Thomas said, then gave Kevin a wicked wink. "That's why I'm looking forward to getting a firsthand glimpse of you and this Shanna you claim you hardly know. I suspect I'll see plenty you're not admitting to me or to yourself."

Yeah, that was exactly what Kevin was afraid of.

* * *

Shanna's cell phone rang so rarely she almost didn't recognize the sound, especially with her purse tucked away in a nook in the back room. By the time she reached her purse and located the phone, it had stopped ringing. And the caller hadn't left a message. When she saw the number of the caller, she muttered a curse, then immediately hit the button for a call-back.

"Hello." Henry's soft little voice was tentative.

"Hi, sweetie. Did you just call me?"

"Uh-huh," he said, then asked, "Is that okay?"

"Of course, it is. I've told you that you can call me anytime." Thank heaven, the court hadn't denied that, just in-person visits.

"But Daddy says I shouldn't bother you, that you're not my family anymore. He gets really mad when I call you Mommy."

"I will *always* be your family, Henry," she said emphatically. "Don't let anyone ever tell you otherwise. You need me, you call, okay? Now tell me how you are."

He hesitated, then said, "Daddy's sick. That's what Greta says, anyway." His voice, filled with worry, gathered steam. "Do you think if he's sick for a long time, he should go to the hospital? What if he dies? What would happen to me?"

She could imagine his precious little face, the expression on it way too serious for his age. "Nothing is going to happen to your daddy," Shanna said, trying to sound reassuring. She knew exactly what was going on with Greg. He was on some kind of a bender and had probably locked himself away in his suite of rooms, leaving the nanny to try to come up with an excuse that would make sense to a seven-year-old.

"But what if it does?" Henry persisted. "Could I come to live with you, then?"

Shanna bit back a sigh, knowing the court would never agree to that. Only Greg or his parents could arrange that, and it would never happen. "You'd live with your grandparents," she told him. "You know how much they love you. They would take very, very good care of you, Henry. But this is not something you need to worry about. Your daddy is going to be fine."

She hoped that wasn't a lie, that Greg wouldn't drink himself to death or wrap his car around a tree on one of the too-frequent occasions when his judgment was impaired.

"I wish you were here," Henry said.

"Me, too, baby. Me, too. But even though I'm not there, I love you and miss you. Don't forget that."

"I gotta go," he said. "Somebody's coming."

"Bye, Henry," she whispered, but she was talking to dead air.

She set the phone aside and rested her head on her arms. Tears stung her eyes. She couldn't help wondering sometimes if it wouldn't have been easier on Henry, on her, if she'd never come into their lives. Henry wouldn't have grown so attached to her. She wouldn't have started thinking of him as her own son. And leaving wouldn't have ripped out her heart and left him scared and alone.

"Shanna?"

Kevin's voice startled her. She glanced up too quickly, without thinking about the fact that she'd been crying. He was at her side in an instant, hunkering down in front of her.

"What's wrong?" he demanded, gently brushing at the tears on her cheeks, his eyes filled with concern. He glanced at the cell phone on the desk. "Bad news?"

She shook her head, afraid if she spoke she'd start sobbing. Since she didn't think she could explain about Greg and Henry and her messed-up mistake of a marriage, she forced a smile.

"Sorry, I was just feeling emotional for a minute." She found a tissue in her purse and dabbed at her face, glanced in her compact's mirror and added a dash of lipstick. "Too many changes, too fast, I suppose. I'm fine now."

He didn't look as if he believed a word of it.

She mustered another smile, hopefully a more convincing one. "How about lunch? I think there's enough of a lull that I can run to Sally's for a half hour. Besides, I want to hear all about how things went with your uncle this morning."

"Are you sure you feel like going out? I could bring something back here."

"Am I that much of a mess?"

He shook his head. "You look gorgeous, just a little sad."

"Like I said, it's been one of those days. Being around people will be good for me." And it would keep her mind off the call from Henry and off the temptation to call Greta and demand to know what was really going on with Greg.

She picked up her keys and purse and headed toward the front of the store. Kevin tagged along behind her, then held the door. When she walked outside, she nearly gasped at the heat and humidity, which had climbed since early morning. It was like a slap in the face, immediately stealing breath and sapping energy.

"How about the Panini Bistro today?" Kevin said as she locked the door. "I think it's time for a change, and Bree says their sandwiches are great."

"Okay," she said slowly, reading between the lines. "Any particular reason you don't want to go to Sally's?"

"Just tired of the same old thing, I guess," he said unconvincingly. "Aren't you?"

She shrugged. "A change will be nice." It seemed they were both in odd moods.

There was enough of a breeze off the bay to make sitting outdoors an option despite the heat, so Kevin led the way to a table. They were silent as they quickly glanced over the menu. Not until after the waitress had taken their order did Kevin face her again.

"Okay, what was the real story back there?" he asked. "You weren't crying just because you'd had a tough morning. You hardly shed more than a few tears when the store flooded, so today would have had to be a doozy to bring them on."

"It doesn't matter," she said.

"It does," he said firmly. "Somebody called and upset you. Was it Laurie? Your folks?"

"Kevin, really, it was nothing," she lied. It was everything and much too hard to explain. Someday she'd tell him everything about the little boy who'd stolen her heart and the man who'd broken it, but not today. Right now she needed to think about something more cheerful. "Tell me about your morning. How did things go with your uncle?"

Though he looked as if he didn't want to abandon his own line of questioning, he couldn't contain the eagerness sparkling in his eyes. "We're going to work together," he told her. "And he'll do your event for you, though I have to warn you he has an ulterior motive."

"What's that?" she asked. "Does he want it to be a fund-raiser? That's okay with me. In fact, it's a fantastic idea. I'll donate a percentage of the sales."

"I'm sure he'd appreciate that, but no, this motive is personal, not professional." He hesitated, then said, "Somehow, he's gotten the impression that there's something going on between the two of us. I swear I didn't say anything to put the idea into his head. Just be prepared to fend off a lot of questions when you see him. It seems he's no more immune to meddling than anyone else in my family."

She was so excited by the prospect of putting together an event at the store, the rest of Kevin's words barely registered. "I'll call him right away and make the arrangements. And I need to call Jess and get her ideas for some easy appetizers that won't be outrageously expensive." She reached in her purse for paper and pen, then jotted down notes. "Can you give me your uncle's phone number? I'll call when I get back to the shop. Or right now, if you think he'll be in. He's probably out to lunch, though."

Kevin placed a hand over hers. "Slow down. You don't need to call him. He's coming to town tomorrow. I'll bring him by the store, and you can finalize all the details."

She paused, startled. "He's coming to the store?"

Kevin nodded, clearly amused that his earlier comments were finally sinking in.

"And he has questions about the two of us?"

"Oh, yeah," he confirmed. "I'm not exactly overjoyed about that myself, but he was insistent."

"Well, there's nothing to tell," she said briskly. "So we don't need to worry."

"You're wrong about that," he told her.

"Which part?"

"Both. We do need to worry because we're both hiding from the truth, and Thomas is going to see right through us."

"I don't know what you mean," she insisted.

Kevin regarded her with skepticism. "Really? If I kissed you right now, what would happen?"

Shanna swallowed hard. There was no denying what a kiss would prove. The attraction between them might be merely simmering for the moment, but it could easily heat to a boil.

"I see what you're saying," she said hurriedly to forestall any ideas he might have of demonstrating his point. "But we won't be kissing in front of him." Or ever again, if they both stuck to their resolution. Right this second, with Kevin's heated gaze on her, it was hard to recall why they'd made that stupid resolution in the first place.

"I don't think the lack of kissing is going to matter," Kevin said, sounding resigned. "Uncle Thomas considers himself to be very intuitive when it comes to this kind of stuff and, unfortunately, I don't think he's overestimating his skill."

"Then just bring him to the door, make some excuse and take off. I can handle the arrangements, and you can come back and get him." She regarded him hopefully. "You and I won't even have to be in the same room."

"Don't you think he'll find that odd? Maybe even make too much of us avoiding each other?" He grinned. "Which, by the way, even I can see would be way too telling. Men and women only avoid each other when they're scared of revealing something."

"Or when they hate each other's guts," she suggested.

"Which we don't," he said. "Quite the opposite, in fact."

"Then we just deal with this," she decided. "If he gets all caught up with some crazy idea that there's something going on between us, we can just laugh it off. I think we're worrying about nothing. Surely, he has more important things on his mind than you and me."

"I don't think he sees it that way," Kevin said, his expression glum. "There's nothing the people in my family love more than a project, and I'm currently at the top of everyone's list. You don't have a chance in hell of avoiding getting caught up in the drama, unless you run far, far away."

Despite the panic his words set off in her, Shanna met his gaze. She even risked putting her hand over his. "I'm not going anywhere."

She couldn't have said why she knew that staying put was the right thing to do or why she wasn't as eager to run as he was for her to do it. She just knew she belonged here. If she couldn't be back in Pennsylvania, making a life with the boy who'd felt so much like a son to her, then this was the home she wanted. Maybe even the man she wanted. She couldn't be sure about that yet.

Kevin sighed, his hand turning over to clasp hers. "Don't say I didn't warn you."

Mick was sitting at the kitchen table with a cup of coffee and one of his mother's scones when the back door opened and his brother strolled in as if he belonged there. Mick frowned at the unwelcome intrusion.

"What are you doing here?" he asked sourly.

Thomas grinned despite the lack of welcome. He went straight to the counter and poured himself a cup of coffee. Acted as if he owned the damn place, in Mick's opinion.

"Nice to see you, too, big brother," Thomas said, meeting his gaze with an unflinching one of his own. "You're as charming as always."

"I'm charming when I need to be," Mick said. "And I'm still wondering what's brought you into my home without an invitation. Did Ma call you?"

"I invited him," Kevin said, joining them.

Mick didn't even try to hide his dismayed reaction. "Now, why would you do that?"

"Because I'm going to work for him, so you're probably going to be seeing a lot more of him," his traitorous son announced. "Today, we have some things we need to do."

"No way in hell!" Mick said, banging his fist on the table as he rose to his feet. He was the same height as his brother, and they had a similar build that came with doing heavy work, often in harsh weather. The similarities mostly ended there. Thomas was a damn tree hugger. Mick respected some of what he did and certainly why he did it, but Thomas would fight to save a gnat that was biting the heck out of him. Mick figured there were some creatures that deserved getting smacked.

"It's my choice," Kevin said mildly, even as Mick glared at Thomas.

"What kind of sneaky, underhanded tricks did he use to convince you of that?" Mick demanded. Given his low opinion of Thomas, who'd backstabbed him more than once when they were getting permits to build Chesapeake Shores, Mick wouldn't put it past his brother to have brainwashed his son.

"He didn't," Kevin said. "Mother did."

That took the wind right out of Mick. He sat down heavily. Megan had had a hand in this? What had she been thinking? She knew how much bad blood there was between him and Thomas, yet she'd gone right ahead and encouraged their son to form an alliance with his uncle. Mick wasn't sure he'd be able to forgive Megan for that. Maybe she'd been paying him back for not being around this past weekend. If so, she couldn't have picked a crueler way.

"She didn't do this just to get even with you," Kevin

said, evidently reading his mind. "She just reminded me of the way I used to ask so many questions whenever Thomas was around, how interested I was in what he did. What she said made a lot of sense."

"And that was enough to send you running off to Annapolis?" Mick asked in disbelief.

Kevin nodded. "I'm really excited about this, Dad. I'll be doing something that matters."

"Being a paramedic mattered," Mick said, even though he could see the handwriting on the wall. Kevin's mind was made up, and if he wanted his son to be happy, there was only so much he could say about this cockamamy plan of his.

Kevin's expression shut down.

"Sorry," Mick said stiffly. "I know you don't want to go back to that, but this? Are you sure?"

"More sure than I am about most things," Kevin said.

"It's what he was destined to do," Thomas said quietly. "Mick, you and I may not see eye to eye about much, but we both love the bay. We both know how close it is to being ruined forever. It's going to take time to get it right, maybe more time than I have. We need the next generation involved."

"And I'm sure it pleases you that it's my son you've enlisted," Mick grumbled.

"Not because he's your son," Thomas said. "Because he cares. He's the right person to do this. If you'll leave me out of the equation for a minute and think back, you'll see I'm right. Kevin grew up on the waters around here. He cares more than most."

Because Mick wouldn't have admitted his brother could be right about anything, he ignored the request and turned to Kevin. "And that boat you bought? Is that just an expensive whim?"

"I'm selling it to Uncle Thomas's organization," he said. "We're going over to the marina in a bit to see what it'll need to make it more functional for their purposes." He hesitated, then added, "You could come along."

"No," Mick said flatly.

Thomas gave him a look of regret, then told Kevin. "I'm going to try to find Ma to say hello and see how she's doing. I'll meet you at the car in a few minutes."

Kevin nodded.

"Ma's outside in her garden," Mick told him grudgingly. "She likes to work out there before the sun gets too high."

Thomas hesitated, then asked, "She's doing well?"

"She is," Mick said, then found himself adding, "You should come around more often, see for yourself. She's not getting any younger, you know. We shouldn't let our differences keep the two of you apart."

His brother looked startled, but thankfully didn't make too much of the concession. He merely nodded. "I'll do that."

After he'd left, Mick felt his shoulders sag.

"I didn't do this to hurt you, Dad," Kevin said.

"I know that," he admitted. "Truth be told, I'm not that surprised. I guess I'd just hoped it would be me you'd take after."

Kevin chuckled. "Oh, I think I got plenty of traits from you."

"Such as?" Mick asked, genuinely curious.

"Stubbornness, for one thing. Your generous nature, for another."

"Sounds contradictory, if you ask me," Mick grumbled.

Kevin laughed. "Tell me about it. It's a constant struggle."

Mick wrestled with himself, then asked, "You think

me going along with the two of you to look at the boat would be helpful?"

"I do," Kevin said. "I seem to recall a time when you and I both went out on the research boat with Uncle Thomas, before the two of you had your falling-out. You had plenty of observations about what was going wrong with the waters of the bay. If the two of you made peace, this could be something all three of us are involved in. It would be something unifying, instead of one more excuse for prolonging your feud."

"Hold on a minute," Mick said, ignoring most of what Kevin said to correct the one thing that stuck in his craw. "It wasn't some inconsequential falling-out. He sold me out. He went right in to the planning officials and told them how to keep me from doing certain things."

"Things he'd already told you were wrong, that would be a detriment to the wetlands," Kevin reminded him.

"So he said," Mick retorted.

Kevin kept his gaze even. "Can you at least try to put that in the past and come with us today?"

Mick wanted badly to be a part of his son's future. This was one way he could do it. "I suppose I can spare the time," he said grudgingly.

"We're stopping at the bookstore afterward," Kevin said. "Shanna wants Uncle Thomas to do a talk there later this summer, so they need to work out the details."

Now wasn't that interesting? Mick certainly didn't want to miss another chance to see his son interacting with the pretty little bookseller. He suspected there was more going on there than Kevin had acknowledged. If so, he wouldn't mind giving the two of them a shove toward each other.

Though he wasn't crazy about the way the morning had started, Mick could admit he was beginning to see some positive possibilities ahead. If Thomas could help Kevin get his professional life on track and Shanna could do the same with his heart, then Mick could finally sit back and relax where his son was concerned. It didn't matter who got the credit. All that mattered was seeing Kevin living his life to the fullest again.

14

Having three O'Brien men underfoot, two of them obviously on a mission, pretty much freaked Shanna out. Kevin didn't look especially overjoyed about the situation, either. For all of her expressed confidence that she and Kevin could control things with his uncle, it was evident in the first few minutes that they didn't stand a chance against the combined forces of Thomas *and* Mick.

Ironically, Mick had hardly said a word. He'd taken a seat in one of the overstuffed chairs and sat watching the rest of them with the look of a cat who'd recently dined on several plump and tasty canaries. It was disconcerting.

She had a feeling that if she and Thomas hadn't had business to conduct, he would have taken the seat right next to Mick's so the two of them could observe Shanna's interaction with Kevin and compare notes. She'd never felt more on display, not even when Greg's parents had looked down their aristocratic noses at her.

When she couldn't stand it another second, she sent a frantic look in Kevin's direction. Since he appeared nearly as desperate to leave as she was, he immediately picked up on the cue.

"Shanna, didn't you tell me that you can check for titles

on the computer in the back?" Kevin asked. "Maybe we could take a quick look for those books Thomas is recommending. Make sure they're available."

"Great idea," she said, seizing the lifeline. She beamed at Thomas and Mick. "Why don't you two help yourself to some coffee? Kevin and I will be right back. Then we'll know whether my distributor has these books in stock."

Thomas gave Kevin a knowing glance, but nodded. "Take your time. I'll have a look around. It seems you have a terrific mystery and thriller section. I can use some new reading material. Scientific journals get tiresome after a while."

Shanna practically ran to the back room. "Thank you for getting me out of there," she said in a low voice to Kevin. "You didn't warn me that your father was coming. I think I could have coped with one of them, but two…" She shook her head. "Not possible."

He nodded. "It was starting to creep me out, too."

She sat down in front of the computer, then went to the distributor's website to check inventory. Five of the six books Thomas had listed were in stock in significant quantities. The sixth was out of print. Still, she'd be able to offer a great selection for customers who attended the event. She placed the order while she was online.

When she finally turned around, Kevin was standing right behind her. He was close. Much too close, in fact. He immediately backed up a step, but not before some kind of invisible force field drew her toward him.

He met her gaze, swallowing hard. "Shanna?"

The questioning note in his voice mirrored the thousand and one doubts rampaging through her head. Still, she couldn't seem to look away. Couldn't bring herself to take the step that might have put her beyond his reach.

He blinked once, then stepped toward her, covering her

mouth with his before either of them could utter the reminder that they'd sworn not to do this again. She felt the shock of the kiss down to her toes, felt the quick rise of need, the desperate yearning for more.

How could it be like this with another man she barely knew, another man whose life was far too complicated? Did she not possess even one single shred of sense? Had she learned nothing from her impetuous rush into an ill-fated relationship and eventual marriage with Greg? Laurie would have a field day answering that one.

When the kiss slowly—reluctantly—ended, her knees very nearly buckled. Kevin steadied her, though he looked a little dazed himself.

"This isn't good," he murmured, mostly to himself.

"I thought it was very good, excellent in fact," she said, mostly because he sounded so somber. She wanted to coax a smile from him.

His lips twitched, but the smile never blossomed, certainly never reached his eyes. "Do you realize that my uncle and my father are probably out there right this second speculating about what we're doing back here?"

"No speculating involved," Mick said, startling them both. He was standing in the doorway, a satisfied gleam in his eyes. Thomas was right behind him, his expression equally smug.

"Not that we were spying," Mick claimed, "but we did get to wondering what was taking so long. I thought it might be something like this." The last was spoken with an air of triumph that left Shanna and Kevin both speechless. "How about we leave you to it? Thomas and I will go to Sally's and grab some lunch."

Kevin sighed heavily. "I'll come with you, make sure you behave civilly."

"No need for that," Mick said. "I think we can keep our

current truce for a bit longer. We'll have a bite, then bring something back for you and Shanna. Let you spend more time together. How's that?"

Shanna's face was flaming. "That's very thoughtful of you," she managed to say.

"Least I can do," Mick said, grinning. "We'll be back in an hour. Shall I put the Closed sign on the door?"

"No, absolutely not," she said, trying to make it clear that there would be nothing happening and therefore no reason to fear untimely interruptions.

He looked vaguely disappointed. "Whatever you say," he said.

After he'd gone, Shanna sank back down on the stool in front of the computer and put her head in her hands. When she'd drawn in a deep breath, she dared a look at Kevin.

"That wasn't good," she murmured.

To her surprise, Kevin chuckled.

She frowned at him. "It is not funny. Even you didn't think it was funny a few minutes ago."

"True, but it is predictable. I just have this vision of the two of them peeking in the door for who knows how long just waiting to catch us doing something compromising. I swear they're worse than my sisters."

"Are you going to find this so amusing once they've alerted Bree, Jess and Abby?"

"Dad won't say a word," Kevin said confidently. "He's going to enjoy holding this over my head way too much to share the information with them."

"If you don't mind, I think I'll just prepare myself for the worst," Shanna told him.

"The worst?"

"Answering to a parade of your sisters before the day's out."

Kevin's smile faltered. "Better you than me," he said wholeheartedly.

"Why? You've had a whole lot longer to practice fending them off."

He shook his head. "There are some things a man can never master. Dealing with meddling sisters is one of them," he said, his glum mood returning.

Shanna lifted a brow. "How about a meddling father and uncle?"

He shook his head. "That's a new one on me. Any ideas?"

"Not a one, unless you want to run over to Sally's and haul some other woman into your arms just to throw them off the scent." Just suggesting such a thing made her feel empty inside.

"Not interested," Kevin said. "There has to be another way."

"Something tells me that unless we stage the mother of all fights and you go storming out of here in a very public and convincing huff, the two of us are doomed."

Kevin nodded. "Looks that way to me, too."

"How are your acting skills?"

"Lousy. Yours?"

"Probably worse," she admitted.

He draped a comforting arm over her shoulder. "Still loving the O'Briens?"

She looked into his eyes, which bore an unmistakable glint of humor along with plenty of the heat that had just gotten them into such trouble. "Not so much," she fibbed. One of them, anyway, had pretty much stolen her heart.

"Not one word," Kevin warned when he, his father and uncle were on their way back to the house.

"I have no idea what you're talking about," Mick claimed. He turned to his brother, who'd miraculously become some kind of coconspirator in the past couple of hours. "You have any idea, Thomas?"

"None. He seems a bit jumpy, don't you think?"

"Guilty would be the word I'd use," Mick said.

"Nothing to be guilty about," Thomas said, his expression thoughtful. "The attraction between a man and a woman is a wonderful, natural thing."

"It is, indeed," Mick said.

"Would the two of you give it a rest?" Kevin snapped. "Don't go making too much of whatever the heck you thought you saw back there."

"It's not as if there was any guesswork involved," Mick retorted. "I recognize a kiss when I see one."

"No question about it," Thomas agreed.

"And I'm glad of it, too," Mick added. "It's time you thought about moving on with your life. Shanna seems like a lovely young woman."

"I thought so, as well," Thomas said. "She's beautiful and intelligent."

"When did you two start agreeing about everything?" Kevin demanded irritably. "A few hours ago, you were barely speaking. I liked it better then."

"Just because we see eye to eye on this doesn't mean we've made peace," Mick said.

"Just a temporary détente," Thomas agreed. "We're of one mind when it comes to you and Shanna."

"Heaven help me," Kevin murmured. Then, because he couldn't contain his curiosity, he asked, "What is it you both think you see when you look at us—beyond the kiss, that is?"

"You never took your eyes off of her, for one thing," Mick said. "That's a sure sign that a man is hooked."

"Same with her," Thomas said. "She kept stealing glances in your direction, even when her attention was supposedly focused on planning that event with me."

"And her expression got all soft and dreamy," Mick added thoughtfully, his gaze turning wistful. "Meggie used to look at me just like that."

"Well, I doubt you'd get that kind of look out of Mom right now," Kevin said, seizing on a way to divert his father's attention. "She's definitely not happy with you. I can attest to that from firsthand experience."

"Don't go using your mother to change the subject," Mick said. "We're talking about you and Shanna. Leave your mother to me."

"I'd be happy to, but you dragged me into the middle of it when you sent me to the airport the other day," Kevin responded, determined not to let go of the topic. "There I was, stuck with trying to defend you after all the promises you apparently made to prove you'd changed."

"I don't need you defending me, either," Mick grumbled, then fell silent, which had been Kevin's goal.

Kevin glanced in the rearview mirror and saw his uncle's lips twitching. He seemed to be getting entirely too much enjoyment out of the entire afternoon.

"Am I going to regret coming to work with you?" he asked Thomas.

Thomas chuckled. "It will give me a few more opportunities to needle you about your love life," he admitted. "But, trust me, the benefits will outweigh the drawbacks. You'll see. Not only will you be immersed in a career you were meant for, but you'll have all my years of wisdom when it comes to women at your disposal."

Mick made a rude sound at that. "Two divorces," he said succinctly.

"At least I learned a thing or two," Thomas said, not taking offense. "Can you say the same?"

"Mom would definitely say no," Kevin felt compelled to chime in, drawing a scowl from his father and a barely contained chuckle from his uncle.

Thankfully they'd reached the house by then, so he could go inside, grab his son and escape from the pair of them. They'd either maintain the peace or come to blows. Whichever way it went, they'd be out of his hair.

Shanna wasn't the least bit surprised when Bree wandered in around four o'clock that afternoon. By then, most of her flower orders had been delivered, Jenny was there and eager to handle any walk-in customers, and Bree had time on her hands. Sometimes she spent the late-afternoon hours in the back of her shop working on her latest play or finalizing plans for her regional theater's debut production. On other occasions, she used the time to pop in to see Shanna and chat.

This afternoon, she poured herself a cup of coffee, then sat down and propped her elbows on the counter. She regarded Shanna with evident curiosity. "Were my father, my brother and my uncle in here earlier?"

Shanna figured the less she actually said, the less there would be for Bree to misinterpret. She merely nodded and kept her attention focused on the day's receipts.

Bree gave an exaggerated look around the shop. "Walls are still standing, so it couldn't have been a total disaster having my father and his brother in the same room. How'd it happen?"

"Your uncle's going to give a talk here in a couple of weeks. We were finalizing the details. Kevin and your dad just came along with him."

"I see," Bree said, though she looked perplexed. "You know there's bad blood between my dad and my uncle."

"So I've heard."

"Then there had to be something monumental going on to get them to share the same space. I doubt it was the prospect of Thomas giving a talk in here."

Shanna merely shrugged.

Bree's eyes suddenly lit up. "You and Kevin! That's it, isn't it? They both wanted to check the two of you out. Oh my gosh, you must have been furious."

Not wanting to acknowledge that there'd been any checking out going on, much less anything for the two men to see, Shanna again shrugged. "They weren't here that long. They went to lunch."

"Really?"

"It was no big deal," Shanna assured her.

Bree regarded her with skepticism. "I wonder if Kevin would tell the same story."

"Why wouldn't he?"

"Because he's more attuned to my family's sneakiness," she suggested. "I think I'll give him a call or maybe stop by the house on my way home."

Shanna debated saving him, then decided to throw him to the wolves. It was his family, after all. "Why don't you do that?" she said cheerfully.

"Oh, boy," Bree said, a grin spreading across her face. "It was awful, wasn't it? I knew it!"

Shanna frowned. "How did you get awful from anything I said? I was so careful."

"Exactly." Bree beamed. "If everything had been as casual and innocent as you were pretending, you'd have offered details. You wouldn't have sicced me on Kevin."

"Great powers of deduction," Shanna muttered, though

she didn't necessarily mean it as a compliment. Actually it was fairly annoying.

"Okay, now that the cat's out of the bag, fill me in," Bree commanded. "What went on in here? Did you and Kevin put on a show for my dad and Thomas?"

Shanna regarded her with a scowl. "You're the one in theater," she retorted. "Kevin and I don't put on shows."

Bree's gaze narrowed thoughtfully. "But something did happen. I can see it in your eyes. You're not looking directly at me. And you're being all evasive and weird."

"Do you analyze everyone you meet?" Shanna inquired testily.

Bree nodded. "Occupational hazard. I like trying to figure out what makes people tick. It comes in handy when I'm creating characters."

"Which reminds me," Shanna said, eager for a diversion. "How's the play coming? Are rehearsals going well?"

"Nice dodge," Bree commended her. "But I'd rather talk about what went on here today."

"Nothing," Shanna insisted. Bree's gaze never faltered. She simply stared until Shanna caved. "Okay, your dad and uncle caught Kevin and me kissing."

Bree's eyes immediately lit up. "Really?"

"And, I'm sure it will thrill you to know that whatever their past differences, they are now united in bugging Kevin and me about that."

"Not surprised," Bree said. "But it does make things tricky for the two of you, doesn't it?"

"Tricky doesn't begin to cover it," Shanna said dolefully. "With those two watching us like hawks, it could very well be the last kiss we ever risk."

Bree seized on her tone. "And you find that upsetting?"

"Yes," Shanna said at once, then blushed. "Really, I mean who wants a bunch of people studying their relationship as if they were specimens under a microscope? If I were in Kevin's situation, I certainly wouldn't want that kind of pressure. I'm not overjoyed by it myself."

"I'll get them to back off," Bree said at once. "I like you and I love my brother. I don't want your relationship ruined by a couple of meddling old men."

"And a few meddling sisters?" Shanna dared to ask. "Anything you can do to keep Jess and Abby out of this? Maybe not mention anything to Kevin yourself?"

"When I first walked in, you were all about me talking to Kevin."

"Only because I did not want to discuss this with you," Shanna told her. "I'm not entirely sure how I wound up blurting it all out, but since I have, maybe you could leave your brother alone. You already know everything there is to know."

"I could leave Kevin alone," Bree agreed. "And I could agree not to say anything to Abby or Jess…"

"But? I heard a distinct *but* in there."

"But they will find out," Bree said.

"Kevin doesn't think Mick or Thomas will say anything about today because they'll enjoy gloating about knowing something that no one else in the family knows."

Bree laughed. "An interesting theory. I'm not sure I buy it. While my father loves knowing secrets, he can't keep them, and he's going to be terrified that Thomas will blab first, so he'll figure he should get the jump on him."

"It was a *kiss,*" Shanna said irritably. "Not some earth-shaking revelation that could change the world. How old are they? Ten?"

"You'd think so, wouldn't you?" Bree said, her expression commiserating. "I'll do whatever damage control I can, but don't expect this to stay a secret for long."

She stood up and gave Shanna a hug. "Whatever you do, remember this. You're good for my brother. Don't let the rest of us scare you off. If we're putting too much pressure on you, tell us to butt out."

"Butt out," Shanna said, testing the effectiveness of the order.

Bree merely laughed.

Shanna stirred more sugar into her coffee as she watched Bree sail out the door. She reminded herself of all the times she'd envied families just like the O'Briens…big, noisy, meddling families. Now she was beginning to see that there was a dark side.

But, God help her, she still wanted to be a part of one. Maybe even this one.

Every time her cell phone rang, Megan jumped. She glanced at the caller ID, determined not to take any calls from Mick. There was nothing he could possibly say about his last-minute absence from Chesapeake Shores that she wanted to hear. It would just be more of the same old, same old.

But as twenty-four hours passed, then forty-eight, annoyance turned to anger. So tonight when the phone rang and she saw his number, she punched the button to turn on the phone.

"What do you want?" she demanded.

"Is that any way to greet the man who loves you?" Mick inquired.

"It's not the way I would greet *that* man," she said pointedly. "However, it's exactly the tone *you* deserve."

"I'm sorry I wasn't here," he told her solemnly. "But

you already know that, if you've listened to any of the dozen or so messages I've left."

"I deleted every one of them," she told him. "Never heard a one."

"Then I'll repeat the gist of them," he said with exaggerated patience. "The trip came up very late at night. I had no choice but to fly out to Seattle first thing in the morning. I called you from the plane to explain. I sent Kevin to the airport to explain. I am very, very sorry. It won't happen again."

She actually bought that he was sorry, but none of the rest. "Of course it will, Mick. Taking off at the drop of a hat without a thought for anyone else is what you do. I wanted so badly to take you at your word when you said you'd changed, but it's evident that you haven't."

"I asked you to meet me out there," he reminded her. "Don't I get any credit for that?"

"I don't have the kind of flexibility that allows me to jet off across the country at the drop of a hat," she countered.

"You would if you—"

She cut him off. "You really do not want to go there right now. I'm not quitting my job to come back to a man who's not reliable."

"I'm just saying it would be easier—"

Again, she cut him off. "Leave it alone, Mick. It's not going to happen."

"You're a hard woman, Meggie."

"I've had to learn to be," she told him. "You gave me lessons."

"Now that's a fine thing to say," he grumbled. "And since we've pretty much beat my sins to death, let's move on to yours."

"Mine?" she said incredulously. "What have I done?"

"You sent our son running straight to his uncle looking for work."

Megan's mood immediately brightened, despite Mick's obvious displeasure. "Kevin saw Thomas?"

"He's going to start working with him next week. He's already transferring the title for that fishing boat over to Thomas's organization, so they can outfit it for research."

"That's fabulous," she said. "This is the perfect challenge for Kevin. I couldn't be happier."

"You're thrilled for him or because you know how much it annoys me to have the two of them working together?"

She chuckled at his miffed tone. "That is an added bonus," she admitted.

"Did you suggest this just to get even with me?" Mick asked.

"No. I suggested it because I've been worried about our son. He needed a new direction in his life and, frankly, I didn't think fishing charters were the answer. Obviously, once Kevin really thought it through, he agreed with me. Come on, Mick," she cajoled. "You know how perfect this will be for him. He and Thomas are like two peas in a pod when it comes to the way they care about the bay. You've been on the water with them, listened to all of Kevin's questions. Your brother was so patient with him. I think he's been counting on this for years, but out of respect for you, he never pushed Kevin. He's waited until Kevin came to him on his own. Give him some credit for his sensitivity about that."

"I suppose," he conceded grudgingly.

"Have you seen him?"

"Who? Thomas?"

"Yes."

"He was here the other day, gloating about taking my son from me."

Megan rolled her eyes. "Oh, please, we both know better. Thomas would never deliberately interfere in your relationship with Kevin or gloat about it, if the two of you did have some kind of a rift."

"Actually, Thomas and I did find one thing we have in common," Mick admitted.

"Really?"

"We think the new bookseller has a thing for Kevin and vice versa. We're in agreement that we need to do whatever we can to encourage it."

The idea horrified Megan. "Mick O'Brien, you keep your nose out of our son's business!"

"I'm just going to nudge a bit," he said. "Same with Thomas."

"Has it occurred to you that your gentle nudging or whatever you want to call it will most likely backfire and keep those two as far apart as they can get? Shanna's the first woman he's shown any interest in, though she's far from the first to try to catch his eye since he's come home. Kevin needs to take this at his own pace."

"Why?" he asked, sounding genuinely baffled.

"Because it's a delicate situation. Kevin's still grieving over Georgia or thinks he should be. In his position, he may view this as some kind of betrayal to her memory."

"Then shouldn't he know none of us see it that way? Won't that reassure him that nothing's wrong with moving on with his life?"

"It might," she conceded. "Or it might not. Do you really want to risk nipping this relationship in the bud before it has a chance to bloom?"

"Sounds as if you're determined to strip all the fun out of my life," he said gloomily.

"Just trying to be realistic," she said.

"Well, there's one way to be sure I won't meddle," he told her. "Invite me to New York so you and I can work on our relationship, instead."

She wanted to tell him not to come, that she was still too furious to see him, but the truth was most of the heat had gone out of her anger just listening to him take a real interest in their son. That alone demonstrated a new, improved Mick.

"When have you ever waited for an invitation?" she said at last.

"You saying if I show up on your doorstep, you won't kick me out?" he asked, his tone cautious.

She grinned, relieved that he couldn't see her expression. "I guess you'll just have to try it and find out."

In the meantime, she could work on her willpower.

15

After getting caught kissing Shanna in the back room at her store, Kevin spent the next few days avoiding her and Main Street in general. He told himself it was because he wanted to spend every possible minute with Davy before starting his job with Thomas the following week. He made the argument so convincing, he almost believed it.

Today he'd met Abby, Trace and the twins on the beach for a family picnic. He also wanted to finalize the arrangements to have Abby's nanny look out for Davy during the week. Though Gram had offered, a two-year-old was too much for her five days a week. Chipping in to pay the nanny made more sense, and Marian had agreed to care for Davy.

"He's no problem at all," she'd assured Kevin.

Now he had only to be sure that Trace and Abby were a hundred percent on board. Trace was the bigger concern, because he conducted his graphic design business from home and it would mean one more child underfoot. Though he claimed Carrie and Caitlyn were no bother, Kevin wondered if he'd be able to say the same about Davy.

As he and Trace put the hot dogs and hamburgers on the grill, Kevin brought up the subject.

"Are you sure it won't be an inconvenience having another kid in the house during the day?" he asked his soon-to-be brother-in-law. "I've heard those three when they get going. They can get pretty loud."

"And most of the noise is generated by Carrie and Caitlyn," Trace reminded him. "That's why I soundproofed my design studio. It doesn't keep out all the commotion, but it mutes it."

"That takes care of the noise, then, but what about the interruptions?"

Trace shrugged. "I actually don't mind having them run in and out. Marian keeps it to a minimum, but the twins are so bright and inquisitive, I enjoy having them around. And Davy loves drawing pictures with me. It'll be fine."

"Until he does one of his drawings on one of your megabuck graphic designs for a client," Kevin suggested.

"A lot of what I do these days is done on computer, and they know not to come near that," Trace said confidently. "It's all good, Kevin. We'd tell you if it wasn't."

Kevin studied him, looking for any sign that he was only saying what was expected. He didn't find it. Trace seemed genuinely content with his professional life and home situation. At least that part of it.

He wasn't quite as resigned to Abby's refusal to set a wedding date. He'd brought it up again this morning, making a joke out of it, but there'd been an unmistakable edge in his voice that Kevin found worrisome.

"How are things progressing between you and my sister?"

"Fine," Trace said unconvincingly. Still, as his gaze sought her out at the edge of the water where she was watching the kids, his expression softened. There was no mistaking the love he felt for Abby. "I just wish we could get on to the next stage of our lives."

Kevin was treading in water so deep he was afraid a single misstep could have him drowning, but he could sense the frustration Trace was feeling. "What would change, really?" he asked. "You'd have rings on your fingers, but you're already living together. You're already a family."

"I want all of it," Trace said, meeting his gaze for the first time. "I want the ceremony, the commitment, more kids."

"Has Abby given you a reason for not setting the date?"

"She has a dozen of them," Trace said, sounding resigned. "All nice, logical reasons that it's hard to find fault with."

"But you don't believe they're the real reason she's dragging her feet," Kevin concluded.

Trace shook his head. "She's scared. I just don't know why. She knows I love her. She knows I'm not anything like Wes. She knows she and the girls are everything I want. I bought a house for us. I thought that would be symbolic, prove to her that I was in it for the long haul." He shrugged. "Maybe she's the one who can't commit to forever."

"You know that's not true," Kevin said.

"It wouldn't be the first time," Trace said direly. "I thought she loved me once before, and she took off."

Alarmed by the suggestion that Abby could bolt from the relationship she'd been destined for, Kevin feared if she kept dragging her feet, Trace would one day tire of the wait and give up. "I'll talk to her," he offered. "Maybe I can get to the bottom of this."

Trace gave him a warning look. "Would you want her meddling in your love life?"

"Absolutely not," Kevin said, thinking of the situation

with Shanna and how badly he wanted everyone to stay out of that.

"Then act accordingly. Stay out of it. Abby and I will figure it out eventually. Now leave me to these burgers and hot dogs. You're distracting me. Go spend some time with your son." He grinned. "You could take over from Abby with all the kids and send her up here, if you really wanted to do something helpful."

Kevin chuckled. "I can definitely do that," he said, heading for the shoreline, where Davy was helping Carrie and Caitlyn dig a moat around their sand castle under Abby's supervision.

"It's a good thing Mick's not around to see this," he commented, studying the lopsided structure and the crooked moat around it.

"Yeah, I think he's doomed if he's hoping the next generation will step up to take over his business," Abby replied. "So far, these three aren't showing much promise."

Kevin slanted a look at her, trying to gauge her mood. "I'll keep an eye on the kids if you want to go up and help Trace," he offered.

Instead of seizing the offer, she frowned. "Did he say he needed my help?"

"I don't think it's a matter of need, but I think he wants you up there with him," Kevin replied, studying her with a narrowed gaze. "What's going on with you two, Sis? Is there a problem? I know all the rest of us have always counted on you for advice, but it works both ways. If there's anything you want to talk about, I can listen at least."

She hesitated, then admitted, "Trace has been pressing me to set a wedding date. He's been mentioning it more and more frequently. I think he's losing patience."

Kevin ignored his very recent vow to stay out of their problems. After all, this opportunity had virtually fallen into his lap. He wasn't going to let it pass. "Okay, why haven't you set a date? And forget all the neat, logical excuses, because I won't buy them."

She met his gaze with a challenging look, then sighed. "You could always see right through me."

"Your fiancé can see right through you, too. Trace isn't buying your excuses, either."

"Yeah, I know," she said bleakly.

He searched her expression, but couldn't read it. "You do love him, don't you?"

"Of course I do," she said fiercely. "More than I ever thought possible."

"Then what's the problem?"

"I'm scared of losing it all. I blew it once before, you know."

"Well, one sure way to blow it again is to keep putting him off when it comes to setting a date for the wedding." Kevin was struck by a sudden insight. "Are you sure you're not testing him?"

She blinked at the suggestion. "Testing him how?"

"Okay, I only saw your marriage to Wes from a distance, but what I saw was a man who had little respect for your career, who always wanted you to be something you're not. Wes expected you to drop everything to become a doting wife and mother."

"True."

"Are you waiting for Trace to suddenly start making demands that you be at home all the time, for him to question your career? Do you think it'll start with a few complaints about how much time you're spending in Baltimore, then escalate to demands that you give it all up?"

She didn't answer at once, but her thoughtful expression suggested she was genuinely considering his explanation.

"You could be right," she said eventually.

"Has Trace even once done anything to hint that he's remotely the control freak that Wes was?"

"Absolutely not," she admitted. "But I never saw that side of Wes till after we were married."

"Therefore if you put off the wedding date, you'll put off discovering if Trace is going to morph into another Wes," Kevin guessed, spinning the theory to its logical conclusion.

Abby stared at him with a shocked expression. "He wouldn't do that," she said, leaping to Trace's defense.

Kevin grinned. "I know that. Obviously, deep down, so do you. Get on with your life, Abby. I think a fall wedding would be beautiful, don't you?"

She grinned and stood up, then bent down to kiss the top of his head. "I love you."

"Back at you," he said, grinning as she ran up the beach to join her hopefully soon-to-be husband.

Whatever she said to Trace had a startled expression spreading across his face. Then, grinning, he gave Kevin a thumbs-up.

Just then Davy crawled into his lap, his thumb poked securely in his mouth. "Daddy," he murmured, leaning against Kevin's chest.

"How's my boy? You getting tired?"

But rather than falling asleep as Kevin half expected, Davy pointed in Abby's direction. "Mommy?"

Not quite understanding, Kevin said, "That's your Aunt Abby. She's Caitlyn and Carrie's mommy."

"*My* mommy!" Davy said emphatically.

Kevin fought the unexpected sting of tears. "No, your mommy's not here."

Davy gave him a sad look. "Want Mommy."

There was no way to explain to a child barely more than two years old that his mommy wouldn't be back ever again. For months now, Kevin had been telling himself that Davy was surrounded by so many aunts, his great-grandmother and recently even his grandmother, that he'd hardly notice that he didn't have a mother of his own. But he hadn't counted on Davy wanting what Carrie and Caitlyn had with Abby.

All he could say was, "I know, son. I miss her, too."

Lately, though, it was getting harder and harder to remember Georgia clearly or to recall why he'd fallen in love with her. With Georgia's parents finally scheduled to come into town in a few days for their twice-delayed visit, he felt even guiltier. He blamed himself not only for his faltering memories of Georgia, but because he was starting to let Shanna into his heart, a place some might say should still be reserved for the woman he'd lost.

Abby walked into Shanna's shop late on Monday afternoon. Her arrival immediately put Shanna on the defensive, preparing to fend off a million questions about Kevin. Instead, Abby merely asked if Bree happened to be there.

"She's not in her shop, and Jenny thought she might have come over here," Abby explained.

"I'm here," Bree called out.

Shanna grinned. "She's back there sitting on the floor looking at gardening and flower-arranging books," she said, pointing the way. "She's figured out which day my shipments of new books come in and she's usually here about an hour later."

Abby shook her head as she walked toward that aisle. "Does Shanna have a book on wedding arrangements?" she asked. "That's what you need to be studying."

Bree squealed, books hit the floor and then the sisters were in each other's arms.

"You set a date!" Bree exclaimed. "Hallelujah! Trace finally got through to you."

"Actually it was Kevin," Abby said. She turned so she was addressing Shanna. "My brother actually has fairly astonishing insights for a man."

Shanna blushed. "So I've gathered."

"Well, this calls for a celebration," Bree said. "Abby, you stay here. I'm going to run out and get champagne."

"In the middle of the afternoon?" Abby said, though she sounded more pleased than shocked.

"Absolutely. Shanna, you don't mind, do you?"

"Not as long as no one goes stumbling out of here," she said. "But shouldn't you go over to the inn and share this moment with Jess?"

"I'll call her," Abby said, immediately pulling out her cell phone and making good on the promise. When she hung up, she told Shanna, "You should be a part of this, too. Since you can't leave the store, we'll celebrate right here."

Shanna felt a warm glow inside at Abby's determination to include her. The glow only dimmed after they'd been left alone and Abby turned to her with a speculative gleam in her eyes.

"Now you and I will have a chance to talk," she told Shanna meaningfully.

"About?"

"My brother."

"Nothing to talk about," Shanna insisted, only to have

Kevin himself walk in the door and pretty much shatter the illusion she'd been intent on creating. She frowned at him. "Isn't today your first day at work with your uncle?"

He looked from her to Abby, apparently guessing at the source of her testy mood. "His workday starts before dawn. I've been to Annapolis and back and put in a full day."

Abby's eyes shone. "That's wonderful. How was it?"

"I have a lot to learn," Kevin said. "But I'm going to love it. Now tell me what you're doing here?"

"I came by to tell Bree that Trace and I have set our wedding date," she said. "Thanks to you." She gave him a smacking kiss on the cheek.

Kevin beamed at the news, but then his gaze narrowed. "You came looking for Bree in Shanna's shop? Why?"

"Bree was in here looking at books," Shanna explained. "And now she's gone to fetch champagne. Jess is on her way over, as well."

"You have to stay," Abby told him. "This is a family thing."

"Looks more like a girl thing," he said, already backing toward the door. "I think I'll leave you to it."

He was gone before Abby could stop him. The interruption had apparently only fueled her speculation. She gestured for Shanna to sit, then moved a chair until they were facing.

"Interesting that my brother would choose to come here right after his first day on his new job," she said casually. "Do you want to stick to the story that there's nothing going on between you?"

Shanna kept her chin up. "Yes, I do."

Abby leveled a look into her eyes, seemed to consider the response, then shook her head. "I'm not buying it."

Shanna shrugged. "Nothing I can do about that."

"Then that kiss the other day meant absolutely nothing?" Abby persisted, her lips twitching as she dropped her bombshell.

"Kiss?" Shanna echoed, displaying what she hoped was a credible amount of innocence.

"You didn't honestly think we wouldn't hear about it?" Abby said. "Dad raced right home and mentioned it to Gram. Normally she's as tight-lipped as anyone I've ever known, but she dropped a hint around Bree, who obviously already knew. I walked in and caught the two of them huddled together. I refused to let up until they filled me in."

If she hadn't been so embarrassed, Shanna would have been delighted by the scenario Abby was describing. Indeed, she would have wanted to be right in the middle of it. But being the subject of such a discussion was a little less enchanting.

Abby apparently caught her dismayed reaction. "I'm making you really uncomfortable, aren't I? I'm sorry. Bree, Jess and I are so used to everyone being in our business, we don't realize how that must feel to an outsider."

Shanna felt her face fall. There it was. Even under these circumstances, she was an outsider. She had to remember that and not get all caught up in thinking she was even on the fringes of this family.

"Oh dear, I've done it again," Abby said. "I didn't mean that you're an outsider, like not one of us, just that..."

"I'm not an O'Brien," Shanna said. "Believe me, I know that."

"But you'd like to be, wouldn't you?" Abby said slowly, her gaze speculative.

"Not in the way you mean," Shanna said at once. "Not by snagging Kevin or something. I just envy all of you having this wonderful big family."

Abby didn't look as if she bought the explanation entirely. "It's not always wonderful. Sometimes it's incredibly annoying."

"But in a good way," Shanna insisted.

"You can say that even after I've come in here pestering you with questions you don't want to answer?"

Shanna nodded.

Abby grinned. "The patience of a saint," she concluded. "You're going to be very good with my brother."

"But—"

"Don't even waste your breath," Abby advised, then beamed as Jess and Bree came through the doorway. Bree carried two bottles of chilled champagne and Jess had a tray of little puff pastries filled with goat cheese and caramelized onion.

"It was the best I could do on short notice. We always have these in the freezer," Jess said. "We can't have a party without some kind of fancy food."

"We need cake, too," Bree declared. "Gram's on her way with the chocolate cake she baked this afternoon."

The next thing Shanna knew, the O'Brien sisters had taken over the coffee area in the store and the champagne was flowing. They waited until Nell O'Brien arrived with the cake before Bree offered a toast to her big sister.

"I may have beat you to the altar, Abby, but I predict your future with Trace will be every bit as long and happy as I intend mine to be with Jake!"

"Hear, hear!" Jess said.

"Now then, I hear a date's finally been set," Nell said.

"The first Saturday in October," Abby said.

"That's less than two months away," Bree said, looking shaken. "What kind of wedding can we pull together on such short notice?"

"Exactly the kind that Trace and I want, small and intimate." She turned to Jess. "We'd like to have it at the inn. Will that work?"

Shanna started to protest that Laurie's wedding was that weekend, but Jess was already nodding. "It'll work."

"But—" Shanna began, only to have Jess shake her head.

"It will work," she repeated, then drew Shanna aside. "Laurie called earlier and canceled everything. I gather you haven't spoken to her."

"Not a word. Everything was still on track when she was here a couple of weeks ago." Upset by the news and even more by the fact that Laurie hadn't immediately called to share it with her, she murmured, "Excuse me. I need to call her."

"Please don't tell her I said anything. I wouldn't have, except you were right here when Abby picked that date."

"It's okay," Shanna assured her. "I won't say a word. I'll just check in with Laurie. I usually speak to her every few days. She won't think it's odd that I'm calling today."

Even as she spoke, her cell phone rang. When she saw Laurie's number on the caller ID, she excused herself again and went into the back room to take the call.

"You busy?" Laurie asked.

"Not at all. How are you?"

"Fine," Laurie said, though her voice trembled.

"You don't sound fine. What's going on?"

"Drew called off the wedding," she blurted. "He says he doesn't want to be married. He wants to go off to some island or something to find himself. Have you ever heard a more ridiculous excuse in all your life? Who does something like that? Why couldn't he just say he doesn't love me?"

"Maybe because he does love you," Shanna said carefully. "Sweetie, Drew was never as ready to get married as you were. He's a great guy, but he's immature. He proposed because he wanted you to be happy, but I don't think his heart was in it."

"Because he doesn't love me," Laurie insisted.

"No, because he needs time to make that kind of commitment. You may not be ready to hear this, but I think he's doing you a favor."

"He called off my beautiful wedding," Laurie said, sobbing.

"Did he call it off, or did he ask you to postpone it?" Shanna asked.

"Same difference."

"No, it's not."

"He doesn't want to marry me."

"He doesn't want to marry you *now*," Shanna stressed. She could almost hear Drew trying to explain that to Laurie and her not hearing a word of what he was saying. From the beginning Shanna had seen the panic in Drew's eyes when the subject of marriage had come up. She'd also seen something else, that he was wildly in love with Laurie and willing to take that leap just because it was what she wanted.

"Tell me what he said," she instructed Laurie. "His exact words."

"He said it was all happening too fast, that he needs to get a better job and start making decent money so he can give me the life I deserve. I told him I didn't care about any of that. I'm making good money."

"But he obviously wants to provide well for you. That matters to him."

Laurie dismissed her analysis. "Forget about it. I can't talk about it anymore. It's too upsetting. I want to hear about you."

"Everything's the same here. Why don't you come up this weekend and see for yourself? It'll do you good to get away for a couple of days. You can put all this in perspective, give Drew some breathing room."

"I won't be intruding?"

"Of course not. Why would you ask such a thing?"

"I saw how things were going with Kevin last time I was down there, despite all of my very wise advice."

"Maybe you should take a page out of that advice manual and put the brakes on your relationship with Drew."

"I'd say canceling the wedding pretty well screeched everything to a halt there," Laurie said wryly.

"How many times have you called him to try to change his mind?" Shanna inquired.

"I can't call him," she said, her tone glum. "I told you, he's gone off to find himself and he wouldn't tell me where."

Obviously Drew knew Laurie well. Going away and hiding the destination from her was the only way she would give him any peace. If her friend hadn't been so upset, Shanna would have smiled.

"Then you really do need to come here for a visit," she told Laurie. "I'll expect you first thing Saturday morning."

"You're sure? I'll probably be lousy company. I'll be all weepy and needy."

"I'll buy lots of tissues and ice cream," Shanna promised. "See you, okay?"

"Thanks, Shanna."

"No need to thank me. This is what friends do." As she disconnected the call, she heard laughter in the front room and walked back to hear Jess, Abby and Nell bantering about wedding plans. Bree was waiting on one of Shanna's customers. Seeing that she'd pitched in without needing to be asked, Shanna felt her heart fill with unexpected contentment. Laurie might always be her best friend, but she'd found friends here, too, people she could count on.

"Come here," Abby called out when she spotted her. "We've been debating about a color scheme for the wedding. Jess thinks fall colors, but I think that'll be too much with a bridal party of redheads."

Shanna studied the three sisters. "Not if you go with something like a soft, shimmering copper for the bridesmaids," she suggested eventually. "That would look great."

"Ooh, I love that," Jess said. "Come on, Abby, say yes. What do you care, anyway? You'll be wearing white."

"I've been married before," Abby protested.

"Oh, for heaven's sake, make it cream, then," Bree said as she joined them. "That first fiasco of yours hardly counts anyway."

"The twins will want to be flower girls," Abby said. "What color can they wear, if you're all wearing copper?" She turned to Shanna. "What do you think?"

"I'd say dark green, but that might be too harsh for them," Shanna suggested. "How about a lighter sage green? It's not very fall-like, but I'll bet it would look great on them, and it would be lovely with the copper."

"With pale pink roses embroidered on their dresses and real pink rose petals in their baskets," Nell suggested. "I can do the embroidery myself."

Abby looked around, seeking consensus, then gave a nod of satisfaction. "I think we have a plan."

"Aren't you going to call your mother and discuss all this with her?" Nell asked. "She's been asking to be involved for weeks now."

Abby flushed, either from the effects of the champagne or guilt. "Of course," she said defensively. "I want her to be a part of this. Last time things were difficult, since Mom and Dad were barely speaking, but everyone's getting along much better now. This will be a real family celebration."

"Hey, what was my wedding?" Bree demanded. "The whole family was there."

"You and Jake got married on the beach at sunset. It was a luau," Jess taunted.

Bree waved her hand with the wedding ring in the air. "Still married," she declared. "All nice and legal."

Shanna let the sound of the good-natured argument wash over her. She wanted this. She just had to be sure moments like this, feeling included with a big boisterous family, weren't the only reason she was slowly, but surely, falling in love with Kevin.

16

To Kevin's regret, Davy was suddenly struck by shyness when Georgia's parents arrived. Not that he expected his son to remember them, but Davy was normally so outgoing, he hadn't anticipated the way he held back at the sight of these two virtual strangers. Merely telling him they were his grandparents wasn't meaningful enough to forge an immediate bond. He needed to be around them, to get to know them.

Georgia's dad seemed to understand, giving Davy time and space to adjust, but clearly emotional, Martha immediately tried to pick him up. Davy screamed and reached for Kevin, tears tracking down his cheeks.

"Daddy," he whimpered, arms out. "Want Daddy."

Martha, looking shaken, handed him over.

"I'm sorry," Kevin apologized. "It's been a long time since he's seen you. He was just a baby."

"Of course he was," John said, putting a comforting arm around his wife's shoulders. "Don't worry about it. That's why this visit means so much. We want to strengthen that bond, make sure Davy knows his mother's family."

When they left the airport, Martha sat in the back next to Davy's car seat. More cautious now, she reached in her carry-on bag and extracted a small, flat, brightly wrapped package with an elaborate bow. "Davy, this is for you, from your Grandpa and me."

Davy's tears had dried, but he still looked uncertain. "Me?"

She nodded. "Want me to help you unwrap it?"

"I do," Davy said, reaching for it eagerly. Kevin watched in the rearview mirror as he ripped at the ribbon unsuccessfully, his frustration obviously mounting.

"Hey, buddy," Kevin called to him in an attempt to forestall a full-blown tantrum. He'd learned the hard way not to bother with ribbon on Davy's packages. The paper was about the most his little hands could manage. "Why don't you let Grandma Martha help? She can take the ribbon off for you."

"No," Davy said emphatically, waving off Martha's eager hands.

She sat back, deflated.

Kevin apologized again. "He missed his nap to come to the airport," he told them. "I'm sure once he's rested, things will be better."

"Of course they will," John agreed.

Just then the package sailed over the front seat and hit the dashboard. Kevin heard the crack of glass, then a shocked gasp from Martha, which immediately set off a bout of noisy sobs from Davy.

What on earth? Kevin thought in dismay. Had Martha actually given a two-year-old something with glass in it? He had to bite his tongue. Not that he had to say anything, because his former father-in-law turned on his wife.

"What were you thinking, giving a child his age something breakable?" he demanded as he picked up the now-bent and broken package. Fortunately the shattered glass was contained inside the wrapping paper.

Martha sniffed. "It's a picture of his mother when she was a little girl," she whispered. "I wanted him to have it."

There was no mistaking the anguish in her voice. Beside her, Davy continued to cry quietly, caught up in all the emotion swirling around him that he couldn't possibly understand.

Kevin stepped in. "Davy, it's okay," he soothed. "We know you didn't mean to break the present. Martha, he'll love it. I'll have the picture put into a new frame. I'll put it on the dresser in his room next to the other photo he has of Georgia. It's up high so he can't break it, but we look at it every night before he goes to sleep and I tell him about his mom and how beautiful and brave she was."

Martha's eyes brightened. "Really?"

"I'll show you. It's our wedding picture. Davy's been looking at it since he was a baby when Georgia first went back to Iraq. He knows it's his mommy. I won't let him forget about her. I promise."

"Oh, Kevin, thank you for that," she said, reaching over the seat to give his shoulder a squeeze. "I've been so worried he wouldn't know anything about his mother. He was so young when she died. He can't have any memories of her."

"I told you there was nothing to worry about," her husband said. "Kevin's an honorable man. He's not going to let his son forget Georgia."

"Absolutely not," Kevin reassured them both.

An hour later, he was relieved to be making the final turn into Chesapeake Shores. He was also glad that he'd made reservations for the Davises at the inn. Something told him that the stress of the drive was nothing compared to what it would have been having them under the same roof. Watching Martha's painful attempts to win over Davy only to be rebuffed had been almost more than he could bear. In some ways John's stoic acceptance of Davy's behavior had been even harder to watch.

Somehow over the next few days, Kevin had to do everything in his power to try to bridge that gap, or it would wind up being one more thing he'd feel guilty about.

Shanna knew that Kevin's former in-laws were visiting for the weekend, but she hadn't expected him to bring them by the store. She was stunned when she looked up and saw them on the sidewalk outside, Davy already waving at her and wriggling to get down from his grandfather's arms.

As soon as Kevin opened the door, Davy bounded straight to her. By the time the others entered, he was already dragging her in the direction of the children's books.

"Story," he commanded.

"In one minute," Shanna promised, turning to greet the older couple who were staring at her with undisguised dismay. "Hi, I'm Shanna Carlyle. I'm a friend of Davy's." Since Kevin had apparently been struck dumb by the awkwardness of the situation, she had to feel her way. "You must be Davy's grandparents."

"Yes," the woman said. "I'm Martha Davis and this is my husband, John. We've come from Texas to spend some time with Davy."

"Well, Davy's a big fan of books. I'm sure you've already figured that out."

"He does love his bedtime stories," the tall, distinguished-looking man agreed, giving her a warm smile, though his wife continued to regard Shanna with displeasure. "That's why we thought we'd buy him a book today."

His wife grudgingly added, "You have a very nice shop. I can see why Davy would enjoy coming here."

"Thank you. I have a large clientele of children, who fortunately drag along their parents."

"Not that I have to be dragged," Kevin said, finally finding his voice. "Shanna's been amazing with Davy. He adores her."

Davy backed up the claim by tugging on her hand and again demanding a story.

"Excuse me," Shanna said to them before hunkering down to help Davy select a picture book. His grandfather joined them.

"Truck, Grampa," he said excitedly, pointing to the book he'd chosen.

"I think you have this book at home," his grandfather said.

Davy nodded. "Like trucks."

Mr. Davis chuckled. "Yes, I know you like trucks." He smiled at Shanna. "His room is filled with them."

"I know. I've seen it," she said without thinking, then winced when she saw his smile fade. She scrambled for an explanation that wouldn't link her to Kevin. "Kevin's sister Jess invited me over one Sunday. Davy immediately insisted on a story."

"I see," he said.

Behind them, she could hear Mrs. Davis questioning Kevin. "How often do you bring him here?" she asked, a vague hint of disapproval in her tone. "Children shouldn't be overly indulged."

"Not even when it comes to books?" Kevin asked. "Seems to me that's an interest that should be encouraged."

"Well, of course," she said, clearly flustered.

It was evident to Shanna that her objection wasn't to the books, but to the bookseller.

Ignoring the adults, she settled in an overstuffed chair with Davy snuggled beside her and opened the book he'd chosen. As Davy pointed at the pictures, she began to read.

Laurie chose that moment to wander in from the back room. She took in the cozy scene before her gaze finally landed on Kevin.

"I was wondering when you'd be popping in," she said, crossing the room to give him a warm hug. "Nice to see you again."

Shanna saw Kevin's discomfort increase as he introduced Laurie to Georgia's parents.

"Do you work here, too?" Martha asked.

"No, I'm just visiting for the weekend," Laurie said. "I live outside of Philadelphia."

"But you must come here often, if you know Kevin."

"I've only visited a few times since Shanna opened the store," Laurie said, either unaware of the tension in the room or deliberately choosing to fuel it for some reason. "But Kevin's usually around."

Martha's frown deepened. "I see." She turned to Kevin. "I think we should get back to the inn. I'm not feeling well. It must have been something I ate."

Or saw, Shanna thought, almost feeling sorry for her. She'd come here to reconnect with her daughter's child, only to find him bonding with another woman. There might be nothing wrong with Kevin and Davy forming new attachments, but it had to hurt.

"I'll take you back now," Kevin said at once. "Come on, Davy. Let's go."

"No!" Davy screamed, verging on a tantrum. "No go!"

"Leave him and come back for him," Laurie suggested,

surprising Shanna. "I'll keep an eye on him if the store gets busy."

Martha turned pale. Kevin looked torn, but Davy was clinging tightly to Shanna, so he relented, probably to avoid causing a scene.

"I'll be back in twenty minutes," he promised as his in-laws walked outside without saying another word. His gaze caught Shanna's. "I'm sorry. I shouldn't have brought them in here."

"It's fine," she told him, meaning it. It had been awkward, not disastrous.

As soon as he'd gone, Laurie sat down in a chair across from Davy and Shanna. "Well, that felt familiar," she declared pointedly.

Shanna knew she was referring to the way the Hamiltons had always treated Shanna—as an unwelcome interloper.

"Cut them some slack," she told Laurie. "Their daughter died. They probably jumped to the conclusion that I'm trying to replace her."

Laurie gave her a wry look, then nodded toward Davy who was contentedly sucking his thumb and leaning against Shanna as he paged through the book in her lap. "Aren't you?"

"Of course not," Shanna said at once, though even as she said the words, she knew they weren't entirely true. She *was* growing attached to Davy and to his father. The lie fell on deaf ears, anyway, because it was evident that Laurie didn't believe her.

Fortunately, a customer came in before Laurie could call her on the lie. Laurie immediately crossed over and took Shanna's place next to Davy. "Hey, buddy, how about I fill in and finish this story for you? It sounds like a good one."

"Good story," Davy confirmed, calmly accepting the change in readers.

After the customer had selected a couple of books and paid, Shanna remained at the register, thinking about the earlier scene with Kevin's former in-laws. She could hardly blame Martha Davis for reacting as she had. What she didn't understand was why on earth Kevin had brought them in here in the first place. He had to know they'd react badly.

A few minutes later, when Kevin returned, he glanced over at Davy to make sure the child was settled with Laurie, then crossed straight to Shanna.

"Is Mrs. Davis okay?" Shanna asked him.

"I don't think she was sick," he said. "She just found meeting you to be upsetting. All the way back to the inn, she kept telling me I was dishonoring her daughter's memory by moving on so quickly." He met her gaze, misery in his eyes. "Maybe she's right."

"Okay, hold on a minute," Shanna said, angry at the woman for trying to make Kevin feel guilty. "First of all, it's not as if you and I are having some wild fling. And second, there would be nothing wrong with it if we were. It's tragic that you lost your wife and they lost their daughter, but it was almost eighteen months ago, isn't that right? You get to move on, Kevin, whether it's with me or anyone else. It's wrong of them to try to stop you."

His lips curved slightly at her heated response. "Remind me not to get on your bad side. You get a little ferocious when you're defending people."

"Yes, I do," she said, thinking of how hard she'd fought to protect Henry from his father. She'd had more than one fairly volatile confrontation, not only with Greg, but with his parents, trying to make them see how awful the situation was for a sensitive little boy. She'd even battled with Greg's lawyer and the judge. She'd known the odds were against her gaining custody, so all of it had been to no avail, but that hadn't stopped her from trying.

She studied him curiously. "You had to know it wasn't going to go well, bringing them in here. Why did you?"

"Davy kept talking about books, so Martha insisted they come here to buy one for him. I couldn't think of any way to talk her out of it."

"I thought she disapproved of indulging him," Shanna said. "You could have used that argument."

Kevin grinned. "That one only came up after she'd gotten a glimpse of you."

She let it go. "Aside from this afternoon, how's the visit been going?"

He shrugged. "I think Martha was expecting too much from it. Davy's still a bit standoffish around her, because she's trying too hard. He's warming up to Georgia's dad, though."

"I could see that," Shanna said. "It will get better with Martha, too."

"I hope so," he said. "That's what I keep telling them, anyway. I do have a plan for trying to improve the situation. We'll try to schedule a few visits closer together, so Davy can get used to them being around."

"That makes sense," she told him. Unfortunately, she could also see the negative side of the plan. Kevin would be bound more tightly to them, as well, and clearly Mrs. Davis already knew how to play on his guilt to get her own way. Would he be able to hold his own against that? She hoped so, for his sake. She didn't want him tied forever to a memory.

"They want to take Davy back to Texas sometime for

an extended visit," Kevin continued, "but I refused to do that until after he really gets to know them. Otherwise it will be a disaster. I don't want that for any of them. I'll take him down there for a weekend in a couple of months."

"They leave on Monday?"

He nodded. "I'll drop them at the airport when I go up to work. They have an early-morning flight." He hesitated, then asked abruptly, "Want to have dinner with me Monday night? We can go to Brady's. I owe you, after this."

Taken aback by the invitation, she said, "You don't owe me anything."

"I think I do," he insisted. "Please."

"Okay, then, dinner would be nice."

His expression brightened. "Great. Now I'd better get Davy and head home. They're coming over this evening for a barbecue. I'd invite you and Laurie, but it would only make matters worse." His gaze pleaded for understanding. "Just so you know, if our relationship—well, if we were committed, I wouldn't try to hide it, not even from Georgia's parents."

"I understand," she said, and she did.

"I wish this were less complicated."

She smiled reassuringly. "I understand that, too."

"I'll see you Monday, then. Shall I pick you up here at six?"

"I'm off on Monday, so I'll be upstairs in the apartment."

"Right. I'd forgotten."

Laurie appeared then with a sleeping Davy in her arms. She held him out to Kevin. "He's a great kid."

Kevin grinned. "Thanks. And thanks, too, for keeping an eye on him. Enjoy the rest of your visit."

Laurie waited until he'd left, then turned to Shanna. "You have a date with him on Monday?"

She nodded.

"Are you crazy?"

Shanna sighed. "More than likely."

Up until now she'd been able to maintain the illusion that they were just friends, but it was hard to do that once a man had actually asked for a date. This wasn't like taking a break and grabbing lunch at Sally's or Panini Bistro. It wasn't anything like having Kevin pick up a sandwich and bring it by. This was dinner, in a restaurant, with a man capable of making her toes curl with a single touch. That he'd asked her right after facing down his former in-laws over Shanna's role in his life made the date seem even more significant.

She was in such trouble, she thought, barely containing a sigh. More worrisome was the fact that increasingly she found she didn't care what kind of disasters might lie ahead.

"You and Shanna seem to be spending a lot of time together," Jess noted Saturday night, with most of the family except for Mick seated at the table. Unfortunately Georgia's watchful parents, who weren't used to the O'Brien family dynamics and penchant for teasing, were there, as well.

Kevin glowered at his youngest sister. "Are you trying to stir up trouble?" he inquired in an undertone, casting a pointed look toward his former in-laws.

Jess immediately backed down, but Bree was less discreet. She turned to Martha and John. "You met Shanna today. Isn't she great?"

"She seemed very nice," Martha said stiffly. She turned

to Kevin. "I know I said this earlier, but don't you think it's a little soon for you to be dating anyone?" She glanced around the table then, seemingly looking for backup, but the others remained silent.

"Shanna and I aren't actually dating," he said emphatically, mostly to avoid another scene in which Martha felt compelled to express her opinion about his loyalty to his late wife or to take off in a huff. "We just see each other from time to time."

Bree snorted indelicately. "From time to time? Ha. Only if you consider most weekday afternoons and Saturdays to be 'from time to time.'"

"Leave your brother alone," Gram said. "It's nice that he's seeing someone." She regarded Georgia's parents with sympathy. "It doesn't mean Georgia didn't mean a great deal to him. She made him very happy."

And very unhappy, Kevin thought to himself. That was what no one here understood, and he could hardly tell them.

Gram continued, "He's a young man. He needs to move on, and Davy needs a mother. Not a replacement for Georgia, of course, but someone to bring a mother's touch into his life."

Kevin groaned as the color washed out of Martha's face.

"Excuse me," she said, and left the room.

John sighed. "I'd better go check on her."

After they were gone, Kevin scowled at his family. "Can't you see that this topic is making them uncomfortable? It's not doing much for my mood, either. Drop it. It's completely inappropriate to be discussing me dating in front of Georgia's folks."

"Do you suppose he's so cranky because Shanna's

holding him at arm's length?" Jess speculated, ignoring his warning. "Going without sex can do that to a person."

"Not a topic for the dinner table," Gram said adamantly, giving Jess a chiding look.

"To say nothing of the fact that it's so not your business!" Kevin retorted.

The problem was, Jess was right. It was increasingly evident that he wanted Shanna, not as a friend, which was the way it had started, but as a woman. He wanted the kissing, the sex, all of it. He thought she did, too. She certainly hadn't held back on the couple of occasions when he'd kissed her.

"Well, despite what Martha said, I think you should just ask Shanna out and get on with it," Jess declared.

"Me, too," Bree chimed in, followed by consensus from Abby.

"Leave it alone, all of you," he ordered, his scowl fierce. "Especially tonight." If they didn't quit, he'd be the next one bolting from the room.

Across from him Trace and Jake grinned sympathetically, but all three of his sisters merely laughed. He wondered what they'd have to say if they knew about his plans for Monday evening. On some level, he knew that invitation had been about a whole lot more than dinner. He wondered if Shanna had known that, too.

"What's going on between you and my brother?" Bree asked Shanna Monday morning after tracking her down in her apartment and luring her to Sally's for coffee. "Is it finally getting serious?"

Shanna frowned. "Serious? After one kiss?" Okay, it had been two, but Bree certainly didn't need to know that.

Bree chuckled. "You are both so pitiful. Kevin was

trying to tap-dance around answering our questions at dinner on Saturday, and I have to tell you he wasn't very good at it."

Shanna recalled the family occasion was to include Georgia's parents. "You brought this up while the Davises were around?" she asked incredulously.

Bree blushed. "Yes, well, that was a little awkward. Martha bolted with John on her heels."

"Who could blame them? What were you thinking?"

"Well, Jess started it, and she almost never thinks before she talks," she said, then shrugged, her expression sheepish. "Then Abby and I couldn't resist chiming in. I have to admit, it was mostly me. Kevin looked so flustered, I couldn't help myself."

Shanna couldn't even imagine how awkward the scene must have been. "Kevin must have flipped out."

"He wasn't happy," Bree admitted. "And Gram got a little ticked that we brought up sex, or rather Kevin's lack of it, at the dinner table."

Shanna groaned. "Maybe this fantasy I have about a big family is all wrong. It sounds awful."

"I suppose that depends on which side of the teasing you're on," Bree said thoughtfully. "Anyway, what I want to know is, when are the two of you going to admit that you're falling for each other?"

"I can't speak for him, but I'm…" She stopped because she couldn't utter a complete lie. She *was* falling in love with Kevin. She just wasn't convinced he was ready for a real relationship. There was a good chance he was with her because she was undemanding and filled the lonely hours in his life.

"You're what?" Bree prodded, refusing to let the topic die. "You care about him, don't you?"

"Well, of course. He's a great guy. He's intelligent, thoughtful, protective, and he's a wonderful dad."

"He's been laughing more lately," Bree commented, her expression pensive. "I think that's because of you. Until recently he'd been pretty grim."

"Can you blame him? He lost a woman who meant everything to him."

Bree shook her head. "He hardly knew her," she said. "I probably shouldn't say this, but you deserve to have another perspective. I think it's guilt, not grief, that he's been feeling all these months. I'm more convinced of that than ever now that Georgia's mom and dad have been here."

Shanna didn't even try to hide her shock. "What on earth do you mean?"

Bree regarded her hesitantly. "He hasn't told you the whole story?"

Shanna shook her head. "He almost never mentions Georgia at all."

"Okay, I probably shouldn't be the one telling you this, but since he hasn't, I will. They met in Iraq."

"I knew that much," Shanna said.

"Well, under those conditions, my impression is that everything's intensified. Emotions run high. People reach out to someone who's there. Georgia was there. The first time they were on leave, they got married, in the middle of the Baltimore airport, no less."

"They must have been very anxious to get married," Shanna said, trying to imagine such a setting for a wedding.

"The only thing worse, in my opinion, would be one of those wedding-a-minute chapels in Las Vegas," Bree said. "Anyway, by the time they came home from their tour of duty, she was pregnant with Davy. Kevin was discharged not long after, but Georgia stayed in the army. They spent a few weeks here before they moved to northern Virginia. Kevin took a job as a paramedic. Georgia was assigned to Fort Belvoir until she had the baby. I think things were okay then. Normal, if you know what I mean. They actually seemed happy."

Shanna nodded.

"When Georgia's orders came to go back to Iraq, with an infant in the house she could have said no, but she refused. They had a huge fight over it, which I know about because she was totally upset when she called me afterward. I told her I agreed with Kevin." She shrugged. "Didn't matter. She was determined to go. If you ask me, that was the beginning of the end of the marriage. Oh, he made a big show around us of accepting it. He claimed he understood, that he admired her for wanting to do her duty."

"He probably did," Shanna said. "At least on some level."

Bree shook her head. "I don't think so. I think he knew the marriage was already over. Our mom left us when she and Dad divorced. Jess was still little, I was just twelve and the others were in their teens, but it had a huge impact. Kevin has a real thing about mothers belonging with their kids. He won't admit that, not with Georgia gone and practically turned into a martyr in his head, but that's the truth. I don't think he would have stayed with her after she chose her job over Davy."

Bree's information gave Shanna a new perspective on Kevin, one that scared her. What would he think when he found out that she'd walked away from a husband and a child, albeit a stepson to whom she'd had no legal rights?

Would Kevin judge her for what she'd done? If he did, his opinion certainly wouldn't be any harsher than what she thought of herself. When it came to guilt, she could match him, maybe even top him. What she viewed as her own cowardice for not staying with Greg for Henry's sake was one of the reasons she'd been keeping Kevin at arm's length. She wasn't convinced she deserved another chance to have a family, especially a family that so closely resembled the one she'd fled.

She was so lost in the troubling thoughts that she almost forgot about Bree's presence.

"Shanna, are you okay? You turned pale. Did I say something to upset you?"

"It's nothing, really," she insisted. "I do have to go, though. I have a million things to do today, since it's my only day off."

Bree covered her hand. "Are you sure you aren't running off because of me and my big mouth? If I upset you, I'm sorry."

"No, you just gave me some information I needed to have," she said.

Information, she thought bleakly, *that could change everything.*

17

Shanna's day only got worse. As she got back to her apartment, her cell phone, which she'd left on the kitchen counter, was ringing. Checking caller ID, she saw it was Henry.

"Hey, sweetie, how are you?" she said.

He didn't reply, but the sound of his weeping was unmistakable. Her stomach sank.

"Henry, what's wrong? Sweetie, talk to me."

"Daddy's going away," he said at last. "For a long time."

"I don't understand."

He said something more, but he was crying so hard she couldn't make out the words.

"Is Greta there? Can I please speak to her?"

The nanny came on the line, clearly almost as upset as Henry. "The ambulance is here," she told Shanna. "Mr. Hamilton, he was drinking. He took some pills. It was an accident, it had to be, but he was unconscious when the maid found him."

"Does Henry know all this?"

"Only that they're taking his dad to the hospital. Mrs. Hamilton is here now. She insisted Mr. Hamilton's doctor be called before she'd allow the paramedics to take him.

They're talking about him going straight to rehab when he leaves the hospital. Henry overheard them before I could get him out of the room."

"No wonder he's so upset. He probably doesn't understand why his dad has to go away. Do you have any idea what will happen with Henry? Has anyone thought about that?"

"I'm to stay here, of course. Mrs. Hamilton said she'd come back later, after she's been to the hospital to get her son settled, and we could discuss what would happen next."

"I'll drive up," Shanna offered.

"I don't think that's a good idea," Greta said, lowering her voice. "Henry mentioned you and Mrs. Hamilton threw a fit, said you were no longer a part of this family and he was not to even think about calling you."

Shanna bit back a curse at the woman's lack of consideration for a scared little boy. She should be reaching out to anyone willing or able to help him. "I'll speak to her," she told Greta. "Let me talk to Henry again."

"He's right here," Greta said, handing over the phone.

"Mommy?" he whispered tentatively, sounding slightly more composed.

"I'm here. I know things must be really scary there right now, but it's going to be okay. You have Greta with you, and your grandmother will make sure nothing bad happens to your dad."

"He's going in the ambulance," he said, his voice catch ing. "He never went in an ambulance before. Do you think he's afraid?"

"No, your dad's very brave. And he's going to the hospital so they can make him well again."

"Mommy, can I stay with you till he's better?"

Shanna closed her eyes against the wave of longing

washing through her. She couldn't bear it when she heard that wistful note in Henry's voice. "No, honey, but you can call me any time you're scared, day or night, okay? Greta will make sure of it."

"I guess," he said, sounding resigned.

"I love you."

"Bye," he said, hanging up on the words he no longer trusted.

Shanna stared at the silent phone, then immediately placed a call to Greg's mother, bracing herself for the chilly greeting she was likely to receive.

"This isn't a good time," Loretta Hamilton snapped.

"Make it a good time," Shanna said. "I know what's happened with Greg and I'm sorry. I truly am. But right now I want to know what you're going to do about Henry."

"That is none of your concern," she said emphatically. "The nanny shouldn't have called you and dragged you into the middle of anything going on here. I'll fire her for sharing this family's business with an outsider."

"I'm hardly an outsider. Besides, she didn't call me. Henry did. Are you going to kick *him* out, because he defied you?"

The comment was greeted by a long pause. "What do you want?" Loretta asked eventually. The chill in her voice had been replaced by weariness.

How many times must she have been through something like this with Greg? Shanna wondered, feeling a surge of sympathy. More times than Shanna had, certainly. It must be devastating for a mother to see her grown son behave in such a self-destructive way.

"I want to help," she said simply. "It's all I've ever wanted."

"Well, there's nothing you can do except make a bad situation worse," Mrs. Hamilton said.

"Greg's going to be okay, isn't he?"

Mrs. Hamilton's bravado slipped. "I really don't know anymore," she said in a rare display of uncertainty. "This time…" Her voice trailed off. "I just don't know."

"Surely this incident will scare some sense into him," Shanna said. "Maybe it will keep him in rehab. Maybe he'll finally want to beat his addiction to alcohol."

"I hope so," his mother said without much conviction.

"I know you don't believe this, but so do I," Shanna told her. "Call me if there's anything I can do for Henry or for you. I mean that."

She sensed Mrs. Hamilton hesitating and waited.

"I know I tried to demonize you when we went to court," she admitted to Shanna. "It was the only way to keep Henry where I thought he belonged. I'm sorry for that. You had no idea what you were getting into when you married my son. I saw the stars in your eyes, and I knew that would never last. I should have warned you. Instead, I kept silent, praying that things would turn out differently after all. Worse, I blamed you when things turned out exactly as I'd anticipated they would."

"I hated what you did, what you all did, but I understood," Shanna told her. "You were fighting for your son. I would probably have done the same. Now, though, maybe you should fight for what's best for Henry."

"Goodbye, Shanna." Once again, her tone was stiff and forbidding.

"Goodbye," she said, wondering if the call would make things better for Henry or if she'd only made a bad situation worse.

Kevin arrived to find Shanna looking distracted and unhappy. Her hair was mussed, she wore no makeup, and it was evident she'd forgotten all about their date. His apparently unexpected arrival would normally have flustered her, but she didn't seem to care.

"Okay, tell me what's happened," he said, walking into her apartment. "Obviously you've had a bad day."

The last time he'd seen her like this, she'd received a phone call she refused to discuss. He wondered if there'd been another one. When she didn't reply to his inquiry, he urged her toward a chair.

"Sit down and tell me what's going on," he said.

She met his gaze with troubled eyes. "I forgot we were going out."

"No problem, though it is a huge blow to my ego," he said dryly. "Maybe if I knew why, I'd feel better about it."

"I can't…" She shook her head.

"Have my sisters been over here bugging you?" It would be just like them.

"I saw Bree this morning for coffee, but she wasn't bugging me."

An even more distressing thought came to mind. "Georgia's mother didn't call you, did she?"

She blinked at that. "No, why would she?"

"To warn you away from me."

Her lips curved slightly. "She couldn't scare me. Believe me, I've known much scarier women."

"Did you happen to run across one of them earlier today?" he asked, feeling his way.

She nodded. "Something like that."

"Want to talk about it?"

"No, but thanks. I really am sorry I forgot about dinner. We could still go. It won't take me long to shower and change, though I can't promise I'll be very good company."

"Your company couldn't possibly be bad, but something tells me you're in no mood to go out. Why don't I pick up something and bring it back here? Thai, maybe? Italian? Whatever you feel like."

She shrugged indifferently. "I'm really not hungry."

"A huge tub of ice cream," he suggested, desperate for something to put a smile on her face.

Her lips twitched. "Not terribly nutritious."

"I think the situation calls for decadent. How about it?"

"A banana split," she suggested. "At least there's fruit in that."

"Can't get much more healthy than a banana split," he agreed.

She almost smiled at that, but it faltered before it could fully form. "I'll walk with you and we can eat them by the beach," she said. "Getting out of this apartment will be good for me."

"Sounds perfect," he said at once, relieved to have her show an interest in something, even if it was only ice cream.

Outside the air was hot and sticky, but there was a faint suggestion of a breeze as they neared the water. Kevin ordered their banana splits with extra hot fudge as she'd requested, then carried them to a bench along the beach. A breeze stirred and kept the mosquitoes away. It even cooled the humid air slightly. To his relief, Shanna dug into her ice cream with enthusiasm.

"This is the first thing I've had to eat since early this morning," she admitted. "I'm starving."

"Nothing like hot fudge sauce to stir the appetite," he said.

"It's comforting," she said, licking the spoon with her eyes closed.

Kevin's blood heated at the rapturous expression on her face as her pink tongue stroked the plastic spoon. Lucky spoon! Who knew that eating a banana split would turn out to be an erotic experience? He shifted, trying to hide his immediate arousal. Given her distress, it was a fine time for him to start thinking about sex.

"I had a call earlier today," she said, startling him. "They took my ex-husband to the hospital. He'd been drunk and he took too many pills. Sleeping pills, I guess, though I'm not sure. They're calling it an accidental overdose."

"I'm sorry," Kevin said, studying her face, trying to discern if this was simply concern for a man she'd once loved or more. Was she still in love with him? "He'll be okay?"

"I hope so."

"Hearing about that must have been upsetting."

She looked at him, her expression bleak. "It wasn't unexpected," she said. "It was only a matter of time before something like this happened."

"Then his problem with alcohol isn't something new?"

She shook her head.

"And that's why you left him?"

She nodded. "I couldn't do anything to help. In fact, most of the time, it seemed I was only making things worse."

Kevin had known a few Iraq veterans who'd turned to alcohol to deal with their memories. He knew that recovery wasn't always easy, not for them or those who loved them. "People with problems like that can't be helped until they're ready."

"His mother's hoping this will scare him so badly that he'll complete rehab this time."

"He's been before?"

"More times than I knew about when I married him," she admitted. "How stupid was I? I completely missed all the signs that he had a problem. I just thought he was a social drinker who overindulged occasionally. I had no idea how bad it was. Talk about naive!"

"Sometimes people with drinking problems are very adept at hiding them."

"Greg certainly was."

"I'm sorry."

She met his gaze, surprise in her eyes. "You really mean that, don't you?"

"It affects you, so of course I'm sorry," he said.

She lifted her hand and touched his cheek. "You really are amazing."

"Hardly," he said.

She gave him a wry look. "Bree told me what happened at dinner Saturday night," she said, shifting gears. "I feel bad for Georgia's parents. Your sisters should have realized they didn't need to hear that you might be seeing someone else."

"They didn't mean any harm," he said. "You know how they are. They like to tease, and this was the first opportunity they'd had to gang up on me since news of the kiss broke. I'm just glad Mick wasn't there to make things worse. He'd probably have given them a detailed eyewitness account."

Shanna groaned at the image that stirred. "Surely he wouldn't have!"

Kevin chuckled at her reaction. "Don't you know him well enough by now to realize that he absolutely would have?"

"Why wasn't he there?"

"He's in New York trying to make peace with my

mother. He let her down a couple of weeks ago, and she's making him jump through hoops to make amends." He grinned. "I have to say I'm finding it more amusing than I thought I would."

She gave him a thoughtful look. "Bree mentioned something about how tough it was on all of you when your mother and father split up and she left."

"Yeah, it was bad," he said, though without the bitterness that once would have been in his voice. He was finally starting to realize that there were two sides to every story, even that one. "Recently, though, I've started seeing my mother's side of things."

"You sided with your dad when she left?"

He nodded. "It was a complicated situation, but I saw it in black-and-white. He stayed. That made him right. She left. Therefore she was the bad guy. Turns out it wasn't that clear-cut."

"Relationships are seldom easy. And it's even harder for an outsider to know what's really going on."

Kevin heard an odd note in her voice, a hint that she was speaking from experience. "Did people judge you for leaving your husband?"

"Some did," she said. "Partly because it was easier than blaming him. I was the nobody who'd married into a prominent family. And partly because we worked so hard to keep anyone else from knowing the truth about how bad Greg's drinking was. Therefore if the marriage was over in less than a year, it had to be my fault. I must have been some gold-digger, eager for a quickie divorce and a lot of alimony. There was even an item in one local paper suggesting that I'd get a bundle because of a prenuptial agreement, which we never had. I could hardly take out an ad in the paper to say I'd taken nothing from him."

"That must have been tough."

She acknowledged it with a nod and a change of subject. "How did things go with the job today?"

Kevin wanted to pursue the discussion of her marriage, but she was regarding him with an expression that begged him to move on.

"The job is great," he said. All day he'd been thinking about sharing this with her. It felt good to come home and have someone around who was interested in how his day had gone. "Uncle Thomas is even more amazing than I realized."

"Tell me," she said eagerly.

"Today I went with him to speak to a couple of Maryland legislators. Tomorrow he has an appointment with the governor, and I'm going along for that, too. Obviously I don't have much to contribute, but he wants me to be up to speed on all these talks before we start a real push for stronger bay cleanup efforts."

"New legislation?"

"No, just stricter enforcement of the Chesapeake Bay Act that's already on the books. It's not just a problem in Maryland, but in all of the states whose waters flow into the bay. I'm not sure if it's a lack of investigators to follow up on violations or a lack of will. Either way, we need to get the states to make this a priority."

She grinned as he talked. "This is the happiest I've seen you since we met," she said. "You're really excited about this, aren't you?"

"It's fantastic," he said. "It's the kind of work that can make a real difference."

"I'm so happy for you." She squeezed his hand. "I can't wait to do my part by holding that fund-raiser at the store. I'm getting so many inquiries about it, I'm afraid it's going to be standing room only that night."

"You could always move it to the inn," he suggested. "Or just count on spilling out into the square. You might have to get a permit for that, but I don't think it would be a problem. Want me to check? I know my uncle would be open to expanding the event. There's nothing he likes more than speaking to a huge crowd about his passion for the bay."

"I love that idea," Shanna said eagerly. "We'd have to have a sound system of some kind in the gazebo on the green, but he could speak from there. People could sit in lawn chairs or on blankets. I'd set up a table to sell books. I'd have to get someone to work in the store, but I could handle the sales outside." Her eyes lit up. "Someone from your group could be there to sign people up for memberships and to take donations."

"I'd do that," Kevin volunteered, catching her enthusiasm.

"This is going to be amazing," she said. She jumped up. "I need to start working on this right now."

"It's after working hours for most people," Kevin reminded her. "There's not much you can accomplish tonight."

"I can make lists, so I'll be set to go first thing in the morning."

He met her gaze. "We're on a date, remember?"

She looked at him, then finally sat back with a sheepish grin. "I got carried away."

He laughed. "I love seeing you like that, but it's hell on my ego to have you so eager to toss me aside for making lists, especially such a short time after completely forgetting that we even had plans for tonight."

She chuckled. "I think your ego's probably just fine. It can withstand a few hits."

He sobered and he touched a finger to the dark smudges under her eyes that not even her excitement and humor could wipe away. "I'm really sorry you had such a tough day."

"I'm better now," she told him. "Thanks to you. The banana split was a good distraction. The idea for expanding the fund-raiser was even better."

"How about this?" he asked, leaning forward to claim her lips. The brief touch set off an inferno inside him. Under his fingertips, her skin heated, as well.

"Is this a good distraction?" he murmured, his breath mingling with hers.

She swallowed hard. "The best."

He met her gaze. "I want more, Shanna. My life's a mess and I can't make any promises about tomorrow, but I want you tonight."

She hesitated for so long, her gaze locked with his, that he thought she was trying to find the right words to refuse him. Instead, she stood up and held out her hand.

"I want you, too," she said simply.

Only as they made their way back toward Shanna's apartment did Kevin start to wonder if she truly wanted him, or if she simply wanted another guaranteed distraction from the news about her ex-husband. Worse, with her hand secure in his, he wasn't really sure it mattered. Right this second, all he cared about was how desperately he wanted her in his arms.

Shanna needed someone to hold her, someone who genuinely cared about her. She especially needed that tonight. Thinking about Greg and his problems and how that had spilled over to make her feel inadequate had been on her mind all day. She knew intellectually that she hadn't failed him, that he'd been troubled long before they'd even met. Still, deep in her heart, she believed there must have been something she could have done, *should* have done, to fix things for him and especially for Henry.

The solid feel of Kevin's hand wrapped around hers gave her a sense of security she hadn't felt in a while. He was a strong man, one she could lean on rather than have to prop up. For all of his grief over Georgia, Kevin had never lost sight of his responsibility to his son. She admired that strength of character more than she could say. It told her the kind of man he was, the kind of man she wanted in her life for the long haul.

When they walked into her darkened apartment, lit only by the soft glow of lights from the street and a bit of shimmering moonlight, a part of her wanted him to sweep her into his arms and make her forget everything else. Another part appreciated the care he was taking, the gentle touch of his fingers on her cheek, the soft caress as he stroked along the bare skin exposed by the neckline of her T-shirt. He was going slow, though his gaze was heated. He was giving her time to change her mind, maybe even to catch up with him.

When he sealed his mouth over hers again, his tongue teasing at her lips, then delving inside to taste, she felt the shock of the kiss melt everything in her. If she hadn't been leaning into him, her knees might very well have buckled.

"Bedroom," she whispered, wanting to get on with it, wanting to feel the length of him stretched out next to her…on top of her.

His hand stilled, almost to the tip of her breast, leaving her tingling and wanting more. His gaze sought hers. There was fire in the depths of his eyes and a need that surely matched her own. "You're sure?"

"Very," she said, leading the way.

Inside the room, though, she grew hesitant, remembering how often things with her ex-husband had gotten exactly this far, sometimes even further, before he lost interest or fell asleep. It had devastated her. Though rationally she'd known alcohol was to blame, she'd been unable to separate that from her own feelings of inadequacy.

"Shanna?" Kevin whispered, a question in his voice and in his eyes.

"It's okay," she insisted, reaching for the buttons on his shirt, rather than her own. She needed to push him past the point of no return, needed to touch and feel his arousal, to know that she could make him desire her in ways she'd begun to doubt herself capable of.

Apparently sensing something a little wild in her, guessing at the tension she was feeling, Kevin let her proceed at her own pace. She heard his breath quicken as her fingers touched his rock-hard abs, then slid lower. She undid the buckle on his belt, the catch on his pants, then slowly lowered the zipper, her knuckle grazing his arousal beneath the soft fabric of his briefs. He moaned then and stilled her hands.

"Enough, sweetheart. My turn," he said, easing off her T-shirt, then lowering his head to suck at her already hardened nipples through the lace of her pale peach bra.

He lifted her onto the bed, then deftly began removing the rest of her clothes before stripping away the last of his.

Shanna waited with bated breath for the moment when something would go wrong, but Kevin's touches became more intimate, his attention never flagging. Her blood was humming, her nerves straining, as he watched her with the kind of masculine appreciation she'd always yearned for.

"You can let go," he told her, stroking her until she

thought she'd fly apart, but she couldn't let go, didn't trust him or herself enough, because it could be over then.

"I want you," she murmured. "Please, Kevin. I need you with me."

He rose above her then, lifted her hips and fit himself to her, then moved slowly, confidently, until he filled her. The sensation was amazing. Too much. Yet not nearly enough. Her hips began to move. He met her, again and again, until at last she dared to let go, dared to believe in him and, finally, in herself, as wave after wave crashed over her, through him.

As the waves finally, inevitably, ebbed, she clung to him, not wanting to let go, not wanting the magical moment to end.

Then, after a bit, magically he stirred inside her and the wild ride started all over again. As they reached the peak and flew over the edge, Shanna's doubts about who she was as a woman fled. No matter what happened from this night on, she would never forget that Kevin had been the one to accomplish that, to give her back the self-confidence she'd thought gone forever.

18

It was three in the morning when Kevin finally awoke and glanced at the clock on Shanna's bedside table. He was immediately assailed by guilt. It was one of the few times ever he hadn't been at home to tuck Davy into bed, or at least to give him a good-night kiss.

Not that he was worried his son wasn't being well cared for. Gram would see to that. Davy'd already been half-asleep when Kevin had left the house, and he rarely woke up during the night. But what if this was the one night he had, and Kevin hadn't been there to comfort him? Even knowing that Gram was right next door wasn't reassuring.

Still, he couldn't regret what had happened here. Loving Shanna had been beyond his wildest expectations. He'd sensed some initial reserve in her that he hadn't understood. It was almost as if she'd been fighting off demons of some kind. If he hadn't known about her marriage, he might have wondered if she was a virgin, because of her hesitancy, then the deliberate nature of her actions. She'd seemed intent on moving forward as if it were a mission, rather than an anticipated joy.

Thinking back on it now, he had the feeling she'd been testing herself—or him—in some way. If she had, they'd both apparently passed, because the night had been filled with sensations and laughter and the kind of passion he hadn't expected to experience again for a long time. The connection between them had been deeper and more meaningful than he'd expected, as well.

What now, though? He'd made no promises, made that very clear, in fact. It was ironic then that he was the one who'd awakened wanting more. He'd never thought of this as a one-night stand, but right this second, he found himself wanting forever. That feeling scared the daylights out of him, especially with another wave of guilt arriving hard on its heels. He could almost hear his former mother-in-law's voice in his head, criticizing him for replacing Georgia in his life. She'd made the accusation often enough before she left that her words were burned into his memory.

He slipped out of Shanna's bed, hunted for his clothes and headed for the bathroom to dress. Not wanting to turn on a light and wake her, he left the door open to let in the glow from the streetlights. Standing there, he could watch her sleep, take in how beautiful she was with the sheet barely covering her, her hair tousled. The idea of joining her in that bed again was way too tempting. He turned away and quickly put on his clothes.

When he was dressed, he paused by the side of the bed, then leaned down and dropped a light kiss on her forehead. She stirred slightly.

"Kevin," she murmured.

"Go back to sleep, Shanna. It's still the middle of the night, but I have to get home, check on Davy and then take off for Annapolis."

"'kay," she mumbled and settled more snugly under the covers, her arms wrapped around a pillow instead of him.

He sighed, forcing himself to turn away and leave. If it was this hard to walk away now, after just one night, what was going to happen as time passed? He'd never been one for casual flings. Mick had instilled a strong sense of honor in his sons, made them understand not to take sex lightly.

Thinking back, Kevin wondered if perhaps that was why he'd raced into marriage with Georgia, because once they'd fallen into bed, he'd assumed that also meant they'd fallen in love. Only much, much later had he realized how wrong he'd been.

Too late, he told himself as he drove home. There was no going back and fixing that at this late date. All he could do was make sure he never made the same mistake a second time. He and Shanna were just getting to know each other on a whole new level. This time he wouldn't rush headlong into anything.

Which meant he needed to take an emotional step back from Shanna whether he wanted to or not. And if that meant staying out of her bed, where his resolve was bound to become a little murky, then so be it.

Mick took an early-morning flight from New York back to Baltimore. He had work to do on the plans for Bree's theater, which was about to start construction as soon as all the permits were approved. She'd do her first, trial-run production at the local high school this fall, then one more over the winter. The plan was to launch a full season in the new Chesapeake Shore Community Theater next summer.

As anxious as he was to get this project off the ground and completed for Bree and for the town, he regretted having to run off yet again and leave Megan. He was increasingly frustrated by her refusal to do the sensible thing and move back home, with or without a ring on her finger. He'd marry her or give her more time, whichever she preferred, but he wanted her close, back in all their lives.

Damn, the woman was stubborn! Even as he thought it, he acknowledged the irony with a grin. That contrariness made her a good match for him, though when they butted heads it definitely made life difficult. Neither one of them had the capacity to give an inch.

Because she was so much on his mind, he pulled out his cell phone as soon as he landed and called her at work.

"I miss you already," he told her. "Fly down here this weekend."

"Mick, that's only a couple of days away," she protested. "You were just here."

"And I can't get enough of you," he responded, then mustered all the arguments he thought might strike a chord. "Think about it, Meggie. You'll be able to look over the plans for the new community theater and talk 'em over with Bree, and you'll be able to get a fix on what's going on between Kevin and Shanna. Then there's the chance to spend time with Caitlyn, Carrie and Davy. Those three grandkids of ours are growing mighty fast. In the blink of an eye they'll be headed off to college and lives of their own."

She laughed. "You're a sneaky devil, Mick O'Brien. You know I can't resist spending time with our children and grandchildren, though I think we have a bit longer than the blink of an eye before the little ones head off to college."

"Push whichever button might work, that's what I always say," he told her. "Will you come?"

"I have to work Saturday morning," she began, then hesitated long enough to make him nervous. "But I'll fly down in the afternoon."

He breathed a sigh of relief. "Not soon enough, but I'll take it," he said at once. "Especially if it means you'll stay through Monday."

She waited a moment, most likely just to torture him, then said, "I can do that."

He chuckled. "Maybe I should have pushed for Tuesday."

"Then I'd have had to tell you no. Take your small victory and be happy," she said.

"I love you, Meggie."

"And I you. Just don't let it go to your head or start making assumptions."

"Not where it's heading," he said dryly, hoping his very physical reaction to her words wasn't evident to any passerby.

"Stop that kind of talk," she said, though she was chuckling. "I'll see you on Saturday."

"Let me know your flight and I'll pick you up," he told her.

"I can rent a car," she protested.

"And I can pick you up," he responded. "It'll give me extra time with you coming and going."

"You just like that I'll be at your mercy once I get to town," she chided.

"Now that you mention it, that is a wonderful bonus," he told her.

He ended the call with reluctance, then went to the parking garage, got his car and headed home. There was no telling what he'd find these days when he got there, and that was exactly the way he liked it. For a man his age, he was discovering he was fond of surprises, especially when it came to his family. It was a huge change from the days when he'd come home out of a sense of duty, his thoughts still on whatever project he'd left behind rather than on what was waiting for him at home. Now the opposite was true.

And recognizing that told him that perhaps he truly was ready for the kind of future that Megan deserved.

Shanna was in touch with Greta almost every day, though she didn't always speak to Henry. She understood that too much contact with the boy could wind up being counterproductive. She was no longer part of his life, not really, and she didn't want to upset or confuse him by acting as if she was. Still, she felt the need to know what was going on with Greg and that Henry was doing well.

Today when she called, Greta sounded subdued. "Mrs. Hamilton has decided Henry and I should move into her house. She says Henry's dad isn't likely to be back home for several months, assuming he stays in treatment the way the doctor's recommending."

"I suppose that makes sense," Shanna said, her heart sinking. The Hamilton home, with its heavy, dark drapes blocking out light, its valuable antiques and expensive breakables, was no place for a young, energetic boy.

Shanna had always suspected that Greg had been told no so often as a child, he'd openly rebelled as an adult and done every conceivable thing that had been forbidden to him earlier in his life. His house had been light and airy with virtually nothing sitting on tables. In fact, the environment had been almost sterile, but he'd encouraged Henry to play in any room he chose. And he rarely, if ever, told him he couldn't do something. With another child, the result could have been disastrous, but Henry wasn't spoiled. He'd somehow always known the limits or simply been so eager to please that he'd been mostly well behaved.

Shanna knew he'd probably be okay wherever he lived, but she worried at the oppressive environment that was the Hamilton home, especially when both of the adults there were bound to be worried sick and totally focused on Greg.

"Mrs. Shanna, I don't want to live there," Greta admitted.

"You have to," Shanna said, alarmed. "Henry will need you more than ever."

"I know," the nanny said with a deep sigh. "But Mrs. Hamilton and I, we never see eye to eye on things. She's entirely too strict with him, but I'm not sure a constant test of wills between the two of us will be good for Henry."

"Please try," Shanna begged. "For his sake. I know she can be impossible, but just agree with her, then do what you think is best."

"What I think is best is for Henry to come and stay with you," she said flatly. "I've been with him practically since his mama died when he was a baby. He was never happier than when you were here."

Shanna's eyes stung with more unshed tears. "Oh, Greta, you know there's nothing I'd like more, but it's impossible."

"Nothing is impossible," Greta said with grim determination. "I intend to tell Mrs. Hamilton what I think until it finally sinks into that thick head of hers. I'll tell her ten times a day and twice that on Sundays, if that's what it takes."

Shanna fought a grin. She'd love to see that, but in the end it would only wind up with Greta getting fired.

"You know you can't do that," she chided. "She won't abide back talk from you."

"Well, I can dream about it," Greta insisted. "And one of these days, who knows what might pop out of my mouth? I know she cares about Henry. She just doesn't want to admit that what he needs to be happy is to be with you, so he can have a normal childhood."

"Maybe this time Greg will get through rehab and pull himself together," Shanna said. "Henry needs his dad."

"Henry needs the man his dad used to be," Greta said direly. "We both know that's unlikely."

"I won't accept that," Shanna said. Because if she did, it would mean admitting that Henry was doomed to a life of chaos and uncertainty.

"It's too bad that man threw away the best thing that ever happened to him," Greta said. "You always believe the best about him, even now."

"I want to," Shanna said. "I loved him. Admitting I'd made a mistake about the kind of man he was, that was hard for me. Even so, there had to be some kind of decency inside him. I don't believe I could have loved him, even for such a short time, if there hadn't been more than good looks and charm."

"Many a woman has been fooled by a persuasive man on his best behavior," Greta said. "Some of them do have good in them. Some are bad right down to the bone. Mr. Hamilton, I'm not so sure about him."

"Well, I am," Shanna insisted. "Look how wonderful Henry is, despite everything he's been through. Some of that has to be due to Greg's influence."

"I suppose," Greta conceded. "I'll call you once we're settled with the Hamiltons. It's probably best if I do that, rather than you calling me."

"Of course," Shanna said, knowing how risky a poorly timed call from her could be. "Tell Henry I love him. I'm not sure he believes it anymore, but it's true."

"He knows. In his heart, he knows," Greta assured her.

Shanna hung up slowly, then looked up to see Bree standing there, openmouthed with apparent shock.

"You're in love with someone named Henry?" she said accusingly.

Shanna winced at her icy tone. "Bree, you misunderstood."

"The words were pretty clear," she insisted. "Oh, Shanna, how could you do this to Kevin? How could you let him fall for you if you're in love with someone else?"

Shanna sighed. "It's not what you think."

"I know what I heard," Bree said, sparks in her eyes, every bit of O'Brien protectiveness kicking in. "You didn't know I was standing here, so what you were saying had to be the truth. Now you're just scrambling to cover it up." She shook her head. "How could you do that to Kevin when you know what he's been through? You've fooled all of us."

Shanna let her rant on for several more minutes until she finally wound down. She realized how Bree could have misunderstood what she'd heard, but if she would just let Shanna get a word in edgewise, she could actually explain.

Bree's tirade finally slowed, but the anger in her eyes hadn't dimmed.

"My turn now?" Shanna inquired.

"Go ahead. Try to explain it away," Bree said, her tone unforgiving and filled with skepticism.

"Henry is seven years old. He's my stepson, the child of my former husband."

Bree looked unconvinced. "Do you swear that's the truth?" she asked eventually.

Shanna kept her gaze level. "It's the truth. I'll get my wallet and show you his picture, if you like."

Bree backed down as quickly as she'd become irate. "Shanna, I'm sorry. I didn't know. You never mentioned having a stepson."

"Because the whole situation is incredibly painful. I don't like to think about it, much less talk about it."

"Does Kevin know?"

"He knows my marriage was a mess, but he doesn't know about Henry. It hasn't come up."

"So, when you divorced, you not only left your husband, you lost someone you'd come to think of as a son," Bree said, putting the pieces together.

Shanna nodded. Close to crying earlier, now her eyes filled up and tears trickled down her cheeks. "Bree, walking away from that child was the hardest thing I've ever done."

"You don't have any relationship with him now?"

"Only by phone. The nanny fills me in, too. She was the one on the phone just now. That's the most the court would allow. Though we'd known each other for quite a while, Greg and I were married less than a year. His entire family fought against my having any visitation rights. They said it would be too disruptive and confusing."

"Oh, my God, I can't imagine how hard that must be," Bree said, instantly sympathetic. "Shanna, I'm so sorry."

"Yeah, me, too. It's even worse right now, because there's a crisis and I *still* can't be there for him."

"If you want to be there, maybe you should just go. What's the court going to do, have you arrested?"

Shanna smiled at that. "The judge might not, but Henry's grandmother would likely give it a try."

"I'll go with you and bail you out," Bree offered. "In fact, all of us will. Can you imagine the combined force of all the O'Briens descending on them at the jail? Or maybe taking on Grandma?"

That image made Shanna laugh. She stood up and hugged Bree. "Thank you for offering. You have no idea how much that means to me."

"You need to fill Kevin in," Bree said, sobering. "You know, the fact that you left behind a child, even a stepchild, is going to be difficult for him to accept."

Shanna nodded. "I figured that out the other day after you told me about your mother and your theory about his feelings for Georgia. I'm scared to tell him," she admitted. "It could change the way he feels about me."

"Not telling him could be worse," Bree advised. "Sooner or later he'll pick up on something or someone will say the wrong thing. It's better if he hears about this from you. After all, this wasn't your fault, Shanna."

"I know, but on days like today, I feel as if it was, as if I've let that little boy down terribly. What if Kevin feels that way, too?"

"He won't if he knows the whole story," Bree said confidently. "Tell him."

"I will," Shanna said. "I'll find the right time."

"*Make* the right time," Bree said. "When Jake and I had some things we had to work through, that's what my dad told me, that I had to insist on talking, that waiting around for the perfect time was a recipe for disaster. No time is ever perfect."

"I'll keep that in mind," Shanna promised.

Bree stood up to go. "You okay now? Want me to bring you some comfort food from Sally's? A chocolate croissant, maybe?"

"I'm okay," Shanna told her. "Thanks for listening and for understanding."

"Which I only did after ripping into you," Bree said ruefully. "Sorry about that."

"Hey, you were being protective of Kevin. I get that. The way you all stand up for each other is one of the things I like best about your entire family. You might give each other all kinds of grief, but when it comes down to it, you're united against anyone who'd hurt one of you."

"True," Bree said. "Just keep in mind, one of these days

I expect you to be a part of this family, so you'll get our backup, as well. All you have to do is ask."

Shanna held back a fresh batch of tears until after Bree had left, then went into the back room and let them flow. When they ended at last, amazingly she felt cleansed. Things were starting to look brighter. And she knew that even if the situation with Greg and Henry worsened, she'd find some way to help…even if she had to charge into enemy territory with an army of O'Briens at her back.

Kevin found excuses to stay later and later in Annapolis just so he could avoid the temptation of spending time with Shanna. No one called him on it the first week, but Abby pulled him aside when he came by late in the evening to pick up Davy in the middle of the second week.

"Sit," she ordered, pointing toward the kitchen table. She set an opened bottle of beer in front of him, probably to help the lecture he knew was coming to go down more smoothly.

"Who died and made you boss?" he inquired lightly, just as he might have in those first weeks after their mother had left and Abby had thought she needed to look out for all of them, despite Gram's presence.

Rather than taking offense, she grinned at him. "I've always been the boss of you."

Kevin merely lifted a brow.

Abby shrugged. "Well, things would go more smoothly if I were, that's for sure. How are you and Shanna getting along these days?"

"Fine," he said cautiously. "Why?"

"I just wondered if she's the reason you've been staying in Annapolis so late every night."

He took a sip of beer, then shook his head. "I have a lot to learn on this new job."

"I'm sure you do, but you don't have to learn it all in the first few weeks." He started to reply, but she held up a hand. "Before you utter some fib, I'll tell you that Uncle Thomas is worried about you, too. He's the one who asked me if something had happened between you and Shanna."

"This family is nothing but a bunch of damn busybodies," he grumbled.

Abby chuckled. "You're just discovering that?"

"No, but it's different when it's directed at you."

Abby gave him a commiserating look. "Tell me about it."

"If you understand, then drop this, let me get my kid and head home." He started to stand.

"Not so fast," she said. "You still haven't answered my question."

Kevin met her gaze evenly. "And I'm not going to," he said. "Anything going on between Shanna and me is just that, between Shanna and me."

His tone must have given something away, because Abby's eyes widened. "Oh, sweet heaven, you slept with her, didn't you? That's what has you all freaked out. Was it awful?"

"It was not awful," he said before he realized his mistake.

A grin spread across his sister's face. "Aha! Gotcha!"

"So help me, if you say one word about this to anyone else in the family, in the town—hell, in the universe—I will cheerfully tell everyone that you used to sneak out of the house and sleep with Trace way back in the day."

She didn't seem overly worried about the threat, which was a disappointment.

"Everyone already knows about that," she said cavalierly.

"Really? Dad knows?"

She faltered slightly at what he'd realized would be a direct hit. "No, but what does any of that matter now? Trace and I are all grown-up. We're living together. We're getting married in a few months."

"Yeah, but Dad always thought you were his precious, do-no-wrong little angel," Kevin taunted. "It will be a sad day for him when he finds out otherwise."

"You're a pig," Abby said, though without any real venom.

For the first time in several uncomfortable minutes, Kevin grinned. He finally had the upper hand. "Pact of silence?" he inquired.

She frowned. "Okay, yes," she said grudgingly. "At least after you've answered one question for me."

Kevin waited.

"Why are you so freaked out that you're avoiding Shanna? Is it because Georgia's parents made such a big deal about you moving on too soon?"

"That's part of it."

"Only part? What's the rest?"

"You never heard the way Dad lectured Connor and me about sex and responsibility, did you?"

"Heaven forbid," she said with a shudder. "It would have been too weird."

He laughed. "You mean because you and Trace were already doing the deed?"

"I mean because it was Dad talking about sex."

"I have to say he was pretty darn impressive once he got started," Kevin told her. "He taught Connor and me both that it was not to be taken lightly, that it wasn't about a few minutes of feeling good or scoring, but about love and respect."

Abby's eyes lit with understanding. "Thus the hasty marriage to Georgia," she said. "And the panic over sleeping with Shanna."

He nodded.

"Oh, Kev, I'm the last person who'd ever suggest that a man should treat sex casually, but a big bolt of lightning isn't going to come down and strike you if your relationship with Shanna doesn't turn out to be the real deal. Is she expecting a commitment?"

"No."

"Then as long as you both understand what's going on, enjoy yourselves. See where this leads. I happen to believe you're perfect together, but that certainly doesn't mean I expect you to try to race me down the aisle. For one thing, Trace would be totally ticked if that happened."

Kevin laughed. "He would, indeed."

Abby gave him a smacking kiss on his forehead. "Go with my blessing," she told him. "Don't shut Shanna out just because you're not ready to take a leap to the next level of your relationship."

Kevin breathed a sigh of relief. "Wise words from an elder," he said.

"I'm barely a year older than you, so don't get carried away," she retorted.

"I love you," he said once again before leaving the kitchen to collect his son and head for home.

As he drove away, he saw Abby silhouetted in the doorway, her hand raised in a wave…or maybe it was another sign of that blessing she'd bestowed on him. Either way, he felt better than he had since the night he'd spent in Shanna's bed.

19

The fund-raiser for the Chesapeake Bay Preservation League drew about two hundred people to the town green, many more than any of them had anticipated. Shanna sold out of books within the first hour and took orders for more. The league increased its membership, and donations amounted to more than two thousand dollars. With everything added together they'd probably top five thousand dollars—not bad for a hastily planned event in a small town. All in all, she considered it a success.

"You did a fine thing here tonight," Mick told Shanna. He was beaming with pride as if he'd had a hand in it. "This is the kind of event that draws a community together."

"It is, indeed," Thomas said, joining them. "I should have you put together a whole series of events like this, not just for the money we could raise, but to educate people about the importance of the bay."

Kevin joined them and slipped an arm around Shanna's waist, an openly possessive gesture that immediately raised Mick's and Thomas's eyebrows.

"It's getting late. I should be driving back to Annapolis," Thomas said hastily.

"I'll walk you to your car," Mick said, displaying an exaggerated amount of discretion for once.

As the two older men scrambled to get away, Kevin chuckled. "It's interesting that they've finally put aside their animosity long enough to be united in this cause."

"You mean saving the bay?" Shanna suggested.

"Oh no," Kevin said. "Don't delude yourself this was a magnanimous gesture having anything to do with the environment. That timely departure and their ready agreement were all about us. They wanted to leave us alone. No doubt they're hoping nature will take its course."

"Kevin!" she protested, not wanting to even consider that Mick and his brother were hoping she and Kevin would run off to her bedroom for a wild and passionate night alone.

"I'm telling you, those two just put a stamp of approval on the two of us, sort of like the FDA puts one on a piece of beef."

"Now there's a lovely comparison," she said, laughing. She lifted her gaze to his. "So, are we going to do it?"

His expression sobered at once. "No," he said firmly.

"Because you don't want to give them the satisfaction of being right?"

"No. This has nothing to do with them," he declared flatly.

Shanna's feeling of exhilaration immediately fled. "Why don't I like the sound of that? Not that you said no to sex, but the way you made it sound so final. Have you had second thoughts since the other night?"

"Third and fourth," he admitted. "Abby says…"

"You've discussed our relationship with your sister?" she asked, shocked by the immediate image of their love life being a casual topic at an O'Brien family gathering. "Who else has chimed in with an opinion?"

Kevin backpedaled at once. "It wasn't that way, not exactly, anyhow."

She studied his flustered expression. "I think we'd better go for a walk and have this conversation."

"Not tonight," he said, his expression dismayed. "This isn't the time for us to have a serious talk. We should be going somewhere to celebrate the success of this event. I doubt you had anything to eat. Let's go to Brady's. We can have steak or crabs and a bottle of their best champagne."

"I'm not sure I want to have dinner with a man who's just admitted he's been discussing our sex life with who knows how many other people," she said. "Nor do I want to spend time with one who's implied that he's never going to sleep with me again." She gave him a hard look. "At least not until I know the reason he made that kind of decision unilaterally."

Despite the way things had gone the last time—or the way she'd *thought* they'd gone—uncertainty crowded in. Maybe she really was no good in bed. Maybe Greg hadn't shunned her because of his drinking, but because she'd been lousy at sex. After all, Kevin was rejecting her, too. The evidence was beginning to mount up.

She met Kevin's gaze to realize he was studying her intently.

"What went on in your head just then?" he asked, his expression puzzled.

"That's not important. You haven't explained what you're thinking, why you're rejecting me."

He regarded her with dismay. "I'm *not* rejecting you," he said emphatically. "Far from it. You scare me." He gestured from her to him and back again. "*This* scares me. I'm not ready for the intensity of what we have." He gave her a pleading look. "Come on, Shanna. You know how complicated my life is. I'm barely over losing my wife. No, wait, I'm not over it at all. I'm a mess. Some days it's all I can do to keep things on track with my son and handle this new job."

"So I'm a complication you can't really handle," she said carefully, understanding but hurting just the same.

"It sounds bad when you put it like that, but yes. It's not you, it's the intensity of what I feel when I'm with you. In a twisted way, maybe you can see that's a good thing," he suggested hopefully.

She almost laughed at that, partly because she could actually see what he meant…in a definitely twisted way. It didn't exactly make things better, but it did make them less awful.

"What do you want to do?" she asked.

"Take a step back," he said at once, proving he'd given this a lot of thought. "That's all."

"Stop seeing each other," she interpreted.

"No," he said at once. "Just no sex."

"I never thought I'd live to hear those words come out of a man's mouth," she said. Under other circumstances, she might even have found it amusing. Weren't most men eager for casual, no-strings sex? And, really, wasn't that all she was offering?

"Believe me, I never thought I'd utter them," Kevin said. "But I can't see any other way to slow this down without ending it."

"And you really think not having sex will work, give you the space you need?"

"I hope so."

She didn't believe for a minute this had been Abby's advice. "Is this what your sister told you to do?"

"No," he admitted. "She told me I should go for it and,

believe me, I would love nothing more than to follow that advice. But I don't think I can. It's not fair to you."

"You could let me worry about what's fair to me. I'm a big girl, Kevin. I know what I can handle. When we slept together, I knew how complicated your life is. I didn't have expectations about the future then or now."

"I'm really handling this badly," he said with obvious regret. "It's not just about my needing space. You forget that I've seen exactly how upsetting it is when you're reminded about anything related to your ex-husband. You still have things you need to work out, too."

"I can't deny that," she said reluctantly.

"Then backing off, at least when it comes to sex, is the right thing for both of us," he said. "It'll be less complicated."

"What if I don't see it that way?" she asked curiously. "Will you walk away for good?"

He met her gaze. "I'm hoping it won't come to that."

She considered going along with his plan, but she honestly didn't feel there was anything to be gained by trying to pretend that the other night had never happened, by fighting the desire for it to happen again.

Eventually, she shook her head. "Nope, sorry. This isn't going to work for me. You seem to hold all the cards, and this is all on your terms, so I'm going to make it easy for you. I'll walk away now. You get your life together, give me a call."

She saw the shock and dismay register on his face and steeled herself against it. This was for the best. He was right about one thing. Her life was in no better shape than his. Even so, she'd been willing to take a risk. If he couldn't do that much, then she needed to cut her losses now. She turned and walked away.

"Shanna," he called, coming after her.

She looked back over her shoulder. "Don't," she said softly. "Please don't come after me. Not now."

All the way back to her store, where there were a hundred details to attend to after tonight's successful event, all she could think about was that she'd somehow managed to find one more man who didn't love her enough, after all. It was a thousand times worse, because she couldn't blame it on anything except Kevin's inability to move forward. Even Greg, with all of his flaws that had made real commitment impossible, had been willing to take the hardest risk of all. To the best of his ability at the time, he'd given her his heart.

Kevin was stunned. The entire scene with Shanna hadn't gone anything like what he'd expected. He'd thought for sure she'd be relieved, or at least that she would understand. Instead, she'd viewed it as some kind of rejection. He'd bungled it badly, but he couldn't seem to regret his insistence that they needed to move forward more slowly, with sex safely out of the equation.

He immediately went back to working late, night after night. This time it was his uncle who called him on it.

"You and Shanna have a fight?" he asked at the end of the week.

"Drop it," Kevin said. "Last time you meddled in my relationship and went to Abby, everything blew up in my face."

Thomas dropped down into the chair by his desk, looking genuinely concerned. "How so?"

"Which part of 'Stay out of this' wasn't clear?" Kevin inquired.

"I'm just asking—"

"Meddling," Kevin said.

"Trying to give you the benefit of my experience," Thomas corrected. "Abby doesn't have half as much as I do."

"For which we can all be grateful," Kevin said.

"Are you with Shanna or not?" Thomas said, his gaze unrelenting.

"Not."

"Now that's a real pity," Thomas said. "I was so sure…"

"Which proves you don't know as much as you think you do."

"I need facts, if I'm to help you."

Kevin groaned. "I'm not discussing this and I don't want your help."

"Well, it's obvious to me you need it." His expression turned thoughtful. "I'll just go and have a chat with Shanna," he said decisively. "Perhaps she'll be more candid and reasonable."

Kevin stood up to block his way. "So help me, if you go anywhere near Shanna, I will quit this job and…" He hesitated, trying to think of the most extreme measure he could take, short of committing murder. "I'll become a priest. Gram's always wanted one in the family. It was a great disappointment to her that none of her sons felt that calling."

Thomas had the audacity to laugh at that. "I'm not worried. You're hardly suited for it."

"Beside the point. I'll do it if everyone in this family doesn't stay out of my business. I think I'll like living in a monastery, preferably one on a mountaintop far, far away."

"And Davy? Your son? Have you forgotten about him?"

"I'll work it out," he claimed. He had no idea how, but surely there would be a way.

"Oh, Kevin, you know there's no priesthood in your future, so let's talk about what really matters, you and this woman you love."

"I don't love her," he insisted. "I can't."

"Why not?"

Because he didn't have an answer that would make a lick of sense to anyone but him, he stood up and headed out the door.

"Work it out, Kevin," Thomas called after him. "Life's too short to be wasting it."

"Right back at you," Kevin said over his shoulder. It was something he should have thought to say even sooner. Because if his love life was a mess, his uncle's was worse. Now *that* was a situation someone in the family ought to jump all over.

"You want us to find a blind date for Uncle Thomas?" Jess said, when Kevin assembled all three of his sisters in the kitchen at the house after dinner one evening.

"More than one," he said. "A bunch of them."

Abby began to laugh. "This is so *not* about our uncle," she said.

Jess turned to her with a blank expression. "It's not?"

Bree chuckled. "Nope, he's trying to get all of us focused on Thomas so we'll leave *him* alone."

"I am not," he flat-out lied. "Think about it. He's getting older. He'd been divorced for a while now. He needs someone who understands what he's doing, who's as passionate about it as he is."

"Then shouldn't you be the one to find him a date?" Abby asked reasonably. "You're working with him. You probably meet all sorts of women who'd be perfect."

"I can't do it."

"Because you made too big a production about him meddling," Abby guessed.

Kevin shrugged. "Something like that."

Jess looked from Abby to Kevin, then back again. "Okay, what are Bree and I missing? It sounds as if you and Abby have discussed this whole meddling thing before."

"That doesn't matter," Kevin insisted. "We're talking about Thomas now."

"No way," Jess said. "I want to talk about you."

"I think I do, too," Bree said, studying him curiously. "Come to think of it, I haven't seen you around the bookstore lately."

Abby sat up a bit straighter at that. "Really?" She turned to Kevin. "I thought everything was okay on that front. Didn't you listen to a word I said?"

"What did you tell him?" Bree asked.

Kevin scowled fiercely at his big sister, all but daring her to open her mouth about their conversation. Abby grinned, but she did stay silent.

Kevin looked around the table at all three of his sisters and realized with a sinking sensation that this little scheme of his had backfired. He should have spoken to them individually, tailored the conversation to what they knew and what they didn't know. Instead, he'd created a matchmaking force.

He stood up. "I'm going to bed. Do whatever you want about Thomas. I just thought you'd want to help."

Though he made it out of the room without any of them trying to drag him back, the buzz of conversation that followed in his wake was troubling. He was going to have to stay on his toes, or Thomas wouldn't be the one whose love life they'd be trying to fix.

* * *

Shanna missed Kevin's afternoon visits. Even more, she missed having him bring Davy by the store. She hadn't realized until now just how much she'd been using Davy as a substitute for Henry in her life. Not that one little boy could ever replace another, but the sensations stirred by being around a bright, inquisitive child were the same.

Greta's calls, frustratingly, had decreased in frequency. The few she made were always brief and unsatisfying. Shanna didn't speak to Henry at all. More and more she was torn about jumping into her car and driving to Pennsylvania to check on him in person. Only the knowledge that the likely scene between her and Mrs. Hamilton could make it worse for him kept her from doing it.

Filled with troubling thoughts, she was sitting at the counter late on Friday when the bell over the door rang. She looked up to see Davy racing toward her. At the sight of him, her heart lodged in her throat and she looked beyond him, expecting to see Kevin on his heels. Instead, it was Mick O'Brien.

"You hoping for someone else?" he asked, his expression sympathetic.

"How could I be when you two are just what I needed this afternoon?"

"Story?" Davy pleaded, tugging on her hand.

Mick chuckled, clearly amused by his grandson's eagerness. "You mind if I take a quick run over to the Town Hall, while Davy's here with you?" he asked. "I just need to drop off some papers. It shouldn't take me more than a few minutes."

"It's fine," she told him, delighted to have some time alone with Davy. "No rush. It'll be quiet for another hour or so till people start dropping in on their way into town for the weekend."

Left alone with Davy, she helped him select several picture books, then settled in a chair with him in her lap. Having his warm, sturdy little body cuddled next to hers eased the ache in her heart.

They'd read two books when the front door opened and Bree strolled in. "Now there's a lovely picture," she said at once, then glanced around. "Where's Kevin?"

Shanna shrugged. "No idea. Mick brought Davy by for a visit."

"For a visit or for some free babysitting?"

"If a babysitter was all he was looking for, you're practically next door," Shanna reminded her. "I think he knew Davy and I were starting to miss each other."

Bree sat down in a chair opposite her. "Why is that?"

"If you're trying to get me to talk about what's going on between Kevin and me, it won't work. I have nothing to say. Talk to your brother."

"I tried," Bree admitted. "We all did."

Shanna stared at her with dismay. "You ganged up on him?"

"I wouldn't put it like that. In fact, he was the one who more or less called a family meeting."

"About me?"

"No, about Thomas, or so he said. The conversation sort of got sidetracked."

"He must have loved that," Shanna said.

Bree's eyes sparkled with mischief. "He walked out, as a matter of fact, which means I'm left with bugging you, if I expect to find out anything."

Shanna shrugged. "Sorry. Not talking," she repeated even more firmly.

Bree regarded her with dismay. "Then it's true, the two of you have broken up?"

"Not talking," Shanna said.

"Does this have something to do with the conversation you and I had about your stepson? Did you tell Kevin about him? Did he react badly? I'll talk to him, make him understand."

Shanna gave her an impatient look. "Still not discussing this with you. It's inappropriate, especially with Davy right here…"

"Oh, he doesn't have a clue what we're talking about," Bree said, then tickled him. "Do you, baby boy?"

Davy giggled and scrambled out of Shanna's arms to reach for his aunt. Shanna felt the ache of his absence almost instantly.

"You're really getting attached to him, aren't you?" Bree said, nodding toward Davy, who'd climbed into her lap.

"He's a great kid," Shanna said.

"He's not your stepson, though, what was his name? Henry?"

Shanna sighed. "No, he's not."

Bree gave her a long, considering look. "Okay, I'm going to ask you something and I hope you won't get offended by it, but is your attraction to my brother because of Davy, because you were missing your stepson?"

Shanna had no idea how to answer that. The truth was pretty complicated. "Maybe at first," she admitted eventually.

Bree regarded her with a worried frown. "But not now?"

Shanna sighed. "Not now. I was starting to fall for Kevin."

"Was?" Bree said, seizing on the word. "Then something did happen. What? Come on, Shanna. I can't help if I don't know what's going on."

"I don't think you can help," Shanna told her. "This was my decision. It's for the best."

Bree's eyes widened. "You broke up with him? Wow! I didn't see that coming. If you were falling for him, why would you do that?"

"Do you recall me saying I wasn't going to have this conversation with you?" Shanna asked with exasperation.

Bree grinned. "My persistence usually pays off. Be glad I'm not Abby or Jess. You wouldn't stand a chance. They'd have had you blabbing away ten minutes ago."

"Doubtful," Shanna said.

"I could call them. Let them give it a try," Bree suggested cheerfully.

"Please don't."

Mick returned just then, took in the scene, gave his daughter a kiss, then pulled up a chair. "What are we talking about?"

"Why Shanna broke up with Kevin," Bree said at once. "She refuses to explain."

Mick sat back, his expression stunned. "I thought Kevin was the one acting like a fool."

"Me, too," Bree said.

Mick looked at his daughter. "She hasn't said why?"

"Not so far," Bree told him.

"I'm still in the room," Shanna said irritably.

"But still not talking, am I right?" Bree said.

Shanna nodded.

"Then for the moment, Dad and I will try to make some sense of this on our own," Bree replied.

As she listened to their speculation grow increasingly

outrageous, Shanna knew exactly what they were doing. They wanted to rile her so badly she'd blurt out the truth. She wasn't going to fall for that.

"It's because we're Irish," Mick said. "She's probably got a bias against that."

Bree shook her head. "There are too many of us, that's it. We intimidate her." She sighed dramatically. "The meddling got to be too much for her."

"Well, if she's not able to handle a little well-meant interference, maybe it's for the best," Mick said.

"Except Kevin's crazy about her," Bree said.

"Davy, too," Mick said sorrowfully, his gaze on his grandson.

"Oh, would you two give it a rest?" Shanna pleaded. "Let Kevin and me work things out on our own."

Mick gave her a hard look. "Are you trying to work things out? Doesn't seem that way to me, since he's been hiding out up in Annapolis till all hours of the night."

"Maybe he's met someone new," Bree suggested, then chuckled at Shanna's dismayed reaction, which she hadn't been quick enough to hide. "Okay, I'm sorry. That was mean. I just wanted to get an honest reaction out of you, and I succeeded. You're still in love with Kevin, no matter what you say."

"I never actually said I wasn't. You drew that conclusion all by yourself. And I am really uncomfortable having this entire discussion with his father and his sister. Go home and have it with him. Don't put me on the spot. I may have been the one to call it quits, but he gave me the reason to do it."

Mick leaned forward, his eyes glittering. "Now we're getting somewhere. What did he do?"

"Ask him," she repeated for what seemed like the umpteenth time.

Mick sighed heavily and stood. “I don’t think we’re going to find out anything more here today, Bree.”

Bree didn’t even try to hide her disappointment. “I suppose not.”

“Let me pay you for Davy’s book,” Mick said, heading for the cash register.

Wanting them out of the store, Shanna shook her head. “It’s a gift.”

“I think she’s in a hurry for us to leave,” Bree said.

Mick actually gave her a commiserating look. “Can’t really say I blame her. You do know we’re only trying to help, don’t you?”

“I know,” Shanna murmured.

But as long as Kevin was determined to keep her at arm’s length, there was nothing anyone could do to help.

20

Kevin knew he couldn't get away with hiding out in Annapolis on the weekends. His family was already starting to ask way too many questions about his late nights at work during the week. Trace, regarding him with sympathy, managed to silence Abby, but there was no one around to keep Bree or Jess from pestering him. Even Gram and Mick had offered their share of opinions about his long absences. It was tedious, but not unexpected.

This morning, as soon as Davy was awake and dressed and everyone else had left for church, Kevin took his son and headed for the marina to check out the modifications being made to his boat. At least that was the excuse he used. Sitting on the deck, even if they didn't leave the harbor, would be more restful than being at home for Sunday dinner under everyone's watchful eyes.

He'd been careful to leave a note for Gram so she'd know he and Davy wouldn't be back for the midday meal, but also made it deliberately vague so it wouldn't give anyone a clue about where they'd gone. He was anticipating a nice, peaceful afternoon with his son.

At least until he looked up and saw Bree headed his way, grim determination written all over her face. He sighed and wondered if he could jump overboard with Davy and swim far, far away before she got here.

"How'd you find me?" he asked as she stepped lightly off the dock and landed on the boat's deck.

"Bwee!" Davy said excitedly, lifting his arms.

"You're not that complicated," she said as she scooped up his son. "You weren't on the beach or the town pier and your car was parked in the marina lot. I'd advise you never to try for a life of crime. You're way too predictable."

"I'll have to remember to leave the car somewhere else to throw you off in the future," he said sourly. "Or maybe I'll just walk everywhere I go."

"That suggests you're actively trying to avoid those of us who know you best," she said.

"Gee, you think?" He eyed her curiously. "Did Gram send you?"

"Nope."

"Dad?"

"I came all on my own," she told him. "I'm worried about you."

"No need. As you can see, I'm perfectly fine."

"Really? Instead of being with your family for Sunday dinner, you're down here hiding out at Harbor Lights. And don't even try to tell me you're working on the boat, because I caught you red-handed doing absolutely nothing."

"Not true," he claimed. "Davy and I are having an adventure, right, kiddo?"

"Uh-huh," Davy confirmed. "Catch fish."

"Really?" Bree said with blatant skepticism. "There's not a fishing pole in sight."

"We're working up to it," Kevin told her. "Right now we're just relaxing, lulling the fish into a false sense of complacency."

Bree merely rolled her eyes, then settled into the chair next to his and propped her bare feet on a railing. "This is fairly peaceful," she admitted after a time.

"It was," he said pointedly.

"You mean before I got here."

He grinned.

"Okay, tell me what I want to know and I'll go away."

"Which is?"

"Why you and Shanna broke up."

"Who says we did?"

"She admitted that much. She even said it was her idea, but that you were somehow behind the decision. And before you get all worked up about her discussing your private business, I want you to know I practically had to use torture to get that much out of her."

He chuckled. "I can imagine. She's a fairly private person and you don't give up easily."

"Dad helped."

Kevin groaned. "She must have loved that."

"She held up okay. It made me like her even more." She studied him. "So, is it really over?"

"I hope not," he admitted.

"What happened?"

Kevin considered evading the question, but it was pointless. Bree would pester him the way she'd pestered Shanna. Why not give in gracefully? Besides, he could use another perspective.

"I got this crazy idea we ought to slow things down," he said. He shrugged at her incredulous look. "Hey, it made sense at the time."

"And now that you've had time to think about it?"

"I can almost see why she interpreted that to mean I was rejecting her."

Bree groaned. "Please tell me you did not come up with this brilliant plan right after you slept with her."

"It wasn't *right* after," he said defensively. "It was a few days later."

"Which is so much better," she said with unmistakable disgust. She poked him in the arm. "What is wrong with you?"

"I'm a little rusty at all this. Besides, dating's changed since the last time I did it," he claimed.

"Really? I never noticed any revised edition of the rule book. Does Shanna carry it at her store? I'm sure she'd be more than happy to sell you a copy at this point."

He frowned at her sarcasm. "In case you haven't noticed, I've been in mourning. My wife died."

Bree sat up straighter and looked him in the eye. "At the risk of sounding callous and disrespectful, baloney! You are not in mourning. If anything, you're guilt-ridden because you're *not* mourning Georgia the way you think you should, or the way her parents think you should."

Kevin blinked at the certainty in her voice. "She was my wife," he protested. "And Davy's mother."

"Do you think I don't know that? And I'm certainly not saying that her death wasn't an awful tragedy," she said. "I also know what it did to you when she made the decision to go back overseas. You sucked it up, but you were devastated by her decision to leave you and Davy."

"She was doing her duty, like thousands of other dedicated soldiers," he said stoically, as he had at least a hundred times before.

"That's how she saw it," Bree agreed. "And a lot of people would agree and admire her for it. But your situation is different. In your case, it reminded you of Mom abandoning all of us. Don't even try to deny it."

"Okay, say I agree that there's some truth in what you say, it doesn't change the fact that she's dead."

"No, sadly, it doesn't," she said with more sympathy.

"I should have stopped her from going back."

"Oh please, you can't seriously believe that anything you could have said would have worked. Georgia was determined. She believed in what she was doing with her whole heart."

"I could have done something," he insisted. "If I had, she'd still be alive."

Bree regarded him worriedly. "You can't go through life thinking like that. You'll make yourself nuts. She's gone. That's a fact. But you're not dead, Kevin. You're alive, and you've fallen in love with a wonderful woman who's ready to explore a relationship with you. Don't you see how huge that is? Don't throw it away by pretending that the past was some idyllic situation. Loving Shanna doesn't negate your relationship with Georgia. It just means that your heart is telling you you're ready to move on."

"How can I, when I know what it will do to Georgia's parents, her mother especially?"

"You can't live your life for the Davises. The best thing you can do for them is to make sure Davy's happy and healthy. And the best you can do for their grandson is to honor his mother's memory, make sure they stay a part of his life, and give him a happy, normal home."

"Surrounded by the likes of you?" he joked, to lighten the moment.

She tickled Davy. "Hey, I'm the best aunt in the whole wide world, right, Davy?"

"Best," he confirmed, nodding emphatically.

"There, I told you so," she said, standing and then handing Davy back to him. "Come home and have dinner with us."

He shook his head. "Not today. Maybe next week. I still have thinking to do."

"Well, don't think so hard that your head explodes," she teased.

"I'll try not to."

Bree gave him a kiss, then peppered Davy's face with butterfly kisses before leaping back onto the dock. "Love you two."

"We love you, too," Kevin acknowledged. "Even if you are a pest."

"But I'm a smart pest," she retorted.

He watched her go, then thought about what she'd said. Cutting Shanna out of his life out of guilt really was absurd. If things between them were so intense, wasn't that precisely the reason to embrace the relationship, not use it as an excuse to back off?

He wondered if it was too late to tell Shanna he'd been an idiot. Then, again, didn't most women live for just such an admission? He'd probably make her day.

It was nearly ten days before Kevin worked up the courage to drop by the bookstore. He had no idea what sort of reception to expect. He just knew that the separation wasn't working for him. He'd also had plenty of time on the drives to and from Annapolis to think about Bree's assessment of the situation with Shanna, to say nothing of her opinions when it came to his relationship with Georgia.

It was certainly true that his feelings for Shanna had grown deeper bit by bit. Especially after the misery of this separation, he didn't want to go through another day without spending time with her. She was a real flesh-and-blood woman, not like the idealized image he'd been clinging to of Georgia.

Bree had all but dared him to take a hard look at his marriage. She'd forced him to see what had been there all along. Caught up in the intensity of a war, he and Georgia had rushed into getting married because of pure lust and a frantic need for connection to another person. Maybe with enough time, they could have really gotten to know each other on another level, but that hadn't happened. Turning their marriage into some romantic fairy tale was revising history.

Not that Georgia hadn't been a good person and a beautiful woman. She had been. But when she'd gone back to Iraq, leaving him behind with Davy, he'd called it dedication to duty for the benefit of anyone who'd questioned the decision, but to himself he'd acknowledged that she was addicted to the adrenaline rush. She loved being a soldier, and the more challenging the situation, the happier she was. Sooner or later, they would have had to face the truth—that they wanted a different future. She might have tried, but she never would have fully embraced the kind of quiet life he wanted for himself and his family.

In fact, he'd found exactly that kind of life right here in Chesapeake Shores. He enjoyed the slow-paced lifestyle and his new work with his uncle. And his sisters might pester him outrageously, but he loved them to pieces. He adored Gram. Even his encounters with Mick, and especially with Megan, were taking on a new tenor. It was a great environment in which to raise his son.

And then there was Shanna. She was steady as a rock, as enamored of Chesapeake Shores as he was. She doted on Davy. And she got to him with those big eyes, that ready smile and a touch that made his blood go from simmer to boil in a heartbeat. He could see himself with her. It was time he admitted all of that to her.

That evening he appeared at the shop, deliberately choosing to arrive as she was closing up so they were unlikely to be interrupted.

"Let's have dinner," he suggested without preamble.

"Excuse me?" She didn't seem impressed by the last-minute invitation.

"Come on," he coaxed. "We can take a drive, find someplace romantic on the water."

There was a flicker of alarm in her eyes, but something more, too. A longing, if he wasn't mistaken.

"What's changed?" she asked, her hesitation plain.

"I'll explain over dinner. If I try to do it here and now, we'll be here till breakfast."

She studied him for a full minute, then nodded. "Okay, sure," she said. "Is there something in particular on your mind?"

He nodded. "You. Pretty much all the time."

There was a flicker of hope in her eyes. "I see."

He was tempted to just explain there and then, lay his cards on the table and beg for forgiveness. But before he could, the door to the shop opened and an unfamiliar woman walked in. There was a boy, maybe six or seven, clinging to her hand. He saw recognition flash in Shanna's eyes, even as all the color drained out of her face.

"Hello, Shanna," the older woman said stiffly.

The little boy looked up at her, his expression guarded. She dropped to her knees a few feet in front of him. "Hi, Henry," she whispered, her voice shaky, tears on her cheeks. Then she opened her arms and, after what seemed an endless hesitation, he ran to her.

"Mommy," he cried, his arms tight around her neck.

Kevin stared at them, shock spreading through him. She had a child? One she'd never so much as mentioned?

One she'd obviously left in someone else's care? Memories of his own mother walking away from her family spilled through him. The ache he'd felt each time she'd flitted into their lives for one of her visits, then left again. And then there was Georgia, who'd chosen her country over her child, an admirable decision perhaps, but one with tragic consequences. Was he doomed to being surrounded by women whose priorities were all screwed up, at least by his standards?

In an instant, everything he knew—or thought he knew—about Shanna was turned upside down. Without a word, he walked out of the bookstore and left her to her reunion, cursing himself yet again for being a damn fool.

Shanna was aware of the shock that registered on Kevin's face right before he turned on his heel and walked out of the bookstore, but with Henry clinging to her and Mrs. Hamilton waiting, she didn't dare run after him. Besides, this moment was too sweet, too long in coming, for her not to savor every second of it.

The boy she loved was actually here, in her arms. He'd grown since she'd last seen him. His hair was streaked blond from playing outdoors in the summer sun, and there were freckles across his nose. His skinny little arms were tight around her.

"I am so glad you're here," she told him again and again, lifting her gaze to include Greg's mother. Mrs. Hamilton might not be her favorite person, but right this second Shanna adored her for bringing Henry here.

When Henry finally released her, he looked around, his eyes alight with curiosity. "Your store is really cool. Can I check it out?"

"Of course," she said at once. "You pick out some

books you'd like, and your grandmother and I can have a chat." She turned to Greg's mother, noted the weariness in her eyes, the resignation in her expression. "Can I get you some tea? Or coffee?"

"I'll have tea if it's not too much trouble."

"No trouble at all," Shanna assured her. "Earl Grey?"

She seemed startled that Shanna had remembered her favorite. "Yes, please."

Shanna busied herself in the back room pouring the hot water and brewing the tea, all the while trying to imagine what on earth Mrs. Hamilton and Henry were doing here. Not that it mattered, as long as she was able to spend even a little time with Henry.

She returned to the main room and found her former mother-in-law seated in the children's section watching Henry with a mix of adoration and sorrow. Oblivious to her mood, he was pulling books off the shelves and chattering about the ones that were his favorites and those he wanted to read. In that moment, Shanna was reminded sharply of just how much he truly was an older version of Davy.

She handed Mrs. Hamilton her tea and settled on the edge of the chair across from her. "I really am glad you came," she said simply. Her gaze wandered toward Henry. "I've missed him so much."

"He's missed you, as well," Mrs. Hamilton said. She hesitated, looking as if she was still undecided about something. Eventually she said, "Could we speak privately? In the back room, perhaps?"

"Of course." Shanna paused long enough to ruffle Henry's already tousled hair. "We'll be right back, sweetie."

"Okay," he said, barely giving her a glance as he chose a pile of books he wanted to read.

In the back, Shanna gestured toward the more comfortable chair at her desk, then drew up a stool. "Is everything okay?"

Tears welled up in the older woman's eyes. "No. Greg isn't recovering the way we'd all hoped. There's been damage to his liver."

"I'm truly sorry," Shanna told her, reaching for her hand. "I mean that."

Mrs. Hamilton looked startled, either by her touch or by the sincerity behind her words. "I actually believe you do."

"I tried so hard to convince him to get help," she said. "He didn't think he had a problem." Though she managed to keep an accusing note out of her voice, she added, "Neither did you.

"His father and I just didn't want to accept it. I suppose we were even a bit embarrassed that it took someone like you to point out that our own son was in trouble. People in our social circle have a few cocktails. We assumed Greg was the same."

Shanna tried not to take offense at the *someone like you* comment. Apparently, though, Mrs. Hamilton realized how she'd sounded.

"I didn't intend for that to sound so demeaning," she said, her tone genuinely apologetic. "I just meant that you hardly knew Greg, yet you saw the problem."

"You're his parents. You didn't want to see it," Shanna said, able to be more generous in her opinion now that she had some distance from the volatile situation. "I didn't want to acknowledge it at first, either."

"Well, I'm sorry for how we reacted when you came to us," she said. "Especially now that I've come to ask you for a favor."

Shanna regarded her with surprise. "What can I do?"

"Look out for Henry," she said. "He's not happy with us. His grandfather and I are too old to keep up with an energetic young boy. There are no children his age living nearby. I'm afraid the situation is only going to get more difficult. Greg will be coming to our house. We're hoping he'll improve, but he might not. At this point, he's not a candidate for a transplant apparently, so there's no telling what will happen. Henry shouldn't have to live with that kind of uncertainty."

Shanna hardly dared to hope she was understanding correctly. "Do you want me to be his guardian? A temporary foster mother? Would you let me adopt him?" The possibilities tumbled out.

The questions seemed to fluster Mrs. Hamilton. "We haven't discussed the legalities among ourselves, though I know we must. I was so anxious to talk to you that I just got in the car with Henry and drove here."

Shanna desperately wanted clarity, but under the circumstances maybe she couldn't expect it, much less demand it.

"Why don't we consider this an extended visit, at least until school starts?" Shanna suggested. "That way Henry won't get his hopes up that he's going to live here permanently, and you all will have time to decide what kind of long-term arrangement would be for the best."

Mrs. Hamilton regarded her with amazement. "You're being very generous under the circumstances. I thought you might turn us down after what happened at the custody hearing."

"All I care about, all I've ever cared about, is what's best for Henry. I love him. If I can do anything to make things easier for him, either temporarily or permanently, I will." She said it without hesitation and with no thought at all to the toll it would take if she had to let him go again.

"I'd want it understood that he'll come home frequently to see his father if the situation allows for that."

"Absolutely," Shanna said at once.

Mrs. Hamilton hesitated. "You have room for him? It won't be an inconvenience?"

"I have a two-bedroom apartment right upstairs. You can see it now, if you'd like to. I can fix the second room up for him."

"You have your store, though. Will you be able to manage that and having a young boy with you?"

"Are you trying to discourage me?"

"No, I'm just being practical," Mrs. Hamilton insisted.

"Well, like I said, the apartment is right upstairs. Henry can come here during the day, or I'll arrange for him to spend time with some other children his age."

"Day care?" Mrs. Hamilton asked, her expression horrified.

Shanna nearly laughed at her reaction. "I have a friend with twin girls who are Henry's age. She has a nanny who looks out for them and for her nephew. I'm sure they'd be delighted to include Henry from time to time." Assuming Kevin didn't flatly veto it, she thought, knowing how upset he'd been when he left earlier.

"I wouldn't have expected families in a little town like this to have nannies," Greg's mother said, sounding every bit the society snob.

"Actually Abby is an extremely successful Wall Street stockbroker who's now running the Baltimore office of her brokerage company. Her fiancé is a graphic designer with an impressive client list of major companies. Her father is the architect who designed this town and many others across the country."

Mrs. Hamilton looked taken aback. "I have to admit I'm surprised and impressed."

"You should drive around a bit before you go home. I think you'll discover that it's a wonderful little town. Henry will have a great time while he's here."

"He'll be with someone who loves him. That's the only thing I care about," Mrs. Hamilton said.

"Were you planning to leave him with me today?" Shanna asked, hardly daring to hope for that.

"No," she admitted, looking flustered. "I drove down here on an impulse. I suppose I wanted to take a look around before making a final decision. I'll speak to my husband and Greg tonight."

At Shanna's suddenly defeated expression, she soothed, "Not to worry. They'll agree that this is for the best, I'll see to that. Why don't I bring Henry back on Friday? Will that work for you?"

It took everything in Shanna to contain her desire to utter a whoop of pure joy. "Friday would be great. It'll give me time to fix up his room."

Mrs. Hamilton put aside her cup. She'd barely sipped her tea. Shanna suspected it had merely been a prop to steady her nerves.

Shanna stood when she did and was shocked when Mrs. Hamilton gave her an awkward hug.

"Thank you for agreeing to this," she told Shanna. "I know I had no right to ask."

"When it comes to Henry, you will always have a right to ask anything of me," Shanna assured her. "Shall we tell him now?"

"If it's okay, let me be the one to tell him," Mrs. Hamilton said. "I'd like to wait until I've spoken to his father and grandfather." Her lips curved slightly. "And it will be nice to be the one giving him the best possible news for a change. He's going to be very excited about this. He's been asking for you ever since he moved into my house. As for Greta—" she gave a little shake of her head "—I swear that woman sings your praises from morning till night. If it would be a help, I'll send her down here. I'd pay for her to have her own place."

Shanna regarded her with amazement. "It would certainly be less disruptive for Henry to have that consistency. Are you sure?"

"Well, I can't very well put the woman out of a job after all she's done for the boy, can I?" Mrs. Hamilton said. "I'll make the arrangements."

"Thank you."

Back in the front room, Henry had winnowed his stack of books down to three that he absolutely had to have. "Is that too many?" he asked worriedly.

"Absolutely not," Shanna said.

He gave her a wistful look. "I wish you could read them with me."

"Me, too," she said, barely resisting the urge to tell him that she would do exactly that in just a few more days. She owed Mrs. Hamilton the chance to be the one to tell him. She knew exactly what it was costing her to make this decision for Henry's sake.

She put the books in a bag, then walked outside with Henry and his grandmother. She knelt down and gave Henry a fierce hug. "I love you."

This time, with his face buried in her neck, she heard him murmur the words, "I love you, too."

Surprisingly, when she stood, she realized that the perpetual ache in her heart, which had been there since the divorce, was finally gone. It had been replaced, miraculously, by hope.

21

Grateful that some of the big box stores were within an hour's drive of Chesapeake Shores, Shanna left immediately after closing the shop to pick up everything she thought she might need to decorate a little boy's room. She'd already put aside several more of the books Henry had been looking at. She would put those beside his bed. Though she wondered if she should wait for a final word from Mrs. Hamilton, she couldn't seem to stop herself from preparing for Henry's visit as if it were a done deal.

By the time she got back home at ten, she'd ordered a twin bed and matching dresser, which required assembly, then picked out sunny yellow paint, sheets and towels, a lamp with a sports theme and posters of his favorite baseball and football teams for the walls. Those were the things she remembered from his room at home. She would have bought even more, but when she was about to go completely overboard, she'd decided Henry should have a say in choosing the remaining items for his new room.

Back home, far too excited to sleep, she stayed up past midnight to put a first coat of paint on the bedroom walls. With only a few days until Henry would most likely be here for an extended visit of at least a month, she wanted everything to be perfect.

In the morning, the boxes with the bed and dresser were delivered just as Mick O'Brien was exiting his car and heading toward Sally's. He immediately detoured in her direction and gestured toward the boxes being carried inside.

"You going to be able to manage those?" he asked. "I assume they're going up to your apartment?"

Shanna nodded. "I had no idea the boxes would be so big."

"How about I watch the store for you, and you can direct the men to take them upstairs and put them where you want them? That way you won't be struggling with them later."

She hesitated, wondering if it was wise to have Mick involved in any of this. Kevin might view it as a betrayal. He was obviously furious with her. She'd tried calling him repeatedly during her shopping excursion last night, but every call had gone directly to voice mail. Other than pleading with him to call her so she could explain what had happened at the store, she made no other mention of Henry. It wasn't something she could clear up in a brief message. The situation was too complicated.

Finally, pushing aside her doubts about Kevin's reaction, she opted for expediency. Mick was here and she could use the help. "Are you sure you wouldn't mind?"

"Wouldn't have offered if I did," he told her.

"Thanks," she said, and immediately directed the men out the back door and up the stairs.

When they'd put the boxes in the spare room, she ran back downstairs to find Mick engrossed in a paperback thriller he'd picked up off the bestseller display.

"Suppose I have to buy this now that it's got me hooked," he said, reaching into his pocket to pull out a twenty. When Shanna started to speak, he stopped her. "I'm not taking it as a gift. You keep giving away merchandise to thank people, you're going to go broke."

"It probably is a lousy business practice," she admitted. "I get so excited about putting books into people's hands, I forget that the object is to make money."

"If you feel that way, maybe you'd be better off working in a library where the books are free," he said.

She laughed. "You have a point. Thank you, though, for looking after the place for me."

"It was a couple of minutes. No big deal. How about that furniture, though? You have any idea how to put it together?"

"I'm sure I'll be able to figure it out."

"I have some time. I could do it for you." He gave her a sharp look. "Unless you were planning to ask Kevin."

"I don't think that's an option," she said regretfully.

Mick studied her intently. "I know he's not exactly skilled with a screwdriver, but your bookshelves have stayed together. He can't be totally inept."

"I'm not questioning his skill, just his desire," she admitted candidly. "He was here yesterday when someone from my past came for a visit. I think he misunderstood. So far, he doesn't seem willing to give me a chance to explain."

"You want to tell me?" Mick asked hopefully. "I could pass the information along."

She grinned at his obvious ploy. "You'd love being in the middle, wouldn't you?"

"I wouldn't mind," he said, his tone noble, a twinkle in his eyes.

"I don't think so. Then you'd know something before he does, and I don't think he'd be happy about that." She shook her head in dismay. "I've made such a mess of this. I should have told him everything weeks ago. Bree warned me about that, but I thought I had time."

Mick nodded. "Life has a way of getting away from you. Seems to me it's always better to get things out there and deal with them." He grinned. "I know a thing or two about that, so you'd be wise to listen to me."

"Hopefully I'll never face a situation quite like this again," she told him.

"Now you've got me even more curious," he said, then waved her off when she started to protest that she wasn't talking. "It's okay. I won't ask any more questions. In the meantime, at least let me help with that furniture. It won't take but a minute to put it together."

She hesitated, then decided it made sense to take skilled labor when it was offered. "Thanks. I'd appreciate it." She handed him her apartment key. "You'll see the boxes in the guest bedroom."

"I'll find 'em," he said.

He was back downstairs in less than half an hour. "You're all set," he said, returning her key. "That bright blue bed and dresser look real good with the yellow paint. It'll make a nice room for a young boy."

She knew he was fishing for an explanation, but she had no intention of satisfying his curiosity. "Thanks for your help, Mick. You've been a lifesaver."

"Company coming?" he persisted.

"Something like that."

He gave her an exasperated look. "You're not going to tell me a blessed thing, are you?"

She laughed. "Nope."

"Tell me this much at least," he said, his expression somber. "Does my son have cause to be upset by whoever's coming to stay?"

"I don't think so," she said honestly. "But from his perspective, he might feel otherwise."

"Well, that's clear as mud."

"I just can't say any more," she told him. "Not yet. The situation could change."

He studied her. "But whatever's going on, you're happy about it?"

"Happier than you can possibly imagine."

"Well, then, Kevin will just have to adapt, that's all."

She gave him an incredulous look. "Coming from you, that's quite a statement. From everything I've heard, O'Briens are not the most adaptable people in the universe. Stubborn as mules seems to be the universal consensus."

Mick laughed. "If you've figured that out, you'll do real well as one of us."

Alarmed by the expectation she heard in his voice, she said, "Mick, things really aren't good between Kevin and me right now. I'm not sure they can be fixed."

"They will be," he said confidently. "Trust me on that. We may be stubborn, but we do know a good woman when we find one. A lot of women in this town tried to catch Kevin's eye when he first moved back. He had no interest in any of them until you came along. You're obviously special to him. Don't give up on him just yet."

As he left to join his buddies at Sally's, she sighed. She hoped he was right, but she certainly wasn't going to count on it.

Not long after Mick left, Shanna's cell phone rang. The minute she saw Laurie's number, she answered.

"Guess what?" she said excitedly before her friend could even say hello.

"Henry's coming to stay with you," Laurie said, though she didn't sound half as thrilled about the news as Shanna was.

"Don't you dare try to bring me down," she told Laurie. "How'd you hear about this, anyway? It's not even official yet."

"There was an item on the society page the other day mentioning that Greg had been hospitalized, so I checked around to find out what was going on. Last night a friend of the Hamiltons told me the big news was that Mrs. Hamilton had decided yesterday to bring Henry to you. Is he there yet?"

Not surprised that Laurie was so well tapped into the society grapevine, Shanna said, "Assuming Greg approves of the idea, he's coming Friday."

"For how long?"

"Until school starts. Maybe longer."

"Oh, sweetie, you're setting yourself up to get your heart broken," Laurie said worriedly. "That family will think absolutely nothing of using you right now, then snatching Henry back the minute it's convenient for them."

"I know that's a possibility," Shanna conceded. "I'm okay with it. I'll take any time with Henry I can get."

"You're too softhearted for your own good."

"The important thing is that Henry needs me right now. He's going to be a part of my life again. I can't wait. Please be happy for me."

"You're being naive if you think it's not going to hurt like hell when he goes back. And he will go back. That's practically a given. The Hamiltons will never give him up permanently."

"He could wind up staying," Shanna said, unable to

keep the wistful note out of her voice. Naturally Laurie seized on it.

"There you go. You're already setting yourself up for disappointment."

Shanna lost patience. "Well, you tell me what I was supposed to do when Mrs. Hamilton asked me to look out for Henry for a few weeks."

"After what those people put you through, you should have said no."

"And who would that have hurt the most? Henry, that's who," Shanna said heatedly. "That little boy isn't responsible for any of this. He needs to be with someone who loves him, especially right now with Greg so sick."

Laurie uttered a sigh of resignation. "Okay, I can see I'm not going to change your mind, so let me ask one last question and then I'll drop this."

"What?"

"How does Kevin feel about this?"

"He doesn't know," she admitted.

"You haven't filled him in on what's happening?"

"Actually, he was here when Henry came for a quick visit yesterday with his grandmother," she admitted.

"So he knows Henry's your stepson."

"Not exactly. Kevin heard Henry call me Mommy and then he took off. Obviously he thought I'd kept something pretty major from him."

Laurie groaned. "Look, I know I haven't been a huge fan of that relationship, but are you going to throw it away over this? Greg and the Hamiltons are your past. Kevin could be your future."

"Kevin's the one who's refusing to talk. I've tried to explain, but he won't take my calls. I don't have time right now to worry about it."

"You're making a mistake."

"Several, according to you," Shanna said. "I can only do what seems right to me."

"Okay, then," Laurie said. "I love you, sweetie. I hope all of this works out the way you want it to. I'll try to get down there in the next couple of weeks to check on things."

"Only if you're going to be supportive," Shanna warned. "I don't want you around here criticizing my choices, especially when they involve Henry."

"Hey, I love Henry, too," Laurie declared. "He's a great kid who's gotten a raw deal. I'm not going to do anything to upset him. That doesn't mean I can't look out for his stepmother."

"I'm going to be just fine," Shanna said.

But having her best friend plant seeds of doubt in her head certainly didn't help her to make the claim with confidence.

Promptly at noon on Friday, Mrs. Hamilton arrived at the bookstore with Henry and what appeared to be enough suitcases for months, not weeks. As soon as the car stopped, Henry leaped out and ran to Shanna.

"I'm gonna stay with you," he announced happily. "For a really long time."

"I know," she said, as excited as he was. "It's going to be so much fun."

"Will I have my own room?" he asked. "It's okay, if I don't."

"You'll have your own room," she told him. "If you give me a couple of minutes to make a phone call, I'll take you upstairs and show it to you and your grandmother."

She called Bree's shop to let Jenny know that she

needed her now. She'd made arrangements for the teenager to shop sit for a couple of hours, while she showed Henry around the apartment and took him out for lunch. Bree had readily agreed to the plan when she'd been told Shanna's stepson was coming for a visit.

"Jenny can watch the store for you whenever you need her," Bree had offered. "I have a new full-time employee, and she'll be able to handle things here if I'm not around. I seem to be spending more and more time these days on theater business."

"If you don't mind me borrowing her, I'll pay Jenny anytime she fills in here," Shanna assured her. "I promise not to take advantage of you."

"You work the payments out with her," Bree had said. "She can balance her hours between us however she needs to."

The arrangement they'd made promised to work out well. Jenny had been delighted to have the possibility of a few more hours of work.

Now, as soon as Jenny arrived to take over, Shanna led Henry and his grandmother upstairs. The minute he saw his room, Henry beamed.

"This is totally amazing!" he enthused. "Look, Grandmother, there are posters of the Phillies on the walls, and the Eagles, too. They're my favorite teams."

"I know," his grandmother said. She smiled at Shanna. "You couldn't have done better at making him feel at home. I should head back to Philadelphia now and leave you to get settled."

"Already?" Henry asked, looking disappointed. "I thought we could have lunch first."

"I thought so, too," Shanna said. "Maybe just a quick one at the café next door?"

The older woman looked pleased by their insistence. "A quick one, then."

Downstairs, Shanna checked to make sure Jenny knew how to handle everything they'd been over. "I'll be at Sally's if you need me, and I have my cell phone with me."

"It's all good," Jenny assured her. "Bree has the same kind of cash register, and you showed me how to scan the price tags and fill in the receipt books."

Shanna grinned. "Sorry. I'm just a worrier."

"Well, there's no need. If I have even a tiny doubt, I'll call you. The cell number is right here."

Satisfied, Shanna led the others to the restaurant, knowing that this public introduction of Henry would be spread all over town by nightfall.

No sooner had they settled in a booth than Sally appeared, her order pad in hand, curiosity written all over her face.

"Well, now, who do we have here?" she asked, grinning at Henry.

"This is my stepson, Henry Hamilton," Shanna told her. "And this is his grandmother, Loretta Hamilton. Henry's going to be visiting with me for a while."

Sally beamed. "That's wonderful." She winked at Henry. "I'll expect to see you in here often. Now what can I get you?"

Shanna glanced toward her former mother-in-law, who was looking at the simple menu with a bemused expression. This was a far cry from her usual country club fare. "I know you love chicken salad," Shanna said to her. "Sally's is wonderful, especially on one of her freshly baked croissants."

"That does sound good," Mrs. Hamilton agreed at once. "With a cup of tea."

"Earl Grey, if you have it, Sally," Shanna added.

"I do." Sally turned to Henry. "What about you, young man?"

"I'd like a hamburger, please."

"What nice manners!" Sally said approvingly. "And Shanna, what about you?"

"I'll have the chicken salad on a croissant, as well."

"I'll be back with these in a minute," Sally assured them.

Despite the promise of a hasty return, though, Shanna noted that Sally stopped to pass along the latest gossip to several of the regulars on her way to the kitchen. By nightfall, half the town would know that Shanna's stepson—not her son—was visiting. Maybe word would make its way back to Kevin, though she wasn't counting on that distinction alone to mend fences with him. It was still evident she'd kept something significant from him.

When she turned back to her former mother-in-law, she saw that she was looking around the casual café with interest.

"I used to go to a place just like this when I was in school years and years ago. My friends and I went every afternoon."

"To check out the boys?" Shanna dared to tease.

Mrs. Hamilton chuckled. "I certainly never admitted that to my parents, but yes. I imagine that sort of thing will never change."

"Is that how you met Mr. Hamilton?"

"Oh no," she said, her expression nostalgic. "Our families had been friends for years. We practically grew up together. It was always assumed we would marry."

"What about love?" Shanna asked, trying to imagine a relationship based on family expectations rather than passionate love.

At one time, her question might have been greeted as impertinent, but now Mrs. Hamilton merely shook her head. "Young people today think love can only begin with chemistry and grand passion. In my day, we had those kind of feelings, of course, but we also knew that love and a strong marriage could grow out of friendship, mutual goals and respect."

"I don't remember about my real mom, but my dad and Mommy were in love," Henry said, his expression sorrowful. "Just not for very long."

Shanna gave him a quick hug. "It was complicated, sweetie. I still care about your dad, and I love you more than anything."

A grin broke across his face. "More than snow?"

"Definitely more than that," she said, playing the once-familiar game.

"More than rainbows?"

"Absolutely."

"More than flowers?"

"You bet."

He paused, his expression thoughtful, before offering the final challenge. "More than hot fudge sundaes?"

Shanna sighed heavily. "Hot fudge sundaes are really amazing," she said as if she were torn. Then she tickled him until he giggled. "Yes, more than hot fudge sundaes."

When she looked up, Mrs. Hamilton was watching them with tears in her eyes. "Excuse me," she said hurriedly. "I need to visit the restroom."

As Shanna watched her go, she experienced a fresh understanding of the woman who'd once held her in such disdain. Though she might seem stiff and unyielding, she truly did love her grandson. Enough to let him go.

Not a day went by that Kevin didn't hear from someone about the boy who was now living with Shanna. Her stepson, it seemed, not her son, but he couldn't see how that made much of a difference. The boy was obviously a big part of her life, and she'd kept his existence a secret. How could he forgive that?

Other people in town obviously didn't have the same dilemma. They were practically bursting with excitement over the news. Mick had hardly been able to contain the fact that he'd put furniture together for the boy. Bree and Jess were the worst, of course.

"He's such a cutie," Bree enthused.

"I know," Jess said. "I saw him with Shanna at Sally's on the day he arrived. He's darling. Don't you think so, Kev? You met him the night he dropped in for a visit, right?"

As he had that night, Kevin walked out of the room without a word. This was not a topic he intended to discuss, much less dissect, with anyone. Least of all his nosy family.

Bree, however, had no intention of letting him off the hook so easily. She was right on his heels.

"I thought so," she said, jabbing a finger in his stomach. "You're in a snit because she kept something from you."

"It's a pretty big something," he growled. "She'd apparently walked away from a child."

"Just like Mom and Georgia," Bree said knowingly.

"Sure, yes, just like Mom and Georgia. Are you saying you approve of that?"

"First of all, I wouldn't be judging her without knowing all the facts. And second, since I do have facts, I'm here to tell you it was nothing like what either Mom or Georgia did. If you would climb down off your high horse and talk to the woman, you'd find out just how different it was."

"There's nothing she could say—"

"Oh, stuff a sock in it and stop being a judgmental jerk without learning all the facts," Bree said, cutting him off. "You won't know if there is unless you actually listen to her." She gave him a knowing look. "Unless you're clinging to this just to put some distance between the two of you because you're scared you're falling in love with her."

Kevin tried to keep his expression neutral so Bree wouldn't see that she might be right. Instead, he challenged her. "If you know I'm wrong, why don't you fill me in?"

"Because you need to be talking to Shanna, not me. It's called communicating, Kevin. You need to learn how to do it."

He scowled at her. "Hey, that goes both ways, you know. It's not as if Shanna has been beating down the door here to fill me in."

"I'm willing to bet she's been leaving messages for you for days," Bree retorted.

He felt his face flush at the accusation. "She left a few," he admitted. "But if she really cared what I thought, she'd have come over here to make me listen."

Bree groaned. "Do you actually hear yourself? That's nuts, even for you."

"Thanks so much," he growled. He suspected he was being irrational, but, dammit, he thought he was justified in being ticked off.

She shook her head. "Heaven save me from two idiots with more pride than sense. Do I have to conspire with Jess and Abby to get you in the same room? Trust me, you won't even see it coming if I have to resort to that. The three of us are a lot sneakier than Gram, and she's already working on her plan to get you back together. You can count on that."

"No question about your capability when it comes to meddling," he muttered. And he didn't mean it as a compliment.

But at least she'd warned him. He'd have to be on guard from here on out, because the last thing he was in the mood for was a cozy chat with another woman who could abandon her son, or even a stepson with whom she'd obviously had a very close relationship.

And no matter what excuses she'd fed Bree, that was the bottom line. He'd seen the way that little boy had looked at Shanna. Kevin had felt his pain, because even though he'd been a teenager, he'd lived something very similar when Megan had walked out on all of them.

As far as he was concerned, what Shanna had done was unforgivable. He'd never understand how believing that somehow turned him into the bad guy.

22

Mick was so frustrated with Kevin, he actually considered driving to Annapolis to confer with Thomas. Maybe if he and his brother put their heads together, they could figure out some way to get through Kevin's thick skull that he was throwing away his best chance at happiness.

Mick knew all about being proud and stubborn. Hadn't he lost Megan by behaving exactly as Kevin was now? Of course, he also knew from that sad time in his life that there wasn't anyone on earth who could have gotten through to him. That was the one thing that kept him from going to Thomas for help. Okay, that and the fact that he didn't want to give his brother the satisfaction of reaching out to him for assistance with one of his own children.

"I don't know what to do to make things right between Kevin and Shanna," he told Megan when they were driving from the airport to the house.

"Maybe there's nothing you can—or should—do," she said. "Kevin has to work this out for himself. You did."

"And it took me too damn long to do it," Mick said. "I don't want to see him wasting that much time."

"Neither do I," she admitted.

Mick glanced over at her. "We could show him by example," he suggested.

She regarded him with suspicion. "Meaning?"

He warmed to the idea. "If we had a fancy wedding, showed him that two people can get past anything if they want to badly enough, he might reach out to Shanna."

Megan actually had the audacity to laugh at the suggestion. "Mick O'Brien, you're incorrigible. I am not marrying you to provide some lesson for our son."

"Did you hear me suggest that it wouldn't be about me loving you? I thought that was a given," he huffed.

"Then maybe you should have included at least a mention of it," she retorted.

"What's it going to take for me to wear you down, Meggie?" he asked with exasperation. "I'm running out of ways to prove to you that we can make it work this time. I'm a different man now. We'll be real partners, share everything. I'll be underfoot so much, you'll be calling around the country trying to line up jobs to get me out of the house."

"Now there's a scenario it's hard for me to imagine," she said.

Though they were miles from the turnoff to Chesapeake Shores and he'd been anxious to get home, Mick made a decision on the spot. He moved the car into the left lane and signaled for a turn. He probably should have taken Megan on this side trip weeks ago.

"Where are we going?" she demanded. "This isn't the way home."

"You'll see," he said, grimly determined to prove his point to her once and for all. If this didn't do it, he was out of ideas.

He drove to the site of a small development of affordable housing being built as part of the Habitat for Humanity program. He'd personally acquired and donated the land and was overseeing the construction. He jammed on the brakes and cut the engine.

"Look around," he ordered. "What do you see?"

She surveyed the scene in front of them for a moment, took note of the bustling activity.

"A construction site for a new housing development," she said, sounding bewildered. "Is it one of yours? It doesn't look like the kind of community you usually build."

He explained about the assignment he'd taken on. "I did this for you, so I could be close to home and still do what I'm best at. It was Ma's idea. She thought I could make a real contribution and impress you at the same time. I provided the land for this one, and I've called in favors from a lot of my friends. They're all pitching in with the construction, and the families who'll live here are helping out, too."

Megan stared at him, then at the houses. "I'm astounded," she said.

He frowned at that. "What does that mean? Shocked beyond belief?"

She nodded. "I can't believe you'd do something like this, Mick. You've always been generous, but this…" Her eyes filled with tears. "Mick, it's wonderful. What an amazing way to use your talent and experience!"

Her praise was nice, but it wasn't what he was after. "So, do you get it now?" he demanded. "I'm serious about you and me, Meggie. I'm not retired, but I am spending ninety percent of my time right here, close to home, at this site and a couple of others." Unable to keep the frustration out of his voice, he asked, "Is that going to be enough for you, or is there some other hoop you need me to jump through?"

She looked shocked by the question, or maybe it was his tone of voice that put that dismayed expression on her face. "Oh, Mick, I never meant for you to jump through hoops proving anything. You certainly haven't asked that of me, though I need to earn your trust again, as well. I just wanted to be sure, wanted both of us to be sure we could make it work this time. At my age, I don't want to go through another divorce because we still can't get it right."

"Do you think I do?" he asked indignantly. "We're both old enough and experienced enough to know that marriage takes work, more work than I was willing to put into it last time. Now, though, I'll do whatever it takes."

Megan's gaze locked with his, hers steady and unblinking. "Ask me again," she said with a hitch in her voice.

Mick regarded her blankly. "Ask you what again?"

She merely lifted a brow.

"Oh," he said, his heart suddenly hammering. He had to gather his thoughts, get the words exactly right. "Megan O'Brien," he began eventually, "will you do me the very great honor of becoming my wife, my partner, my soul mate? Will you call me on my mistakes and share everything with me?"

Her lips curved slowly and tears trickled down her cheeks. "Yes, Mick O'Brien, I believe I will."

Mick tried to sweep her into his arms, but in his big SUV, the gesture was more awkward than romantic. Too bad he hadn't picked her up in the classic convertible, but this moment was sweet enough. He wasn't going to waste too much time on regrets.

"I love you, Meggie," he said, stroking her cheek. "Always have, even when I was being a damn fool."

She laughed at that. "Me, too," she admitted. "But maybe this time, two old fools can avoid the same mistakes."

"I'm counting on that," he told her, right before he found a way to get his arms around her and kiss her without the dadgum gearshift skewering either one of them. "I can't wait to get home and share the news."

"No," she said at once. "We need to keep this to ourselves for now."

His temper stirred. "You tell me why we shouldn't tell the world."

"Think about it, Mick. Our daughter's getting married in another few weeks. We shouldn't steal any of Abby's limelight. And with our son's romance currently in a precarious state, it might be like rubbing salt in his wounds."

Mick sighed. "Are you always going to come up with one excuse or another?"

"No," she promised, lifting his hand and pressing a kiss to his knuckles. "The minute Abby and Trace are married and Kevin's sorted things out with Shanna, we'll make the big announcement." She grinned. "Though knowing your mother, she'll figure things out long before then."

"Ma does have a sixth sense about everything going on in our family, doesn't she?" he said. He consoled himself by saying, "Well, maybe this will give her time to adjust to the idea."

Megan nodded. "I want to be sure she understands that my coming back will never displace her."

"That'll work itself out, Meggie," he said with confidence. "Ma loves you."

"And I, her," she said. "But the two of us under one roof will take some compromises. I don't want her to be unhappy, Mick."

"She won't be, not as long as she can see how happy we are."

"I think you're being overly optimistic, because it's what you want. You know she's been fretting about this since we first started seeing each other again."

"True," he acknowledged. "But I also know that the two of you will work out the details so you're both happy. And I'll do my part to make sure she understands that we want her right there with us. She'll offer to move back to her own cottage, but she'd be miserable away from all the commotion, I think."

"Okay, then, we're agreed," Megan said. "We wait and we make sure things are right with Nell."

Mick wasn't overjoyed by the wait, but he could see the sense in it. "Agreed."

Megan squeezed his hand. "This will be a good thing, Mick. We can take our time and figure out all the details."

"What details?"

"I have a job in New York," she said, as if he needed reminding.

"You'll quit."

She frowned at that. "Not without something else lined up," she said emphatically. "I'm not going to sit around and be dependent on you for my happiness, the way I was before."

"Then you'll open an art gallery in Chesapeake Shores. Maybe that boss of yours will want to expand down here and open a branch or whatever you'd call it in your business. You could manage this one for him. Or start your own. Whatever you want to do, I'm behind you."

"Really? You won't object to me working?"

"Not as long as there's plenty of time for the two of us. You'll need an assistant you trust, too, because I want you to travel with me, Meggie. No more separations."

She nodded. "Agreed."

He grinned. "See how smoothly things are going to go? We've already negotiated through some tricky territory."

Megan laughed. "We have, haven't we?"

"It's going to work out just the way we want it to, Meggie." He thought of his inability to compromise in the past. Combined with her inability to ask for what she really wanted until it was too late, it had been a disaster. This time was going to be different. "It'll be smooth sailing."

She gave him a wry look. "No, it won't, but every bump will be worth it. I do believe that."

Mick nodded, satisfied. Maybe that was the key to a successful marriage, knowing there'd be many a bump in the road, but believing that, in the end, love was worth it.

Kevin knew he was in for a hard time when Trace and Jake showed up at the house on Saturday morning, apparently unified in some mission by Abby and Bree.

"I don't suppose the two of you are here to play a little one-on-one on the basketball court," he said as he deliberately sipped his coffee.

Jake and Trace settled into rockers on either side of him and set them in motion. They probably looked like three old men about to discuss the weighty issues of the world, but Kevin knew better.

"No basketball," Jake said. "I have to get to a landscaping job in an hour."

"And I'm taking the girls over to Myers's farm to ride ponies," Trace added.

"Then you're here because Bree and Abby sent you," Kevin said glumly.

"Exactly," Trace said.

"Can we just agree that I already know everything you're likely to say, and leave it at that?" Kevin asked hopefully.

Jake shook his head. "Nope. They're worried," he said.

"I know that."

"We need to reassure them," Jake added.

"They think you've misjudged Shanna and that you owe her a chance to explain what's going on," Trace added.

"I'm aware of that, too," Kevin said, gathering they were going to work through the entire lecture, no matter what. "Anything else?"

"I believe there was quite a bit more," Jake said. "But I tuned it out." He scowled fiercely at the other two men. "Which I will deny if either of you dare to repeat that."

"They won't hear it from me," Trace said. "I pretty much missed the rest, as well."

"Thank heaven for small favors," Kevin muttered. "You can go now. Your duty's done."

"Are you going to see Shanna?" Jake asked, his expression hopeful.

"Nope," Kevin replied.

Trace heaved a sigh. "Then our work here isn't done. We're supposed to make sure you go to see her and work this out."

"Are you supposed to drag me into town?" Kevin asked curiously, wondering if they'd actually dare to try. It had been years since he'd willingly been drawn into a brawl, but lately he'd been itching for something to pummel. Maybe these two men would do.

"I believe Bree would recommend force, if necessary," Jake said. "I'm not for it."

"Me, either," Trace said.

"Okay, then. Now what?" Kevin asked.

Jake shrugged. "Beats me."

"Any more of that coffee?" Trace asked. "I could use some before I go back for the girls."

"Wouldn't mind some, either," Jake said.

Kevin looked at the two of them and shook his head. "Do Abby and Bree have any idea how pitiful the two of you are?"

"Thankfully, no," Trace said.

Kevin laughed. "I'll get the coffee. Then, in the interest of brotherhood and all that, maybe I'll give you a few tips on dealing with my sisters."

"That would be welcome," Trace said. "Because the closer the wedding gets, the less and less I seem to understand Abby."

Jake nodded in commiseration. "Even after all these years, Bree's still a mystery to me."

"It's not just them," Kevin said before he left. "It's women, my friends. They're all an enigma."

"Amen to that," Jake said.

Kevin clapped them both on the shoulder. "There, you can go home and tell my sisters that the three of us ended this conversation in complete agreement."

He figured that would keep his sisters off his case, at least until they compared notes and started asking more detailed questions about why this cozy chat hadn't led to a reconciliation.

A month after Henry's arrival, Shanna stood in the doorway of her guest room, which was now decorated to appeal to a little boy. She still couldn't get over the fact that Henry was actually here, that it was entirely possible he could be here to stay, if the court approved the arrangement that she and Greg had come to last week, thanks to his family's determined intervention.

Henry was already enrolled in school here. She was going to legally become his guardian and, eventually, if Greg got through rehab and stayed on track under court supervision, he would be allowed unsupervised visitations with his son again. Time would tell about all that. In the meantime, Shanna or his parents would be there for all of Henry's visits with his dad. A judge was scheduled to rule on the arrangement next week, but with everyone involved in agreement, it seemed unlikely he would overrule the plan.

Henry stirred, rolled over and caught sight of her. A gap-toothed grin split his face. That smile was coming more frequently as the days went by and he felt increasingly secure.

"If you get dressed, we have just enough time to go to the town pier fishing before I have to go to work," Shanna told him. "What do you think?"

His answer was to scramble out of bed and tug on shorts and a shirt, then throw his arms around her. "I love you. I love fishing."

"I'm glad I come first," she teased. "Come on, there's cereal waiting in the kitchen."

Twenty minutes later they were at the pier. The sun filtered through the remnants of early-morning fog. There was already a hint of fall in the air, though it was still the early days of September. Henry scrambled up onto a bench, waited for Shanna to cast his line, then took the rod from her and clasped it tightly. She sat beside him, smiling at the little frown of concentration that knit his brow. She reached over and brushed his soft-as-silk hair back from his forehead, then looked up and straight into Kevin's wary gaze.

"I wasn't expecting to see you here," he said.

"We come here most Saturday mornings," she said. "Henry loves to fish."

He looked as if he didn't know what to say next and she didn't help him out. As time had passed and she'd realized that he had to know the truth, she'd come to accept that he simply didn't care about her enough to want to make things right. She'd recognized that her explanations would fall on deaf ears. He had no intention of forgiving her for keeping Henry's existence from him.

Now his gaze shifted to the boy beside her and the hardness in his expression softened slightly. It was back again, though, when he turned to her.

"Your stepson, I gather?" he said, proving he had heard at least some of the story by now.

She nodded. "I hope to be his legal guardian soon."

Confusion darkened his eyes. "What does that mean? What about his father?"

Henry looked up just then. "My daddy's sick. If the court says so, I'll get to stay here forever and ever."

Kevin looked from her to Henry and back again. "I don't understand."

"It's a long story."

"Something tells me it's one I need to hear," he said with obvious reluctance.

"I have a hunch Bree and Abby have been saying that for weeks now," she said.

He nodded. "I hate when they're right."

She chuckled. "I'm sure you do."

"Will you fill me in?"

"Another time," she said, pointedly looking toward Henry.

"Of course." He hesitated, then met her gaze. "I'm sorry

I apparently jumped to the wrong conclusion in the store that day, then compounded it by digging in my heels and refusing to listen when you tried to explain."

"You were just being an O'Brien," she said wryly. "Though I have to say it's one of the least attractive of the family traits."

"My sisters have mentioned that a time or two." He gave her a hopeful look. "I'll listen now, if it's not already too late."

"Henry's going to spend tomorrow with his grandparents and his dad," she said at last. "Jenny's going to watch the shop for me. Would you like to have lunch?"

"Lunch would be good. I'll pick you up at noon."

She nodded. "See you then." She turned to Henry. "Come on, sweetie. I have to go to work."

Disappointment spread across Henry's face, but he dutifully reeled in his line and climbed down off the bench.

"I have an idea," Kevin said. "I was going to take Davy fishing off the dock at the house in a little while. Maybe Henry would like to come along."

Shanna looked to Henry, but he was inching closer to her, obvious fear in his eyes. It was one thing for him to talk to Kevin while she was nearby, quite another to trust a man on his own. Living with his father's unpredictability had cost him his innocence. Quite possibly that was the worst of what Greg had done to his son.

"Another time," she said. "We can talk about that when I see you tomorrow."

"Sure," Kevin said. He smiled at Henry. "Maybe Shanna will come with you on my boat one day."

At that, Henry's eyes lit up. "You have a boat?"

"I do. It was a fishing boat, but now it's a research boat. It's being used to study the bay."

"Study how?"

"We test the water for pollution. We check on the oysters and the crabs and the fish. We want to be sure all of this is in good shape when you grow up and want to bring your kids here to fish."

"Awesome!" Henry said and turned eagerly to Shanna. "Can we?"

"Of course," she said, ruffling his hair. She glanced at her watch. "We have to run."

Kevin nodded. "I'll see you tomorrow, then."

She had the sense that his eyes were still on them, his gaze speculative, even after they'd left the pier and headed for Main Street.

"Is he your friend?" Henry asked Shanna as they walked back to the bookstore.

She nodded. "He's a good friend, yes."

Henry studied her. "Like you and daddy used to be?"

Shanna was at a loss. "In a way."

"Oh," he said, a faint tremor in his voice.

Shanna stopped walking and hunkered down in front of him. "Does that bother you? Didn't you like him?"

Henry seemed to be struggling to form his thoughts into words, but there was no mistaking his troubled, unhappy expression. Shanna waited.

"He was okay, I guess," he said eventually. "And it's cool that he has a boat."

"Then what's bothering you?"

"You and Daddy got married," he said, looking down at the ground. "And then you went away. What if he goes away, too? Will it be my fault?"

The giant leap he'd taken was a shock. "Henry, first of all, Kevin and I are not going to get married. We've never even talked about that. Second, you had absolutely nothing to do with why your dad and I got a divorce, and you certainly won't come between Kevin and me. You're a terrific boy. Your dad and I are both very lucky to have you in our lives. You do know that, don't you?"

He shrugged. "I guess."

She hesitated, then said, "You know, Kevin has a little boy, too. You heard him mention Davy. Well, he's almost three. And just like you, his mommy died. You know what that's like. You could be his friend and help him out. You have a lot in common. You both love to read. I know he'd love it if you'd read to him sometimes."

"It would almost be like being a big brother," he said, excitement slowly threading through his voice. "I mean, if you change your mind and get married."

"Hey, slow down," she said with a laugh. "You're getting way ahead of things. Let's just focus on all of us trying to be friends, okay?"

For now, having Kevin back in her life as a friend was all that mattered. After the way Kevin had shut her out of his life, she wasn't sure *she* was ready to forgive *him* now. Tomorrow's lunch would tell if that was possible. After that, well, they'd both have to see what came next.

23

When Kevin got back to the house on Saturday morning, he found Davy already on the pier fishing with Mick. He walked out and joined them.

"I see the two of you got a head start on me," he said, ruffling his son's sun-streaked hair.

"Fish don't wait around all day," his father said.

"Caught anything so far?"

"Look in the bucket," Mick suggested, a gleam in his eyes.

Kevin glanced in and found a tiny fish swimming in circles in the salty seawater in the pail. "Nice one," he said wryly.

"Davy's first catch of the day," Mick informed him.

Kevin grinned at his son. "Good job, kiddo, but I'm thinking he ought to be back swimming with his family and friends."

"Dinner," Davy insisted, his jaw set stubbornly.

"Believe me, I tried to convince him," Mick said. "He wants Ma to see. Apparently he promised her he'd bring back lots of fish for dinner."

Kevin barely held back a grin. "She'll be impressed, no doubt about it."

"So, where'd you run off to so early?" Mick asked as Kevin baited a hook and tossed his own line into the water, then settled down on the other side of his son. The warmth of the sun seeped into his shoulders and relaxed him after the early-morning jog that had taken him to the town pier.

"I went for a run," he said.

"See anyone interesting?" Mick asked with exaggerated innocence.

As Kevin studied his father's expression, his gaze narrowed. "You already know I ran into Shanna, don't you? How the heck did you find out so fast?"

Mick chuckled. "Cell phones, pal. I not only got a call, I saw a picture of the two of you on the town pier. Bree could hardly wait to share the news that the two of you are speaking again."

Kevin shook his head. "I really am thinking more and more about moving into a monastery."

Mick howled. "Yeah, Thomas mentioned something about that. I have a tremendous admiration for the priesthood, but I'm thinking you'd be better off working things out with Shanna. That's where you belong."

Kevin regarded him curiously. "You sound so sure about that. Why?"

"Love's a precious commodity," Mick said. "I can see it in your eyes when you're around her. She's brought you back to life after a real sad time. That's not something to be taken lightly. It's certainly not something you throw away because you've had a disagreement."

"We never had a disagreement," Kevin said.

Mick rolled his eyes. "Because you never gave her a chance to even tell you what's been going on in her life," he said. "Hard to disagree when one of you's sitting around in the dark."

"Save the lecture. I've heard it before."

"But apparently it didn't sink in," Mick said unrepentantly.

"We're having lunch tomorrow," Kevin said. "I'm surprised Bree didn't tell you that, as well."

"Sadly, she wasn't close enough to hear what the two of you were saying."

Kevin laughed at the obvious frustration in his voice. "That must have driven her wild. You, too."

Mick nodded. "It did. But lunch tomorrow is good news. I'll be sure to tell your sister."

Kevin was about to make a rude remark, but just then Davy's line began to jerk. He reached over and helped his son hang on, then reeled in the fish. This one was a legitimate catch, big enough for more than a mouthful.

"Good job!" he praised.

"In bucket," Davy ordered.

Kevin added the fish to the pail, then watched as Davy squatted down to watch them, his expression filled with delight.

"See, Daddy, friends," he announced, pointing.

"Uh-oh," Mick murmured. "Those fish are going home with us for sure now."

Kevin sighed. "Afraid so, but at least they're not likely to wind up on the dinner table. Something tells me we're going to have to do some fast talking or these two will become pets."

Mick shook his head. "Not to worry. I'm a clumsy guy. I might just trip over that bucket, send it flying right into the water."

Kevin stared at him. "Is that how my fish always ended up back in the bay?"

"Are you kidding me? You tossed 'em back the second

we got 'em off the line. If I wanted fish for dinner, I had to catch 'em when you weren't around and get your mother to cook 'em when you weren't looking."

"Come to think of it, that's exactly what Mother said when she suggested I work with Thomas."

Mick regarded him with a disgruntled expression. "I suppose she was right about that," he admitted grudgingly. "You're happy with this new job, aren't you?"

"I am," he said. "A lot happier than I would have been running fishing charters."

"You and Thomas get along okay?"

"Sure. He's a reasonable man."

"And I'm not?" Mick said, instantly taking offense.

Kevin stared at him. "I did not say that. Look, I know you were hoping that either Connor or I would take an interest in your company, but you know neither of us has the skill."

"You learn skills. You're not born with them," Mick grumbled. "Do you think I came out of the womb with a hammer in my hand?"

"No, but the work suited you, just as this research suits me."

"I suppose." Mick studied him. "Does it make you happier than being an EMT?"

Kevin nodded. "For now, absolutely. Maybe one of these days, I'll be ready to do that again. The local squad can always use trained volunteers," he said. "I know I have skills that are needed, but given everything that's happened, this new career makes sense for me. It's not something I ever shared with Georgia. It's a fresh start."

"Can't argue with that," Mick said. "I'm a big fan of fresh starts myself these days."

"You and Mom?"

Mick nodded. "We're making real progress. I hope you're going to be okay with that."

"I've gotten used to the idea," Kevin admitted. "Having her around again has been better than I expected. If the two of you can work things out, that's all that really matters. I shouldn't have been judging you."

"Or her," Mick reminded him.

"Okay, true."

Mick stood up. "Seems to me we already have the only two fish out here that are biting this morning. What say, we go inside and get something cold to drink? Davy, you ready for some juice?"

Davy nodded, stood up and went straight to the bucket and tried to get a grip on the handle, but it was too heavy for him.

"I'll take it," Mick said, then awkwardly juggled it and let it drop. It landed on its side and rolled off the dock.

Davy ran to the edge, but Kevin caught him before he could fall in after it. His son looked up at him with a sad expression.

"Fishes gone," Davy announced sorrowfully.

Kevin nodded. "Fishes gone, but you know what? It's a good thing. They're home where they belong. We'll catch some more another day."

Davy immediately brightened. "'kay."

Mick shook his head as he watched his grandson. "That ability to let go and move on is a wonderful thing to see."

Kevin nodded. He hoped he'd be able to do the same after he saw Shanna tomorrow.

After sending Henry off with Mrs. Hamilton on Sunday morning, Shanna checked to make sure Jenny had things under control at the shop, then went upstairs to get dressed for her lunch date with Kevin. A half hour later, Laurie appeared at her door, Drew at her side. They both looked as if they were bursting with excitement. They couldn't seem to take their eyes—or their hands—off each other.

"Well, you're the last two people I expected to see this morning," Shanna said, stepping aside to let them in.

Laurie beamed at her. "We're getting married," she blurted as soon as she was inside. "Today, if you can spare the time to be my maid of honor."

Shanna blinked at the announcement. "I thought the wedding had been postponed indefinitely. What happened?"

Drew gave her a chagrined look. "I woke up and realized I was being a fool. I came home last night and told Laurie I wanted to go through with the wedding, if she'd still have me."

"And I said yes," Laurie added, "but only if we didn't wait. So, here we are. We have the license and I've found a notary who is willing to perform the ceremony. All we need is you." She looked over Shanna's dressy outfit. "And here you are, all dressed up. It's perfect. I consider that a good omen."

Shanna debated telling her that she had plans with Kevin and her own reconciliation, but why ruin Laurie's big moment? "I'll need to make a quick phone call," she told her. "Then I'm all yours."

As self-absorbed as Laurie could be at times, in this instance, she immediately read between the lines. "You were going out, weren't you?"

"As a matter of fact, yes, but it's no big deal. Kevin and I can reschedule."

"Bring him along," Laurie said, glancing at Drew for approval.

"Absolutely," Drew said. "I can use a best man. Maybe he wouldn't mind filling in."

"I don't know…"

"Come on, Shanna. Maybe it will give him ideas," Laurie said. Given her objections to Shanna's relationship with Kevin, the remark just proved she was in a love-induced haze. "We're going to go to the inn for lunch after the ceremony," she continued excitedly, "so it will almost be the wedding we originally planned, just smaller and less expensive. I want both of you there to celebrate with us."

Before Shanna could agree, there was another knock on the door. She opened it to find Kevin standing there.

"Am I too early?" he asked.

"That depends. It seems Laurie and her fiancé have decided they're getting married today, and they want us to stand up for them. You can run for your life or come inside."

"Of course he's coming inside," Laurie said, joining them. "Come on, Kevin, you can't let us down."

Laurie introduced Kevin and Drew, then linked her arm through Drew's. "Okay, everyone, let's get out of here and seal this deal before Drew makes another run for it."

Kevin cast a helpless look in Shanna's direction, but she merely shrugged. Once Laurie set her mind to something, comparisons to a steamroller came readily to mind.

"Here's the address of the notary," Laurie said to Kevin. "Do you know where this is?"

"I do," he said. "Why don't I drive?"

"Perfect," Laurie said. "Drew and I can ride in back and pretend we're in a limo. No looking in the rearview mirror, though, because we're probably going to make out."

Kevin chuckled. "I promise not to look."

"But I will," Shanna warned, "so behave yourselves."

The drive took barely five minutes, and the ceremony was only slightly longer. Despite the lack of formality, Laurie looked radiant when the notary pronounced them man and wife. Drew looked faintly dazed, but nearly as happy. Shanna wondered if that wasn't the way to do it—simply make a decision to wed and dive in, rather than dragging things out and allowing time for a million doubts to creep in.

"Now to the inn," Laurie said imperiously. "I spoke to Jess, and she already has champagne on ice for us."

When they reached The Inn at Eagle Point, they were directed to a small private dining room, which Jess had miraculously managed to decorate with flowers, the inn's best china and beautiful crystal to celebrate the occasion. She even had music playing in the background.

Shanna turned to Kevin. "Your sister's amazing. I know she had practically no time at all to pull this off, but look how beautiful this is!"

"Jess is a romantic and Bree does flowers. I suspect she pitched in, too."

"It's absolutely gorgeous," Laurie said. "I couldn't have asked for a lovelier wedding reception."

Shanna drew Laurie aside and studied her friend's face, looking for signs that she was disappointed not to have had the big fancy wedding she'd initially wanted. All she saw was a woman practically glowing with happiness. Shanna gave her a fierce hug. "I am so happy this worked out the way you wanted it to," she told her friend.

Laurie beamed. "I still can't believe he changed his mind, that he really missed me."

"Sometimes absence really does make the heart grow fonder," Shanna said, wondering if their separation had made Kevin miss her, as well. "Drew obviously just needed a little time to get used to the idea of being married."

Laurie laughed. "Oh, I think that part still scares the hell out of him, but at least he got through the wedding."

Shanna smiled. "Maybe anyone getting married should have a little fear. It's a huge step, and it is forever."

Laurie clapped a hand over her heart dramatically. "Now you're scaring *me!*"

"Nothing scares you." She glanced toward Drew, who hadn't taken his eyes off Laurie, as if he hardly dared to believe his luck. "Why don't you go and dance with your new husband?" Shanna suggested.

"Only if you'll dance with the best man," Laurie said, leading her across the room to where the men stood.

Kevin hesitated, then asked, "Would you like to dance?"

Shanna nodded and moved into his arms. The moment she was there, she remembered exactly how safe and secure he made her feel and how much she'd missed that feeling. She lifted her gaze to his.

"Thank you for doing this. I know it's not the way you planned to spend today. We still have a lot of things to talk about."

"And we'll get to those," he told her. "But for now, it's kind of nice being with two people who are so happy." His expression turned nostalgic. "I remember feeling that way once."

"When you married Georgia?"

He shook his head. "The night I spent in your bed."

Tears immediately filled her eyes. "Kevin, you shouldn't say things like that."

"Why not? It's true."

"So much has happened since then," she reminded him. "I know I've made you miserable."

"You didn't," he said. "I made myself miserable by not trusting you. I took the worst memories from my past and imposed them on you without bothering to find out the truth. You tried to explain, but I was too stubborn even to listen. That's all on me."

She pretended to consider his words. "You know, you're right," she said with an exaggerated display of drama. "You were a jerk."

He laughed. "I was." His expression sobered. "But I do want to know the whole story. Maybe when we leave here?"

"If there's time," she agreed. "Henry will be back around six."

He gestured toward Laurie and Drew, who were in a tight embrace and barely swaying to the music. "Something tells me they'll hardly notice if we leave."

"I don't think you're supposed to walk out on the bride and groom," she said. "They have to go first. That's the tradition."

"This isn't exactly a traditional couple," Kevin said wryly. "I doubt it will take much to convince them this party is over and they're free to move on to the wedding night, or the wedding afternoon, as it were."

"I could suggest they have their meal served in their room," Shanna said.

"Do it."

She waited until the song ended, then tapped Laurie on the shoulder. "I think maybe you should take this party upstairs and have room service deliver your lunch. You two can enjoy it in privacy."

Laurie's expression filled with dismay. "We invited you here for a reception, and now we're ignoring you."

"You just got married," Shanna said. "We're not insulted. Honest."

Laurie glanced at Drew, blushing. "It would be nice to go upstairs."

Drew's gaze never left her face. "Works for me."

"Then go with our blessing," Shanna told them. She hugged Laurie. "I'm so happy for you." She turned to Drew. "Be good to her, you hear me?"

"Always," he promised.

Kevin kissed Laurie's cheek, then shook Drew's hand.

"Thanks for being a part of our wedding," Laurie told him. "Next time, I expect to be dancing at yours."

Shanna felt heat flame in her cheeks at Laurie's words. "Pay no attention to her. Women in love say crazy stuff."

"I'm serious," Laurie said.

"Go," Shanna ordered, blaming champagne and the romantic aura of her wedding for Laurie's change of heart about her and Kevin.

As soon as Laurie and Drew were gone, she turned to Kevin. "Now what?"

He reached for her hand. "Let's get out of here."

"We could just have lunch here."

"Not with my sister lurking about the premises," he said. "Lunch is one thing, but there's no way we could have a private conversation."

"You probably have a point. Where, then?"

He hesitated. "You know, I'm not sure. I have it on good authority that my sisters have spies everywhere. Do you know that Bree took pictures of us on the pier yesterday and sent them out with her cell phone?"

If she hadn't been so appalled, Shanna might have laughed. It sounded like something an O'Brien would do.

"My apartment then," she suggested. "We could pick up sandwiches or pizza and take them to my place. Unless one of them climbs a tree on the town green with a zoom lens on a camera or binoculars, they won't be able to see us."

Kevin nodded. "That'll work. Why don't I drop you off, then pick up the food. Any preference?"

"Quiche and a caesar salad sounds good to me. Is there anything on the menu at the French café that you like?"

"I'll find something."

He let her out in the alley behind the bookstore, where the stairs led up to her apartment. "I'll be back shortly."

Shanna was halfway up the stairs when the back door to Bree's shop opened and she popped her head out.

"Trying to sneak past me?" she inquired.

Shanna laughed. "Going home. You didn't enter into the equation."

"Where's my brother going? I thought you'd be together all afternoon. You didn't have another fight, did you?"

"Actually we were in a wedding," Shanna told her, resigned to supplying enough details to satisfy Bree's curiosity.

"Oh, that's right. I ran the flowers over to the inn earlier. Your friend Laurie got married. How was it?"

"Fast-paced, but, you know, I think the impulsive nature of it suited her just fine."

"Is Kevin coming back?"

Shanna gave her a wry look. "Not if he knows you're lurking in the alley."

Bree chuckled. "Okay, I get it. I'll go back inside and mind my own business."

"Really?" Shanna asked skeptically. "Is that possible?"

"For a good cause, yes," Bree assured her. "This is a good cause, right? The two of you are going to work things out?"

"I hope so," Shanna said. "I want us to be friends again."

"Friends?" Bree exclaimed indignantly. "This better be about more than that. You both need to get serious."

"How about laying off and letting us take one step at a time," Shanna said, her message pointed, but her tone gentle.

Bree sighed. "I suppose you're right. Meddling's usually counterproductive."

"Yes, it is."

"Okay, I'm gone," Bree said, stepping back inside and shutting the door.

Before Shanna had climbed another couple of steps, Bree's door opened again.

"One more thing," she said. "Then I'll disappear for real."

"Yes?"

"Kevin loves you. I know he does. So, even if he messes up the words, listen for what's in his heart, okay?"

"I think your brother's perfectly capable of speaking for himself," Shanna told her. "But, unlike his recent behavior, I *will* listen. I promise."

"All I'm asking," Bree said, closing the door again. This time it remained shut.

Shanna sighed as she continued up the steps and went inside to wait. She was beginning to understand the kind of pressure that Kevin lived with every day. He had this wonderful, well-meaning family, but all those expectations, all that certainty that they knew what was best for him, must be exhausting. She felt it, and she could pretty much tell them to bug off, if she wanted to. He had to sit back and listen.

Not that he had to heed their advice. She'd seen evidence that he had the same independent streak the rest of the

O'Briens had. She supposed it was a necessity in that family.

But despite all the potential drawbacks she foresaw, the bottom line was that she wanted to be one of them. She wanted to be Kevin's wife.

The admission, phrased for the first time in exactly that way, with no hesitation, startled her. She'd allowed herself to acknowledge missing him, even loving him, but this was the first time she'd looked into the future and seen so clearly what she wanted.

Even as she had the realization, she could hear Laurie's voice reminding her that she'd wanted the same thing when she'd rushed into marriage with Greg. The two men, however, could not have been more different. And their families, well, the O'Briens were warm and welcoming. The Hamiltons had been stiff, cold and unyielding, at least until recently.

Convinced not only of what—*who*—she wanted, but that it was the right decision for her, she couldn't help wondering if what Kevin had to say this afternoon would open the door to that kind of future for the two of them. Or, once he heard more about her past marriage and the complicated situation with Henry, if he would slam the door on the two of them forever.

24

Kevin noticed that the back door to Flowers on Main was ajar as he took the steps up to Shanna's apartment two at a time. He knew instinctively that his sister was standing just inside that door. Upstairs, on the landing, he leaned over the railing and hollered, "Close the door and go back to work."

He heard Bree chuckle, but the door closed quietly. Only then did he knock on Shanna's door.

When she barely opened it a crack to peer out, it was his turn to laugh. "Making sure the coast is clear before you let me in?"

"Something like that," she said, stepping aside so he could enter.

"Did Bree spy on you, too?"

"Accosted me with questions is more like it," she said. "You?"

"Nope. She stuck with peeking out the back door of her shop."

"I love your family, but they're a little obsessed when it comes to the two of us."

"Tell me about it. I've had Mick, Trace and Jake on my case recently. You should probably be happy to know they're all on your side."

"I didn't realize our situation called for taking sides," she said, as she reached into the bags he'd brought and put their food onto dishes she'd already set out on a table by the window overlooking the town green.

Kevin shrugged. "We're talking O'Briens here. They take sides over everything, which is one reason my father and uncles rarely speak. I'm pretty sure Uncle Jeff's daughter, Susie, is the only cousin who defies the rules. She speaks to all of us. Her brothers barely nod if they pass us in the street. The only time there's detente is on holidays, when Gram's around."

"But isn't the fight between your father, Thomas and Jeff?" she asked, regarding him with bewilderment.

"That's how it started," he acknowledged. "Like I said, sides were chosen. Facts and logic had little to do with it. All that was required was ingrained family loyalty."

"But you're *all* O'Briens," Shanna protested.

Kevin chuckled. "There you go, trying to impose logic on this."

Shanna sat down at the table, picked up her fork, speared some romaine lettuce, then chewed thoughtfully. "Doesn't it make you crazy?" she asked after a while. "Who can work up the energy to keep a grudge going after all these years?"

He leaned forward. "You'd never know it to see them now, but my father didn't speak to my mother for something like fifteen years after the divorce. Most of us kids didn't speak to her, either, unless Gram forced us to when Mom came to visit."

"So that's what I could have looked forward to, if you hadn't decided to listen to my side of the story about Henry? You'd have frozen me out from now till doomsday?"

"What can I say? It's a family tradition."

"That's just nuts."

"I know," he agreed. "But I'm here now, and I want to know everything. Before you even start, I apologize for misjudging you, jumping to conclusions, refusing to listen to your explanations and all of the other idiotic things I did."

"Okay, do you want to hear the long version or the short version?" she asked.

"Whichever one you want to give me," he told her.

She began haltingly, but eventually the words started to spill out. Kevin cursed as Shanna told him about her disastrous marriage to Henry's father.

"Let me be clear about one thing," she said. "Greg was never physically abusive to me or to Henry, but his unpredictability and verbal abuse was almost as bad. Eventually I realized that I couldn't stay. It was only the thought of what might happen to Henry if I left that kept me there even as long as I stayed."

"You should have left the minute you realized how bad his addiction to alcohol was," Kevin said.

"I'd made vows," she said simply. "More important, there was Henry to consider." She met Kevin's gaze. "I loved him as if he were my own."

"You should have taken him with you."

"I thought about that, believe me, but with absolutely no legal right to him, I would have been charged with kidnapping. Since no one—not even his own family—believed me about Greg's drinking and his abuse, I knew they'd never believe that I'd done it to keep Henry safe. We'd have been on the run for the rest of our lives. How could I do that to him? In some ways that seemed as cruel as leaving him with his dad. It was a no-win situation."

"Surely the law would have been on your side," Kevin protested. "There must have been evidence, something. You would have been protecting a child, for heaven's sake."

"Nothing," she told him. "Leaving Henry behind was the hardest thing I've ever done in my life. If the nanny hadn't been there, I don't think I could have done it. Every day since, I've prayed that his family would wake up to what was going on and keep Henry safe. His father never hit him, but his yelling used to terrify Henry. And that was if he was even around. The nanny was the only person in Henry's life most of the time."

"How did he wind up here with you?"

She explained about the accidental overdose, the hospital stay, Greg's liver complications, and the decision by Greg's family that Henry needed a more stable environment. "He'd bonded with me. Even before Greg and I were officially engaged, Henry was calling me Mommy. At first we both tried to discourage it, but it made him so happy. I think that was part of why we finally decided to marry, because we knew how thrilled Henry would be."

She sighed, thinking back to the time when they'd actually been a real family. It had been so brief. Then Greg's drinking had started again in earnest.

"So, after keeping you from him for over a year, they suddenly realized you were the parent he needed? And you agreed to step in?" he asked incredulously.

"I think Greg's family knew all along, but they would never admit such a thing to the world. Then the circumstances changed, and they've been forced to take drastic steps to ensure Henry's happiness." She grinned. "The nanny helped. Greta kept insisting that Henry would be better off with me. I have to give Mrs. Hamilton credit, though. In the end, she was the one who brought him here. It had to have been humbling for her to admit that I'd been right, but she did it."

"She was the one with him in the store that day?"

Shanna nodded. "She finally realized that Greg wasn't able to provide Henry with the kind of life he deserved and that getting Greg well again was going to be all she and her husband could possibly contend with. She convinced Greg to agree to let me become Henry's legal guardian. We'll see where it goes from here. She even offered to send Greta here to help me look out for Henry, but in the end, Greta decided to accept a position with another family."

Kevin was stunned. "Hold on a minute. Are you saying Henry could wind up back with his father?"

She nodded. "But only if Greg's health improves."

"You're taking a huge risk. Are you sure it's worth it? Do you love this child?"

"Of course I do," she said. "As far as I'm concerned, he's my son, no matter what the law says. I know it's a risk, but it's one I have to take. Leaving him behind before left this huge hole in my heart."

Kevin couldn't help wondering where this left the two of them. "You have a lot on your plate right now. I know I've made it worse."

"Not worse. I just wanted so badly for you to understand. When you wouldn't take my calls, I thought there was no way we'd ever get back the friendship we had before." She met his gaze. "I hated the thought of that."

"It wasn't much of a picnic for me, either," he admitted. "I had no idea how much I'd miss you. I kept telling myself it was for the best. Bree suggested I was using this situation to keep from admitting how much I love you."

He stood up, walked around the table and held out his

hand. Shanna placed hers in his and stood up. The air between them sizzled.

And then the door opened and Henry came bursting in, followed by his grandmother. He skidded to a stop at the sight of Kevin. Shanna tore her hand out of his grasp and knelt to give the boy a hug.

"How was your day?" she asked him. "Did you have fun with your dad?"

Kevin caught the subtle shake of Mrs. Hamilton's head, even as Henry's eyes welled up with tears.

"Greg wasn't feeling well," she said stiffly.

Shanna gathered Henry close. "I'm so sorry, buddy."

"It was okay," he said, putting on a brave face. "Grandma and Grandpa took me to a baseball game." He sighed. "But the Phillies lost."

"Oh, dear, you really aren't having a good day, are you?" Shanna said, brushing the tears from his cheeks.

"I'll bet I know a way to make it better," Kevin said, not entirely sure he should intrude, but unable to stand by and watch the boy's misery. "Why don't we pick up my son and go out on that boat trip I promised you?" He met Shanna's gaze. "What do you think? We won't stay out late."

"I think that's a wonderful idea," Mrs. Hamilton said, regarding him with sudden approval. "Henry loves boats, don't you?"

Henry nodded eagerly.

"Okay, then," Kevin said. "Shanna, you know where the marina is. Why don't I meet you and Henry there in an hour? I'll go get Davy."

She smiled at him. "We'll be there."

As he passed Mrs. Hamilton, she stopped him with a touch on his arm. "Thank you," she said in an undertone. "He really needed something to turn this day around."

Kevin nodded. "I'm happy I can help."

And though everything he'd learned here this afternoon made his heart ache for both Henry and Shanna, he was filled with determination to see that their lives got better from here on out. He'd been raised to be protective of those he loved. Now, it seemed, he counted Shanna and that little boy among them.

Henry couldn't stop talking about going out on Kevin's boat. The trip seemed to have wiped out all of the day's earlier unhappiness.

"It was so fun, wasn't it, Mommy?" he said again as he climbed into bed.

"It was great," she agreed.

"And Davy's really smart for a little kid, huh?"

"He is."

"Kevin knows lots and lots of stuff about the bay. Did you know all those things he was telling us?"

"No, I didn't."

"I want to learn all that, so I can do what he does someday," he announced.

It sounded to Shanna as if he'd developed a serious case of hero worship. On the one hand, she was glad about that. Heroes had been in short supply in his young life. On the other, there were no certainties about what role Kevin might continue to play in his life.

"Kevin says he'll see me after school tomorrow," Henry announced. "He says he brings Davy by the store sometimes when he gets home from work and that we can go for ice cream."

This was news to Shanna. "He told you all that, did he?"

"He promised," Henry said, his expression serious. "Does he keep his promises?"

"He's kept all the ones he ever made to me," she assured him.

"Cool."

She leaned down and pressed a kiss to his forehead. "Get some sleep, kiddo. It's way past your bedtime and you have school in the morning."

"But I wanted to look at one of those books you have on the bay," he protested.

"Tomorrow," she insisted.

"Okay," he said readily and closed his eyes.

Shanna stood there for a moment, lost in the joy of knowing he was here with her and safe. In a few days she'd know if this arrangement would last.

"I can't sleep if you're going to stare at me," he murmured.

She laughed. "Sorry. I'm turning out the light right now. Love you."

There was only the slightest hesitation before he whispered, "Love you, too."

Outside his door, she leaned against the wall and blinked away tears. Every time she earned those softly spoken words, she felt blessed. One of these days, she hoped he'd learn to say them freely, filled with trust in the love surrounding him.

The house was in a total state of chaos. Abby's wedding was two hours away. Megan was in an absolute frenzy over last-minute details. Jess had run off to make sure everything at the inn was under control. Bree and Trace's sister Laila were trying to keep Abby calm, no small task with Carrie and Caitlyn underfoot and practically dancing with excitement.

Kevin spent one minute in the midst of the frenzy, then

headed outside, where he found Jake, Connor and Mick trying to keep Trace calm. Kevin looked at his soon-to-be brother-in-law and shook his head.

"What's your problem, pal?" he asked the groom. "You were the one who couldn't wait for this day to get here."

"I'm not relaxing until Abby's walked down the aisle and actually said *I do,*" Trace said. "There's still time for her to back out."

"She's not backing out," Mick told him. "I won't allow it."

Kevin chuckled. "Don't let her hear you say that. She'll be on the first plane to anywhere, if she thinks you're issuing edicts."

"Good point," Mick said, reversing his stance at once.

Just then Carrie and Caitlyn ran outside, the ribbons in their hair already coming undone, curls escaping.

"Mommy looks really, really beautiful," Carrie told Trace.

"I'll bet she does," he said.

Caitlyn reached for his hand. "Wanna see?"

"Nope, it's bad luck," Trace said, holding back.

Both girls stared at him, not comprehending. "How come?"

"It's just a silly superstition," Mick said. "But women believe it, so men have to act accordingly."

"I don't get it," Carrie said.

"Neither do I," Mick said. "How about I take you two over to the inn? We can check and make sure everything's ready for the ceremony. Trace, you want to come along? We're just in the way around here."

"I'll grab Davy and meet you there," Kevin said. "I want to go over his duties as ring bearer again. Otherwise the wedding rings are likely to wind up at the bottom of the pool."

Trace frowned at him. "Don't even joke about that."

Kevin patted his shoulder. "Settle down. Everything is going to go smoothly. Davy is going nowhere near the pool, with or without the rings."

"Okay, fine," Trace said, wiping his brow.

Mick shook his head, his expression pitying. "For a man who was so intent on getting on with this wedding, you're in a sorry state today."

"I'll be fine after the ceremony," Trace repeated. "Has anyone heard from my folks?"

"They're meeting us at the inn," Kevin reminded him.

Trace nodded. "Right."

"In case you were wondering, your sister's inside with Abby," Mick added. "Now that everyone's accounted for, can we go?"

"Sure," Trace said, following Mick and the girls to the car.

Fifteen minutes later, Kevin found them on the lawn at the inn where chairs had been set up on the grass for the ceremony. Tents had been set up for the reception following the service. The bay, splashed with the colors of sunset, would serve as a backdrop for it all.

There were only about fifty guests expected, and most had already arrived. He spotted Shanna, holding Henry's hand, standing off to the side. He crossed to her. She saw Davy and immediately knelt down.

"Don't you look handsome," she told him, adjusting the collar of his tiny tuxedo. Then her gaze met Kevin's. "How are you doing? You look almost as nervous as the groom."

"I have a lot of responsibility making sure my kid makes it down the aisle with the rings," he told her. "Trace is already freaking out about it."

She chuckled. "Based on what I saw, Trace is freaking out about everything."

"If you ask me, your friend Laurie and Drew had the right idea. Do all this on impulse and get it over with."

"Now there's a romantic notion," she commented.

"Georgia and I put our wedding together in two days and got married in the airport," he said, then wished he'd kept his mouth shut when he saw Shanna's expression. She looked dismayed. "I suppose you had a big, fancy wedding."

"It was really, really big," Henry confirmed. "I was there."

Shanna sighed. "Which just goes to prove that it doesn't really matter what kind of wedding you have. There are no guarantees."

"True," Kevin said, suddenly feeling deflated. Lately he'd been feeling more optimistic, about his life, about the two of them. Now, in less than a minute, he'd brought them both down.

"Look, I'd better get Davy over there with the rest of the wedding party. I'll see you after the ceremony, okay?"

She nodded.

He started away, then turned back. "You look beautiful by the way. I don't think I mentioned that before."

She smiled self-consciously.

"Even prettier than the bride," he added.

She chuckled then. "Don't you dare say anything like that to Abby. She'll be justified in hurting you."

"I'll try to remember that."

As he walked away, he fingered the jeweler's box in his pocket and wondered if somehow before the end of the day, he'd find the courage to ask Shanna to marry him.

Shanna stood on the inn's lawn, openmouthed with shock, when Abby's bouquet landed in her arms. She hadn't even been aware of reaching for it.

"Well, I guess that all but seals things," Bree said in an undertone. "You have to marry my brother now."

Shanna laughed. "I don't see his name tucked among the flowers."

"Well, you certainly can't run off and marry someone else," Bree said indignantly. "It wouldn't be right."

Kevin walked up just then and scowled at his sister. "Go away, Bree."

"I'm just saying—"

Kevin cut her off. "Go away. I'll take it from here."

"You know she's just looking out for your interests," Shanna told him.

"She's implying that I can't figure out what I want and go after it," he said. "Come on. I feel like taking the boat out."

"But the boys—"

"Gram and Mick are taking them back to the house."

"You were so sure I'd agree to go with you?"

"I was hoping. Well? Are you coming with me?"

With her heart hammering in her chest, she nodded and followed him to his car. Minutes later they were on the boat and he was casting off.

When they were in the middle of the bay, surrounded by sparkling water, stars and moonlight, he dropped anchor and let the boat drift. Then he joined her at the railing.

Shanna turned to face him and lifted her gaze to his. "What do you want, Kevin?"

"You," he said without hesitation.

She blinked at the certainty in his voice. "Really?"

"You had to know that," he said, studying her. "What about you? What do you want?"

She'd risked her heart by taking Henry in. It had paid

off, too. The court had agreed to let him stay indefinitely. Now she dared to risk it again. "You."

"I wasn't sure after the way I treated you."

"I've wanted you for a long time," she admitted candidly. "But I wasn't sure I had the right to love anyone or to be loved after what happened with Greg and Henry."

"I can't think of anyone more deserving of being loved," he told her. "Can we start fresh, Shanna? Can we move forward from right this moment with no secrets between us, and see where we go?"

"I already know where I want us to go," she said, not willing to wait. Life could be all too short, something he should understand even better than she did. She regarded him with a moment's uncertainty. "You do know that Henry and I are a package deal, right?"

"I knew it the first time I saw you with him," he said. "I think Davy will like having a big brother. I know I'll love having a stepson when the time comes."

When the time comes? His words sent a chill through her. He was hedging his bets. She could tell. He wasn't all in, not the way she was.

"I thought you knew what you wanted," she said. She gestured around them. "I thought that's what this was all about."

"I do know," he insisted. "But I rushed into marriage once for all the wrong reasons. I want to take my time with you, savor every step. When you and I get married—and there's not a doubt in my mind that we will, just so you know—it will be because we're both a hundred percent ready for that kind of commitment. We have two boys to consider, too. They need a family they know will last."

Shanna saw his hesitation as an unwillingness to commit, as an inability to trust what they had. He was looking for guarantees that were impossible.

"Kevin, I've already said I love you and I meant it, but—"

A look of pure panic crossed his face. He cut her off. "Marry me," he blurted.

Shanna reeled from the sudden change. "What?"

"I don't want to lose you. Just now, I saw that look in your eyes and realized you might walk away. I can't let that happen."

She studied his face intently. "Are you sure?"

He nodded. "I started thinking about this weeks ago and then Henry appeared and I started coming up with a thousand and one excuses for waiting. Bottom line, just like you, I know what I want. Why wait?"

She regarded him doubtfully. "Less than a minute ago, you wanted to wait, to make sure you weren't making a mistake like the one you believe you made with Georgia."

"I can't argue with you about that. The timing, the circumstances…" He shrugged. "I believed Georgia and I had something special. I wanted to believe it. And I'll never regret that I have Davy because of that decision."

"Of course not," she said.

"I know what I want," he insisted. "For real this time. There's not a shred of doubt in my head or in my heart. I want you and me and those boys, forever. Maybe a couple of girls of our own."

"You don't get to pick," she reminded him.

"Girls, more boys, it won't matter. The point is that you're the wife I want, this is the family I want. Waiting won't change that."

She wanted to believe him so badly. "You're sure? A hundred percent?"

"A thousand percent," he said. He reached in his pocket and pulled out a box. "See. I've been carrying this around. I walked down Main Street at least three dozen times planning to come in and propose."

"But you didn't."

"Something held me back," he admitted.

"Paralyzing fear maybe?"

He shook his head. "No, I was waiting for this. You and me, with stars in the sky, a path of moonlight on the water. I wanted to give you the romance. Being out here on my boat, with the lights and stars sparkling on the water, beckoning us back to shore, to home, it just seems right." He brushed a strand of hair from her cheek. "We're both always so darn practical. For once I wanted things to be special. I wanted to do something you'll remember always."

Her lips twitched slightly. "You proposing is pretty memorable. The setting is just the icing on the cake."

"And this?" He slid a diamond onto her finger.

She studied the ring in the moonlight, seemingly fascinated with the way it sparkled. "How could I not say yes to a man who just gave me the stars?" she whispered. "Who knew you had that kind of magic in you?"

"It's not me. It's love. It brings out the magic in everyone."

And as he looked into her eyes, Shanna knew it was true. What they had was magic. Maybe even strong enough to guarantee forever. But even if magic alone wasn't enough, she knew with everything in her that they had what it took to make it. They just had to keep their hearts open and listen.

* * * * *

Don't miss the next CHESAPEAKE SHORES novel when Sherryl Woods brings the O'Brien family home for a heartwarming Christmas...

After years apart, Mick and Megan O'Brien are finally ready to make it official...again. But not all their grown-up children feel able to give this union their blessing. The last thing Megan wants to do is hurt her family again. After all, is she really sure she and Mick can make it this time around? And when an unexpected delivery causes chaos, it seems only a miracle can reunite this family.

Luckily it's Christmas—the season of miracles.

Read on for a preview of

A CHESAPEAKE SHORES CHRISTMAS

1

It was only the second time in the more than twelve years since her divorce that Megan O'Brien had been home in Chesapeake Shores during the holiday season.

Newly divorced and separated from her children, Megan had found the memories had been too bittersweet to leave New York and come back for Christmas. She'd tried to make up for her absence by sending a mountain of presents, each one carefully chosen to suit the interests of each child. She'd called on Christmas Day, but the conversations with the older children had been grudging and too brief. Her youngest, Jess, had refused to take her call at all.

The following year Megan had ventured back to town,

hoping to spend time with the children on Christmas morning. Her ex-husband, Mick O'Brien, had agreed to the visit. She'd anticipated seeing their eyes light up over the presents she'd chosen. She'd even arranged for a special breakfast at Brady's, a family favorite, but the atmosphere had been so strained, the reaction to her gifts so dismissive, that she'd driven everyone back home an hour later. She'd managed to hide her tears and disappointment until she was once again alone in her hotel room.

After that, she'd made countless attempts to convince the children to come to New York for the holidays, but they'd stubbornly refused, and Mick had backed them up. She could have fought harder, but she'd realized that to do so would only ruin Christmas for all of them. Teenagers who were where they didn't want to be could make everyone's life miserable.

Now she parked her car at the end of Main and walked slowly along the block, taking it all in. Even though it was only days after Halloween, the town was all decked out. Every storefront along Main Street had been transformed with twinkling white lights and filled with enticing displays. The yellow chrysanthemums outside the doorways during the fall had given way to an abundance of bright red poinsettias.

Workers were stringing lights along the downtown

streets and readying a towering fir on the town green for a tree-lighting ceremony that would be held in a few weeks. The only thing missing was snow, and since Chesapeake Shores hadn't had a white Christmas in years, no one was counting on that to set the scene. The town created its own festive atmosphere to charm residents and lure tourists to the seaside community.

As she strolled, Megan recalled the sweet simplicity of going Christmas shopping with the kids when they were small, pausing as they stared in wonder at the window displays. There were a few new shops now, but many remained exactly the same, the windows gaily decorated in a suitable theme. Now it was her grandchildren who would be enchanted by the displays.

Ethel's Emporium, for instance, still had the same animated figures of Santa and Mrs. Claus in the window along with giant jars filled with the colorful penny candy that was so popular with the children in town. Once again, Seaside Gifts had draped fishing nets in the window, woven lights through them and added an exceptional assortment of glittering nautical ornaments, some delicate, some delightfully gaudy and outrageous.

At her daughter Bree's shop, Flowers on Main, lights sparkled amid a sea of red and white poinsettias. Next door, in her daughter-in-law Shanna's bookstore, the window featured seasonal children's books, along with a selection of holiday cookie recipe books and a plate filled with samples to entice a jolly life-size stuffed Santa. Inside, she knew, there would be more of the delectable cookies for the customers. The chef at her daughter Jess's inn was sending them over daily during the season, some packaged for resale as enticing gifts.

In fact, all along Main Street, Megan saw evidence of her family settling down in this town that had been the creation of her ex-husband, architect Mick O'Brien. Though all of their children except Jess had fled for careers and college, one by one they had drifted back home and made lives for themselves in Chesapeake Shores. They'd made peace with their father and, to some extent, with her. Only Connor, now an attorney in Baltimore, had kept his distance.

It should have been gratifying to see an O'Brien touch everywhere she looked, but instead it left Megan feeling oddly out of sorts. Just like Connor, she, too, had yet to find her way home. And though her relationship with Mick had been improving—she had, in fact, agreed to consider marrying him again—something continued to hold her back from making that final commitment.

Megan shivered as the wind off the Chesapeake Bay cut through her. Though it was nothing like the wind that whipped between New York's skyscrapers this time of year, the bitter chill and gathering storm clouds seemed to accentuate her odd mood.

When she shivered again, strong arms slid around her waist from behind and she was drawn into all the protective warmth that was Mick O'Brien. He smelled of the crisp outdoors and the lingering aroma of a spicy aftershave, one as familiar to her as the scent of sea air.

"Why the sad expression, Meggie?" he asked. "Isn't this the most wonderful time of the year? You used to love Christmas."

"I still do," she said, leaning against him. Despite all those sorrowful holidays she'd spent alone, it was impossible for her to resist the hopeful magic of the season. "New York is always so special during the holidays. I'd forgotten that Chesapeake Shores has its own charm at Christmas."

She gestured toward the shop windows. "Bree and Shanna have a real knack for creating inviting displays, don't they?"

"Best on the block," he said proudly. There was nothing an O'Brien did that wasn't the best, according to Mick—unless, of course, it was an accomplishment by one of his estranged brothers, Jeff or Thomas. "Why don't we go to Sally's and have some hot chocolate and one of her raspberry croissants?"

"I was planning to start on my Christmas shopping this morning," she protested. "It's practically my duty to support the local economy, don't you think?"

"Why not warm up with the hot chocolate first?" he coaxed. "And then I'll go with you."

Megan regarded him with surprise. "You hate to shop."

"That was the old me," he said with the irrepressible grin she'd never been able to resist. "I'm reformed, remember? I want to do anything that allows me some extra time with you. Besides, I'm hoping you'll give me some ideas about what you really want for Christmas."

Given all the years when Mick had turned his holiday shopping over to her and later to his secretary, this commitment to finding the perfect gift was yet more evidence that he was truly trying to change his neglectful ways.

"I appreciate the thought," she began, only to draw a scowl.

"Don't be telling me you don't need anything," he said as he guided her into Sally's. "Christmas gifts aren't about what you need. They're about things that will make those beautiful eyes of yours light up."

Megan smiled. "You still have the gift of blarney, Mick O'Brien." And over the past couple of years since they'd been reunited, his charm had become harder and harder to resist. In fact, she couldn't say for sure why she'd been so reluctant to set a wedding date when he'd shown her time and again how much he'd tried to change in all the ways that had once mattered so much to her.

When they were seated and held steaming cups of hot chocolate, topped with extra marshmallows, she studied the man across from her. Still handsome, with thick black hair, twinkling blue eyes and a body kept fit from working construction in many of his own developments as well as his recent Habitat for Humanity projects, Mick O'Brien would turn any woman's head.

Now when he was with her—unlike when they were married—he was attentive and thoughtful. He courted her as only a man who knew her deepest desires possibly could. There was an intimacy and understanding between them that could only come from so many years of marriage.

And yet, she still held back. She'd found so many excuses, in fact, that Mick had stopped pressing her to set a date. She had a feeling that a perverse desire to be pursued was behind her disgruntled mood this morning.

"You've that sad expression on your face again, Meggie. Is something wrong?" he asked, once more proving he was attuned to her every mood.

She drew in a deep breath and, surprising herself, blurted,

"I'm wondering why you've stopped pestering me to marry you."

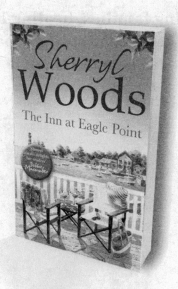